# SHANGHAIED

## GREG MUTTON

GREG MUTTON AUTHOR

Book Cover by Gail Rust

Cover Concept by Elyse Nation

1st edition2024

ISBN Paperback:  978-0-6459789-2-6

ISBN eBook:     978-0-6459789-3-3

Memory is the diary we all carry about with us.


OSCAR WILDE

# ONE

T he fog of unconsciousness started to dissipate.

Slowly his brain began to function. He could feel something, a movement—a slight undulation that seemed out of place. As consciousness took command of his senses, he could feel his surroundings. Even with his eyes closed he could sense light—a pinkish glow behind his eyelids. The air felt different, cool, and slightly damp. And it smelled different—something he was trying to remember, an aroma that always made him feel good.

He was lying on something very comfortable, something pliant yet firm. Deliberately and with caution, he opened his eyes. He had to blink a couple of times to clear any residue and lubricate them. Then he gazed around the room. It was different from anything he knew or thought he knew. Rich, warm, wood panelling, muted grey leather, and fabric greeted his gaze.

He sat up and looked to his right. Three vertical windows in the wall revealed his location. Windows was a generous description; they were vertical portholes. He now realized he was on a boat and from the décor, a very nice one. This cabin was obviously the master, but he couldn't remember owning a boat. In fact, he couldn't remember much at all.

'Must have been one hell of a night!' he said to himself as he climbed out of the bed, the ache in his bladder transcending any other needs. The head was behind the bed, separated by a wall covered in grey velour. When he'd finished, he washed his face and re-entered the bedroom, walked to the opposite side of the bed, and stood in front of a full-height mirror.

Another shock; the face that looked back he vaguely recognized, but the body ... well, it just didn't go with the head. The face was middle-aged, the hair was long and grey, the green eyes surrounded by lines that only came with years. But the body—it would suit a man in his late twenties or early thirties—someone who looked after himself, someone who worked out.

Then another shock, he couldn't remember his name and the disparity between the face and body only confused the situation more.

He shook his head, trying to disperse the fog that was blocking his memory. It didn't work. His identity remained lost. 'Yep, must have been one fucking huge night.'

Then his nudity finally hit him. He turned and opened the wardrobe to his left, and another surprise, the door had a name plate "Clyde Robinson", now he had a name, even though he didn't recognise it.

He was greeted by clothes. 'Well that's what one expects to find in a bloody wardrobe,' he chided himself, then turned again and opened the drawers behind him. Again, what he'd expected—underwear, socks, and the usual bits found in drawers. Everything was new and what he believed to be his size. He quickly dressed; even this felt new, as if he hadn't done it before. He checked himself in the mirror again, pleasantly surprised by the result.

'For someone who doesn't have a fucking clue who he is, you don't look too bad.' He turned back to the drawers. Something drew him to the cupboard above. It was locked but, as if by some premonition, he opened the bottom drawer. He saw a small indentation on the bottom. He pressed it and the section popped up. Inside was a key.

'How in hell did I know that?' Gingerly, he took the key and unlocked the cupboard, almost dreading what he'd find. He opened it; a light automatically came on and revealed a thumb and eye scanner.

He placed his left thumb on the pad and his right eye against the eye cushion; why he chose this combination, he had no idea. But it worked, with the sound of a locking mechanism opening. He stood back as the inner door swung open.

He let out a slow whistle at the contents. An armoury, with several weapons he somehow recognized. Reaching in, he selected a Glock G40, something in his mind telling him he knew this weapon. It felt good to hold it, like he was being reunited with an old friend, but he couldn't remember ever using one before.

Instinctively, he took the gun to the dressing table. There on the leather insert, he quickly stripped it, went back to the cupboard, opened a drawer at the bottom, and withdrew a cleaning kit.

After cleaning and reassembling the Glock, he went through other drawers until he found one that contained several leather items. He removed one—a hip holster pack and, again, back to the weapons safe. Opening another drawer, he discovered several magazines, withdrew four, picked out a box of bullets and loaded them. He even knew that the bullet design was called RIP and understood how they worked; this day was becoming stranger by the minute.

He put a light cotton shirt over his tee shirt, giving some concealment to the weapon. It felt imperative he take it with him. Finally, he tied his long hair back in a ponytail and, satisfied with his appearance, picked a pair of expensive-looking sunglasses off the bed stand and left the room.

Five steps up and he was in a wood-lined corridor. The colour was warm and inviting. He turned again. Up five more steps and he was in the saloon – still no sign of other life. Absentmindedly, he brushed his hand against the Glock, as if for reassurance.

Again the décor was similar to the bedroom. Two-toned grey leather lounges, a warm teak table to seat eight, and more wood to the stern, concealing the galley.

*Coffee!* His mind screamed, so he went directly to the galley. Somehow he knew where everything was and soon had a steaming brew in his hands.

He opened the large bi-fold doors and walked out onto the rear cockpit and looked around. Water everywhere he looked, no land, no other boats, just ocean. Noticing twin doors in the stern, he opened the closest and stepped down onto the swim platform, and turned back to look at the boat. There, embossed in the lazarette door, *"Maritimo M70"*. Now, although he knew what type of boat he was on he still couldn't remember owning a boat or even knowing anyone who owned one this big. The day was just one confusing discovery after another.

He decided to check things out from a higher vantage point and returned to the cockpit and took the internal staircase to the fly bridge. Here, again, the same elegant décor, but he was more interested in the view. Finding a pair of powerful binoculars on the second helm seat, he started to scan the ocean around the boat.

Nothing, it was totally empty.

His heart sank, a little. 'Just what the fuck is going on?' he asked himself. Again he scanned the sky and ocean, desperately looking for something, as it was, he could be the only person left on Earth. A cold shiver ran down his spine at the thought.

He sank into the main helm chair, despondency starting to claim him. Casually, he reached into a recess in the dash and withdrew the ignition key, inserted it into the switch and turned it. The three large displays in front of him came to life. He first checked the boat's systems. One generator was running to supply power and a message flashed across the screen.

DROGUE DEPLOYED

Someone had deployed a sea anchor, which explained the rope tied off at the stern cleat. *Someone's gone to a lot of trouble in this,* he thought.

Next, he checked the radar. It reinforced his visual sighting—the screen was clear. The sonar was next; he needed to know how much water he had under the keel. The result was as expected—plenty. He was somewhere in the middle of an ocean.

Now the chart plotter; he hoped to see the journey the boat had made to get to its current position. It revealed nothing; whoever had dumped him there had erased any clues. 'Arseholes,' he cursed under his breath. Still, he should be able to get a good GPS fix and then figure out where he was.

A noise from the saloon startled him.

He wasn't alone.

Carefully, he stood and headed for the stairs. How did he handle this? Should he surprise whoever was there or act as if this was a pleasure cruise? He chose the latter, mainly because he didn't want to shoot anybody – just yet. He casually climbed down the staircase and turned into the saloon.

'Who the fuck are you and what am I doing here?' an enraged female voice demanded. 'And where are my clothes?'

She was sitting on the lounge to his left, with the table between them. He was tempted to laugh—her hair was dishevelled and she was wrapped in a sheet, looking both forlorn and threatening at the same time.

'First, if you go back to the cabin you're in, you'll probably find clothes and everything you need in the cupboards. As for who I am, maybe I should ask you the same.' He decided to play boat owner.

'Obvious, isn't it? You brought me to your boat last night, probably drugged me. Who knows what you did to me, arsehole!' she screamed.

He decided that wasn't his best move so he started again. 'The truth—I have no bloody idea who I am or how I got here. I think I was out with some of my mates last night, but how I got here or even where here is, I'm stumped. And before you start again, I don't recall owning a boat like this, so I suggest you get some clothes on and we can start again.'

The woman seemed to calm down. She nodded and disappeared down the stairs, while he busied himself with making a fresh pot of coffee, just finishing it as she returned. She was dressed in a similar fashion—cotton slacks, tee shirt with a loose cotton shirt over the top, and she was better colour coordinated than him. He did notice the holster at her hip and the Glock G2o nestled in there.

'Fully accessorized, I see,' he quipped.

'Well, I don't want to be outdone, do I?' she fired back. 'Look, I'm sorry I exploded earlier. But you know what it's like, waking up and not remembering anything.'

'So you're blank as well?'

'Totally; I have no idea who I am but I'm a bit confused as to when I am,' she said in a serious tone.

'What do you mean, when?'

'Look at me. I've got a body I think I would have killed for in my twenties, but I have an old face that is familiar. I can't remember my name or anything else, so something is very hickey.'

He shook his head. 'Yeah, tell me about it. I didn't recognize the person in the mirror. The face I kind of recognise, but the body… well; let's just say the face and the body don't match; and the weapons.' He nodded to her hip. 'I had this thing stripped and ready to clean in a few seconds. I can't remember ever handling a Glock G4o before, let alone knowing what it is. And the ammo, I loaded this with RIP rounds; I know that on impact they break into nine flechettes. A small hole going in, a huge amount of damage inside, and usually no exit wound,' he said as he poured two coffees.

She took the mug and they sat in silence. At last, the woman looked up. 'We just can't keep calling each other you, or whatever. We need names; any thoughts?'

He sat for a few minutes before answering. 'Well the name on my wardrobe was "Clyde Robinson" did you see anything similar in your room?

'Well, the name "Bonnie Masterton" was on the door, as well as inside the locker where I found this,' she tapped her pistol as she spoke.

'Then we have names,' he said as he stood and offered his hand. 'Hi, I'm Clyde, pleased to meet you Bonnie; now how about some breakfast, I'm starving.'

<h1 style="text-align: center;">Two</h1>

Breakfast was a quiet affair, even though they had decided on names, they were very cautious of each other.

Clyde prepared some ham steaks and scrambled eggs, he found in the fridge. Bonnie made a fresh pot of coffee and they sat to eat. With the hunger pangs now sated, he sat back and gave his companion the once over.

'I must say, Bonnie, if I had to choose anyone to share amnesia with, I don't think I could've done any better.' Clyde broke the silence.

'I suppose that is some sort of complement?' she retorted. 'I'll reserve my judgment, but I will say this, if you can cook other things as well as those eggs, I'll end up fat again.' Bonny's face betrayed her confusion.

'So you think you were over weight?' Clyde replied. 'I don't know, but I'm sure I wasn't as well built as this. Something in my memory says I had the start of a middle-aged spread. I think we are both remembering some things, things we are supposed to remember.' He reached for his coffee as they both retreated to silence.

Bonnie was the first to speak. 'I think we should do a complete sweep of the boat. Every cupboard, every drawer, see what other surprises are in store for us. And we should do it together.'

The look on her face told Clyde she didn't trust him – yet; he stood and cleared the table, rinsing the plates and placing them in the dishwasher. 'Sounds like a plan. Shall we start in my cabin?'

Bonnie nodded and they went down the stairs to the corridor that led to the accommodation, turned right, and went down to the master cabin. They started in the head, checking every space, Bonnie deliberately commenting on his choice of toiletries. 'At least you'll smell nice,' she said with a cheeky grin.

Back in the cabin, they repeated the process. The wardrobe was full of casual clothes that would suit a boating life but the weapons cache was quite amazing —several different types of knives, shotguns, and a couple of assault rifles, complete with grenade launchers and ammunition.

'Looks like you're intent on starting a war!' Bonnie said as she held one of the rifles, automatically, confidently stripping and reassembling it, before returning it to its hiding place. Clyde was impressed with her skill and familiarity with the weapon. The look of confusion and fear on her face stopped Clyde in his tracks.

'I know. How do you know how to do that, right?' he said.

Bonnie just stood still, staring at the weapon cache as if it would give her answers. 'Yeah, something like that,' she whispered.

Clyde moved to her side, placed his arm around her, and drew her in. 'I know this is all so strange. Remember, I'm in the same boat.' Although his pun was unintentional, it broke the tension and they both started to laugh and continued with the inspection.

They next moved to the VIP cabin, in the bow—Bonnie's cabin. Here they repeated the process. Clyde deliberately inspected some of the gadgets he found in the head cabinets. Bonnie stormed in and grabbed what he held. 'Come on, you've had enough fun.'

Clyde resisted feigning indignation. 'How do I know that this isn't a weapon of some kind?' he said with a smile.

Bonnie stood, hands on hips. 'Stop being gross! A lady has to tend her garden once in a while.' She grabbed the item, pushed him out, and replaced it in the cabinet.

They found similar weapons caches before heading to the next stop, the guest cabin. It was definitely not a guest cabin.

'Looks like an operating theatre,' Bonnie said. She was correct—it could be used for that but was well-equipped as a battlefield trauma centre. Together they worked through the sterile-looking cupboards and equipment, Bonnie naming each piece and describing their use.

'Looks like I should call you doc?' Clyde said as he closed the last cupboard.

'Maybe that's what I was,' Bonnie replied quietly.

Next, they went across the corridor to the crew cabin where things got more interesting. Instead of twin bunks, they found a complex communication system where the top bunk should have been.

Bonnie began inspecting it immediately. 'This is very complex. It's military communications, satellite coms, but I know how to operate it.' The scared-little-girl look was back. The expression only lasted a second or two; then she was back to business. 'We should be able to contact anywhere in the world from here, but what in hell's name is it doing on a pleasure boat?'

Clyde chuckled. 'Well, let's reserve that *pleasure boat* concept for the moment. We still have a lot of boat to examine.'

The cupboard in the corridor outside housed the laundry and supplies; no surprises here. So far the only weapon caches had been in their cabins.

Back up the stairs to the saloon, again, all normal for a pleasure boat. Next, they climbed the stairs to the fly bridge. Clyde took control—somehow he knew how everything worked. There was also a commercial communication system, including satellite comm systems installed here.

Bonnie sank into the plush leather lounge opposite the helm station. 'I could get used to this life, if I knew what this life was.' She gazed around, taking in the décor and the view. The upper lounge, as Bonnie had called this area, was finished in perfect detail—soft muted cream and grey palette with warm wood for the cupboards and table. Like the rest of the boat, it oozed luxury and relaxed living, but under the lounge she was sitting on, Bonnie found two RPG launchers and several cases of grenades.

'This must be for very unpleasant guests.' She giggled.

Clyde finished playing with the controls and turned to her. 'Come on, still a few places to check.' He bounded down the stairs and out to the rear saloon area. He opened the stainless steel gate down to the swim platform and the lazarette. He lifted the hatch just as Bonnie caught up with him.

'What's this?' she asked as he started down the short ladder into the lazarette.

'Lazarette – basically, a storage area for less attractive items, and water toys,' Clyde was correct—they found a number of things there—a large freezer full of food, scuba tanks, and a tank-fill compressor. Plenty of fishing gear, spear guns, and two Fostech semi auto shotguns. Clyde handed one to Bonnie. 'Get the feel of this, baby.'

She took the short weapon and pulled it into her shoulder. 'Feels good, any ammo?'

Clyde handed her a ten-round magazine. She inserted it and turned away, out to the stern. Thankfully, it was equipped with a suppressor otherwise Clyde was sure he'd be deafened down in the lazarette. The Fostech, reputed to be the fastest cycling semi-auto shotgun available, didn't disappoint. As fast as Bonnie could squeeze the trigger, the gun fired and the magazine was empty in no time.

'I like it!' Bonnie said, smiling as her eyes filled with excitement.

'Good. You used it, you clean it,' Clyde replied. 'I'm going to the engine room.'

He climbed out of the lazarette and went back up to the rear cockpit, opened the hatch to the engine room, and climbed down. Everything was as he expected, neat and functional. The two engines were a bit of a surprise, as were the cramped quarters. *Time to make a few calculations,* he climbed back out and closed the hatch.

A few minutes later, he heard Bonnie call. He answered and she joined him at the helm.

'This is no ordinary boat,' he said. 'First, there are two bloody large, strange-looking engines in her belly. Next, the engine room feels small to me—you know, too cramped—so I came up here to try and work some things out. This boat has something like triple the fuel capacity of a standard boat.

'Next, these boats are usually shaft drive, not this one. She's running a counter-rotating turbine propulsion system. A high-volume, low-pressure type of water jet, very efficient and should be very fast. Now, before you carry on, most of this is on the computer. There's a huge amount of data that's been left for us, including a range and speed graph. From this, we can work out how fast we can go to reach a destination and how much fuel we'd use.' He sat back, feeling a certain amount of pride in his discovery.

'Okay, genius, now tell me just where we are,' Bonnie fired back.

This question rudely stripped away any self-congratulatory feelings Clyde had. 'Haven't got to that yet,' he said quietly as he switched on the displays in front of him. He spent a few minutes calling up the chart plotter and located their GPS coordinates.

Any sense of victory was soon dissipated when Bonnie spoke. 'So you've managed to discover that we're in the middle of the bloody Pacific Ocean; anything else?'

He didn't answer. Instead, he checked through the boat's data. 'I don't get it. We're here in the middle of nowhere but we have full fuel tanks, so how'd we get here?' He didn't want an answer, he was thinking out loud. He brought his attention back to the chart plotter, changed the range resolution, and started a search for any land masses.

Bonnie simply asked. 'Anything I can do?'

Clyde nodded absentmindedly. 'Yes, check the food stores and work out how many days of food we have. I'll keep checking to see where we can go.' He didn't look up; his concentration on the instruments was total.

Bonnie left and Clyde continued to work, searching the charts for any land close enough for them to reach. By his calculations, the boat had a safe range of over two thousand nautical miles, but the problem was he couldn't find anything in that range. Frustration was building in him, his thoughts getting darker all the time. *Why would anyone stick us out here with all this, just so we can go nowhere?* It didn't make sense.

He was about to leave when he noticed a piece of paper tucked into the second helm chair. Clyde gently pulled it out, unfolded it, and read it—GPS coordinates, but not for their current location.

'Clyde, have a look at this.' Bonnie was climbing the stairs holding a familiar looking piece of paper. 'I found this under one of the food packets. What is it?'

Clyde took the paper and compared it with his—same coordinates. 'Seems we are meant to go here,' he said, pointing to the chart plotter. 'I found the same up here, under the seat.'

'What's there? It looks like nothing.'

'Wrong, there's a small chain of islands, that's all I can get of the system,' he replied before Bonnie could ask more. 'So what do we do? Go or not?'

'What other alternative do we have, where else can we reach?' Bonnie asked.

'There's nothing else. Those islands are well within our range and I can't find anything else. So I suppose we really don't have any choice, do we?'

There was no need to answer. Either they sat where they were, hoping they would be found, set off the EPIRB and wait for rescue, or they went where they seemed to be being pushed.

Clyde busied himself entering the destination into the chart plotter. Now all they had to do was start.

'We'd better pull the drogue in before we try and leave,' he said as he left the helm.

Ten minutes later, the drogue was stored and Clyde was sitting back at the helm. He activated the control console and started both engines, port first then starboard. They sprang to life, there was no vibration, but he could hear the muted rumble of the exhaust.

He looked over to Bonnie and smiled. 'The die is now cast,' he said as he moved both drive controls to forward and then opened the throttles. The big boat surged ahead and was soon sitting on the plane, the fuel usage now matching the optimum he had calculated. He switched the radar and sonar systems on, noting that both the sky above and the sea ahead were empty. Satisfied that everything was under control, Clyde switched on the autopilot and sat back from the helm.

'This is an amazing boat. I reckon I'd have loved to own one. Look at this—the sonar can be configured to scan forward and to the side out to one hundred meters and a depth of fifty meters. If it detects anything that could impact the boat, it sets off an alarm, drops the speed, and can even alter course. I've never heard of anything like this on a pleasure boat.' Clyde was fascinated by the gadgets.

'But we both know this is anything but a pleasure boat,' Bonnie replied. 'So we don't need to be up here?'

'No, not really,' Clyde answered absently.

'Good. I'm going to do what one is supposed to do on a boat like this, sunbake. Oh, by the way, I figure we've got at least four weeks of food, but I don't know about water,' Bonnie called as she started down the stairs.

'Plenty of that—the whole pacific; we've got a desalinator that'll automatically keep us supplied with fresh water,' Clyde replied. Bonnie just nodded and left.

# THREE

Sunlight glinted off the gently undulating sea.

The swell was mild and the view was something one could only imagine, or so Clyde thought. He checked their course and speed for the thousandth time, still 073 degrees and speed 18.5 knots. Fuel consumption was very good, so much so, he now believed they could increase speed without any detriment. But he was enjoying the solitude, just sitting at the helm, gazing lazily over the ocean.

A sound behind him broke his daydream.

'I thought you might be hungry,' Bonnie enquired as she placed two plates on the table.

Clyde turned around and stopped, totally stunned by what he saw. Bonnie stood by the table, clad only in the tiny bikini she wore to sunbake.

'Wow,' was the only word he could utter.

'Wow, it's only a quick salad,' she replied, a teasing grin on her face.

'I wasn't talking about the salad.'

Bonnie smiled and did a slow turn, giving him a great view of her body. 'This is just what I always wanted to look like, I think, but I have a feeling that nature didn't agree. Unfortunately, I don't think I've ever looked like this. But now...' her voice trailed off.

Her body was definitely younger than her face and would turn heads at any venue. She was relatively tall and curvy, not a stick figure but what Clyde termed a real woman, just what he preferred.

Bonnie wasn't trying to be provocative; Clyde could see she was genuinely intrigued by her new figure, and that she loved the reaction from Clyde. Then she stopped and her face lost its childlike demeanour. 'How is this possible? It doesn't fit.' Tears started to build in her eyes.

'I don't know, but I do know that we're here now and we look like this.' He removed his shirt and tee shirt as he spoke. 'I don't remember having a body like this either. And my face doesn't fit but guess what, I don't give a shit. This is me now, and I'm gonna enjoy it while I can.'

Bonnie smiled, wiped the tears away, and took his shirt. 'Put the tee shirt back on. You can't come to my table bare-chested.' She laughed as she wrapped his shirt around herself.

Lunch proved to be very good. Crisp salad and a bottle of Chardonnay improved their moods; Bonnie sat back, glass in hand, gazing through the large windows and out the back of the boat. 'You know, this should be terrifying. We have no idea who we are, where we are, or where we're going, but I find it strangely exhilarating.'

Clyde nodded, his mind obviously deep in thought. At length, he spoke. 'Who, what, when, where, how, and why? That's what we need to work out.'

'What are you talking about?'

'Simple. Don't ask how I know this, I just do. To figure out what's going on we need to ask those questions – and find the answers.'

Bonnie thought about this before answering. 'Who, what, when, where, how, and why. I see what you're getting at, what were you, some sort of strategist, military, corporate what?'

'No fucking idea, but it sounds like we now have something to do,' he replied. 'Get down to the comms room, start listening. Scan frequencies, see if there's someone else out there but don't transmit yet. I'll stay here and see if I can get anything with the boat's computer.'

Four hours later Bonnie returned, the look on her face telling Clyde it had been a fruitless four hours. 'Any luck?' Even as he spoke he knew it was a redundant question.

'Nothing, what about you?'

'Except for general information about the boat and the weapons, there seems to be nothing. I couldn't even hook into the internet and I know we have some of the most sophisticated satellite comms available, for my money, I'd say someone finally broke it. I did find out about the launch date for the boat, which was only a couple of months ago, in April. Thing is, I think I remember going out last Friday night, Friday, July 20. If that's so, then how did I end up in the middle of the Pacific on Saturday, July 21? That's what I can't figure out. The logistics of getting us here are huge. How was it done?' The question nagged at Clyde's mind and he was sure he wouldn't like the answer, if he ever got one.

'So your assumption is that today is Saturday, July 21?'

Bonnie's question twigged something in his mind; Clyde started working on the keyboard. 'Every system has an internal clock, none more than GPS. It'll record the time and date of each reading. It doesn't store it, but it needs accurate time to calculate locations.' He kept working through various layers of the computer program.

Finally, he stood back. 'There, today's date.' Clyde stood aside so she could see the screen.

'Bullshit, that's not possible. What the fuck did you do?'

'Nothing, that's the correct date according to the computer, it's hard to accept, but that is the date the systems are working to.'

They stood quietly, not wanting to believe what they saw on the screen.

TUESDAY 14:09:2065

'So you're saying that somehow, we've lost what, nearly forty years years?' Bonnie asked, her voice betraying the fear she was feeling.

'No, I'm not; all I'm saying is that's the date the computer recognizes as today. Anything else will need proof. It could be just an elaborate joke, a stupid prank. But if we look at what we've discovered, it does make sense, of sorts,' Clyde replied. 'At the moment, all we have to go on is this bloody computer. Maybe when we get to wherever it is we're heading to, it'll all be explained, but for now, we have to keep our heads and not jump to any conclusions; and if you need another conundrum, the launch date of this boat was June 17, twenty-twenty five.'

'How do you know that?'

'Simple, it's recorded in the computer and on the registration plate.' He lifted a small access panel on the dash, exposing the plate. 'Either this is the most elaborate prank ever or...' Clyde didn't need to finish the sentence, they both grasped the meaning. He returned to the helm. 'We'll be starting our first night underway. I think someone should be up here, just in case.' He looked out through the large windscreen, the light slowly fading as dusk approached. Part of him wanted to stop, send out the drogue again, and wait until morning to continue, but another part of his mind was desperate to find out what had happened, and any delay wasn't in his calculations.

Bonnie interrupted his thoughts again. 'I've thawed out a couple of really nice steaks, so how about we have dinner and settle in here for the night? We can take turns to sleep so we can both be awake tomorrow.'

Half an hour later, Bonnie returned with a tray bearing their dinner. Clyde throttled the engines back until they were moving at ten knots. 'Just to be safe, I think we should run slower at night.'

They sat at the table and ate their meal, Bonnie constantly gazing out the rear deck. The sun was setting off the port rear quarter, a huge orange ball slowly dipping into the ocean. With the boat now running in displacement mode, there was little wake to disturb the serenity of the scene. Colours ranged through the spectrum as the sun lost its battle with the planet's rotation and finally disappeared behind the horizon.

Bonnie stood and went out onto the upper deck. 'God, that was beautiful. I don't think I've ever seen anything as wonderful.' Her voice sounded almost reverent as she spoke. 'If we are the last two people on Earth, that scene makes it worthwhile.'

Clyde chuckled. 'Well, I don't believe we're the last two here, but you're right, that was spectacular. However, now we need to lock the boat down for the night.' He led her out to the deck, stacked the chairs, and moved them inside. He repeated this with the two small tables before he joined her at the railing.

The sea behind them betrayed their course, phosphorescence revealing their passage. The sun was gone and the moon still to rise, the only light was from the boat and its wake.

He felt Bonnie shiver slightly. He moved closer and placed his left arm around her tentatively. She responded approvingly by snuggling in closer.

It felt good, like they had always been together. They didn't speak. Bonnie turned her head toward Clyde, her green eyes sparkling in the light. Slowly, they moved closer until their lips met, and then the passion took over. Clyde felt his pulse quicken as he wrapped her in his arms and crushed her to his chest. Bonnie responded, her lips parting and her tongue darting tantalizingly against his; the desire flooding his loins. Slowly, deliberately he removed her bikini top, gently caressing her breasts, his teeth nibbling her neck and ears.

Naked, they stood back to examine each other. Clyde reached forward and cupped her breasts, gently massaging her nipples between his thumb and forefinger, her moans spurring him on.

Bonnie reached down and took hold of his erection, stroking it as his fingers parted her velvety folds. Her moans increased as he stroked her clitoris, his left hand still tweaking her nipple. Bonnie kissed him again, harder this time, the urgency of the moment transmitted through her insistent tongue. He spun her around, bending her forward, his hard cock ready for action.

'Yes, now.' Bonnie cried, almost breathlessly and Clyde responded. He entered her, almost violently, her gasp of surprise and pleasure inflaming his passion even further. She braced herself against the railing as he thrust hard into her, the rail allowing her to force herself back against his onslaught. They slammed into each other in reckless abandon, all caution thrown away. All that mattered was the rising passion and the desperate desire for release.

'Yes, harder, fuck me harder!' Bonnie cried. 'Oh God yes, yes!' she screamed as Clyde felt her muscles begin to grip him as her orgasm wracked her body.

Clyde groaned and thrust harder, his hands gripping her hips like a vice. Then he let out a blood-curdling cry and slammed his pelvis into her, crushing himself against her buttocks. He held there and repeated the thrust a few more times as his own orgasm raged through him.

They held the position for a couple of minutes before Bonnie slowly stood up. She turned and kissed Clyde again, this time tenderly. 'Damn, I needed that.' She giggled as they melted into each other.

Finally, they broke apart, Bonnie noticing the stickiness on her thighs. 'I need a shower,' she whispered.

'I think we both do; my room or yours?' Clyde asked.

'Each to our own; we need to get back up here.' She turned, collected her clothes and weapon, and walked to the stairs. She stopped and looked back to Clyde, who was still ogling her. Bonnie replied by sticking her tongue out at him before skipping down the stairs.

Clyde collected his clothes and locked the doors to the deck, returned to the helm station, and turned on the navigation lights. *Who knows? There might be someone else out here.* He moved the casual chairs on the aft deck inside, locking the large bi-fold doors when he'd finished. The boat was now secured for the night, so he left the saloon. The sound of Bonnie's shower was inviting, but he decided that discretion was the best move here and turned down to his cabin.

Clyde showered quickly, dressed, and retied his hair. His clothes consisted of jeans, tee shirt, and a cotton jacket. On his feet, he chose a sturdy pair of joggers, the soles neutral so as not to damage any of the wood flooring. But something nagged at him. He opened the weapons locker again and examined the items before selecting an M4 Carbine equipped with a grenade launcher. He took four magazines and half a dozen grenades and put them into a sports bag. Finally, he inserted a fresh mag into the carbine and cycled one into the chamber.

He left his cabin just as Bonnie entered the corridor. She was also carrying a bag but what was slung under each arm was telling. Each side of her now sported an Uzi machine pistol.

'Get a funny feeling too?' Clyde asked.

They headed back to the fly bridge, Clyde turning off the lights as they went. Then they set up their positions on the bridge. Bonnie placed four mags for her Uzis in one drawer, keeping another four in her bag.

Clyde set the M4 in a recess beside the helm, a recess that looked suspiciously like it had been specifically designed for the purpose. In the bottom of each of their bags, they had body armour, night vision and comms gear, just in case.

The uneasiness Clyde felt grew with each minute, as if his gut was trying to warn him of something. He switched all lights off on the bridge and dimmed the readouts. Slowly his eyes adjusted to the new level and his vision outside the boat improved.

Bonnie decided to test her night vision gear and placed the set on her head, dropped the ocular lens into place, and scanned the sea ahead of the boat. She repeated the process with Clyde's unit.

'Okay, I'll take the first watch,' Clyde announced. 'I'll wake you in five hours. Sleep fast.'

Bonnie agreed, leaned over, and gently kissed Clyde on the cheek before curling up on the lounge. Within minutes, her rhythmic breathing announced she was asleep.

# FOUR

O 1:00—the time glowed weakly in the top right corner of the main display.

Clyde studied the ocean in front of them, night vision goggles firmly attached to his eyes. He had been on watch for five hours and it was becoming difficult to concentrate; he needed to sleep.

As this thought passed through his head, he felt something touch his shoulder. Bonnie was awake. 'Anything to report?' she asked as she stretched the kinks out of her body. The lounge was comfortable for sitting, but definitely not designed for sleeping.

Clyde removed the NV gear. 'Nothing – we're still alone.' He stood and made way for her to take the helm. 'Course is constant; speed is now twelve and a half knots, all the alarms are set so you should have a quiet time. Oh, I made a flask of coffee about an hour ago.' He pointed at the silver vacuum flask on the sideboard. 'I'll get some kip. Believe me, I need it.'

Bonnie settled into the helm chair as Clyde removed his shoes and stretched out on the lounge. Minutes later soft snoring told her Clyde was asleep; she stood and walked to the rear doors. Their wake stretched behind them like a phosphorescent line that slowly dissipated in the distance.

The moon was past its zenith and added an almost mystical glow to the ocean. *This is the stuff of legends,* she thought as she bathed in the scene. She returned to the helm and began her watch.

***

*The man was standing in the centre of a crowd; at least twenty faces looked back at him, faces he thought were familiar but he couldn't name one of the owners. The mood was happy, a celebration of some kind – a birthday? He held a knife in his hand, he was being told to cut it. Cut what? His mind screamed.*

*'The cake, blow out the candles and cut the cake.' The chorus came from the crowd.*

*A man's face was now in front of him. 'Come on, stop stuffing around. Blow out the candles and cut the damn thing! You can't avoid the inevitable—age creeps up on us all.'*

*The voices and faces were familiar; but he still couldn't put names to them.*

*He turned back to the table; there in the centre was a huge dark brown cake, the number sixty-five etched in the centre in white icing; he couldn't count the candles, but there were heaps of them.*

***

Something was shaking him; gripping his arm, tightly. 'Wake up, Clyde. Wake up.' The voice was also familiar, but he didn't recognize the name.

'Come on, wake up. We've got company!' the voice cried again.

Slowly his eyes opened. It took a few seconds to remember where he was. Then, as realization dawned, he sprang to his feet, the faces from the dream fading into obscurity again.

'What'd you say?' His voice was groggy. He looked at the clock—04:00 was displayed.

'The radar, it picked something up, at extreme range.' Bonnie pulled him toward the helm console. 'Here, see for yourself.'

She was correct. The radar showed something large on a parallel reciprocal course. The fog began to clear and he focussed on the screen in front of him. He checked the data and rechecked it.

'If this's right, we'll pass within a few hundred meters of it in a couple of hours. Did you check the radio?' He glanced at the VHF and UHF systems, both on and in search mode.

'No need, they're both scanning constantly; nothing so far.'

Then Clyde had another idea. 'What about the gear below? We've got heaps more stuff than this. Maybe they're on a different system.'

Bonnie handed him a mug of coffee and turned to leave. 'I'll go down and check. I know—just listen, no talking,' she called as she started down the stairs.

A cold feeling of dread and apprehension gripped Clyde. He had no idea why, but he wanted to change course and accelerate away at full speed. Something in the back of his mind was screaming for him to get out. Instead, he poured a fresh coffee and took a long draw from his mug; the hot liquid revived him almost as soon as it hit his stomach. He knew it was psychological, but he still appreciated the feeling.

He checked the plotter again. Closing speed was just over twenty-two knots, meaning they would pass around 05:30. The sun would be rising to their starboard, silhouetting the boat, but, anyone on the bigger vessel would be looking directly into it.

Clyde picked up the carbine, checked it, and loaded the grenade launcher. He went to the lounge to his left, lifted the seats and removed the two RPG units, and set about loading them. Satisfied, he leaned them against the lounge, cradling them in the centre of the L joint.

He remembered that they hadn't checked the lounge seating at the table. He lifted the lounge seat and was rewarded with two more Fostechs and heaps of ammunition. He grabbed two thirty-round drum mags and a couple of boxes of ammunition, loaded the magazines, and assembled each weapon. He stood back to inspect his work and immediately decided to set up another two spare mags.

Clyde had just finished when Bonnie re-entered the bridge. 'What the… ' she started. 'Clyde, are you expecting a bloody war?' She gazed around the room. The RPGs cradled in the lounge joint, the two Fostech shotguns now on the table and the spare mags beside them.

Clyde looked round the room and pointed at the radar. 'I saw this – I just want to be prepared for any eventuality.' A cold shiver coursed down his spine as he spoke.

Bonnie stood, hands on hips. 'And I don't suppose you could find any nukes, could you?' Clyde saw through the bravado as she tried to conceal the feelings that were etched on her face.

She must have felt self-conscious, berating Clyde, with the Glock on her right hip and two Uzis hanging from her shoulders. She shook her head. 'Sorry, you're right.' She patted one of the Uzis with her left hand. 'I have the same feeling.' She moved to the lounge, picked up one of the RPGs, and examined it. 'This is bloody weird. I can't ever remember seeing one of these, except in movies, but I know how to use it. How's that possible?'

'Don't ask me, I only work here!' Clyde responded as a beep sounded from the console. He checked the equipment. 'Well, they know we're here. We've just been picked up on their radar. You better get back down to the comms room.'

'No need, I piped everything up here. If they call we'll hear it here but we can only respond from down there. Now, what are we going to respond to?'

'Easy, recreational or commercial only, nothing on any of the military bands,' Clyde replied. 'The last thing we need is for anyone to find out what's on this boat.'

The next forty-five minutes passed relatively quickly and quietly—Clyde and Bonnie scanning the sea and keeping their thoughts to themselves.

*'Unidentified vessel, this is the freighter* Poulsen, *please respond.'* The dismembered voice from the speakers broke the silence.

'That's on a ham frequency,' Bonnie said.

*'This is the freighter* Poulsen *calling the unidentified vessel at coordinates ...'* the voice read out the GPS coordinates for their boat. *'Do you need assistance?'*

Clyde had the binoculars up to his eyes, scanning the ship. Although it was still a way off, it loomed large in his sight, still running dark. He put the glasses down and turned to Bonnie. 'I think we should answer.'

Together, they left the bridge, Clyde turning the proximity alarm volume up as he passed. In the radio room, Bonnie took her position at the console, switched the mic on, and spoke, 'Freighter *Poulsen*, this is the vessel off your port bow. How do you read us?' She switched the mike off and looked at Clyde. 'What's the name of the boat?'

'Fucked if I know,' he answered as he opened a drawer in the desk. Luck was still with them, he pulled out a book titled *Journey of the Minerva*. 'That'll have to do, we're on the *Minerva*.'

'*Unidentified vessel, your signal is loud and clear, what is your name?*'

'Inquisitive bastard,' Clyde said. 'Give me the mic.'

Bonnie handed it over.

'Freighter, this is Clyde Robinson on the MV Minerva, who am I speaking with?' Clyde tried to sound official.

'*Minerva this is radio operator Anthony Stevens, over.*'

'Thank you, Mister Stevens, we are fine and require no assistance. But thank you for the offer. Minerva out,' Clyde replied.

'Minerva, *please wait. Our captain would like a word.*' The radio went silent as though there was a change of person at the station.

'*MV Minerva, this is Captain Juan Rodregas. We are surprised to find a vessel such as yours so far out to sea.*'

The hackles on the back of Clyde's neck rose. Something was very wrong

'*This is why we are concerned for your safety. Do you have enough fuel for your journey?*'

Clyde looked at Bonnie. 'He's stalling.' Then into the mic, 'Captain, I assure you this boat is built for long haul voyages. We have plenty of everything. Again, I appreciate your concern, but there's no need to delay either of us. Again I thank you – Minerva out.'

As Clyde replaced the mic the sound of a proximity alarm howled through the boat.

'They're trying to board us.' He turned and leaped out the door, drawing his Glock at the same time. They raced from the radio room. Clyde was up the stairs to the saloon in two leaps and racing for the rear door. He quickly unlocked it just as a rubber-encased figure stepped up from the swim platform. The Glock barked twice and the head exploded. Clyde shifted his gaze to the other door and fired again, with a similar result.

'Bonnie,' he called as he leaped for the stairs to the bridge, taking the steps three at a time. The staccato burp of the Uzi reassuring him Bonnie was taking care of business. He reached the helm as a heavier machine gun opened up. Bullets bounced harmlessly off the large windows. *Bullet-proof glass*, Clyde thought as he slid to the helm chair, pushed the throttles to the stops, and held on as the large boat leaped forward, the speed quickly reaching thirty knots.

Another burp from the Uzi and Bonnie quickly raced to his side. 'They had tied a rubber ducky to the back, it's not there now.' She was breathing quickly and her eyes had an excited mist in them. 'We're not going to let them get away with this?'

'Not on your life. Grab one of those RPGs,' Clyde commanded as he turned the boat around. They headed back to the freighter at thirty knots, Bonnie standing on the rear upper deck, RPG to her shoulder. 'Aim for the water line,' Clyde called as she aimed, waiting for the range to fall.

Clyde picked up the Carbine and opened the window beside him, leaning the weapon on the sill. The range was now less than two hundred meters and Bonnie braced herself and fired.

The instant the projectile left the launcher she raced inside and grabbed the other unit, just as Clyde opened up on the freighter's bridge area. He flicked the autopilot on and sent a forty-millimetre grenade flying toward the ship.

The first RPG hit exactly where Bonnie had aimed, the delayed armour-piercing round ripping into the ship before exploding. She fired a second time, aiming further forward this time.

Clyde's grenade landed on the bridge, entering through the shattered wing door window; the effect in an enclosed space was devastating. In his mind, Clyde saw the mayhem that must have been wrought on those manning the bridge, everyone there would either be dead, or very seriously injured. He shuddered, maybe he had been too quick to fire; he shook his head to clear his doubts.

Bonnie's second shot was as good as the first. It hit about twenty meters behind the bow, detonating in the same manner. Clyde turned the big boat around again and they sped away from the now doomed freighter.

'Wait!' Bonnie cried as she quickly reloaded one of the RPGs. 'Give me a good shot at the stern.'

Clyde slowed the boat and turned to run closer. As they cleared the freighter's stern, Bonnie fired. This time, her aim was much higher than the waterline. The missile impacted just where the rudder shaft exited the hull and supported the huge rudder below. The explosion was unspectacular—the grenade simply slammed through the hull plating and detonated inside, as it was designed to do. But inside, it destroyed the ship's steering system, the hydraulic motors, and the mechanical linkages that turned the ship.

'I do hope we just did the right thing,' Bonnie said as she walked back inside.

Clyde's confidence returned as he handed her the glasses. 'Take a look at the stern. Tell me what flag you see and what is painted under the railing.'

Bonnie scanned the ship as they passed. 'The flag is square with yellow and black squares.'

'And what's painted on the stern?' Clyde asked.

Bonnie looked again before slowly putting the gasses down. 'Danger, Plague ship,' She was quiet as she sank into the lounge. 'Was that a body hanging there?'

'Yeah, I think they caught the sign writer,' Clyde replied solemnly.

Then Bonnie started to shake, uncontrollable sobs racking her body. Eventually, she regained her composure as Clyde moved to her side.

She brushed him aside and stood. 'Think about the last twenty hours. First, we wake up on this boat, our memories are gone, but we know everything about the weapons we find. We meet and start to investigate our situation and all we end up with are more damn questions.'

She held her hand up as Clyde tried to speak. 'No, let me finish. Next, we end up screwing on the deck only a few hours after we met. And this morning, not twenty-four hours later, we kill half a dozen people and severely damage, if not sink, a large freighter. And I almost forgot, the damn computers on this boat believe this is 2065 and we know the day before yesterday was 2032. Go fucking figure!' she yelled, her voice cracking with emotion.

Clyde wrapped his arms around her and drew her close, Bonnie's body shaking uncontrollably as she sobbed into his chest. He didn't speak—there were no words to help. He knew she just had to come to terms with what had happened. He glanced back to the helm. The autopilot was running the boat, they were back on course and running at twenty-five knots; even the fuel usage wasn't causing problems.

*Whatever those engines are, they run on the smell of an oily rag.* He was correct—the engines and drive system, according to the computer, had been developed in New Zealand and gave huge increases in efficiency over conventional diesel/prop systems. The figures he was seeing on the engine monitor were over thirty percent better than he had predicted. He relaxed; they could keep this speed up for a couple of hours without affecting their reserves.

Eventually, the sobbing stopped and Bonnie pulled back. She wiped the tears from her face and looked into Clyde's eyes. 'Sorry, must be a silly female thing.'

Clyde dismissed her words. 'What a load... you were amazing and I don't believe in that *silly female* crap anyway. You're way stronger than you give yourself credit for. Plus that was a rather intense time.'

'But you haven't been reduced to a blubbering mess?'

Clyde looked deep into her eyes – that's when she saw it.

'Not on the outside,' he whispered. Bonnie saw the truth of his words. Generations of male conditioning was at work here; outwardly, he was showing a tough persona, but inside, she saw something different, almost a scared small boy, she smiled and moved back into his arms.

Eventually, they broke apart and both sat in the helm chairs and checked the instruments, nothing had changed, even the freighter was no longer showing on the radar, indicating it was either out of range or it had sunk. Either way, she was now reconciled with their actions.

That's when she realized she was hungry. Looking at the console clock, she shook her head. 'Looks like brunch will be the order of the day.'

10:36 displayed on the screen, so Clyde gently reduced the throttle position until the boat settled back to eighteen knots, he checked all the indicators again, and set the alarms.

'Then, brunch it is,' he said as Bonnie led the way down the stairs.

# FIVE

They entered the saloon and Clyde went to the large doors, opened them, and stepped out.

'We should check, just in case they left any surprises,' he suggested. Bonnie followed him to the back of the cockpit—everything looked normal. Clyde moved down through the starboard door onto the swim platform.

'Blood!' he said as he drew his Glock, Bonnie raised her right-hand Uzi. She moved behind him and checked the starboard side of the boat; then continued across the deck and made sure no surprises were hiding to port.

The blood trail stopped at the lazarette door. Clyde motioned for Bonnie to stand to his left as he flicked the latch. He pressed the raise button on the control and the door opened, the lights coming on automatically.

Clyde spun across the opening, instantly scanning inside. He stopped. There, lying on the floor was a body. Somehow, it had managed to open the hatch and fall inside; slowly he climbed down the ladder, his gaze and the Glock not leaving the body. Bonnie moved to the opening to cover him. He checked for weapons, found an AK74, and quickly removed it before checking for a pulse.

'No pulse,' Clyde said.

Instantly Bonnie was at his side, a knife in her hand. She cut the wetsuit hood away, revealing a young woman's face. She reached down and checked the neck, moving her fingers around until she stopped. 'Wrong, it's there, very weak.' She turned to Clyde. 'We've got to get her to the medical cabin now.'

Bonnie's demeanour made it clear she was in no mood for discussion as he holstered his pistol. He climbed back up the ladder as Bonnie lifted the woman and held her upright. Clyde reached down and took her under the armpit and as gently as possible hauled the limp form out of the lazarette; Bonnie followed and helped by taking the legs. Together, they carried the body down to the cabin. Once inside, Bonnie quickly set up one of the beds and they laid the woman on it.

'I can handle things now. Go and clean up the mess,' she directed Clyde as she began to cut the wetsuit off.

Clyde returned to the lazarette, grabbing a mop and bucket on the way. He mixed up some disinfectant and began cleaning down the swim platform and the lazarette floor. When he was satisfied the area was clean, he hosed any residue away. He climbed back up to the cockpit, closing the access gate behind him, and began a methodical search for any more blood and spent casings.

Clyde placed the confiscated weapon on the table and stood looking out to sea.

*The engine room, I didn't check there.* He cursed himself. He stepped back out and opened the hatch. It lifted slowly on its hydraulic struts. Instinctively, he drew his pistol and quickly moved to port, just in case. Clyde slowly climbed backward down the ladder, the Glock covering the room.

It was hot; both engines had been running all night and one generator was always on duty. Carefully, he checked around the starboard engine – nothing there. Then he moved over to the port side. Slowly, he checked the port engine and finding nothing, holstered his pistol. He climbed back out of the engine room, satisfied that it hadn't been breached and returned to the swim platform. He climbed back down the lazarette, checking it again before returning to the saloon. He picked up the confiscated weapon—noting how light it was—removed the magazine and inspected it.

*Empty?* He was confused. 'Why would anyone try to take a boat with an unloaded weapon?' He cycled the action and checked the breech. It hadn't been fired. Now he was getting suspicious.

Clyde placed the rifle on the lounge and climbed the stairs. The boat was equipped with a 360-degree security system so he pulled up the feed from the encounter. He ran through it several times until he found what he wanted. He sat back, scratching his head. 'Fuck me,' he whispered.

'Maybe later; I'm too tired at the moment.' Bonnie's voice lilted from the stairs.

'How's your patient?'

Bonnie smiled and held out her right hand; Clyde frowned as he reached over and took what she was holding. 'Three seven point six two rounds; she was shot by her own people.'

Clyde took the three deformed bullets. 'I know – watch.' He re-ran the video feed. It showed the woman being forced off a small inflatable that drew away from the stern of the boat. She disappeared behind the stern lounge then someone fired from the inflatable. 'Three shots,' he smiled as they continued to watch and the inflatable returned to the boat. Three disembarked and two started to climb up to the stern deck. Next, the action exploded. The reports from Clyde's Glock were recorded, as were the two miscreants disappearing over the stern.

He stopped the feed. 'There, that's the lazarette door. That arsehole dumped her down there.' Clyde started the recording again and watched as Bonnie effectively despatched the third intruder and the small inflatable.

'But why shoot her if she's one of them?' Bonnie cried.

Clyde answered. 'She was a decoy, bait, if you like. She was supposed to draw us out, we throw down on her, she surrenders and that would have given them an indication of our capability. The least it would have done is distract us long enough for them to storm the boat. But she didn't do what they wanted. She hunkered down behind the lazarette and that bastard shot her for it. So do you still think we did the wrong thing back there?'

Bonnie's reply was dead cold. 'No, I think we did the only thing we could.'

'So how's the patient? Will she be all right?'

Bonnie nodded. 'Yeah, she'll survive. She lost a lot of blood but she's strong and we have plenty of plasma and blood on board. As soon as I have her type matched, I'll start her on whole blood. She'll be okay.' A cloud of concern seemed to float over Bonnie. Her face reflected how serious she was feeling.

'Clyde, what have we been chucked into? This boat, it's specifically designed for this job. The engines, the weapons, and the medical room... it's so bloody well-equipped. Every time I open another cupboard I find new gear. But the weird thing is; I know how to use it, not in any polished TV version, but in a real-world, battlefield way. Shit, how do I even know there's a difference?'

Clyde stood and moved to her side. He took her face in his hands and tilted it up so he could look into her eyes. 'Truthfully, I have absolutely no idea. I know no more than you do, but I'm glad we can do these things. All we can do is keep moving forward. Eventually, we'll figure it out... together. It's bloody obvious we've obviously been brought here for a reason, hopefully when we reach those islands, we'll get some answers.'

Bonnie took his hands in hers and held them tight. She smiled and nodded. 'Thank you. That's what I needed to hear. I'd better get back to our guest. Oh, I don't know about you, but I'm bloody hungry. So far we've missed breakfast and lunch. Think you could rustle something up?'

They left the bridge, Bonnie heading to the medical room and Clyde the kitchen. Fifteen minutes later, he opened the door to the med room and announced that a meal was ready.

They sat quietly while they devoured a plate of sandwiches and only started to talk as they poured coffee. Bonnie catalogued their guest's injuries and her prognosis for recovery – Clyde listened, struggling to comprehend all Bonnie was saying but, from her words and demeanour, it was obvious she knew what she was talking about

Bonnie saw the dark rings under his eyes, and then she remembered. 'Clyde, you need some sleep, you didn't get much last night.'

'Can't; we need to keep an eye on things out there and then there's your patient. You can't leave her alone for long. Don't worry, I'll be fine.'

'Bullshit. It appears that I've been selected as ship's doctor and you'll do as I say. No macho crap, so listen up. There's a spare bed in medical. You go down there and sleep. I'm sure that if our guest wakes, you'll respond. I'll keep an eye on things up here and wake you if I need to. No arguments just do it.'

Clyde knew she was right and followed meekly as she led him to the room. The spare bed was made and ready, all he had to do was remove his shoes and lay down. Bonnie busied herself checking the patient and five minutes later as she prepared to leave, she knew Clyde was already asleep. She smiled and quietly closed the door behind her as she left.

*** 

'Clyde, wake up!' Bonnie's voice echoed in his ears. 'Wake up!'

He felt someone shaking him and his eyes flew open. Momentary disorientation took hold. He felt slightly nauseous and unsure of his surroundings, but only for a few seconds.

'We're not moving,' Clyde said as he sat up.

'No, the proximity alarm went off and the engines stopped. You need to see this.' Bonnie's voice was fast and agitated. She dragged on his left arm, forcing him off the bed. Clyde glanced at the other bed. The patient was still there but he noticed the transfusion line had been removed.

'Is she getting better?' he asked, not actually expecting an answer.

'Yes, I'll explain later. Come on.' Bonnie was almost frantic as she dragged Clyde towards the bridge stairs.

They raced up to the top deck, Bonnie now standing aside and pointing out to port. Clyde stopped dead. 'What the hell is this?'

'Exactly, the boat just stopped,' Bonnie replied.

Stretching out to port and ahead of the boat was a debris field. Bits of boats floated everywhere—wood, sails, chunks of fiberglass, and clothing bobbed on the gentle swell. Even in the fading light of early evening, the extent of the field was huge.

Clyde leaped to the helm and checked the screens. He worked quickly, scanning the field as best he could.

'There must be ten or twenty boats wrecked here. What the hell happened?' Clyde picked up the binoculars and began scanning, searching ahead and to each side of the boat. At length, he put them down, defeated by the available light. He checked the time; 19:00 was displayed on the screen.

He turned to Bonnie. 'What do you want to do?'

'I don't know, that's why I woke you.' Bonnie threw the problem back to Clyde.

He walked out to the top deck, again scanning the field, achieving the same result. 'I think we should wait until it's fully dark and use the night vision gear to check this out. After that, we can look for a way through this mess, or go around it.'

Bonnie took this decision and her attitude changed. 'I'll go and check on our guest. If you want, you can find something for dinner.'

Bonnie left and Clyde set about checking the security settings before leaving the bridge. He didn't feel much like cooking, so he checked the freezer, found a large Meat Master pizza, read the instructions, placed it in the oven, and selected the pizza program.

Ten minutes later, Bonnie walked back into the saloon to the delicious aroma of pizza. 'You read my mind.' Her voice was filled with anticipation. 'Pizza is one of my favourite indulgences.' She sat and eagerly took a slice.

Conversation was minimal until each had finished their last piece. Clyde closed the box while Bonnie was busy making coffee. He glanced over to the liquor cabinet, wondering if a stiff Scotch would be a good idea. Eventually, he decided that it could wait. The time was now 20:05 and the ocean outside was dark and foreboding.

Clyde took the mug Bonnie offered and sank into the leather seat. A groan from a speaker behind him had him up and scanning the room instantly.

Bonnie chuckled. 'Our guest seems to be waking. I'll go check on her.'

They both stood and Clyde took the stairs up to the bridge. He switched all the internal lights off and took the night vision headset out of its case. The night was clear and the moon hadn't risen so Clyde had a good view of the debris field.

He put the set on and allowed his vision to adjust, then began scanning the wreckage. His heart was heavy—the devastation was worse than he'd first thought. He re-estimated at least thirty boats were wrecked here, and his mind began to race. *What could have caused this?* The question raced around inside his head, with the nagging fear that whatever caused this, could still be lurking in the vicinity and their boat could be at risk. *The longer we stay, the greater the risk.* Then he remembered what the boat was equipped with. He sat at the helm and brought up the system menu. 'YES!' Clyde cried out loud.

The boat had a full suite of electronics, including FLIR (Forward looking Infrared) thermal imaging cameras. Quickly, he reviewed the operating instructions and initialized the system. He selected the greyscale setting and began to scan the field. Clyde didn't really know what he was looking for; he just felt it was imperative that he looked.

He started to port and systematically scanned the wreckage, taking his time. He was so intent on his search; he didn't hear Bonnie come up the stairs. She placed her hands on his shoulders. Clyde jumped from his seat. 'Shit, you startled me,' he said, much to the mirth of Bonnie. 'Our guest?'

'Awake and hungry, luckily the bullets missed anything important, blood loss was the main issue but she should make a full recovery; she's in the saloon.' Bonnie looked at the display. 'What's this?'

'Thermal imaging; don't know why, but something inside said I had to do it. It looks for heat signatures.'

Bonnie pushed past him, staring at the screen. 'What does a white blob mean?'

Clyde turned back to the screen, adjusted the resolution, and zoomed in on the blob Bonnie had seen. He worked the controls until he had the image as good as he could get it.

Now there were three white blobs.

'Well?' Bonnie was more insistent this time.

'I don't know,' Clyde replied.

'They're people.' The breathless voice came from the stairs. Bonnie leaped around and caught the young woman as she began to sag. The effort of climbing the stairs had been too much.

'I told you to stay down there. You're far too weak to climb those stairs,' Bonnie chided, as she helped the young woman to the lounge and immediately checked her wounds. 'You're bloody lucky you didn't rip these open.' Bonnie turned and headed down the stairs, leaving their guest with Clyde.

Clyde studied their guest. She was young, he estimated in her mid to late-twenties, with brown hair and eyes. Her face was long and angular, but still very attractive.

'Those signatures are people, my people,' she gasped through breaths. 'We've got to help them, please.'

Her eyes pleaded in a way that tore at Clyde's heart, but common sense won the day. 'There's nothing we can do for them tonight, it's just too dangerous. I'll monitor them and we'll see what we can do in the morning.'

'But they might not survive!' she said.

'And if this boat is disabled, or worse, neither will we – no we'll wait until it's light.'

Bonnie returned just as Clyde finished. She had blankets and pillows and quickly made up a bed on the lounge before she went back downstairs. Returning with the pizza box, Bonnie placed it on the table and opened it to reveal the last three pieces. The girl didn't have to be asked a second time and soon had a large slice on her plate.

'Now,' Bonnie said. 'I think you should tell us what's going on.'

The girl hesitated as she took a bite of her pizza. 'Maybe that should go both ways,' she suggested quietly.

Clyde looked at her. She seemed so young and vulnerable. He just couldn't consider her a threat. 'My name is Clyde and this is Bonnie. Two days ago it was 2032 for us. We woke up on this boat and things started to get crazy; truth is even our names may not be ours. We can't remember who we are, but those names were in the cabins we woke in.

'So far, we've discovered skills neither of us knew we had before; found weapons we instinctively knew, we killed half a dozen bad guys, oh, and we sank an old freighter. Now the fucking computer says it's 2065. That's our story, what's yours?' Clyde stood back and waited for her to speak.

'First, your computer is correct, it is 2065, so what has happened to you I don't know. My name is Allison Denham. My father is Professor Reginald Denham.' She seemed to be looking for some recognition. Getting none, she continued. 'I was part of this refugee convoy, heading to some islands he is supposed to have found.'

'Bullshit. From your accent I'd say you're a Kiwi, a New Zealander. How can you be a refugee?'

Allison looked bemused. 'You really don't know, do you?' She looked from one to the other. 'Neither of you have any idea of what's happened, do you?' She sat back, looking at her hosts as though they were children. 'Look, I'm too weak to go into detail, so here's a summary.' She took a long drink of water.

'During the twenty twenties, we had construed pandemics. It turned out to be the first attempt to control the entire world population by administering a vaccine that killed people, or at best made them very dependent on further pharmaceuticals. Sadly, for the elitists who were in charge of the attempt, it failed dismally when their final *saviour vaccine* proved to be more dangerous than the virus it was to fight. There were mass riots and governments fell; an ideal time for a civil war.

'In twenty – twenty five, Islamic Jihad groups began a campaign of terror in every western country they could. At that stage, Europe had thirty million refugees to deal with, most of whom sided with the Jihadists. England finally closed all points of entry and began forcibly deporting militant refugees; then the UN retaliated and tried to blockade the country.

'Next, civil wars started in America and Australia. New Zealand was overrun because of the socialist policies of our government. In twenty – twenty six, the war in America spread to Europe. Germany fell and France, as usual, surrendered. Hungary, Poland, and a few others joined forces with England and broke the UN blockade. The UN and one of the Elitist organisations, declared its total government of the One World, as it then called Earth, and refused to accept or even recognize any national borders. It tried to invade America and was defeated. You must have lived through all this and still have no memory?

Both Bonnie and Clyde responded with a shake of their heads. Allison continued.

'Anyway, things calmed down for a while, twenty – twenty seven saw a kind of ceasefire. Everything continued this way until twenty thirty five, when someone, we still don't know who, released an airborne pathogen. Some suggested it was a desperate attempt by religious fanatics to bring on the end of days. There was one report that it was a final act of some mad Jihadist. There were reports of them declaring they had been given a mighty sword by Allah—a sword to destroy all unbelievers.

'All I know for sure is that the pathogen is like every apocalypse movie on steroids. The infection took different paths in different people. It has different symptoms, even in the same families, and it totally confounded all the authorities.' She had another drink. 'By twenty forty, the population of Earth was reduced by eighty percent and everything broke down. All infrastructures started to fail because there was no one to monitor or repair it, but some survived. Some, like our group, have a sort of natural immunity that helps our bodies fight off the plague, and we then became the most valuable commodity ever.

'The UN, or what was left of it, decided to hunt us down and use us to find a cure. They captured hundreds of us; used us in the most horrible experiments, even resorting to draining the blood from living people, to try and find their cure; but couldn't find one. There was nothing they could do to stop the devastation. By then, almost every country was uninhabitable—decaying corpses were everywhere. So the authorities took to the sea. Ships like the freighter have been scouring the planet for years, tracking us down. They found us and that is the result.' Allison pointed to the debris field. 'Now they have given up trying to find a cure. They are completely insane and are hunting down any survivors and killing them, an *end-of-days* fervour has taken control.' She slumped down on the lounge, exhaustion etched on her face.

Bonnie went to her, adjusted the pillows, and within minutes, Allison Denham was asleep.

# Six

Allison's news shocked both of them.

Bonnie retreated to the other lounge and lay down, trying to sleep. Clyde knew that would be a total waste of time for him, so he set to and kept a watch on the instruments. Nothing new was showing.

Boredom soon got to him and he left the helm and went to the cupboards opposite the table. They hadn't had a look in these as yet, so he opened the first one. Inside there were four boxes, each one containing a state-of-the-art drone. These were much more than toys, each was unit fitted with a hi-res, low light/infrared camera. He unpacked one, being careful not to make any noise, as he didn't want to wake either of his companions.

The light was far too low for him to make out the instructions, so he took the drone down into the main saloon, switched on the lights, and began reading. The units were advanced. He remembered something, just a flash of him playing with earlier versions, but they were dinosaurs compared to the unit before him; still, many of the functions seemed familiar. They could be flown manually or in autonomous mode, allowing them to search a predetermined area.

An idea sprang forth—now he had an option.

He checked the battery pack, only half-charged. Clyde attached it to the charger and plugged it into a power point. Next, he went back upstairs and checked the GPS coordinates of where he wanted to search, entered the pattern into the controller, and sat back to wait for the battery to charge.

Twenty minutes later, a soft chime from the saloon told him the battery was fully charged. He retrieved the pack and inserted it into the drone. Following the pre-flight instructions, he moved each of the rotor support arms into the correct position, connected the controller, and moved the unit to the rear fly bridge deck. He set it on the small table and activated the learn function—with this the unit "learned" where it was, this would now be the reference point for all subsequent navigation.

Clyde activated the camera and checked its operation. The image on the small screen on the controller showed his face. He chuckled quietly. 'Let's hope you find someone better looking than that.'

He stood back and initiated the program. The drone's rotors began to spin and it lifted gently off the table, hovering for a couple of seconds before lifting to a height that cleared the boat's superstructure. It paused while the program plotted a course, then set off towards its destination.

Clyde moved back inside and took the USB cable from the drone box and plugged it into a port on the helm station. He selected that as the source for the screen and instantly the feed from the drone was displayed in front of him. At eight meters off the water, he got a great view of the debris field—bits of boats floated everywhere, but his main interest was below the water, and this wasn't being shown.

The drone arrived at its programmed destination and Clyde saw his objective. A small dinghy, undamaged but well-concealed by the wreckage around it; three white dots appeared on the screen. Switching to manual control, Clyde dropped the drone lower, trying to get a better view of who was in the small craft. The drone dropped until finally, at about three meters above the water, a better image was possible. He set the drone to hover mode and changed from IR to low light function.

Now he could see his targets. Three bodies lay huddled together, partially hidden under a tarp. Two looked like adults, but the third was a small child. Clyde thought it looked about five years old. No-one moved; even though the drone would be clearly audible at the height it was currently hovering.

He checked the battery status of the drone, still ninety-six percent. He activated the return to base function and set the decision parameter to ten percent battery capacity. Next, he moved to the radar and checked for any other vessels and weather fronts.

What he saw didn't make him feel better. A large storm front was moving in from the north, and it looked deep. 'Fuck!'

'Fuck what?' Allison's voice carried from the lounge. Then Bonnie was beside him, watching the drone feed.

'Yes, Clyde, fuck what?' she said.

He pointed to the radar screen. 'Looks like it'll hit in about three hours and we don't want to be anywhere near this debris field when it does.'

Bonnie looked at the time readout. 'Well, that settles it, we go in now.'

'Are you totally mad? If we get hung up, it's goodnight for us all, them included!' Clyde pointed to the drone feed.

Bonnie stood, hands on hips. 'Clyde, you said yourself that we don't have any propellers or rudders, so there's nothing to snag. Why can't we just push our way through the debris and pick them up?'

'It's not that simple. We still have the jet outlets at the back of the boat and the intakes. And before you carry on, yes, we can clear them with the rake, but we can't see under the boat. What if we hit something that holes us? Where are we then?'

Everyone fell silent. Clyde was sure they knew he had a valid point, but neither woman said so.

Clyde turned back to the helm, despondent at the thought of not being able to do anything. He sat looking at the controls and switch banks, hoping something would magically jump up and save the day.

There were two switches he didn't recognize, one labelled UWL and the other UWC. He had no idea what they were for, but he decided to flick them anyhow. First, he flicked the UWL button. Nothing seemed to happen. *Maybe they're just spares*, he thought, and absentmindedly flicked the UWC switch.

This time he got a result. The screen showing the drone feed changed and displayed an underwater scene. Not just one, but six separate views.

'What did you do? Get the drone back!' a frantic Allison cried.

Clyde studied the screen. 'Hang on a minute.' He picked up the drone controller and disconnected the USB cable. The small screen now showed the dinghy. 'I'll be...' he started, 'these are under the boat; underwater lights and cameras, now we've got a chance.'

Tentatively, Clyde switched the station-keeping function off and selected reverse. The boat responded immediately. He studied the screen as they slowly moved away from the wreckage. When he was satisfied he had enough information, he brought it back to neutral and all motion faded away.

'These two are in the bow, one above the water and one below.' He pointed to the top two images. 'This one is mid-ship and these three are at the stern, two below the waterline and one above. Now that we can see, we can try and reach them.' He selected forward and the boat started moving in that direction.

Clyde switched on the bow lights and the two floodlights above him, illuminating the water in front of them. At least now he should see any obstacles before they collided. Slowly, the big cruiser moved forward, Clyde using only a minimal throttle setting. Allison was glued to the drone control and Bonnie helped Clyde with the underwater vision.

'Stop,' Bonnie called, and Clyde pulled the controls back to neutral. 'There, what's that?' she asked.

'Looks like a sail, just under the surface.' Carefully, he joggled the controls, orienting the boat for the best chance of missing the sail. When it was pointed where he wanted, he engaged forward again, and they moved in that direction.

Clyde used the forward sonar to help. The proximity alarm was off because it would be going crazy now. Then he saw something else, pulled the controls back to neutral, and allowed the boat to drift.

Allison was behind him. 'That's our boat, but they sank it.'

'Must have an air pocket,' Clyde replied as he studied the cruiser. It was inverted, lying just ten meters below the surface. 'Damn, that's weird. Sends shivers down my spine. Thankfully, it's too deep to worry us.'

He again engaged forward. They were into the worst part, where the smaller craft, or what was left of them, were bunched together. Worse still, many were tethered to each other, creating an underwater spider web of ropes to contend with. Clyde's solution was simple. He retrieved a boat hook from the rear deck, attached a combat knife to one end, and handed his finished masterpiece to Bonnie.

'I can think of a few things I could do with this, but I bet you have a specific task in mind,' she said.

Clyde brought two of the comm units out of their bags, handed one to Bonnie, and took the other himself. 'Correct. You take this up to the bow. Any rope we encounter, either move out of the way with the hook or cut it with the other end. Simple.'

'Yeah simple,' Bonnie replied, Clyde saw the understanding in her eyes, but he also saw her reluctance to hanging over the front of the boat trying to saw through ropes. She tested the edge of the knife and was reassured that it would do the job; anything short of a steel cable would be no match for it.

Ten minutes later, with Bonnie securely tied to the bow stanchions; Clyde called her on the comm system. 'Ready?'

'*As I ever will be.*'

Clyde edged the big boat slowly forward. Every now and then, Bonnie called a halt as she dealt with an obstruction. Their progress was painfully slow—the debris field was a chaotic tangle—but with every passing minute, the dinghy got a little closer.

'We might have a problem,' Allison said. 'What's this mean?' She turned the drone controller to Clyde. The battery level meter was showing yellow, down to twenty-five percent.

'That's okay; we should be there by the time it needs to return.' Then he remembered the drone was programmed to return to the boat, but the boat was no longer where the drone was programmed to return to.

'You're right, we do have a problem. I'll need to bring it back manually, keep an eye on this figure.' He pointed to the battery indicator. 'When it reaches fifteen percent, call me. I'll bring it back then.' He was hoping they would be at the dinghy by then.

They were less than twenty meters from the dinghy when Bonnie called a halt. There was a mass of ropes in front of them and she had to clear them all before moving. Clyde used the time to bring the drone back. He checked one of the battery packs in the other drone boxes. It was fully charged, so he installed it and sent the drone back on station.

It took Bonnie twenty minutes to clear the ropes. Clyde tried to help, but there was little he could do. But with the barrier gone, they had a clear run to the dinghy, and their worries were just beginning.

Clyde checked the weather radar again. The storm was huge and moving faster than he had first predicted. They had less than an hour to rescue the survivors and clear the wreckage before it hit.

Slowly he approached the dinghy; any sudden manoeuvre could be a disaster. Gently, he let the small craft touch his boat. Clyde held the cruiser on station as Bonnie secured the dinghy with her boat hook and held it firm as she walked it to the stern. Clyde and Allison joined her as she tied the two boats together before stepping down into the small craft. Carefully, she moved the tarp away and checked their vital signs.

'They're alive, just.' She gently lifted the small child, a girl, and handed her to Clyde, who took her into the saloon and handed her to Allison.

Together, Bonnie and Clyde lifted the two adults onto the boarding platform and then into the saloon. Clyde returned to the dinghy, noting that it was moving strongly in the increasing swell from the approaching storm. There were a few items he retrieved that looked like the people's possessions, and then he cut the small boat free. Immediately, it began drifting away.

He removed the folding table and chairs in the cockpit and stowed them in the lazarette, closing the large doors as he entered the saloon. The boat was moving, rising, and falling with the swell, as he approached Bonnie. 'Sorry, but I'll need you upfront. We've got to clear this debris now. That storm is too bloody close.' Bonnie nodded and took her tool, opened the doors again, and stepped out.

The sea around the dinghy's position was full of ropes, so Clyde knew that Bonnie had her work cut out to try and clear the mess.

'*Come forward, slowly.*' Bonnie's voice crackled with static from the approaching storm. Clyde engaged forward, but the boat didn't move. He looked up at the display. There was the problem, the one thing he'd been dreading—a large sail had somehow been caught up on the intakes for the drives and both were blocked.

'Hang on; we've picked up a sail. I'll try and clear it.' Clyde activated the rake but nothing happened. While the rake was designed to clear flotsam from the intake, the sail remained stuck.

'The engines, maybe they need to be shut down?' Allison suggested. Clyde was reluctant to shut the engines off. If Murphy's Law was in action, they wouldn't start again, but he knew he had no choice.

Hesitantly, he reached for the key and shut down the port engine. It made little difference. Next, he shut down the starboard engine. Still no effect, so he operated the rakes again. This time the sail moved, but it still covered the intakes.

The boat heaved with the swell. In the distance, Clyde could see white caps, something he didn't want to see with no engines and Bonnie still tied to the bow. Again the rakes moved the sail back, but the intake was still blocked.

*'What the hell are you doing? I'm getting drowned out here!'* Bonnie's voice was furious. Then a particularly large swell lifted the boat and a shrill cry echoed in Clyde's head. He looked up, Bonnie was still tied off, but she was drenched and water was running off her and the bow.

Clyde chuckled—a nervous reaction—as he watched the sail drift back behind the boat. He reached for the port engine key and turned it, holding his breath. He felt it catch and watched the rev counter settle at idle. He repeated this with the starboard engine. He finally let his breath out when the rev counter showed him it was running.

'Coming forward, Bonnie,' he announced as he raised the buckets from the neutral position. Gently, the boat moved ahead, both Clyde and Allison intent on the screen. They had to stop twice more so Bonnie could clear ropes before clearing the debris field.

With the field falling astern, Clyde handed the helm to Allison and hurried down the stairs, out the rear of the saloon and raced to the bow. Bonnie was working on removing the tether when he arrived.

A blast from the horn warned them that something was amiss. Clyde looked ahead and saw a large swell still forming, with no whitecap, heading straight for them. He grabbed Bonnie and she wrapped her arms and legs around him just as the bow lifted. He felt Allison increase power, trying to keep momentum, and next the bow crashed down, into the following trough.

*'Get moving, there's more of that ahead.'* Allison's voice boomed out of the speakers on the top of the fly bridge. Clyde didn't need any encouragement. He grabbed the knife end of Bonnie's stick and deftly cut her free. Holding each other for support, they carefully moved back to the stern and the safety of the saloon.

Clyde stood back and looked at his companion—she was soaked and looked totally miserable.

'Talk about drowned rats.' He chuckled as he moved past her and up the stairs.

'Next time you can clear any fucking debris!' she yelled as he raced away, taking the stairs three at a time. Allison was holding the wheel tightly, her face drained of colour, as she tried to keep the boat on an even course. Outside the sea was a mess. Swells and waves, driven by the chaos of the storm, rushed toward the boat from every direction. Keeping to a course was almost impossible.

Clyde was impressed with the way the young woman handled the boat. She hadn't been joking when she'd told them she had some experience. 'You right there?' he asked.

'Yes. Believe me, I've run through worse than this. When I was younger, I used to sail with my father, how are our survivors?'

'The guy is semi-conscious, but the other two are still out. Bonnie's with them now,' he answered as he studied the approaching sea.

'I think you should get down there. Bonnie will need your help,' Allison said. Clyde saw the reason. Large masses of dark water were visible, rearing up higher than the boat. He didn't waste time as he slid down the polished banister rail.

'Bonnie, we need to get our guests secured now,' he called as he landed in the saloon. She scooped up the small girl as Clyde reached the woman, and they rushed to the medical cabin. They placed their charges on the beds.

Bonnie turned to Clyde. 'You should get back to Allison. I'll take care of these two.' As she spoke, Bonnie felt the bow rise as they assaulted another huge swell.

'I'll help,' a thin reedy voice announced. The male of the trio was only just standing in the doorway;—the doorway was all that was holding him upright, but the look of determination on his face told Clyde that arguing was a waste of time, so he accepted the offer and left.

✳ ✳ ✳

Bonnie smiled as she gestured for the newcomer to take the chair in the corner of the room while she busied herself setting up two saline and electrolyte feeds.

'You're all badly dehydrated. How long were you in the dinghy?' she asked as she handed him a bottle of prepared electrolytes.

He took the drink gratefully, opened it, and drained the contents before speaking. He was tall and, Bonnie thought, good-looking. His dark hair was matted and salt-encrusted, and his grey eyes were tired in a way she hadn't seen for a long time.

'I don't know, a week, maybe ten days. We had a small survival pack, but it ran out after a few days.'

'But you must have had water?' Bonnie was curious. If the pack had run out after a few days, water would be a huge problem.

'We rationed it from the start. Plus, we had a small filter system in the pack, but it finally failed two days ago.' He looked slightly embarrassed. 'We saved our urine; the last two days we had to drink that. Do you have any idea how futile that can feel – all the water of the Pacific Ocean, and all you have to drink is piss?'.

Bonnie laughed, seeing the irony of the situation. Thankfully, she had the woman and child now hooked up to the intravenous feed and everything securely locked down. She sensed something coming and called out, 'Hang on!' just as the bow of the boat lifted violently and the engine speed increased.

At the helm, Allison and Clyde hung on tightly. Clyde pushed the engine controls to their maximum, the rev counters showing at red line. The angle increased as the boat climbed the wall of water in front of them.

'I didn't see it. It came from nowhere!' Allison cried as she fought the helm.

They were racing up a forty-five-degree wall of water. Clyde could see the top of the huge wave, still several meters above them. His mind was cool as he ran through a few scenarios. This could be a freak wave and if so, he needed to be ready to drop the engine revs as they broke through the top. It didn't matter if they were props, jets, or even with their advanced turbine system; if the intakes came out of the water, there would be no load for the engine to drive. With no load, engine revs could climb to dangerous levels almost instantly.

His other scenario was much better. If this was a surge driven by the storm, there was a possibility there would be some larger top to the wall they were climbing. In that case, they would come off the top and slide gently down the back of the swell; a much better result than crashing through the top of a wave. *Boats this big don't fly very well* he thought.

He felt the angle increase. He held tight to the back of Allison's chair for support. His mind raced as he tried to remember what angle the boat could take before it flipped. The engines roared and drove them harder, still fighting to tame the monster they were riding.

The bow ripped through the top of the swell. Clyde waited for the right moment to pull the throttles back. Too soon, and the boat could be sucked back down the face of the swell. Too late, and the engines could be damaged. He didn't try to rationalize his actions. When his instinct told him to reduce the throttles, he did.

The boat started to fall, the drive intakes now out of the water and the engines idling. The beams from the floodlights lit their course. It was a storm-driven surge. The water behind the swell was full and a mess, almost a maelstrom, but the boat landed gently and Clyde applied more throttle. The intakes now flooded, it surged forward easily, handling the confused sea in their path.

Clyde began to relax. He smiled as he gripped Allison's shou der. 'You weren't joking. You really have done this before – bloody good job!'

'I've seen some big seas, but that was way above anything I've ever seen before,' Allison replied.

Clyde could see her hands were shaking from the excess adrenalin now coursing through her system. 'How about you go below and check on Bonnie? I'll take it from here.'

Gratefully, she accepted and disappeared down the stairs. The worst was over—the huge storm was now behind them and, barring any new weather issues, they all should be able to relax, at least for a while.

# SEVEN

The sea began to settle as soon as the storm front had passed, and an hour later they were again in relatively smooth waters. With only a gentle, even swell to contend with, Clyde was able to set the boat at twenty-two knots and altered their course back towards the desired destination.

The newcomers were all now conscious, although Bonnie kept the woman and child in the med cabin for observation and recovery. She was amazed they had survived, and wanted to make sure they were strong enough before letting them leave the beds. The male was doing much better. The fluids and electrolytes had revived him sufficiently for her to allow him to return to the saloon.

The first rays of sunlight splashed across the horizon as Clyde heard footsteps on the stairs to his left. He turned as the man he rescued appeared at the top of the stairs. 'Good morning. You definitely look in better shape than when we found you.'

'Yes, thanks to your partner. Interesting boat you have.' He held his hand out. Anton, Anton Garibaldi.'

Clyde shook it. 'Clyde – Clyde Robinson, I think – and yes she definitely is interesting.'

'Allison gave me a short version of your story; puzzling, to say the least. What do you know of the current situation?'

'Only what Allison told us. Some sort of pandemic seems to have wiped out most of the population.' Clyde again checked the instruments. Nothing was showing, so he switched all the alarms back on and turned to his companion. 'Must be time for breakfast; or at least coffee.'

Anton agreed and they descended the stairs again.

Allison was busy in the galley; they weren't the only ones who were hungry. Clyde opened the rear doors as the aroma of bacon and eggs wafted through the boat. Bonnie and the others joined them and introductions were made. Clyde was busy making toast while Bonnie took charge of the coffee supply.

Once they were all seated at the table, Anton began relating their story. They were part of a large group of survivors who'd been heading for the same location as Bonnie and Clyde. Unfortunately, they'd run afoul of the freighter and lost most of their people. A few had managed to leave in three larger cruisers while the rest had been either captured or killed.

Anton continued. 'We were all in New Zealand; it seemed that things there had quietened down. Then we got word from Allison's father that he had found and settled the islands, so we decided to make our way there. We have known the Professor and his family for years and when he asked us to find Allison, we agreed. We located her and the refugee fleet set off. Believe me, it was wonderful to be away from all the madness of the round ups.'

Clyde finished his meal and reached for the coffee pot. 'None of this makes any bloody sense. Why kill people who are immune to the plague, and where did it come from anyhow?'

Anton pushed his empty plate away, his eyes filled with pain and anguish. 'I think you need to know a little more. What Allison told you is the official story. The truth is somewhat different.' He filled his mug with steaming coffee. 'I'm a microbiologist and immunologist. Zena is a microbiologist and geneticist. We were working on a universal vaccine delivery system. Ours was a binary system. First, the patient is given a carrier vaccine. This bonds to the DNA of the subject and nothing else; it's totally inert and harmless. If there's an infection, say something like measles, all we had to do was deliver the universal vaccine and the carrier would use it to attack the foreign body, the measles virus, in this case.

'The secret to our research was the carrier. This was DNA-specific. It attached to the host's DNA and could modify the vaccine for any invader. It also was unique to the subject. Once bonded to that, it could ignore infections that posed no threat, allowing the body's immune system to do its job. Add to this, it could also reject the vaccine if it was not needed, so all the problems that vaccinations may have caused were gone.'

'Holy crap; that would've been worth billions to Big Pharma,' Clyde said. Then he realized the story hadn't finished. 'So what happened? I take it this didn't end well.'

Zena continued. 'Correct. When our results were published, well, you can imagine the bidding war. Pharma companies, med-tech operations, everyone wanted a piece of it; we were set to become billionaires. Then the government stepped in, or so we thought. We were feted by politicians, generals, and all the usual bureaucratic detritus.

'They pitched something that we thought was the best result. Instead of selling to the highest bidder and allowing that company to control the health of the world, our government offered to buy our discovery and distribute it to the world. The offer was generous and we would be given huge research budgets.'

'A con, I take it?' Bonnie asked.

'Totally – we agreed and handed over our data. We were paid, but the research funding was held up in red tape. That's when it all went pear-shaped. Anton?' Zena handed the floor back to her husband.

'That's when the bloody UN got involved. I think even back in your day it was a very one-eyed organization.'

Anton's comment brought a flood of memories to Clyde. 'Yeah, I remember now. It was predominantly owned, for want of a better word, by totalitarianism and was critical of anything that didn't support the spread of that ideology. Sadly, the fools we had as politicians were either too stupid to see, or complicit in what was going on. There were calls for the western world to pull out, but I don't think it happened.'

Anton shook his head. 'That's where you're wrong. Islamic Jihadists had flooded the west. Millions of young men were dumped, purporting to be refugees. They soaked up all the welfare and started to agitate. Finally, America had enough, and civil war broke out. Australia wasn't far behind and soon every western nation was involved in another world war, this time fought on each country's own soil.

'But that wasn't the worst of it. Every damn religion got involved. We had the New Templars, the Holy Mother warriors, Soldiers of Zion, even Buddhist fighters, so you can see the problem we faced.

'Sadly, the UN was in control of our invention. They distributed the catalyst globally, the first part of the system. Now every human being was "infected" with half the solution to disease.

Unfortunately, that's when the UN finally fell apart and one of the Jihadist groups got hold of the vaccine and mutated it into a biological weapon. They went out to the world, saying that they had a mighty weapon from God and only the true believers would be spared. So either we surrender and convert or face their god's retribution. Sound familiar?

'The leaders of every other religion, from the Pope down, started saying the same thing, pray, become pious and God will save you. Mass religious conversion broke out and reignited the war. But it wasn't the end. When the vast majority of the surviving world governments basically told the terrorists to go fuck themselves, they released the virus.

'Blind faith is a dangerous thing. The so-called true believers started dying, including the Jihadist leadership. Actually, they were some of the first to die. The Pope followed soon after.

'People everywhere started dropping like flies and we had no idea of how to save them; the problem was the mutated virus. It bonded with the catalyst and the host's DNA, and symptoms were individual. Families wouldn't get the same symptoms, even identical twins exhibited different problems. There was nothing we could do, as the Jihadists who'd stolen the virus killed anyone who was involved with the research, and, with their leadership now dead, we had nothing.

'There were some of us who had a form of immunity. Maybe the catalyst didn't bond with our DNA, maybe we had something different in our immune system, nobody knows. All we do know is that the virus mutated with each host it infected and that strain died with each individual host. In truth, we have no clue as to how it operated or why. Eventually, entire nations were devastated. With effective infection rates of over ninety-five percent and mortality rates of over ninety percent, our best option was isolation and survival. And here we are today.'

Bonnie spoke for the first time since Anton had begun. 'But what about now, what's happened to the virus? Has it spread to different species?'

'No, it's keyed to the human genome. As for the rest, I have no idea. We do know that there was a massive loss of life. There are probably fewer than half a billion humans left alive. Whole countries became massive open graves. Bodies were everywhere and the risk of secondary infection became too great. That's why the professor decided to find the islands, up until then it was just a rumour, something very few believed existed. You can imagine how we felt when he contacted us and told us about the islands and where to find him.'

There was silence for several minutes until Clyde stated the obvious. 'Okay, that's how the world died, but how the hell did we get here?' He looked at Bonnie; her face told him she wanted the answer as well.

Anton lowered his head. 'The only one who can answer your questions is Reginald Denham. Hopefully, he'll be at our destination. I'm sorry, but I just don't have the answer for you.'

Clyde looked at Bonnie again. The almost imperceptible shake of her head told him to drop the subject. If the Garibaldis couldn't—or wouldn't—answer, there must be a reason. 'Okay, looks like we have to wait,' he said as he refilled his coffee mug. 'I'll head back up to the bridge, see what's happening.' He had just reached the top of the stairs when the radar pinged. Something was almost dead ahead, at the extreme range of their system.

Clyde reached for the binoculars, but the range was still too great for him to see anything. 'What now?' he grumbled. Then he remembered the drones. He took one out of the cupboard and started to assemble it.

Allison's head appeared at the head of the stairs. 'Something wrong?'

Clyde looked up. 'Don't know yet. There's something out there, something large. I thought it might be prudent to allow the drone to have a look, before we run into something we'd rather avoid.'

Next, he checked the target's location—it wasn't moving. He programmed the parameters into the controller and took the drone out to the upper deck. He turned it on and set it on its programmed flight path. The target was at the extreme range for the drone. The controller had a maximum range of fifty kilometres line of sight; and the target was just under that.

Time was another factor—the drone had to travel the forty-six nautical miles to the target and then investigate. Maximum duration for the unit was listed, in the manual, as 2.5 hours. Time to target would be approximately fifty minutes. Investigating it would probably account for another forty-five. With a safety reserve, it would give forty-five minutes to retrieve the unit, provided nothing went wrong.

Clyde left the camera switched off, as he wanted to conserve as much power as he could. He busied himself at the helm, checking the fuel status, distance to their destination, the current fuel burn rate, and the fuel remaining in the tanks. The results were pleasing, the engine and drive system again proving to be frugal.

He could still see the drone just ahead of the boat, but it was pulling away with every second. Gently, he increased the boat speed slightly, until he reached twenty-eight knots. While this wasn't the most efficient speed, in terms of fuel use, but was the best compromise he could work out, given the need for speed and fuel conservation.

'Are we in a hurry?' Anton's voice emanated from the stairs. Next his head appeared, and he joined them at the helm station.

Allison answered. 'There's something out there; something big. Clyde sent a drone to have a look.'

Clyde was busy with the binoculars, trying to see what the target was. What he saw was huge and grey, but still not distinct enough to identify. Time passed slowly until curiosity finally won out. He plugged the USB cable into the port on the dash and activated the camera. The image flickered and then settled.

'You must be kidding,' Clyde said quietly. 'A bloody aircraft carrier; what's it doing just sitting there?' The drone still had several miles to go to reach the target, but already Clyde had a heavy feeling of dread. They sat, eyes glued to the screen, as the huge ship loomed closer.

When the drone was within one hundred meters, Clyde reverted to manual control, lifted it up, and scanned the flight deck. The scene was one straight out of an old urban horror flick, decaying corpses strewn around the deck haphazardly.

Bonnie's gasp of horror announced her arrival on the fly bridge. 'What's this?'

'An aircraft carrier, a bloody big one,' Clyde answered.

'Get closer to one of the bodies,' Bonnie demanded. Clyde obeyed and soon the scene was filled with the image of rotting flesh. Allison turned away, retching.

Bonnie was all business. 'No sign of any predation, this is natural decomposition.'

Clyde watched her, amazement in his eyes. 'Sometimes you scare the crap out of me. How do you know all this shit?'

'No Idea. I just do, okay?' Indignation filled her voice. Clyde made the drone gain altitude and when it was high enough, he switched the camera to heat sensing. He did a complete pass of the flight deck before speaking.

'She's cold. I think someone has shut the reactor down.' He quickly checked the battery level – still plenty – so he moved the drone to the island. Still no heat, so he switched back to normal vision.

The scene inside the ship's bridge was similar to the flight deck—everyone in there was dead, their bodies decaying at a slower rate because of the lack of exposure.

'I can see it!' Allison yelled. They all looked up and sure enough, there on the horizon was the ship. Clyde landed the drone on the flight deck, switched it off, and went back to the helm.

There was silence as they approached. Each minute that passed, it grew larger and as the minutes dragged by, the enormity of it was rammed home.

When they were fifty meters away, Clyde dropped their speed and began a slow circuit of the ship.

'What's that hole in the side of it?' Allison asked.

'Elevator access, that's where the planes are taken to the flight deck.'

'Did you see any planes up there?' Allison again seemed to notice things the others missed.

'Good question. I was too busy inspecting bodies, so I didn't look. Take the wheel.' Clyde handed the helm back to her as he activated the drone again. The answer was quick—the deck was free of any planes. He turned the drone for the elevator platform, dropped down under it, and slowly moved the unit into the gaping hole that was the access port.

He moved the drone cautiously until it was hovering just inside the opening. The camera scanned the interior, but it was so dark nothing was visible. Clyde switched to low light enhancement mode and the scene changed. Except for a few more bodies and aircraft tugs, the huge space was empty.

'Looks like they just left it here,' he said quietly.

'Take the drone in further. Let's have a good look,' Anton suggested.

'We can't go too far. This vessel is a big tin can. The control signal will get screened and we'll lose the drone.' Clyde moved the drone slowly further inside; an eye always on the signal strength graph in the drone's feed; when the strength started to drop he set the drone to hover. He panned the camera a full 360-degree sweep. The scene was chilling—more bodies, and more ancillary equipment but besides that, the entire hangar area was empty.

'We should board her, make sure there's no one left. Maybe they're in there but we just can't see them.' Zena had come up the stairs and was shielding her daughter from the screen as she spoke.

Bonnie brought them back to reality before anyone could try something stupid. 'Nobody is going anywhere near that ship. I know you said the virus dies with the host but take a good look at the bodies.'

Clyde repositioned the drone closer to one of the corpses.

'Take a good look, don't hide from it,' said Bonnie. 'That pool of muck around the body is the remains of a human being, and it will be the source of heaps of nasty possibilities. Decomposing bodies are a death trap, and even if we had the proper gear, I would still advise against it.'

Everyone was glued to the screen—the body was in an advanced state of decomposition, skin, muscle, and organs had begun to liquefy as they decomposed, forming Bonnie's *pool of muck*.

Anton moved to his wife's side, taking her into his arms to comfort her. 'We've seen enough horror for ten lifetimes. Going over there will serve no purpose and Bonnie's right; it could get all of us killed.' He took her face in his hands. 'Listen to what I say, Zena. The reactor has been shut down, so that means no power. No power means - no ventilation - and that means there will be pockets of fetid, probably deadly air. If there are any bodies in those areas, and there will be, just breathing the air could be fatal. For the reactor to get as cold as it is would take ages, probably months, so the refrigeration will be another issue. All the food that was on board will be rotting. No, Zena, there's nothing we can do. If anyone is still alive, they won't be for long.' He turned to Clyde. 'Please bring the drone back and get us out of here.'

Clyde nodded, lifted the drone up, and flew it back to the boat. Before he landed it, he turned to Bonnie. 'Is it safe to bring it back? I did land it a couple of times.'

Bonnie took the binoculars. At this range, they would be like a low-power microscope. She scanned the unit and had Clyde turn it a couple of times before she spoke.

'I think it's okay, but just land it downstairs. I'll get some stuff I have in the medical room and disinfect it, just to be sure.' Clyde agreed and landed the small craft delicately on the rear deck.

Allison turned the boat away from the carrier and applied enough throttle to have them running at twenty-two knots, back on their original course.

Clyde stood just inside the saloon door as Bonnie took a couple of swabs from the drone before cleaning it and the spot where it landed. She headed back to medical to analyse what, if any, pathogens may have been brought back. Her efforts were rewarded with a no-risk result, and she quickly returned to the fly bridge and advised the others. 'We're safe; the drone didn't come into contact with anything bad.'

Her words brought a collective sigh of relief.

Zena changed the subject. 'Look at the time. Anybody interested in lunch?'

Even though they had just left what was in all probability the most horrendous thing any had seen, they all agreed that lunch was a good idea.

'That's something we need to think about. Do we have enough food and water?' Anton asked.

Clyde answered. 'Water isn't an issue; we have a desalinator. Food should be fine also, we have three freezers full of food and we might even be able to do some fishing, but it shouldn't be necessary. By my calculations, we are less than a thousand miles from our destination and if we run at eighteen knots during the day and ten at night, we should get there in about three days. Fuel at that speed isn't an issue either; we should arrive with plenty in reserve.'

'Did you allow for the extra weight we now have?' Bonnie asked.

'Yes, I redid the calculations this morning, so I'll change the speed and set the autopilot' As he spoke, Bonnie, Zena, and Anton went down to the saloon and started fixing lunch.

Allison was still at the helm. She appeared to enjoy driving the boat. 'What's your heading?' Clyde asked as he sat in the second seat.

'Zero-four-five.'

Clyde began adjusting the autopilot settings. 'Just setting the autopilot; can you bring the revs down and make eighteen knots?'

'Why?' Allison sounded a little scared.

'Lunch is almost ready. We'll discuss it then,' Clyde said as he activated the autopilot. Allison let the wheel go and followed him down to the saloon.

# EIGHT

Over lunch, spirits rose with every mile that separated them from the horror of their last encounter. The meal was simple: crusty bread, cold meats, and a large green salad.

Clyde spoke, his voice serious. 'I still can't fathom why Bonnie and I are here. We have skills neither of us remember gaining, we don't know our real names or identities, but we are certain of some things. The last thing I remember is going out with a couple of mates. I definitely don't remember ever owning a boat like this.'

'As I said before, the only person who can answer your questions is Allison's father, Professor Denham. We haven't been to the islands before, plus we haven't been part of whatever the Professor has planned. We have known him and his family more from various academic conferences and some social interaction, but neither Zena nor I have been part of what he's been doing since everything fell down. I understand how confusing this must be, but hopefully you'll be able to ask him yourself in a few days.' Anton appeared to answer the question as best he could, or was he just backstopping the narrative? Clyde wasn't sure which.

'Then we'll just have to wait a few more days,' Bonnie added. 'Right now, there are some other things we need to discuss. First, sleeping arrangements; there are only two bedrooms and two queen-sized beds. Clyde and I will take his room, freeing the front cabin up for you and Zena.' She turned to Allison. 'There is still the lower bunk in the comm room; the radio gear is all on what should be the top bunk, and there is one bed available in the med room which Sarah can use.'

She looked at Clyde, who just gave a slight shrug of his shoulders. 'Second, we have a small arsenal on board. You have obviously noticed that we are both armed. Now, here comes the big problem. We don't know each other and, so far since we woke up, we've already had to kill boarders from the plague ship. I suppose what I'm saying is that we need to form a basis of trust. We have no idea what we will encounter and everyone needs to be able to defend themselves. How do we resolve this?' She slumped back in the seat.

There was a prolonged silence. Anton was the first to comment. 'Maybe, until we know each other better, one of you should be awake with us.'

'Not going to work,' Clyde said. 'Bonnie and I've been awake for nearly three days, with only a couple of hours of shut-eye. I don't know how she feels, but I'm totally knackered. I think we both need a good eight hours' sleep.'

Bonnie sighed. 'He's right; we're both running on adrenalin. If we don't get some sleep, we run the risk of making mistakes, even hallucinating. Out here that could be fatal. No, we have to start trusting now or we may all end up dead.'

'I've never even held a gun, let alone shot one, so I'd be more dangerous to us than anyone else,' Anton said.

Zena nodded a wry smile on her face. 'He's right. I'd feel a lot safer if Anton didn't have access to any weapons, at least not until he's had some training. I grew up on the land and I could shoot before I started school. But I don't know if I could shoot another human being. I'm willing to be armed, but I may not be much use.'

Allison stood, her eyes glaring at the new arrivals. 'I don't believe you two. You know what we're up against and still the pacifist bullshit comes out.' She turned to Clyde. 'I've done some sport shooting, skeet and the like. Show me what to do. I'd be more than willing to shoot any of those bastards that want to hurt us.' Her voice was full of confidence, so Clyde agreed.

He took Allison out to the deck and retrieved one of the Fostechs and a couple of magazines. After a quick intro to the weapon, he told her to squeeze off a few rounds, just to get the feel. She did. Five spouts of water erupted off the port side. Next, he gave her some more instructions, went forward, and called, 'Now!'

Clyde hurled a large used plastic storage box out to port. It hit the water and Allison opened fire. Five rounds, five hits, and the box was in a thousand pieces before Clyde was back at the stern.

'You'll do me; bloody good shooting!'

Next, he took his Glock out and handed it to her. Allison took the large pistol and felt the weight. She again squeezed off a few exploratory rounds and Clyde went forward again. This time, the gun was a little more difficult to handle. Only four of the five rounds she fired hit the target. Still, at the speed they were traveling, Clyde was happy with the result.

He turned to Bonnie. 'Kit her out the same as you and introduce her to the Uzi.'

Clyde holstered his gun as the two women headed to the forward cabin. They returned a short while later, Allison now sporting a hip holster and her own Glock. Bonnie carried an Uzi and a few spare mags.

Soon the air was filled with the unique staccato burp of the machine pistol, Allison quickly taming the small, but deadly weapon. Bonnie instructed her on how to strip and clean all three weapons she had used working her like a drill sergeant would, until Allison got her nod of approval.

Clyde quietly cleaned his weapon at the other end of the table, watching the lesson before him with interest. Where their skills came from he had no idea, but he was glad they had them.

Allison went back up to the bridge, and Bonnie forward to transfer her things to Clyde's cabin. Zena took Sarah to the medical cabin so she could sleep. In all the drama, the small child had been overlooked and now she was exhausted.

Clyde and Anton stood on the rear deck. 'I want to explain,' Anton started. 'I've never been a physical type, always a nerd I suppose. Anyway, I never had any interest in guns, so I never learned.'

Clyde remained silent, allowing his companion to speak his mind.

'But what young Allison said resonates with me. She's right—we have no room for pacifism now. When you're rested, would you show me how to use the weapons?'

Clyde stood back, studying him. 'Is it what you really want?'

Anton's reply carried a strength that surprised Clyde. 'Yes. When the freighter discovered our little flotilla, we had little to no defense; they simply came and took who they wanted and killed anyone else they found. We hid in that dinghy, cowering in fear. Allison's words made me see that and I never want to feel like that again. Maybe if we had taken the time to arm ourselves we might have saved many more. That's something the Professor said, that if we are to survive, we have to be willing to fight. I'm only just starting to see what he meant.' There was steel in his words and his demeanour. Clyde could see that the man before him had made a life-changing decision, one he could never hide from again.

'Okay,' Clyde answered. 'I'm going to get some sleep. Tomorrow we start.' He clapped Anton on the shoulder as he went back into the saloon, leaving his companion gazing out to sea.

As he entered the cabin, he saw Bonnie sitting on the lounge to port, gazing out the large portholes. She held something in her hand and had the look of someone with a problem.

'Anything I can help with?' Clyde asked.

Bonnie turned to him. 'How old do you think I am?' Now Clyde knew he was in trouble; no woman ever asked that question wanting an honest answer.

Bonnie clearly saw his dilemma. 'I'm not fishing for compliments. We both need to come to terms with our situation.' She held up the small box in her hands. 'Tampons; if I'm as old as I think, then these are redundant, but if I'm as old as my body seems to be, they could be very useful, if you get my drift.'

'So you think you've already gone through menopause? Okay, assuming that's true, those could just be something from previous tenants.' Clyde knew his answer was weak.

'Don't be dumb. Everything has been designed for us, you and me specifically. The clothes all fit perfectly and you have huge feet, yet all the male shoes are the right size. Come on, Clyde, surely you're not that dumb.' Bonnie's words smashed through his defense.

'Okay, okay. Say you're right and somehow, we've been magically rejuvenated, so bloody what? Don't you think it'd be great to be as young as our bodies' say we are, with the skills and abilities we have?' His eyes lit up and his voice was excited.

'Yes, I agree. But I can't find any contraceptives. No pills, no condoms, so what does that say?' She didn't wait for an answer. 'We have to be careful. I don't think our guests have told us everything. So until I can confirm this body's cycle, if any, sex is now out.'

She stood in front of him, fear in her eyes. Clyde reached for her and she melted into his arms. 'All right, that makes sense, not that I like it. Remember, you're the only woman I have ever had sex with, at least, the only one I can remember.' He let his hand slide down and gave her left buttock a playful slap. 'Besides, I think we can find other ways to enjoy ourselves.'

Bonnie pulled away, smiling, and gave him a gentle punch to the ribs. 'Men – all you ever think of is your stomach and the little thing that hangs off it.' She turned and stepped into the bathroom as she spoke.

The sound of the shower started and Clyde quickly stripped off his clothes, he locked the door, just in case, and then looked down at the Glock. He picked it up and entered the bathroom, placed the gun on the vanity, and stepped into the shower.

Bonnie stood, letting the water cascade down her body, washing away her fears. Clyde moved behind her, reached around, and cupped her breasts in his hands, his growing erection pressing against her backside.

'Is this what you call little?' he asked jokingly.

Bonnie turned and placed her hands around his neck. 'Well, I suppose it's the biggest I've ever seen.' Her words were mocking. 'At least the biggest I can remember, but you'd better put it away. I'm way too tired for anything.'

They finished showering and went to bed. It was still late afternoon and the light streaming through the portholes to starboard made it difficult to settle. Clyde reached for a controller on the bedside table. He pressed one of the buttons and the cabin lights dimmed and the portholes turned opaque. He replaced the controller and Bonnie snuggled into him. Within minutes they were both asleep.

The clock by the bed showed 00:35 when Clyde woke. He rolled over to try to get back to sleep. Ten minutes later, he gave up, rose, and dressed quietly so he didn't disturb Bonnie. He clipped on his holster and two spare magazines and left the room.

Something was wrong; he didn't know what, but he felt it. He entered the saloon. It was empty, and the lights were out. He quickly climbed the stairs to the bridge. There was a figure at the helm, obviously asleep, slumped back, and the chair reclined. Clyde approached. It was Anton, and he was sound asleep.

Clyde checked the nav system. The GPS was offline. Next, he checked the compass. Their course was wrong. It should be 045 but the compass showed 272. They were way off course.

'Fuck!' Clyde exclaimed, waking Anton.

'What's the problem? Oh, shit, I'm sorry, I must have dozed off,' Anton croaked.

'Yes, and we're way off course.' Clyde pulled the throttles back to idle, and checked the instruments. There was no signal from the

GPS satellites, something Clyde had been thinking about, but he didn't know why.

'How can we be off course? Yes, I fell asleep, but I didn't touch anything,' Anton said defensively.

'No, it's not your fault, well, not entirely. We don't have a GPS signal. The autopilot lost its point of reference. I'll need some time to figure out where we are.' Clyde rummaged through the chart drawer for the chart he needed.

He checked the chart plotter. It took two feeds, one from the GPS and a second from the compass. He traced their wanderings back to the point where the course had changed, noted the coordinates, and went back to the paper chart. He asked Anton to help hold the laminated chart down while he found the spot where they'd changed course. He went back and forth between the plotter and the chart a few times until he was satisfied he'd figured out where they were.

'Damn it!' Clyde cried. 'We're over fifty miles off course.' He leaped to the helm, disconnected the autopilot, and began to change course. He opened the throttles and the boat began to change direction.

The changes to the boat's attitude must have woken Bonnie and Allison; they entered the bridge together.

'Problems?' Bonnie asked.

'Yeah, you could say that. We lost the GPS signal and the course changed. We're fifty miles out of position. I've been wondering who is monitoring the system, and now we may have the answer; no one... they're all dead,' Clyde replied.

'The system is satellite-based and there's nobody on a satellite?' Allison responded.

'No, not on the satellites, but someone has to operate the ground stations, monitor and adjust satellites… or I think that's what should happen. Without the GPS, it's back to a good compass and charts.' Clyde monitored their speed over the water, now showing twenty-two knots. He did some calculations and announced, Our new course is zero-four-eight and it should only delay our arrival by about three hours.' He reduced their speed to eighteen knots. 'Now we'll need two on watch all the time. I'll try and see if I can alter the autopilot so it takes its reference from the compass only, but we still need two here now, just in case.'

Bonnie spoke up. 'We've had our rest. Allison, you need to go back down and Anton, you'd better get to sleep as well.' There was no argument and the others left.

Bonnie took the helm while Clyde consulted the manuals to find a way of reactivating the autopilot. He poured over the schematics and instructions for over an hour before he had a possible answer.

'You've got to be kidding.' He chuckled as he moved to the keyboard. He printed four pages from the manual and read them again. Then he started entering commands into the system. The changes only took seconds; the difficult part had been finding the answer.

'Right, Bonnie, switch the autopilot back on.'

Bonnie complied and instantly their course deviated, first to port, then to starboard, before settling back on the correct heading. She looked at Clyde, who just shrugged his shoulders.

'Don't ask me, I just work here. Sit there and watch things. I'll go and rustle up some coffee.'

The rest of the night passed without incident. Bonnie and Clyde took two-hour shifts, one awake at the helm, the other catching up on some sleep.

At 05:35, Clyde woke just as the first rays of sunlight began to invade the darkness. They both watched as the sun slowly edged above the horizon, to starboard. Colours raged across the ocean, dancing and shimmering as the huge red orb battled with the darkness of the night. Soon the battle was over and the sun dominated the sky.

'Damn, that was beautiful,' Bonnie quietly announced.

'Yeah, kind of makes you glad to be alive.' Clyde smiled as they settled into the helm chairs, eyes still fixed on the rising sun.

Soon sounds from below signalled that the others had also risen.

The day passed quickly, every minute drawing them closer to their destination. Anton proved to be a quick learner and soon had the Glock mastered. The M4 was a different proposition, and by the end of the day, he still hadn't mastered it. Overall, though, Clyde was pleased and impressed with his progress. Bonnie was similarly happy with Zena's ability and attitude. She was sure that Anton had discussed things with her the night before.

Allison's cry from the helm startled them all. Clyde leaped from the aft lounge and raced up the stairs as the boat began to slow, the sound of an alarm assailing his ears as he reached the top.

'What is it?' he cried as he reached the helm.

'The underwater proximity alarm; there's heaps of stuff underwater here.' She pointed at the sonar screen. It was set to scan the path in front of the boat, looking for any submerged dangers. It was something Clyde had dragged from his memory—shipping containers. Thousands were lost every year, or so he remembered.

Many made landfall, but there was still a vast number in the ocean not accounted for.

Some sank to the bottom; others reached a state of neutral buoyancy and sat suspended at different depths. Clyde had set the alarm to a depth of twenty-five meters, much deeper than the boat's draft, just to give them fair warning. He watched the screen. It looked like a wall of sunken debris, containers close together, almost as if deliberately set there.

'They're too deep to hurt us, but we'll take it easy just in case.' Clyde reached over and switched the radar back on. It settled quickly and returned a clear screen. As he moved back to the sonar screen, he noticed something. 'Great, the nav system is back. At least I can check if my manual calcs were correct.'

'Ali, come port ten degrees,' Clyde instructed. 'There's a container we might like to avoid just ahead.'

As she adjusted their heading, Allison replied, 'Aye, Captain,' a cheeky grin on her face.

They passed the submerged container easily. It was standing on its end, just a meter under the surface. Clyde called below. 'Anton, just off to starboard, you'll see a partially submerged container. Use the grenade launcher. See if you can put a hole in it.' He turned back to Allison. The look she had demanded an explanation. 'It's too dangerous to leave it that shallow, what if there're other boats like ours? If they don't have our toys, they'd hit it and sink.' His answer ended just as the pop of the launcher sounded. A second later, there was an explosion and the container was holed.

'Good shooting Anton!' Zena's voice echoed up the stairs. Clyde checked the sonar again, only a few more obstructions were evident, and they were too deep to cause any problems.

'Okay, Ali, back to our original course,' Clyde announced as he watched the screens in front of him. The radar was clear, and the sonar revealed that they were now passing the last two containers; when they were clear, Clyde increased the speed back to eighteen.

The rest of the day was very quiet. Allison wanted to stay at the helm. Bonnie and Zena donned bikinis and took the opportunity to sunbake on the forward deck. Anton and Sarah found a chess set and were engaged in the game as Clyde came down the stairs. Anton looked up. 'Don't ask. I'm down three games already,' he chuckled.

Sarah looked up and for the first time since coming aboard, she spoke to Clyde. 'Daddy's not very good at games. Are you any better?'

Clyde laughed. 'Sorry, but I can't remember ever being into chess.'

'Oh well, if you want to learn, I'll teach you,' Sarah answered with no arrogance; just a small child wanting to help someone else.

Her response triggered something in the depths of his memory; nothing specific, just a feeling, one he couldn't recognize. 'Thank you, Sarah. I'll think about it,' he answered, dismissing his thoughts.

He stood, watching the game, stunned by the child's skill. Clyde seemed to understand what was happening, as if he knew the game even though he had no memory of ever playing it. He was so engrossed that he almost didn't notice Bonnie brush past heading for their cabin as Sarah coolly set her father up for yet another checkmate. Inevitably, Anton saw his impending demise and surrendered.

Clyde shook his head. 'That's one hell of a daughter you have.' He looked at Sarah. 'Well done. Maybe I will let you teach me, one day.'

Remembering Bonnie's passing, Clyde left the table and went to the cabin. She'd been in there a while now and his sixth sense was tingling.

As he entered the room, Clyde saw her sitting on the bed dressed in a pair of jeans and a tee shirt. She sat vacantly staring at the small box of tampons she held, turning it over in her hands.

'Is everything okay?' he asked, not really wanting an answer.

'Depends on your definition of okay,' she looked up, her face showing evidence of tears and also confusion. 'I don't understand.' She stood and faced him. 'This,' pointing to her face, 'tells me I've passed my use-by date. In my head I know I've gone through menopause, but what's happening down here...' She dropped her hands to her belly. 'Well, that tells a different story.' Her eyes bored into Clyde and all he saw was confusion. 'Shit, do I have to spell it out? I've got my period. Now, do you understand?'

Something must have changed in his countenance.

'Oh, finally the male of the species gets it.' Her voice was sharp and filled with sarcasm. 'I'm sorry, that's not fair.' She gazed into his eyes, hers pleading for understanding. 'I know that this should be over for me. I know I've passed all this crap, but now I'm back in my twenties. What the fuck is going on, Clyde? What's happened to us?' The tears flowed freely now, as he reached out and pulled her close.

They stood, clinging tightly for ages, until Clyde finally disengaged. 'I'm sorry, but I don't have any answers. All I know is that we're here and we have little to no memory. I was just watching Sarah play her father at chess, flogging him, actually, and for a moment, I had a flash of something. I don't know what it was, just the possibility that I may have had children—nothing solid.

'I don't believe we've been told everything. In fact, we know that. Anton keeps referring to this bloody professor, so all we have is each other. We need to watch our backs, at least until we find out what's going on.'

Bonnie simply agreed and went to the bathroom, where she washed her face, re-did her hair, and slapped on some makeup. When she emerged, she looked fresh and there was no evidence of her ever crying.

It was 17:00 as they entered the saloon.

# Nine

Clyde busied himself setting up the barbecue.

Zena had thawed some beautiful T-bones and it was his duty to cook. Allison and Anton had been at the helm and Bonnie enlisted Sarah's help to make a couple of salads. Earlier in the day, Bonnie had started the ice maker; when she'd had enough ice, she had put a slab of beer in the large cooler box in the aft cockpit. With the steaks sizzling on the grill, and a beer in his hand, he was happy. 'This is the life,' he said quietly.

'I couldn't agree more.' Anton replied as he too cracked a beer. 'If only life could be so simple.'

They set up the table out on the deck. The evening was calm and balmy, just right for dining alfresco. The conversation drifted around, everyone trying to avoid the inevitable.

Bonnie finally broached the subject. 'Zena, Anton, tomorrow we should arrive at our destination. What can you tell us?' Her voice was commanding, leaving no doubt that she wanted as much information as she could get.

Anton looked to his wife for some assistance but, finding none, began to speak. 'To be honest, we don't know, as I said before, we've never been there.'

'That's what I don't understand,' Clyde said. 'You've never been there and yet you take off on a journey, and you have no idea of what's waiting for you?'

Anton glared at Clyde. 'Yes, we did because there was nothing for us at home. Our friends were dying in droves. We were being hunted just because we were alive, and believe me, anywhere is a better prospect than that.' He stopped, Clyde watching closely as he took several deep breaths, to calm down. 'All I know is that it's an old military and research base—at least, that's what he told us — and the Professor suggested we'd be better off joining him. I told you this all before. Evidently the site is capable of sustaining a small group for many years and it has research facilities. The location has been kept secret and it's in the middle of nowhere, off all shipping routes. He contacted us and told us there was a place for us and that he was engaged in some research to save mankind. That's all I know.'

'There's something you're not telling us. Why are we here? What's been done to us?' Clyde asked.

'I don't know. I wasn't involved! All I have is conjecture, and that could just be an overactive imagination.'

'Bullshit. You know more than you're saying.' Clyde slammed his fist onto the table.

Zena held her hand up for calm. 'Yes, you're right, there is more, but we've been told not to say anything to anyone. We couldn't even tell those who were in our little flotilla.' Her eyes misted over.

Clyde felt like a total arsehole. 'Is it that bad?' he asked quietly.

Zena nodded. 'Yes, Clyde, it is.'

'Zena, no – you can't say more,' Anton cried.

'And why not – we did it, not the crazy professor. We're the ones who wiped out the human race! Why shouldn't they know; Denham doesn't own us; we're still free agents.' She turned back to Clyde, then to Bonnie. 'I'm sorry, but there is more and I suspect it's the reason why you are here and in the youthful condition you are.' She smiled at Bonnie. 'You know what I'm talking about.'

Anton placed his hand on his wife's arm. 'Sit down,' he suggested gently. 'I'll make the confession now.' Zena sat, tears flowing down her face. Anton looked out the back of the boat before he continued.

'Beautiful, isn't it? And to think that humans did their best to destroy it all – pollution, over-taxing the natural resources, all in the name of profit – in the end, it's human arrogance that has destroyed us. We were so determined to beat every disease, so determined to extend our lives, we forgot why we have all those horrible things—population control. Whether you believe in God or any other deity, it's pretty clear that these things were created to control our mad procreation.

'The world was overpopulated. Take your country—all the ecological minds and all the scientific data told your government that it could support no more than twenty-five million. Even to do that, they needed massive infrastructure works, especially in water and food security. What did they do? Fucked it all up, imported millions of refugees that overtaxed every system. Food, housing, welfare, and water, everything started to fail. Even in your time, it was evident that things were out of control. Ten years after you, it was a disaster and there we were, Zena and I, desperately working to eradicate the only thing that could save us—disease.

'The funny thing is, while we found a cure, human stupidity and greed took over and we've told you the results. We're the ones who are the real criminals; we're the ones who will be credited with wiping out the entire human race.' Anton slumped back in his chair.

Clyde stood and walked to the stern rail. He watched the phosphorescent trail left behind by the boat. It would be even more defined when the sun finally disappeared. He turned and sat on the lounge and cracked another beer. 'Stop feeling sorry for yourself; you admitted the human race isn't finished yet, —massively depleted, yes, — but there are still survivors. Give us a couple of generations and it'll be business as usual, everyone trying to screw someone else over for a few bucks.'

Zena looked sadly at Clyde. 'No, you're wrong. One of the side effects of anyone who has been given the binding virus is sterility. We were so focused on eliminating disease we failed to see the true nature of our work. Every human who has been infected with the first virus, and that's every person alive in July 2037, is now sterile, so we are responsible for wiping out the human race. In less than a century, there will be no humans left on Earth.'

The words stunned everyone. Clyde sat, his mind reeling from what he heard. Allison stood and walked to the rear lounge, sat beside Clyde, and asked for a beer. 'I don't believe it. I'm no different, if you get my meaning, so if my body is functioning normally, how can I be sterilised?'

Zena answered. 'I know what you mean, but what has happened is your DNA, and the DNA of every human has mutated. Once the binary virus bonded to your DNA, it effectively sterilized you. How it works, we still don't know. We had all our research money frozen, if you remember. So we've had no time to investigate the issue. I'm sorry, but as it stands, you can never have children.'

'But didn't you say my father said he was going to fix all the problems. He said he had a solution for the virus and its effects,' Allison said.

Zena responded. 'Allison, we haven't seen your father for a few years. All our communication had been via email and after that all failed, by ham radio.  Hopefully he has all the facilities he says he does, we just need to wait and see.'

Bonnie stood and moved to Allison. 'Look, we still haven't met your father, so we shouldn't jump to any conclusions.' She looked at Zena. 'Who knows; this base he's found may have all the research stuff you need to cure this. You just said you haven't had time to fully investigate. No, I think it best if we wait and see before we jump to hasty conclusions.' Her words lightened the mood and the issue was put to rest, for the time being. Clyde suggested that they clean away the dinner mess and he and Bonnie would take the night shift. He started by example, cleaning the barbecue before locking it down for the night.

With the plates all cleared away and the table and chairs stored, he closed the doors and locked them. Zena put Sarah to bed before wishing the others goodnight; Anton followed her. Now only Allison was left. She was at the helm when Bonnie and Clyde entered the bridge, watching the sea in front of the boat.

'Looks smooth,' Clyde observed.

'Yes,' Allison answered. 'And the radar shows nothing, so I think it'll be a quiet night.' She turned to Bonnie. 'You know, it's not fair. I've never considered having children; I've been too busy—studying, working towards my doctorate. But with what Zena has told us, I'll never have the opportunity. I feel cheated; empty even; the fact that someone else can take that decision away from me is wrong – It should be my decision, or at least mine and my partner's decision, not some scientist in a lab.'

Bonnie took her hand. Clyde decided that a strategic withdrawal was in order and stepped away from the conversation. 'You're wrong, they didn't do it. They were trying, however deluded it may seem now, to save humanity. It is a horrible thing, but don't give up. Your father may have a solution or at least the facilities for one to be found.'

Allison seemed to pick up at these words. The two women sat and talked for ages before Allison finally decided that she needed some sleep. 'Can I stay up here? I think I'd rather be with you two tonight.'

Bonnie agreed and sent her to get some bedding. Clyde took the first shift on the helm; Allison took the main lounge, while Bonnie curled up on the one beside the helm station. With all the lights switched off, and the displays dimmed, the fly bridge was soon quiet; the sound of steady breathing and a little snoring was all that could be heard.

*** 

The time readout showed 05:00 when Bonnie woke. Slowly, she stretched the kinks out of her body, the lounge again proving to be second-rate for sleeping. Clyde was still at the controls, but she noticed the earphones leads dangling, ending in his top pocket. He was watching to starboard, the direction of sunrise, the sun just beginning to demand its position as master of the day. She gently placed her hand on his shoulder.

'Shit!' Clyde yelled as he leaped out of the chair. 'You scared the crap out of me.'

Bonnie pulled the earbuds out of his ears. 'No need to shout,' she said quietly, but the damage was done—Allison was stirring. She woke quickly, jumping to her feet, looking around the bridge.

'Clyde, are you OK?' she asked as if expecting him to be badly hurt.

'Yes, just Bonnie scaring me. Sorry, I woke you.'

'It's 5:00 am. You were supposed to wake us a couple of hours ago. What happened?' Allison inquired.

Clyde sat back down and again looked to starboard. 'I was just enjoying the quiet, and then it was almost sunrise, so I let you sleep.' He stopped talking and concentrated on the light show dawn could bring. He wasn't disappointed—the first rays sliced through the darkness, announcing the arrival of the light. Like swords, they carved the sky into a brilliant palette of colours. But it was a fleeting show; the huge orb seemed impatient to make its dominance felt.

Bonnie looked at Clyde. 'You need to get some sleep. Your eyes are hanging out of your head.' Clyde suddenly realized he was too weary to argue and he followed her meekly down the stairs, leaving Allison to man the helm.

They entered their cabin and Bonnie left to use the head. Clyde simply lay on the bed and was sound asleep when she returned. Rather than risk waking him, Bonnie removed his shoes and darkened the windows. She gave him a gentle kiss on the forehead before quietly leaving.

Anton had just left his cabin and they met at the landing. 'Thought I might make some coffee, interested?' he asked.

'Great idea I'd love some; Is Zena awake?'

'Yes, she's a bit shaken after last night's discussion.'

Bonnie understood. 'I think I might have a chat. You know, girl to girl, sort of clear the air.' Anton agreed and they parted, Bonnie heading for the forward cabin.

She knocked and Zena opened the door. Bonnie entered and quietly locked the door behind her. 'Zena, it's time to talk.'


***


It was around midday when Clyde woke with a start. He heard raised angry voices and the main one was Bonnie. He leaped out of bed, slipped on his shoes, and grabbed his Glock. He carefully opened the cabin door, checked the passageway, and seeing it was empty, cautiously made his way into the saloon.

Bonnie's agitated voice echoed down from the bridge. 'And just what did you think we would say? What gave you that right?'

'Bonnie, it's not like that. We're trying to save our species,' Anton pleaded.

Clyde made it up the stairs quickly, his Glock extended in front of him. The sight of him emerging from the saloon stopped all conversation. 'What the fuck is all the yelling about?' he said, his weapon moving with his eyes as he covered the group.

'Put the gun down,' Bonnie commanded. 'You don't need it... yet.'

Slowly, Clyde lowered his weapon, holstered it, and moved to Bonnie's side. 'Okay, will someone please explain?' His eyes moved to the helm. Both engines were switched off; the boat was stationary. The only movement was the gentle undulations of the passing swell.

Bonnie turned to him, her eyes filled with tears of anger. 'We were brought here to be stud cattle. It seems that this mad professor somehow came back to our time, kidnapped us, and took us to his research facility. There he somehow rejuvenated us, including my bloody ovaries. That's all he's interested in—my ovaries and your nuts. He intends to use us as some sort of hybrid breeding program.'

Clyde looked at the faces in front of him, he felt the confusion building. 'Bullshit! Even I know that's impossible. Once a woman has used up all her eggs, it's over— no more kids'.' He moved away from them, took his seat at the helm, and sat staring out to sea.

He knew for certain that it was impossible, but deep in the recesses of his mind, a small doubt was festering. What else could explain how they looked? He shook his head, trying to clear the thoughts. It didn't work, and doubt still rambled around his mind.

He turned to stare at his guests. 'And you knew this all along?' As he spoke, his hand slipped down to his weapon.

'No, not all of us, just Zena and me,' Anton answered. 'And we weren't party to the program, we were told only after we agreed to join Denham's group, plus he never told Allison any of this.'

Allison reached out to Clyde, her hand resting lightly on his shoulder. 'I'm sorry, really. If I'd known I'd have told you. This plan is nothing short of monstrous.' She lowered her head, as if from shame. 'I can't believe that my father could do something like this. I always thought he was a good man, sometimes a little too arrogant, but essentially good.'

Clyde didn't get to respond. The radar pinged as Allison finished. He quickly checked the display. 'Two fast movers inbound, approximately twenty miles out!' He checked again. 'At present speed, we have about thirty minutes before they arrive.' The Glock was in his hands and he trained it on Anton and Zena. He looked at Bonnie. 'Tie them up, secure them to the table.' He looked at Allison, the unspoken question hanging in the air.

'Don't worry; I'm on your side. This madness has to end, and if that means I must defy my father, so be it.' She moved quickly towards the saloon.

Minutes later, she was back, a packet of zip ties in her hand. She made Anton and Zena sit at the table, then she deftly secured them to it, locking both their hands and feet with the ties.

'Clyde, this is a mistake, we can help,' Anton pleaded.

It was Allison who answered. 'Yes, you're right; it's all a huge mistake. You two and my father trying to play God, all the time justifying your crimes as some sort of higher purpose. Believe me, it ends now.' As if to emphasize her point, she opened the cupboard and extracted two of the Fostechs and half a dozen thirty-round magazines. She placed them on the table and began filling the drums. When she'd finished, she spoke again. 'One hundred and eighty explosive rounds; if he tries anything that should convince my father.'

Bonnie retreated to the cabin and returned with her Uzis and both gear bags. Clyde loaded several magazines for his M4 and set a box of grenades beside the helm.

Zena looked at them, fear in her eyes. 'Just look at yourselves. Look at what you're contemplating. Is the alternative so horrible, so repulsive, that you'd resort to murder to escape?'

'Murder? The alternative is slavery! I don't really want to kill anybody but if it comes to that, yes, we will defend ourselves,' Bonnie answered, her voice steel-hard and cold.

Clyde returned to the fly bridge and watched as Bonnie went to the sun lounge on the foredeck. Allison took her position aft; both women concealed their weapons under towels and cushions. Clyde reset the controls to autopilot and they were moving again. He stayed at the helm, for the moment. Each wore a small communicator, allowing them to monitor the other's actions.

'Five minutes,' Clyde said softly, his words repeated in the other's earpieces. The minutes dragged, the small RIB assault craft getting larger each second.

'Please,' Zena pleaded, 'let us help you.'

'Like you helped the rest of humanity? I don't think so. Now shut up before I gag you,' Clyde said 'And don't think of shouting or warning these clowns; if it goes south remember Sarah is downstairs and could be in the line of fire. Just be cool and this'll all work out.' His words had the desired effect. Although he knew he could never harm the child, they didn't, so their silence was now guaranteed.

The two RIBs had slowed, still a couple of hundred meters away. They were taking a more cautious approach.

'*Hello, Genesis. Please respond,*' the usually silent UHF radio boomed.

'That's the professor!' Zena announced. 'Please, we'll be quiet. Don't let our daughter be harmed.'

Clyde gave her a weak smile. 'At least we know the name of the boat. A bit dramatic, though — *Genesis.*' He picked up the radio mic. 'Hello, please identify yourself.' He had a good view of the boats. Each carried six, each armed with the same weapon as Clyde—the M4, although he couldn't see any that were equipped with grenade launchers.

*'My name is Professor Reginald Denham. I'm the reason you're here. Please, can we come aboard and talk face to face?'* the voice replied.

Clyde looked down at Bonnie. She simply shrugged, leaving any decision up to him. 'Thanks for the help, Bonnie.'

Allison answered, *'Let him aboard, not the others. They're armed. Do not allow anyone other than him on board.'*

Clyde picked up the mic again. 'Professor, please proceed to the rear of our boat. We'll discuss you coming aboard then.' The lead RIB responded by accelerating towards Genesis. 'And Professor, don't come any closer than twenty meters for the moment.'

Clyde watched as the second boat started to move forward much slower. 'Bonnie, I think you'll get the first company.'

*'Yeah, but I have a very warm reception for them.'* As she spoke, Bonnie stood, dropped her shirt, and moved to the boat's tender. Now clad in only her bikini, distracting the men in that RIB from their plan.

She stopped at the tender, checking that the shotgun was still where she'd placed it. She started to wave to the approaching boat. *'It's amazing what a brief glimpse of tit and arse does to the male of the species.'* She chuckled into the comm system.

The professor's boat stopped the required twenty meters from the stern of Genesis. Clyde dropped the jet buckets into the neutral position but kept the engines running. He checked their fuel status, not liking what he found. They were in the middle of the Pacific Ocean and the only known land he could find was the professor's islands. With their fuel status, the only option was those islands.

'Professor, we seem to have a problem. You know who we are, but we have no idea about you. Since we woke up, Bonnie and I have been attacked by a plague ship, pirates have attempted to board us, and we came across a derelict aircraft carrier. So far, we have survived and rescued some survivors. Now you turn up here, close to a location that was locked into the nav system, but you turn up with armed goons. Some might call me suspicious, but that worries me. What do we do?' Clyde replaced the mic, moving to the rear deck for a better view, and waited for an answer.

*'This bloody boat is getting too close,'* Bonnie's voice echoed in his ear. *'If we're going to do something it had better be in the next sixty seconds.'*

It was Allison who turned the tide. As Clyde watched from the upper deck, she leaped up from the lounge, the Fostech aimed directly at her father. 'Hello, Dad. I really don't like your armed idiots this close. They either chuck their weapons overboard, or I shoot. And Father, the first shot is aimed at you.'

'Allison, you're alive.' There was genuine joy in his voice, but it didn't sway his daughter.

Bonnie retrieved her shotgun and trained it on the second boat. No one in either boat had raised their weapons; Bonnie took advantage of their mistake.

Clyde took the lead. 'Now, Professor, we have a better situation. Here's what you and these idiots with you are going to do. You will all throw your weapons overboard. Anyone not obeying will see all of you killed.' To emphasize his words, Clyde lifted and aimed his M4 at the professor. 'Allison, I have him covered. Aim your gun at the engine. Bonnie, you may take the other boat out at your discretion.' Clyde flicked the safety off and fired a burst into the water a few centimetres from the hull. Bonnie sent three rounds toward the second RIB.

The reaction was instantaneous. It turned sharply away and accelerated, exposing the hull just behind the bow, Bonnie fired and this time she hit her mark. Both shotguns were loaded with explosive charges so the impact tore a large hole in the bow of the second boat. If they decelerated, the bow would settle and the boat would fill with water; their only option was to keep it up and leave the area. To reinforce the decision, Bonnie sent a volley of five shots after the retreating boat.

'Now, Professor, what's your decision?' Clyde asked.

The answer was simple—all weapons were thrown overboard. Then the professor looked back at Clyde. 'Anything more?' he asked.

'Yes, remove your clothes and swim over here. I'm sure you can manage twenty meters. When you're in the water, that boat is to leave and return to wherever it came from. You, Professor, will be joining us for the rest of the trip.' Clyde watched as the professor began removing his clothes down to his jocks. He instructed the helmsman to return to base and dived into the water.

'Now get moving and remember, one false move and I'll send you all to hell,' Allison yelled at the boat. It started to move and her shotgun remained trained on it as it sped away. She returned to the stern just as her father climbed out of the water. He approached her but Allison kept the gun pointed in his direction.

'Is that any way to greet you father?' he spluttered indignantly.

'My father would never have kidnapped these people. He would never have planned to use them as stud animals. I don't know who you are.' Her voice was filled with cold rage and the gun was kept pointed at his head.

Clyde stepped in. 'Allison, please go forward and make sure both those boats keep going.' He handed her the binoculars and she reluctantly headed back to the bow.

'Professor!' A small voice exclaimed from the saloon.

Denham turned 'Sarah, how did you get here?'

'They found us. Mummy and Daddy are here too.' She leaped into the waiting and wet arms of the professor. 'You're all wet. Did you go for a swim? Mummy won't let me. She thinks a shark might eat me.'

'You know, I never thought of that. Where are they?' he asked, looking at Clyde.

'Up here.' Bonnie's voice floated down the stairs, followed quickly by Anton and Zena. The three embraced, with Sarah caught up in the middle of it all.

Clyde motioned for them to move inside. Bonnie covered them while he went forward to speak to Allison. The conversation was short and soon everyone was sitting around the table. Zena and Bonnie made coffee, but Allison couldn't be convinced to drop her guard. She kept her distance from her father but she had dispensed with the Fostech. Instead, she kept her Glock pointed at him. 'Just in case the boats return, you'll be the first to die.'

Denham answered. 'They won't.'

Professor Denham didn't fit the image Clyde had built up in his mind. He was tall and good-looking with a closely cropped haircut.

His body was lean and well-muscled. He looked more like a marine than a mad scientist.

He accepted the offered coffee and tasted it immediately. 'A good brew, thank you,' he said to Bonnie.

Allison arced up. 'Don't think that you can charm your way out of this; it won't work, especially on me.' She almost spat the words, contempt oozing from each of them. 'We know everything— your dark plan to use these people. How could you?' Her voice was quivering and so was her weapon; her anger was becoming a real problem.

Bonnie turned to Allison. 'I'll watch him; go and grab a coffee.'

Allison accepted, holstered the weapon, and moved to the galley. When she returned her mood was a little better.

'You're right, Allison. I did plan to use these people, just as you said. But it's a waste of time.' Denham seemed to deflate as he spoke. Gone was the arrogant posture and the intellectual superiority. He looked like a defeated man.

'The grand plan was to return to a time before the virus was released, come back with viable subjects, and use them as donors. The women were to be fed fertility drugs and their eggs harvested, the men were to donate sperm. Once this process was underway, the lab would fertilize the eggs and implant them in host mothers. The problem was that the modified DNA saw this as a threat and attacked the zygote, terminating the pregnancy almost before it began.

'The next attempt was to mate the newcomers with survivors, but the result was the same. Zena, you were one of the lucky ones, you must have had Sarah just before the major effects became clear, either that or you have some impossible immunity.

'So you see I failed; there's nothing we can do, the human race is finished.' The professor's voice was heavy with sadness. 'I'm sorry for what I've done, but I fear it can't be undone. I'm afraid you may be stuck here with us.'

'So we're not going to be your breeding slaves?' Bonnie asked.

Denham seemed to cheer up a little. 'No, Bonnie. You're free to do as you wish, but I think you'll see that our small community is a far better place than any alternative.'

It was Clyde who asked the hard question. 'So how many have you kidnapped and what happened to them?'

'Ten couples just like you; and they're all still with us, on the islands,' Denham replied.

'So somehow you managed to travel back in time, kidnap twenty people, return, and modify us. Then you try your breeding experiment. That fails, so now we are all supposed to just accept an apology and live happily together?' Clyde asked. 'Why the hell can't you just take us back and let us live out our lives as we were?'

Denham seemed to recover some of his attitude. 'It's better to show you, it involves science and physics far beyond me. How far are we from the islands?'

'Probably about one hundred and fifty miles, why?' Clyde enquired.

'I suggest that you get back on the helm. From here on in, it gets interesting.'

As if his words were a cue, the proximity alarm sounded and the engines dropped back to idle. Clyde leaped up and raced up the stairs to the helm station, the professor close behind.

The reason for the alarm was clear—shoals. The water shoaled sharply, rocks broke the surface and the depth of water dropped dangerously.

'This is one of the reasons no shipping ever came close to these islands.' Denham pointed at the shoals in front of the boat. 'There is a way through, a deep entrance, but if you don't know it, you'll never find it.' He turned to face Clyde. 'Now you must decide to trust me or not. I know the way through. Trust me and we get there. Don't and you'll just burn fuel for nothing.' He offered his hand to Clyde. 'Please, I promise no harm will come to you, and I'll show you the way through, you can record all the way points then you'll be able to leave whenever you want.'

Clyde hesitated. Here was their kidnapper, asking for his trust, and against all reason, his gut told him he should. Clyde took the offered hand, and the deal was struck.

# Ten

The islands had a natural, almost perfect defense.

Shoals, reefs, and rocky outcrops were all interlaced in a way that made navigation almost impossible and stretched out to more than one hundred and fifty nautical miles. There was no easy path through; no way to just find a patch of deep water and drive straight in. It was almost as if the reefs had been designed and installed as a defensive maze.

Professor Denham showed he was up to the task. First, he motored south for ten miles, the shallow reef clear of their port beam. Then he found what he was looking for—a deep channel. He waited while Clyde marked this on his chart while the GPS system was still operating; it was a given that it would eventually fail so the chart was marked with GPS locations and the alignment of two huge rock outcrops.

Once this was complete, Denham turned the boat into the channel and accelerated. Timing was as important as location. The normal tidal movements were critical in entering and departing the chain. Clyde checked their progress, using the forward sonar and a stopwatch, as Denham sped the boat to the next waypoint.

When they arrived, he reduced speed, changed course, and slowly picked his way through another area of shallows. The water under the boat was deep but the channel was narrow. To bring a large vessel through there would take incredible skill and a good set of balls.

'How big a ship could get through, Prof?' Clyde enquired.

Denham chuckled. 'I think you'll be surprised at what we have in here. You'll see soon enough.'

'So this is the only entrance?'

Denham studied Clyde carefully before answering. 'For large vessels, yes – there are a couple of entranceways for small boats, like the RIBs. But this is the only way we know for larger vessels.'

He checked his stopwatch, looked at the sonar, and changed course again. This time they were heading back out to sea. So far, Clyde noticed that the channels weren't wide or deep, so the idea of larger vessels entering was hard to comprehend. They continued toward the destination, constantly monitoring the channel, the tides, and the time.

The sun was sinking fast and the light faded much quicker than Clyde liked; he turned to Denham. 'Is the light going to be a problem?'

Denham's face told the answer. 'In a way, yes; I'm not confident in traversing the last three passages in the dark but I can have one of our pilots join us. We do that and we'll be home in time for supper.'

'Great plan. Trap us in here and have your goons take the boat,' Allison leapt up from the lounge, drawing her Uzi in one smooth movement. 'Was that your plan all along? Well, it won't work.' Her weapon once again pointed it at her father.

'Allison, take it easy.' Clyde moved between them.

'Take it easy? You know what he had planned for you. How can you trust him?'

'Because I have no choice, but that doesn't mean we can't proceed cautiously. Now lower your gun,' Clyde pleaded.

Allison lowered the weapon and moved away, the gun still in her hands.

'Professor, call your pilot and tell him to come out alone. If we detect any others, I might just let your daughter sort that out.'

Denham's face showed he knew what Clyde meant. He called the island and instructed the pilot to come out alone; no other craft was to accompany him.

Twenty minutes later, the sound of a small craft alerted Clyde to the imminent arrival of their pilot. He moved to the helm and switched on the boat's floodlights. The pilot had done as ordered—he was in one of the RIBs and alone. He tied the small craft to the stern and under the watchful eye of Allison and her Glock, climbed the stairs to the bridge.

'Thom thanks for coming. Thom, meet Clyde. Clyde, Thom.' Denham made the introductions.

'Bloody nice boat Clyde,' Thom said as they shook hands. 'Damn, Reg, this is one hell of a kidnap bonus!' He took the helm and began moving her through the last three channels.

'What's he mean?' Clyde asked.

'You don't know? Shit, man, this is your boat. Every person the prof brought back came with their own boat. Hell, we even got to choose which one, although in your case I think Reg made an educated guess.'

Clyde stood and absorbed the information; he had no recollection of asking for a boat, no recollection of actually being considered in any of the events leading up to his arrival. He filed this new information away, deciding to wait for the right time to ask the questions.

Denham slowly shook his head. 'Thanks Thomas! Clyde, it's a long story, something for another day, but I will explain in time.'

It was just after eight when they cleared the final reef. Thom pushed the throttles to maximum; the acceleration and speed seemed to impress him. 'As I said, can I have one of these?' He chuckled as he lowered the speed and turned toward shore.

There was no dock that Clyde could see and they were making a mad rush toward a sheer rock wall. He was about to demand that Thom stop when the boat began a gentle turn. There was a gap in the cliff and a rock wall was now on both sides of the vessel with a wide, deep channel between them.

Thom slowed more and guided the boat through the entrance to a lagoon. It was huge—over two kilometres wide and even longer. To port Clyde could see a large cave—Thom steered directly into it—and a good-sized dock, complete with cranes and a rail system.

'Awfully well set up Professor?' Clyde said.

'Let's say the previous owners didn't spare any expense on construction.' Denham smiled. There were several large boats already at anchor and another two tied up where Thom was parking Genesis. Two at anchor were easily over sixty meters and one was even larger.

'Pick them up cheap?' Clyde asked.

'Sort of – their previous owners didn't survive. It seemed a shame to waste such beautiful things,' Denham replied.

'Clyde, we need to tie the boat off; you or me?' Thom asked.

'You—and I'll be watching,' Allison replied, using her gun to point Thom in the direction of the stairs.

'Just like her mother,' Denham said softly. 'If she was here, I think I'd have a couple of holes in me. But then again, she'd have never let me think I could save the human race.'

With the boat secured, Denham invited all to follow him. Allison hesitated when he suggested they leave their weapons aboard. 'Only our security guys are armed,' he explained.

'That's why we're keeping ours,' she replied through clenched teeth. 'Until I can trust you, these are my best friends.' She had her Glock, six spare magazines, Bonnie's twin Uzi harness, and eight spare mags for them. Bonnie and Clyde had their Glocks and spare mags, but Clyde opted to take his M4 and the backpack with additional mags and grenades, just in case.

The sight seemed to amuse Denham. 'Believe me, you don't need them, but if it makes you more comfortable, feel free to bring them.' He stepped off the boat, Allison close behind, next the Garibaldis, and last, Bonnie and Clyde. The small troop followed Denham, Clyde still cautiously scanning their surroundings with Bonnie and Allison also keeping a close eye out for any signs of treachery.

They walked toward a large structure—obviously some sort of office complex. Denham opened the door and indicated that they should enter. Inside were a number of people, all unarmed, who it appeared were completing normal daily tasks. They recognized the professor, but the sight of his armed companions caused them to stop what they were doing.

'Don't be alarmed; these are friends, they just don't know it yet. Please ignore us and keep working.' Denham led his party to a bank of three elevators, selected the centre one, and pressed the call button. Moments later, the doors opened. Clyde and Bonnie drew their weapons and took flanking positions on either side of the doors.

Denham chuckled. 'You two really know your stuff. Do you remember anything else?' The car was empty and Denham motioned for them to enter, reluctantly, they complied.

'Remember what exactly, Professor?' Clyde responded.

'I don't know; what you did, who you are. I mean the Bonnie and Clyde routine is good, but do you have any recollections of before?'

'No, we don't,' Bonnie snapped.

The elevator rose quickly and stopped at the floor Denham had selected. He reached forward and pressed the door close button. 'Please shoulder your weapons before we alight. You saw the reaction below. If they've called security, as they should have, we could end up in a firefight and I don't think any of us wants that.'

Denham was right; a firefight in an area they didn't know would be disastrous. Clyde nodded and shouldered his M4. Bonnie secured her Glock. But Allison lifted her right-hand Uzi and pointed it at her father's lower spine. She kept the one in her left hand free to operate. 'Okay, open the door. If there are any problems the first shots will remove your lower spine!' she hissed through clenched teeth.

Denham obeyed and the doors slid open. Clyde looked to the right of the car and then jumped to the other side and scanned the left. He pressed the door close button and turned to the professor. 'Seems you were right; I can see at least six armed guards flanking the elevator. We step out and we could be in deep shit. Problem is, the longer we wait, the more guns we could be facing – any suggestions?'

Denham stood tall. 'Yes. Let me exit first, I'll call them down and disperse them. Look, I know that you're suspicious, and you have every reason to be, but I assure you there's no hidden agenda. We tried to do something, it failed and now you're stuck here with us. Like it or not doesn't really matter, neither of us has any choice.'

He was right and deep down, Clyde knew it. 'Okay, we open the doors and you clear the way, the guards have to disarm, lay their weapons down and walk away. Got it?'

Denham agreed and the doors opened, he stepped through and called to the guard commander – a short conversation turned into a louder one with Denham finally pulling rank and ordering all security guards to stand down, lay their weapons down, and walk away. Their response left no doubt as to who was in charge, as they quickly obeyed and left the area.

Denham turned back to the elevator car. 'They're gone. Please can you shoulder your guns and come out?'

Clyde moved first. He shouldered his carbine, but not as Denham asked. He used the sight optics to scan the area to the left and above before repeating to the right. Satisfied he stepped out, securing his weapon at his side.

With the path now clear, Denham led them across a wide tiled area. The ceiling soared twenty meters above their heads and directly in front was a huge expanse of glass. The view was incredible. The building had been both constructed and hewn out of rock, the construction had taken advantage of natural caves and the builders had used these and enhanced them to create an incredible area.

Denham watched as the magnitude of the place sunk in. 'We were very lucky in finding this place. The original owner was a reclusive billionaire, probably someone you've never heard of. Simon Castilian?'

'Castilian's father made his fortune during and after the Second World War. Simon consolidated it and grew the empire. He hated the idea of fame, so he was never photographed and he went to extraordinary lengths to maintain his privacy. It's said he poured over six billion into this complex. Then various agencies joined him. This place has been home to many secrets, some we know about, some we are still discovering. There is another version that says the whole Castilian thing is a fabrication, that he was invented as a convenient cover for CIA black ops and fundraising.

'I know this has been a harrowing time for you. Please come with me, we have accommodation ready. This discussion can take place later.' Denham beckoned them to follow. Clyde and Bonnie agreed but Allison held back.

'Look, Allison, I have had enough of this,' Denham said. 'There's no way I can make you accept what I say—you're too much like your mother for that—so here's how it's going to go. The others are tired, they need to have dinner and sleep, and they seem to accept this. If you want to keep this up, fine, but I think you'll be alone. I'd never do anything to harm you and, as I've said, the original plan didn't work so your friends are just like the rest of us. Please, let's just get tonight over. We can discuss things tomorrow.'

Denham's words had little success. 'How can I believe a word you say? Remember, you told me that the treatment Mum was having would save her. Instead, it killed her. You lied then, you could be lying now.' Allison again brought the Uzi to bear on her father.

Bonnie stepped between them, placed her hand on the top of the weapon, and calmly asked Allison to lower it. They stood staring at each other; tense seconds passed before the weapon slowly started to lower. Finally, Bonnie took both Uzis and the harness from Allison and they started to move toward the far end of the atrium. 'Allison, I don't trust him yet either, but we need to get some sleep, we can sort this out tomorrow.'

Clyde held back; he took Denham aside and they had a whispered conversation before he re-joined the others. 'I just spoke to Denham. We've got a double unit with two separate bedrooms. This whole thing is suspicious, but we don't have an alternative, at the moment, I think we should keep Allison with us, at least until she settles down. The last thing we need is her going off the rails and shooting someone. Also, with the three of us together we can have some sort of watch set up.' Bonnie nodded her agreement and moved closer to Allison to discuss Clyde's option.

The accommodation was impressive. Their apartment consisted of a main entry foyer, tiled in muted grey and blue tones. Off to the right was the first bedroom; a large king-sized bed dominated the centre and a separate wet room was located to the right of the bed. The left wall was taken up with artwork and a concealed door led into a huge wardrobe and dressing room. Allison claimed it immediately.

The entry continued into a lounge area complete with a large entertainment wall almost entirely covered by a huge screen. Clyde slowly shook his head. 'I can't actually remember anything from the past, but I have a feeling that TV was crap; I hope what you have here is better.'

The answer from Denham made him smile. 'The truth is, we don't have any TV, all the networks are gone and nothing works. The screen is only good for playing our video library, but that is quite extensive.'

To the right was a well-appointed kitchen and at the rear was a large curved window, giving a private view of the surrounding landscape. Bonnie and Clyde's room was to the left featuring a spectacular view. The layout was much the same as Allison's but with the addition of a large spa in the corner of the bathroom. Bonnie let out a sigh of gratitude. 'Just what I need, come on, all of you out; I need a soak.'

The professor showed Clyde how to program the door lock; then he and the Garibaldis left for their quarters. Soon the sound of running water filled the room as Clyde inspected the kitchen, finding a good supply of food and other consumables. He saw Allison sitting on the sofa, her Glock in her hand; she repeated his idea that someone should stand watch, she wanted to know who was going to be first. Clyde agreed and told her he would take the first shift. Allison bid him goodnight and returned to her room as he poured two large whiskeys and carried them to the bedroom.

Clyde entered the bathroom. Bonnie was blissfully enjoying the massage from the water and air jets; he placed the drink close to her.

'Great idea,' she took the glass and sipped the liquor. 'Now, what do you want?' she cooed.

Clyde answered by standing and heading for the door. 'I think we should have at least one of us awake during the night, I've decided to take the first shift and Allison will relieve me in a few hours, then we will see about your invitation. Don't soak too long, in six hours you'll be on watch.

***

Bonnie woke as the sun was just beginning to defeat the darkness of night. Dawn was her favourite time of day.

She rolled to her side, gazing out the window, but her eye was drawn to Clyde's back, to the tracks her nails had carved into him last night. She smiled, reliving some of it as she climbed out of the bed. Clyde rolled onto his back, giving her a good look at the similar marks she had inflicted on his chest. Her smile broadened.

Quietly, she retraced the steps to the bathroom, closed the door, and began inspecting herself in the mirror. Her breasts were tender and from the very faint marks, she smiled as she remembered the time after Clyde came to bed and when she had risen to take her turn at watch. Her smile widened as she continued to inspect her body.

She felt a tingling in her loins. 'Damn, that's the best sex I've ever had.' she whispered before the rational part of her brain asserted itself. *Well, the best I can remember.* Again, this thought brought a chuckle.

Bonnie entered the shower and briskly washed herself. She was letting the water cascade off her body when Clyde opened the door.

'Good morning. Room in there for another?' he asked and then made a silly growling noise in his throat.

Bonnie shook her head. 'Down, tiger; I need food. We didn't get any last night and I'm hungry. Now can you please hand me a towel?'

Clyde gave her an evil smile, retrieved one of the towels, and held it just out of reach. 'Come and get it.' In no mood for games, she reached out and grabbed it, quickly dried herself and wrapped the towel around her before she left the bathroom. 'Now get showered and come out for breakfast,' she called, leaving Clyde with a dejected look on his face.

****

There was an outfit laid out on the bed. 'What's this – dressing me now?' he called, but he was actually wondering where the clothes had come from. They hadn't brought any from the boat.

'Found them in the wardrobe. Put them on and we'll see how they look,' Bonnie called from the kitchen, 'and hurry, breakfast is almost ready.'

He obeyed and was soon standing in front of the mirror dressed in shorts, an open loose-fitting shirt over a singlet, and canvas boat shoes. Bonnie had thought of everything, even a belt that would allow him to clip his holster onto.

Satisfied, Clyde entered the living area. Bonnie and Allison were busy in the kitchen so he went to the large window. Outside was a terrace complete with table and four chairs and a couple of lounges.

'To your right on the wall there's a switch. Press it and open the door,' Bonnie commanded as she left the kitchen carrying a tray with three plates of food. Clyde did as instructed and the huge window began to rise until it was fully retracted just below the ceiling.

'And before you ask, there is a comprehensive layout legend in the kitchen, shows just where every switch and gismo is. Help Allison with the rest of the things,' Bonnie called as she placed the plates on the table. Clyde and Allison soon joined her and all tucked into the meal enthusiastically.

Scrambled eggs, bacon, and roasted tomatoes made up the main part of breakfast but to Clyde, the most important thing was the coffee pot. By the time he'd finished eating, he was pouring his third cup.

'So what's on the agenda today?' Clyde asked.

'Can we please just enjoy the morning? All that will come later,' Bonnie responded. 'Besides, we need to find out just what is going to happen to us, and I can wait a little for that.'

They continued to eat in silence until their door intercom buzzed. Clyde went to the viewer to check who was there; he drew his own pistol before opening the door.

'Morning Professor,' Clyde said to Denham as he let him in. 'To what do we owe this early visit?' Clyde motioned for Denham to go through to the balcony, the Glock in his right hand hidden from view, while he retrieved another coffee cup.

'I thought an early start to our tour was in order. Thomas wants to take you on a training run through the reef this afternoon,' Denham answered. 'And please, my name is Reginald or Reg, as I prefer.' He turned to his daughter. 'And how are you this morning, Allison?'

Allison gave her father a withering look. 'I slept well, thank you.' She lifted the top she was wearing enough to expose the Glock at her hip. 'I kept this under my pillow, just in case.'

Bonnie defused the situation. 'Well, we'd better get going. Come on, Allison, help me clean up.' She stood and they took all the breakfast things back to the kitchen.

'I see you are also wearing your gun?' Denham observed.

'For now, Reg – we'll see how the day proceeds,' Clyde answered.

*** 

The morning tour only covered the central building that they were staying in. It consisted of twenty levels, with accommodation at the top and building services at the bottom. Between them was a myriad of functionalities—huge hydroponic gardens, four massive levels for raising animals, and another dedicated as a slaughterhouse.

'Some find this level disturbing,' Reg said, 'but if we want to eat, we have to grow and prepare food. Castilan knew this, that's why he designed the place like it is.'

'But how much did he spend on the facility?' Bonnie asked.

'I really don't know. After about six years he got involved with some quasi-military group, probably the CIA or others. Originally, he just wanted a quiet place to live. I have no idea why he wanted to work with them, but he did, and we believe they all eventually spent over sixty billion on the facility.'

'Sixty billion?' Clyde's voice was almost a screech. 'Well, they got ripped off. There's no way even an organization as stupid as the CIA could waste that much on this. Sorry, Reg. It's a nice place but that's a bit over the top.'

The professor just smiled. 'Clyde, if this was all there is to it, I'd agree, but there are seven islands in this chain and they all have facilities. Plus, they're all linked by a subterranean tunnel system. The rubble was used to form part of the reef system. When you see all of it, and eventually you will, I think you'll see it in a different light.'

They continued the tour, the power stations being one of the last sites they saw. The chain sat on an active volcanic region. The two outer islands made ideal sites for geothermal power stations and each facility had additional solar and wind power systems. Even motive power was taken into account with three massive diesel storage facilities holding millions of litres of fuel. Clyde questioned the wisdom of this—diesel, like all hydrocarbon fuel, could deteriorate—but he was assured that the facility had the latest in preservation technology and that their fuel was good for several decades to come.

At 12:30, Denham called the tour closed and they took the elevator back to the main accommodation area. The elevator doors opened to a completely different scene. The entire area was filled with people, some sitting at tables that had been set up, while others mingled. The sight of Denham and his group hushed everyone and a path to one of the tables cleared. When the group was seated, everyone else also took their seats.

Denham rose to speak. 'My friends, we are here to greet and meet our newest arrivals. First, I am grateful that my daughter, Allison, has survived and is here with us, and I have two people to thank for that—our newest arrivals from the past. Bonnie and Clyde rescued Allison and sank the cursed plague ship that had taken so many survivors. Our drones have confirmed this so we are forever indebted to both of you.' A round of applause coursed around the room.

'Next, they also rescued my good friends, the Garibaldis, two people who may be able to find the answer that I, sadly could not. So we have new friends—people we hope will want to stay and become part of our community. Now, please enjoy the meal we have ready.'

A group of people stood and moved to a long set of tables on the far side. They removed the covers to reveal a bountiful buffet.

Clyde felt a hand on his shoulder. It was Thomas. 'I'd advise eating sparingly. We have a reef run later and it'll be a pretty rough one.' Thom smiled as he made his way past and on to the buffet.

# ELEVEN

The buffet was, indeed, bountiful.

Like the gathered guests, the food represented every culture one could imagine. Choosing was difficult, to say the least. With Thomas's warning echoing in his head, Clyde chose carefully and sparingly.

When he returned to the table Bonnie seemed surprised at his constraint. 'Not hungry?' she asked, her plate filled with a number of exotic dishes.

'I have a reef run with Thom later and he warned me to eat sparingly.'

They tried to eat in silence but were constantly interrupted by people introducing themselves. Clyde's head reeled from all the names and questions, most of which he couldn't answer. It was a great relief when, ninety minutes later, Thomas tapped him on the shoulder and indicated it was time for them to leave. Clyde followed him to the exit, still being harangued by people wanting to greet him. Finally, in the elevator, he breathed a sigh of relief.

'The early days can be a bit much,' Thomas stated. 'Everyone wants to meet you, wants to be your friend. But please understand, they mean well, and faced with the future as it is now, I think it's understandable.'

The elevator descended, finally stopping at the dock area. The two men exited and walked toward a long structure that had twin rails running down a ramp into the water. Clyde scanned the dock – no Genesis.

Thomas smiled. 'We moved her to the maintenance dock. She's been through a bit and we always keep the boats in top condition. Don't worry; she'll be back in a couple of days, good as new.' Clyde simply nodded; he had no option but to accept Thom's words at face value.

Thomas opened the door in front of them and led the way in. Inside was a real surprise for Clyde—there were twelve large RIB fast assault boats, each equipped with seats for a dozen heavily armed troops, plus four of the smaller craft he had seen previously.

'We used to have five of the smaller boats, but someone blew the bow off one.' Thomas smirked.

'Yeah, sorry about that Thomas,' Clyde responded.

'Don't worry, we can replace it and it was the professor's fault. He shouldn't have gone out there until he knew what he was facing, but that's Denham for you. If anyone ever had a God complex, it's him,' Thomas replied calmly.

Clyde stopped walking. 'I thought you were on his side?'

'Look, first, drop the full name, it's Thom. Second, yes, I'd follow Reg to the end of the earth, but only because I understand him and part of that is accepting his flaws. Believe me, anyone who has done what he's done has to have a huge ego, and he does.' Thom stopped and turned to face Clyde, studying his companion in a way that made Clyde feel like a microbe under a microscope. Finally, he spoke again. 'Come on, let's get going.'

They climbed aboard one of the smaller RIBs, attached the slings that were dangling from a crane parked overhead and activated the crane. The boat started to rise and move to the launching ramp; then gently lowered into position on a cradle. Thom showed Clyde how to release the slings and they were ready to go.

'When you're ready to launch, just enter your code here.' Thom indicated a keypad on the stanchion beside the boat and entered his code. 'Don't worry, you'll get yours as soon as I certify you to run the reef and you'll get your boat back at the same time. We really don't want anyone sinking anything in one of the channels.'

The boat began to reverse into the water; as soon as the boat began to float Thom started the engine. He ran through a series of checks and, satisfied all was OK, gently urged the boat forward, instructing Clyde to remove the final tether from the cradle. Now free, he dropped the bucket into the reverse position and throttled up enough to move a safe distance from the launch ramp.

The RIB was powered by a single V8 diesel engine, running a twin counter-rotating turbine drive.

'This boat uses a smaller version of the drives on your cruiser. It is highly manoeuvrable and bloody fast.' Thom smiled as he slammed the throttle to full. The RIB leaped out of the water. Clyde was prepared; he'd taken a firm grip on the grab rail on the centre console. Within seconds, the boat was up on the plane and flying toward the dock entrance.

They had just reached top speed when Thom lowered the revs and dropped the bucket into full reverse, then opened the throttle again. The RIB stopped in a little over its own length, the large stern wash simply lifting the RIB as it passed under the hull.

'Now we have entered the controlled zone, speed is regulated to four knots from that point,' Thom's extended arm lined up with a marker buoy, 'to one hundred meters outside the entrance.'

Clyde studied the buoy. The sign was a large yellow background with the numeral '4' emblazoned in black, leaving no doubt as to the maximum speed in the zone. He let his gaze drift from the buoy and began scanning behind them. The dock area was huge, but the waterway seemed to go far beyond what he could see.

'How far back does this cave system go?' he asked.

Thom smiled. 'All in good time – for now, you need to master this entrance.' As he spoke he stood aside and handed control of the boat to Clyde. 'Now the lesson begins.' They left the speed-controlled sector at exactly 2:00 pm and Clyde opened the throttle, obeying Thom's command to get a feel for the boat. He revelled in the ability of the small open craft, throwing it into tight turns, even a full 360-degree doughnut. He practiced the crash stop that Thom had done in the dock area before finally turning the bow for the sea entrance.

Thom proved to be a great instructor, stopping at each waypoint and explaining the best way of navigating it. They reached the open sea an hour later and Thom again took the lead and began talking Clyde through the return trip. Each waypoint had a number of markers, invisible to the untrained eye, but obvious when they were revealed.

The markers were rock outcrops, reference points on the island, some with specialized lights only visible through sensitized lenses, making sneaking through the entrance very hazardous.

The trip back was carried out in the same manner—Clyde driving and Thom instructing. By then Clyde had a good grasp of the landmarks and Thom didn't call for any stops to explain. Once again, they exited the reef system and entered the calm waters of the outer lagoon.

'I usually don't say this, but you're a fast learner. If you and Bonnie are to stay with us, and I'd suggest you seriously consider that, you'll need to be capable of running the entrance. As it stands, I reckon I'll have you certified within the week; then we can revisit your long term plans. Well done.' Thom smiled his approval. He stood for a few moments, as if trying to make a decision. 'Let me drive. It's time to show you something.'

Thom took the controls and soon had the boat flying across the glassy blue surface. The cliff face was growing every second. Clyde was beginning to feel a little apprehensive; they were heading away from the concealed entrance to the dock lake, as Clyde had christened it, straight toward the cliffs. Larger and larger the rock wall grew; still Thom raced the boat toward it.

It looked like they would hit in a few seconds and as Clyde's nerve was about to fail, Thom veered to starboard and raced parallel to the wall. He lifted a small lid covering a switch on the dash, held his finger above it, and waited, still racing close to the rock wall and counting. Clyde could see his lips moving, silently. It was a countdown and when it reached zero, Thom pressed the button and started counting again – five; four; three; two; one.

When he reached zero, Thom threw the boat into a sharp left turn. Still at full speed, they raced toward the rock wall again, now only fifty meters away. But the wall started to change. It seemed to be breaking apart, and when it seemed that their fate was sealed, the boat raced through an opening in the sheer rock face; the door closed rapidly behind them, the roar from the diesel engine shattering the silence of the tunnel they had entered.

Thom reduced his speed and lights started to come on as they progressed.

The tunnel was massive, well over one hundred meters high and three times as wide. 'What is this place?' Clyde whispered, as if the sound of his voice might wake some ancient demon.

Thom chuckled as he steered the boat down a narrower tunnel to port. 'Wait and see.' They continued for another few minutes. Clyde lost track of time. He was mesmerized by the sheer scale of what he was seeing. Thom guided the boat into a dock that appeared to have been designed for smaller craft. Clyde tied the boat off and they stepped ashore.

Without speaking, Thom took the lead and Clyde followed behind. He had absolutely no idea where they were or what their destination would be, but his curiosity won the day.

Ahead was a structure, smaller than the one they had taken the boat from, and security was much tighter. Thom entered his code into the keypad and a section of the wall opened, a console emerging from the wall. Thom placed his right hand on it and looked into an iris scanner. A green light bathed his eye and Clyde heard the door unlocking.

He turned to Clyde. 'You need to do the same. Trust me, you're in the system. After it recognizes you, you have twenty seconds to enter.' Thom's voice disappeared with him through the door. Clyde hesitated, but once again his curiosity won out.

He placed his hand on the console and looked into the iris scanner. He waited; a thin green beam of light scanned his eye.

Nothing was happening; maybe Thom had set him up. Slowly, he started to try and reach his Glock with his left hand; he couldn't without disturbing the scan.

Panic started to rise, but Clyde dismissed it. If Thom wanted him dead, he'd had plenty of opportunity to do it. As he started to calm down, the unmistakable sound of the door lock reached his ears. He leaped to the now-ajar door, pulled it open, and stepped through.

'Sorry that took so long,' Thom said. 'Sometimes it takes the system a while to recognize new people the first time. Follow me.' He strode off and Clyde fell in step behind.

'I noticed you're carrying,' Clyde half-stated and asked at the same time.

'Well spotted. Yeah, I usually do when I leave the compound, but not in the main areas. Eventually, you'll be the same.' Thom stopped at an elevator and turned to Clyde. 'It's about time we had a long chat and I've got just the place.' The elevator opened and they entered.

This was an express unit and Clyde felt his stomach drop as it sped upwards. Moments later, the doors opened and they stepped out into a large, well-appointed lounge. Thom led the way to a well-stocked bar, went behind the counter, and selected a bottle of Wild Turkey and two glasses.

'Come on, let's have a drink and I'll explain some things.' Thom moved to a table in front of the huge glass wall that stretched the entire length of the room. He poured two very generous measures and handed one to Clyde. 'Have a good look down there. What do you see?'

Clyde stood and went to the glass. It was black; he could see nothing. He was about to turn when lights started to come on many meters below him. Slowly, the darkness was defeated and he could see, but he refused to accept what he saw.

'That's not possible. You just can't get ships that big in there.' He shook his head in disbelief.

'Why not; the cave and the entry tunnel are large enough. What better place to hide them?' Thom replied. 'We're about two hundred meters above them. The mountain above us rises another five hundred. Sit down and I'll fill you in.'

Clyde returned to his seat, as Thom repeated the same story. The billionaire recluse, Simon Castilan, had started to terraform the natural islands to build his ideal hideaway. Unfortunately for him, certain government agencies and the military found out and made a deal with him to assist in his project. The use of the term deal was very generous; evidently Simon had a past and the deal was that if he allowed the agencies and military to build their base there, his past would disappear. He had one proviso; the location of the base would be kept very tightly controlled, only those with a direct 'need to know' would be privy to the details. This was agreed and soon billions of dollars started pouring into the project.

'It took ten years and, I believe, over sixty billion, but this is what we ended up with. Those ships down there are mainly nuclear-powered. They're cold at the moment because we don't have the people to run them, but we're training. We have one submarine that's active. It's due back in a few days and one of those destroyers will be crewed soon. The problem is people. We just don't have enough.'

'So how many are on these islands?'

'About three thousand – the main facility can support up to ten—but we can't find them, or at least find those we would want to bring here. The convoy that you found the wreckage of would have bolstered our numbers by almost another ten percent, if they had made it,' Thom added as he sipped his drink. 'Down there, in the military complex, there's housing for another fifteen thousand as well as the ships themselves.' His voice trailed off as he too gazed down on the dead fleet below.

'But what about logistics,' Clyde asked. 'Food, water and, well grog – everything seems to be here in abundance?'

Thom explained. 'I don't know all of it, but Reg says that this place has some very serious stores; even perishables are well stocked in things he calls "*stasis lockers*". His explanation is that these are something like refrigerated storage, but I don't know how it all works. The areas you saw yesterday, hydroporics for fruit and vegies, and the grazing sector; remember this was designed to support many more than we have, so I don't think we even have scratched the surface. Plus, whenever we find a relatively safe area we can raid, we do so and as long as we can, we will continue to do so.'

A sound entered the room. It sounded like a plane. Clyde looked up, almost startled. 'Planes as well?'

'Yeah, mainly recon and surveillance,' he checked his watch. 'That'll be a Hawkeye returning from a patrol. We send them out once a week just to see what's out there and give the crews some flight time. Mostly we use drones. They're more efficient and we don't need the crews.'

Clyde drained his glass and reached for the bottle, refilled his, and offered it to Thom, who did the same. 'So what's your story? You know mine so how about some reciprocity?'

Thom took a long swig before he answered. 'Well, I suppose you should know. I'm like you, I was brought here as a breeder.'

Clyde looked up from the window 'When? How long have you been here?'

'I came here from 2025 along with a woman, Candice. Unlike you, we were fully aware of what Denham wanted. I had no ties so I was happy – I mean the thought of breeding with as many women as I wanted... well, I'm just a normal hetero male.

'My companion, on the other hand, took a higher view. She believed that God had selected her and that she was to be the new Mary. Don't get me wrong, Candy was great and a really nice person, she just fell in with Denham's rhetoric. Anyway, we had one child of our own two years ago, and that started things in earnest. Denham believed he had the answer and so the rest of you were recruited. Only he knew how to use the technology so he didn't need to take the time to... seduce you, I suppose is the best phrase. He just went back to the time before the infection and brought you forward, not asking if you wanted to. He just grabbed who he wanted.'

'So you just came here of your own free will?' Clyde asked.

'More or less, the way Reg sold it, well, it was believable. You must remember what it was like, the Elites trying to take over, the UN a total waste of time and the western world far more concerned about false ideologies than the actual survival of the race. I suppose that when he found us, we were both so disillusioned we didn't need much convincing.'

'So where is Candy now?' Clyde asked.

Thom looked sad as he replied. 'Dead... she took this Mother Mary thing too fucking far. She jumped into the breeding program, which was hard on her. To do what they wanted, they needed to put her on some rather heavy drugs. They harvested her eggs in bulk and fertilized them, then implanted them into hosts. That's when it all hit the fan. That's when Denham and his cronies discovered that they couldn't make it work. Virtually all the pregnancies self-terminated in the first few months, but some went full term. What was born wasn't human. The virus attacked the foetuses, deforming them in horrible ways. It was all too much for Candy. She blamed herself and took a dive off the top of this mountain.' He stopped; the emotion in his voice raw and naked.

'I'm sorry, I shouldn't have asked,' Clyde could almost feel Thom's pain and loss; his eyes told Clyde everything he needed to know.

'No, you didn't know and you have many more questions. Come on, we still have over half the bottle; what else do you want to know?'

'Okay, you and Candy have a child. Now, why did he bring us here? He knew his plan was a failure. What use can we be?' Clyde refilled both glasses.

Thom stood and paced to the end of the room and back. 'You were already here, undergoing the transformation, but for some reason he decided to use the boat; I think he wanted the two of you to form a sort of bond. Don't ask why, but you need to understand that everything is one-way. I've been informed that the machine that brought us all here is stuffed, and before you ask, I have no idea, how it worked – you'll need to discuss that with Reg.' Thom took a long swig from his glass. 'Even your boat was specially built. The engines and drive systems were almost experimental in your day. Both originated in New Zealand and offered huge efficiency gains over conventional diesel and shaft drive. Denham went back and arranged for it to be built and transported it here exactly where he wanted it. By this time both you and Bonnie had been finished—sorry, but that's the best description I have—the prof simply took you out to the boat and left you there. What his detailed plan was, I have no idea. But here you are.'

Clyde's head was reeling, questions kept forming, but he decided to let them rest, for the time being. 'So, what now?'

'Fucked if I know; all I can suggest is that I introduce you to the others and we discuss our future. But understand this—we're the only ones with a future. We're the only ones who can breed. Fucking sad, isn't it? The future of the entire human race is us.' Thom threw his empty glass at the wall, smashing it into a million pieces. Immediately, a small robotic cleaner scooted out of its docking bay, cleaned up the mess, and retreated until needed again.

Thom grumbled something incomprehensible as he went to the bar and retrieved another glass, filling it to the brim on his return. Clyde refused the offered bottle, deciding that one of them should slow down.

Thom drained the glass in one gulp, refilled it, and repeated the process, probably trying to drown some memory. He stood, staggered, and fell back into his chair. 'Fucking thing's heavy,' he grumbled almost incoherently as he exposed his pistol and dragged it out onto the table between them.

'That's a bloody cannon, may I?' Clyde asked as he reached forward and picked the weapon up.

'When I shoot someone, they stay fucking shot. Better than that pea shooter you carry. If you like, there are a few more in the armoury. I'll get you one,' Thom mumbled just before he passed out.

Clyde held the gun, dropped the magazine out, and cycled the action to clear any round in the chamber. The gun was huge and heavy. Clyde stood and tried to mimic a combat sequence in the room, picturing potential assailants hiding in various places and trying to quickly target them. It was difficult, the weight and size of the gun making for clumsy movements.

He inspected the ammunition, a soft whistle escaped from his lips as he did. *Hand-made*, Clyde thought as he turned the bullet over in his fingers. He stopped moving it and looked intently at the slightly flattened end of the projectile. Something about it made his skin crawl.

He replaced the round into the magazine and the gun onto the table; then he turned and went back to the window. He gazed down at the gathered fleet of vessels and suddenly felt annoyed; there was another memory, buried deep, but he couldn't bring it back.

A sound came from behind him, a warning. Clyde spun around; his Glock seemed to leap into his hands.

The door opened and Denham stepped into the room. He ignored the gun pointed at him and walked to the lounge where Thom was snoring loudly.

'Passed out again... still, it's been a while and,' he surveyed the room, 'no damage. Believe me, that's a bonus.' Reg picked up the now almost empty bottle, turned it in his hands, and smiled. 'Just one; you've shown great restraint. I suppose he's been telling you his story?'

'Yes, you could say that.' Clyde answered coldly.

Reg reached into his pocket, pulled out what looked like a mobile phone, and handed it to Clyde. 'This is yours – standard issue, everybody gets one. I suggest you call Bonnie, tell her where you are.' He glanced over to Thom again. 'Probably better tell her you'll see her tomorrow. I don't think he'll be going anywhere tonight.'

Clyde agreed and made the call, all he needed to do was say Bonnie's name and the call was made. Bonnie indicated that she was not very happy about the situation; Clyde ended the call and returned to Denham.

'Now I think it's time we had that discussion.' Reg smiled as he poured each of them a drink. 'From the frown on your brow, I'd say you have some questions?'

'That's an understatement, there are so many, I don't know where to start. One of the main issues we have is trust. You admitted you kidnapped us for a purpose you found didn't work; you were so convinced that you could save the human race that actual people became commodities, nothing more than a way for your end to be realised. The result is that we're trapped here, or so the general opinion says, and you now ask that we simply forget what you've done and trust you – why the hell should we?'

Reg indicated the meal on the table; he waited until Clyde sat and started to eat. 'I'll go back to when the world fell apart. It was a tragic and terrifying time, people got sick and died in their thousands, the health systems of almost every nation failed, and anarchy and violence became the norm; at least for a short while until those people died as well. I wasn't there. I was already looking for this place so my recollections are from what others told me. I tried to contact Allison, but I couldn't and the Garibaldis had gone to ground as some wanted their heads believing they were the perpetrators. Then we found this place.'

'Yeah, that's another question; where were all the former inhabitants?' Clyde asked.

'There was no-one here except the elusive Simon Castilan; he was an actual person. He died soon after we arrived and so did a number of my crew, but enough survived to start exploring this place. I won't dwell on the gory details but we found another fifty or so bodies, and quickly burned them, fearing we were facing some sort of contagion.' Reg paused while he took a swig from his glass.

'We found Castilan's communication system and began trying to contact other people; when we did, we gave them co-ordinates for them to head for.'

Clyde looked up. 'So you just gave the location of these islands to anyone you contacted?'

'No, we gave them a set of co-ordinates then we waited to see just who showed up. We did pretty well as only one group was off.  We saw immediately that they were a problem and we simply left them where we found them. Looking back, that probably wasn't the best idea as I believe these people were picked up by the Poulsen and took that ship; after that, they did everything they could to find us and destroy anybody heading for our islands. Several months later we picked up a group of brilliant scientists who were immune and they are the ones who cracked the code for the time travel thing. I set about returning to the past and recruiting people for my grand plan, as you called it. Then I went back and grabbed you and Bonnie, rejuvenated you and set up the boat for you. While you were in the process, I found the Garibaldis and helped them to put together a small fleet of pleasure craft to head here from New Zealand. Next, I put the two of you on the boat and came back here, but when I returned the news was devastating; my grand breeding plan was an absolute disaster, and the machine we used was out of action.'

Clyde had finished his meal and sat back. 'What I don't understand is, why put us on that boat, with all the attendant capabilities? Why not just wake us up here and see what happened?'

'We thought it would be better if we simply left clues for you to find; the GPS data for the islands for one. We wanted the two of you to form a bond before we brought you here.' Reg held up his hand, stopping Clyde's next question. 'Don't ask me, I'm not the psychologist who made the decision. Maybe in a few days you can ask him yourself. But you're here now, and if we can't repair the machine we used to get you, you're stuck here with us. When you have been certified by Thom to run the reef, you can take your boat and see what else you can find, if that's what you need to do; the decision will be yours. I can't do anything more about trust; either we start down that path or we don't; for me I would rather we did. Now, I think we should get some sleep, tomorrow will bring another surge of questions I'm sure.'

'Just one more question; Allison, she has a huge amount of anger towards you. I think she blames you for her mother's death; we need to know what happened?'

'There's not much to say; my wife contracted a very aggressive cancer, it literally ate her up. I tried everything I could, every treatment, every drug, but nothing worked. Ali was in the final stages of her studies and I thought that seeing her mother as she was would only cause her too much grief, but the decision was left to her mother, Maggie. She was the one who decided that Ali should finish her studies, without seeing her as she was. She tried to sound upbeat when they spoke on the phone, but the end was speeding toward us and she couldn't hang on long enough for Ali to see her.

In Ali's mind, I'm to blame and there's nothing I can say or do that will change that. Now, can we get some sleep?'

# TWELVE

B onnie ended the call and turned the unit off.

She quickly recalled the last words Clyde had spoken, something about having some girl time with Allison. She smiled as she realized what he meant and rammed the phone back into the pocket of her jeans and swore. 'Typical fucking men,' she swore again, for effect.

Allison rushed from her room. 'What's up? What's Clyde done now?'

'Nothing really, just that he and Thom have found a bar somewhere; Thom's passed out and Clyde says he can't just leave him. Typical, we arrive here and the first thing he does is find a drinking buddy and gets pissed.' Bonnie hoped she wasn't hamming it up too much.

'Is that all?' Allison sighed. 'Good riddance. Gives us time for a girl's night in; we'll have some dinner, maybe a bottle or two, and talk—really talk—and get to know each other. By the way, I've managed to circumvent their door lock over-ride. Once we lock the door, nobody but we can unlock it; that should give us some piece of mind.'

'I have a better idea,' Bonnie added with a wicked glint in her eye. 'We have a huge spa in our bathroom. How about we take a bottle and relax there?'

Allison agreed enthusiastically and went to the kitchen to select the wine while Bonnie began filling the tub. When Allison returned, she brought two wine glasses and a bottle of red wine. She stopped, took in the room, and selected a small table that she moved to the side of the spa. There she filled the glasses and placed the bottle beside them.

The spa was filled to the correct height and Bonnie turned on the motors. Immediately, the water began to bubble and froth. 'I added some spa bubbles. It amazes me just what this place has, but I'm not about to complain.' Bonnie stripped her clothes off and moved to the spa.

'Bonnie, stop, just for a moment. I'm sorry, but can you let me look at you?' Allison asked, embarrassment reddening her face. Bonnie understood immediately and went to her side. Together they turned and stood gazing into the full-length mirror.

'I don't know how to ask, so I'll just do it. Are you angry with my father for what he's done to you?' Allison blurted out.

Bonnie smiled and looked at the reflections. They could be sisters, physically. Their bodies had the same youthful radiance, the same sexual attractiveness that nature intended.

Bonnie slowly lifted her hands to her breasts, cupped them, and lifted them. 'I really don't know. I'm bloody sure that these weren't like this when he took us, but I'm not complaining. I know the face and hair give things away, but overall, I like what I see.'

She released her breasts and ran her hands down her body. She reached her hairless mound and then retreated to her belly. 'I'm not so sure I'm okay with what's inside. I have a strong conviction that I'd finished with the breeding issue, and now it's back, and there's no contraception here.'

Allison looked glum. She repeated Bonnie's movements, cupping and examining her breasts and finally holding her hands on her belly. 'I hate the fact that I'll never have children. As I've said before, when there was the possibility of it, I had a choice. Now some arsehole has taken that away, and it pisses me off!' Her voice broke and tears flowed freely down her cheeks. 'It's just so fucking unfair.'

Bonnie reached out to her and they embraced, Allison racked with sobs. 'Don't give up. If the research facilities here are as good as Anton and Zena hoped, they may be able to find a solution. Remember, we're human beings; throughout history we have faced massive challenges and that's been the time we shine as a species – this is another challenge for us to rise to. Now, stop this crying, and let's have a drink.'

Allison smiled weakly and they climbed into the spa, took their glasses, and toasted the future. 'It's like you're a mother and sister in one body. I'm so grateful you saved me.'

'So am I. I don't think I had a sister or daughter so maybe that's one reason I have this body. Physically, I could be your age and your sister, but the face has age and I hope, a little of the wisdom that's supposed to bring.' Bonnie raised her glass again.

For a while they just giggled and drank, the wine eventually loosening tongues and breaking down inhibitions. Allison asked a lot about Clyde. It was clear she had more than a passing interest in him, and she wanted specifics. Bonnie initially changed the subject but as the bottle emptied, her answers became more truthful. Allison seemed to be hinting at something; she actually mentioned the word threesome a few times. Try as she might, Bonnie couldn't get that image out of her mind and what was more intriguing, it actually excited her.

'So how do you handle the pregnancy issue?' Allison asked.

Bonnie gave her what was probably her last serious motherly look of the evening. 'Perhaps I need to know something. Have you had any boyfriends?'

'Yes, heaps,' Allison began, but then she stopped. 'But I never screwed them without protection. I was always focused on my studies and a bit afraid...' her voice trailed off, but only for a second. 'Still, how do you handle it?'

Bonnie sobered up, just for a second, before answering. 'Listen, a girl has more than just a vagina, if you get my drift.'

Allison giggled and her face turned red again. 'Yes, I know. I've watched porn. You're talking about oral, anal, and other things.'

Bonnie splashed her. 'You cheeky bugger – you knew so why did you ask?'

'Just to see if you would answer, what you'd say.' Allison giggled. 'Now, more about Clyde; does he have a big one?'

Bonnie answered on the proviso this was the last question about her sex life, Allison agreed and picked up the empty bottle. Bonnie stood and quickly dried her feet, went to the kitchen, and returned with the last bottle they had.

For the next hour, they drank less and talked more. Allison took Bonnie on a tour through her life from her childhood to now. Her father had always been driven. He had come from a wealthy background and his two brothers had joined their father in the family financial business. There had been a bit of trouble over Reginald Denham's decision to follow a scientific career, but his mother had supported it and in the end, everything worked out for the better.

Allison had been born and Maggie, her mother, doted on her, knowing that she'd never have another child. Allison had proved to be an excellent student and progressed rapidly through her schooling, winning not only academic accolades but also the title of most popular girl, something that her father hated.

Allison continued the story. 'I was always a top student, and I completed my first degree when I was only twenty one. I then went back for my doctoral studies and another four years of hard work.' Bonnie refilled their glasses as Allison continued. 'I was in my third year when my mother took ill and Dad kept telling me that she would get better. I tried to see her whenever I could— Mum understood and didn't want to interrupt my studies— and Dad kept telling me she had the best care and would beat the disease.'

'A year later, the day after I graduated, she died, and because of him, I didn't get the chance to say goodbye. All his promises, all his guarantees that he would beat the disease—all lies just to keep me focused on my studies. He's an absolute bastard,' Allison spat, her words filled with venom; she drained he glass and used the last of the bottle to refill it. 'That's when I left him, he was never around anyway and our home was so empty. I bummed around for a while then the Garibaldis vaccine was announced. Six months later, everything went pear shaped, and the rest is what led us here.'

'How old are you now?' Bonnie asked.

'I'll be thirty in a few weeks, that's why we could be sisters; you look about the same age— well, from the neck down anyway.' Allison's answer brought a new wave of sobbing from her.

Bonnie didn't say anything. She had the answers she wanted, but for the girl in the tub with her, the wound was still open and festering. She placed her glass beside the tub and moved across, taking the sobbing form into her arms again.

'Allison, please listen to me. You need to tell your father all this. Let him know how you feel.'

Before Bonnie could continue, Allison pushed her away. 'What's the fucking point? I'd rather put a bullet in his damn head.' Her eyes seemed to glow with rage.

Bonnie knew she had to get this out, for all their sakes. 'Bullshit. Remember back to the boat when he came aboard. You had him covered and he just stood there; if you really wanted to kill him that much, that was your best chance – and you let it pass.'

'What a load of shit,' Allison snapped back.

'Really?' Bonnie raised her voice and stood, giving herself a more commanding position. 'Do you want to know what we saw, Clyde and me? We saw a man in extreme pain, a man who was prepared to risk his daughter shooting him; even if that was the only way she would see how much he loved her. Not only that, we could see the pain of defeat, and now we know why. His grand plan had been a total failure; but his daughter had been returned to him and she wanted to shoot him. But you couldn't pull the trigger. Deep inside, you saw it too,' Bonnie's voice dropped and now held compassion. 'You knew, at that moment, he suffered as much as you, and probably more.'

Bonnie reached out and placed her hand on Allison's shoulder. Allison stood and almost melted into Bonnie, her sobs turning into an almost primordial howl of pain as she released all the grief and hate she had kept bottled inside her for years. Slowly, the sobs retreated and pain gave way to exhaustion. Bonnie helped her out of the tub, assisted her to dry, and took Allison to her bedroom. It seemed that her head hit the pillow and instantly she fell asleep.

Bonnie retreated and went back to her room, quickly pulled on a flimsy nightgown, and went back to the kitchen. Her stomach was grumbling she was so hungry. Checking the clock, she realized why.

'It's after midnight; we were in the tub for over four hours. No wonder I'm starving.' A quick meal of poached eggs on toast and she was in bed herself.

***

Clyde woke slowly. His head hurt and his mouth was dry and sandy, like the bottom of a bird cage; he also thought it tasted like one. There was a loud buzzing sound filling his head. He opened his eyes and looked toward the source; Thom was on his back snoring loudly on the lounge.

Gently, Clyde stood and tried to stretch the kinks out of his body, his mind wondering how many before him had slept off an evening on these lounges.

Reg was nowhere to be seen, but the need for water to slake his thirst and the urgent pressure in his bladder forced Clyde forward. He went to the bar, found some bottled water in a fridge, and downed a full bottle. He scanned the room, his eyes finally fixing on a sign that read 'HEAD-MALE'—his next stop.

The head wasn't just a toilet—it also held showers and change rooms. Clyde emptied his bladder before checking out the rest of the room. There were about twenty lockers. None had any locks so he opened the first one. It was empty. Clyde opened the next. Inside was a supply of small, single use toiletries. He took what he needed and headed for the showers, picking a towel off a rack at the entrance of the shower room.

He stripped off and soon had a good head of hot water cascading over his body. This was always his best hangover cure—a hot, hard shower. Fifteen minutes later, he turned the water off and began to briskly dry himself. Clyde dressed and tied his long grey hair into his signature ponytail. He walked out of the head a new man.

Food became his concern.

He checked Thom, who was still buzzing on the lounge, and turned toward the door marked 'GALLEY'. Before he could walk through, the galley door swung open and Reg walked in carrying a loaded tray.

'Thought we should have something to eat before Thom wakes,' Reg smiled as he moved to one of the tables at the window. He laid the table while Clyde stared down at the fleet below.

***

Last night had been a revelation to him—Reg had been open and believable but Clyde didn't have any information or memory of events to dispute him. He'd given his recollection of his falling out with Allison and the death of his wife. From there, they'd covered the geo-political events that had eventually led to today. The aroma of breakfast snapped him back to the present—a plate of scrambled eggs, bacon, and hash browns greeted him.

Quietly, he began to eat, the food helping to assuage the results of last night's binge. Neither man spoke until the meal was finished and coffee poured.

Clyde stood, taking his mug to the window. 'Reg, there's something that's been niggling at me; something about that fleet that seems off.'

Reg joined him. 'The destroyers down there – I think they were called Zumwalt class in your time.'

Clyde stared down at the three ships below, a glimmer of a memory glowing in his mind. 'Yeah, I seem to remember them being a white elephant—way too expensive—and I thought only one or two were built. If I remember correctly, there was a compromise with the stealth capability, defeating the reason they were designed in the first place. After that, they canned the program, or am I mistaken?'

Reg slapped him on the shoulder. 'No, Clyde, you're not mistaken. The Zumwalt class destroyer was too expensive for the general military. What you need to realize is that the agencies that funded and equipped this place... well, let's just say they had very deep pockets and little to no oversight.'

'But Thom said they're all nuke boats, or so Thom told me? Somewhere in my mind I seem recall that the Zumwalt was powered by gas turbines?'

Reg smiled reassuringly. 'It appears some of your memories are returning. Yes, the ones that were designed for the navy were. These are a little different, same with all the others—different design, for a different purpose. Tell you what, let's get sleeping beauty up and back to the compound. When he's sober, we'll talk more. He might even give you a tour of some of them.'

Together they woke Thom, well almost—he was still like a dead weight, unable to stand and walk on his own—as they bundled him into the elevator. The elevator stopped and the doors opened. It wasn't at the dock.

'We're on the wrong level. We left the boat at the dock,' Clyde said. This was another dry cave that looked like a mini train station.

'No, we're at the right spot; I had some of the boys pick the boat up and take it back, I knew where you two would be. What we have here is part of the transportation system they built.'

Clyde felt the unmistakable rush of air announcing the imminent arrival of an underground train. Silently the train, if it could be called that, slid into the station. It was sleek and streamlined. Suspended from a single rail in the roof of the tunnel, it consisted of four carriages, each with doors that led into a compartment with eight comfortable seats.

They entered, took their seats, and propped Thom up near the opposite window just as the doors closed. The train started to move, but there was little sensation—it was smooth and quiet, the only real indication being the passing of tunnel lights, and they passed very quickly.

'It can reach speeds of over four hundred kilometres per hour, but we have limited it to two hundred. It runs to every point of the island chain and is almost entirely underwater.' Reg seemed proud of his toy. 'We have other ground transports, but this is the most efficient.' As he finished, they started to decelerate and although it was a rapid deceleration, Clyde felt very little of it.

They exited the train and were met by a couple of nurses and a wheelchair. Thom was placed into it and they turned to leave.

'Be gentle with him. You know what yesterday was.' The nurses nodded and left pushing Thom.

'So what was yesterday?' Clyde asked.

'He didn't tell you? Yesterday was the anniversary of Candice's and Steven's death,' Reg explained.

'Candice I knew about. Who was Steven?'

'His son,' Reg's words stunned Clyde. 'When Candice jumped, she was holding their infant son. She couldn't accept that she had a child while others couldn't. She believed that somehow, she had caused their miscarriages or deformities; so she took her perfect son and they died together. Thom still can't get over it and every anniversary, he goes back to where he was when it happened, drinks himself stupid, and passes out. I'm glad you were with him; last time he almost killed himself.'

Clyde took the words in silence. He was unable to imagine the depth of grief that Thom was holding. But along with the grief, was guilt; Thom also took the blame, believing he was guilty of something that caused Candice's break with reality.

Clyde stood for a moment before speaking. 'Something's bothering me. All this virus stuff happened years ago but Sarah Garibaldi, she's only about five, and if I am any judge of age, Zena is very close to menopause. If she was exposed to her own virus, surely she wouldn't have been able to conceive?'

Reg simply smiled. 'Yes, that is an anomaly, one I can't explain.'

Together, the two men ambled through the station, took an elevator, and parted company. Clyde headed back to his apartment.

# Thirteen

Reg decided to walk the short distance to the administration section of the complex.

The journey was pleasant, with most of the walkway open and exposed to the elements. Lush semi-tropical bushland surrounded it, giving the impression of being totally in the wild and not in a man-made structure. Here he could relax and let his mind wander away from the issues and responsibilities he dealt with every day. He savoured the aroma of the bush he was now walking through. *The smell of life*, he thought as he slowed his progress. While the walkway gave the impression of being part of nature, it wasn't. In fact, it was totally enclosed in insect-proof mesh, one of the trade-offs living here required.

All too soon the end of the walkway loomed ahead. He sighed, *Time to face the music*. The door ahead slid quietly aside. As he stepped through the door an assistant hurried toward him. She was young, probably in her late twenties casually dressed in denim jeans and white shirt. 'Professor, please.' She stopped in front of Reg and began to speak hurriedly. 'Four councillors are waiting in the main meeting room and they don't seem happy.'

'Are they ever?' Then he saw the look on her face. 'Don't worry, I'll see them.' He thanked her and changed direction, heading for the meeting room.

The politics of the group were based on a collective—everyone contributed according to their abilities and everyone was rewarded according to their needs. A third of the current council wanting to see him didn't bode well. *Either they have a very serious issue, or it'll be the usual suspects trying to force their ideas, again,* Reg thought. Of twelve people currently sitting on the council, he had a good idea of just who would be waiting for him.

He stopped at the door of the meeting room, gathered his thoughts, and pushed the doors open, deliberately leaving them in that position.

He smiled inwardly when he saw who was waiting—his suspicion was correct, the same four clowns who were trying to take control of the colony. After all the human race had been through, these four wanted to become despots. *Some things never change*, he thought as he smiled his greeting. 'Good morning. And what desperate issue must we discuss today?' Reg asked, his voice filled with sarcasm.

It was the lone female, Zuri Malabo, who answered. 'You know very well what is needed.' Zuri was African American and had once been an activist for black rights in that country. Since being elected to the council, her angry left-wing political views had been spewed forth at every opportunity. She had a small base of supporters who wanted to change things. She believed that the group needed a strong leader, a permanent leader, who would forge ahead.

Her view of someone like Denham was poor. She and her group hated academia, and with some reason. After all, it had been academic researchers who had condemned the race to extinction.

Her view was extremely one sided—believing that black females should be in power.

'And, my dear Zuri, please remind me what you mean.' Reg knew that eventually, there would be a showdown with her and her cronies. Malabo was an impressive figure. Tall, voluptuous, strikingly beautiful, and she knew how to use her assets.

She stood, dramatically placing her hand on her hips and then raised her head so she was looking down her nose at Reg. To anyone who had just met her, this was intimidating, but Reg simply took his seat and allowed her to impress herself.

'This Clyde – what have you told him and when will he leave?' she demanded.

'Told him? Everything I can. And as for when he's leaving, I have no idea. I haven't even broached the subject with him. He and his companion have been through a lot. They need time to acclimatize to the new world they have been thrust into. Now, if there's nothing else, I have more important things to do.'

Reg stood to leave. Malabo blocked his way. 'Listen, that bastard is going to do what we ask. Just take his woman and hold her as collateral. He'll obey.' Hatred and venom filled her words.

'And then what? Are you and your few going to kill the rest of us? Because if you want to follow your own advice, that'll be the result. Maybe you or one of your brave followers would like to volunteer to carry out the mission, become heroes, like you constantly tell yourself you are.'

Reg gave her time to speak, but instead, she seemed to whither a little.

'I thought not. You're all so brave and filled with shit when you're in a safe and protected environment, but not so when there's a risk to take. Now understand this, I'll discuss the issue with Clyde when I think the time's right. He'll decide whether he helps or not. It's his decision and as this whole meeting has been recorded, if anything happens to either him or Bonnie, we'll all know who to call on. Now get out; this meeting is over.'

Malabo sneered. 'The meeting may be over, but the issue still needs to be rectified and if you won't – I will.'

Reg breathed a sigh of relief as the four left. While he hated her ideology, she had a point, if there was to be any future for the human race, Clyde was their best hope.

He left the meeting room after he had sent the recording of the meeting to three different servers, and walked to his office.

***

Clyde left Reg at the station and went toward the accommodation section and had a pleasant stroll through the bush. He arrived at the main foyer and followed his instincts to his apartment, arriving just after 10:00. He opened the door and stepped through, instantly noting the drawn curtains and the sonorous sounds emanating from Allison's room.

He quietly walked to his bedroom door and opened it. Bonnie was still asleep, naked but partially covered by a sheet. He stopped, half-convinced he should wake her, but he had other more pressing needs and with a final look, he went into the bathroom and quietly closed the door.

The bathroom was divided into three sections—the bathing area, a vanity area, and a separate toilet. That was his destination.

He closed the door behind him and looked at the toilet. There was no paper, just a remote control at the side. He lifted the lid and sat down, picking up the control as he did. There were three buttons, 'RINSE', 'CLEAN' and 'DRY'. He decided that 'CLEAN' was the correct one and pressed that.  Immediately, his backside was sprayed with warm water, followed by a pulsing, soapy flush, another rinse and then the dry cycle started.

'Damn, first time I've had my arse blow-dried.' Clyde chuckled. With bodily functions taken care of, he left the cubicle and proceeded to wash his hands. He moved back to the main bathroom area. The evidence of the previous evening's revelry was obvious in the two empty wine bottles and glasses, the spa still circulating the water.

'Looks like these two had fun,' Clyde sniggered, his mind building pictures he knew it shouldn't. 'What the hell. I'm allowed a fantasy or two.' He decided to change. After all, he'd been in the same clothes since yesterday, so he set the spa to recycle and left the room.

Back in the bedroom he selected fresh clothes, locked his pistol in the safe and returned to the bathroom. He changed quickly, placed his clothes in the hamper and picked up the empty bottles and glasses, and as quietly as possible, left the bedroom, closing the door behind him.

Clyde deposited the empty bottles in the disposal chute and started to brew coffee. He had just finished and was about to go out onto the balcony when a buzz from the door stopped him. He put his coffee down and went to the vid panel, activated it, and looked at the scene before him.

A tall, attractive black woman and three men stood there. He pressed the talk button and spoke. 'Hello, who are you?' he enquired.

'Zuri Malabo, a member of the ruling council of Eden. You will allow me to enter.'

*Eden. Fuck, these people have delusions of grandeur.* He was about to open the door when he saw the men were carrying pistols. 'Sorry, Zuri, but I have absolutely no idea who you are and I don't like armed men at my door.'

Clyde thought he had her stopped when he heard, 'Then you leave me no alternative.' She turned to one of the men. 'Open it.'

The sounds of the door lock releasing galvanized Clyde into action. He reached for his Glock, only to remember he had left it secured in the wardrobe safe. He backed away from the door as it opened.

The three men entered, their weapons held on Clyde, the woman was last and she locked the door behind her.

'Now, you will give me your weapon and do as I say.'

The woman seemed to like her control and Clyde simply lifted his shirt. 'I'm not carrying.'

Allison's door burst open and she emerged, wearing only pyjamas and her two Uzis, which she trained on the invaders.

'I think you should all drop your weapons. Believe me, I can drop all four of you before you can react.' Allison released the safety on each gun as she spoke.

One of Malabo's goons spun, trying to bring his weapon to bear, three nine-millimetre slugs from Allison's left Uzi dropped him before he'd half-turned. The other two tried something similar and suffered the same fate—a short burst from each Uzi finished any argument.

Bonnie's door flew open and she stood in the doorway, similarly dressed, with her Glock trained on Malabo. 'What the hell, Clyde? I was sound asleep. You could have just shaken me.'

Clyde ignored her and went to each of the bodies, checking them for any signs of life. It was just an automatic response; he knew that if Allison had shot them, they were dead. He collected each weapon and inspected them—three Desert Eagles.

'Heavy artillery for a social visit,' He held his hand out. 'Clyde – we haven't been formally introduced.'

Malabo had a look of utter confusion on her face as she took his hand; her mistake. Clyde spun her around until she was facing Bonnie, put one of the Eagles to her temple, and called. 'Bonnie, come and frisk this bitch.'

Bonnie complied and found she was unarmed.

There was a frantic buzzing and knocking at the door. Bonnie covered their prisoner while Clyde checked the viewer. Denham and other security people were outside.

'Reg – seems we're very popular today,' Clyde joked.

'Is everyone all right?' Denham asked.

'Yes, the three of us are, but I can't say the same for this Malabo woman's goons. They're toast. Now, just give us a couple of minutes. There are two ladies in here wearing only PJs and I'm sure they don't want everyone to see them like that.' He signalled for Bonnie and Allison to dress. Bonnie left quickly while Allison held back.

'Maybe I should wait until Bonnie comes back?' she asked, both Uzis now trained on Malabo.

Clyde smiled and held up the Desert Eagle. 'I think I can handle her. Now get dressed.'

Allison gave him a cheeky grin and leaped back into her room. Clyde opened the door and let Reg and the others in.

The three dead men were sprawled on the tiled floor, but there were two robotic cleaners desperately trying to clean up the mess; finally, they were defeated and they retreated back to their docks.

Both men turned their attention to the woman sitting on the lounge.

'I'm glad you're here. Arrest this murderer and that psycho daughter of yours,' Malabo blustered.

'I don't think so. Reg, watch this.' Clyde activated the large screen on the wall, selected the feed, and replayed the events of the morning.

Reg and the others watched before he spoke. 'Zuri, I didn't need to see that to know what you were up to, I just didn't think you were stupid enough to try anything so soon. Seems your standing with your fellow council members is not the best. They came to me and asked me to intervene; it appears that the only person who wants you as a dictator is you.'

'Then man up. Tell this fool why you brought him here. He's just a tool. Tell him his job,' Malabo shrieked.

Clyde moved in front of him, just as Bonnie and Allison re-entered the room, fully armed. 'Lady, I think it's you who needs to listen. I know I was brought here for a reason. I'm in no doubt about that but, since I've arrived, I've been shot at, and attacked by homicidal pirates on a ship that I sank. I found the two people who engineered the destruction of the human race and now I arrive here, at a place that is supposed to be safe, and then I find an arsehole like you who'll do anything for power.'

He raised the pistol to her forehead. 'And I don't give a flying fuck about anything you think you know. Under the present circumstances, I have every right to end you here.' Clyde flicked the safety off and cocked the hammer. He placed his finger on the trigger, watching as the face of Malabo drained of colour. He smiled and released the hammer. 'But I won't because unlike you, I have morals and a conscience.'

Thom stepped through the doorway, pursed his lips, and let out a slow, tuneless whistle. 'I leave you alone for an hour and look at the trouble you get into.' He moved through the room until he faced the prisoner. 'Malabo, I should have known your skanky arse would try something stupid.' He turned to Clyde. 'You should have shot her first, save us the trouble later.'

'Enough of that; Thom, please take her to the brig. We'll decide what to do with her later,' Reg ordered.

Thom obeyed and soon had Malabo handcuffed and in the middle of the three guards as they marched her, with great flourish, out of the apartment, creating a show for all to see. The medical team was busy with the bodies and cataloguing the scene.

Reg suggested they all go out onto the balcony to allow the investigation and clean-up to proceed. Clyde made a new pot of coffee and they left the room. As they sat outside, Bonnie handed Clyde his pistol and holster; showing him she was in no mood for any more surprises.

The balcony protruded out from the structure like all the others in this accommodation wing, and gave a fantastic perspective of the island terrain below. Also, like all outdoor areas, it was covered in the insect-proof mesh.

'The original owner had a thing about insects. He had this mesh specially constructed for the job,' Reg said nonchalantly. He was stalling, Clyde could see that.

Clearly, Allison wasn't in the mood for any bullshit. 'Come on, Professor... cut to the chase, fill them in on what you're hiding.' Allison cut a commanding figure, even dressed as she was in tiny denim cut-offs and a tee shirt – the two Uzis dangling at her side emphasized her authority.

'Allison, remember what we discussed last night?' Bonnie said.

Allison softened her tone. 'Father, please, what's going on?'

The professor showed a look of relief as he spoke. 'Can it wait until Thom returns? He'll be able to corroborate the information'. It was agreed and the mood seemed to relax, the coffee was good and the pot was soon empty. Allison volunteered to make a fresh one as the door buzzed, Thom had returned. With everyone now settled, and with a fresh mug of coffee, Reg began his explanation.

'This facility is far more than a simple black ops base. It houses much of the most controversial equipment from places like Area Fifty One and the equivalent from a number of allied countries, Australia included. Among these artefacts was one very exciting piece of kit—a machine that allowed me to travel back in time.'

'I embarked on a program to bring as many healthy people here as I could and I managed to bring ten couples before the machine failed.'

'Okay, we're here, so that part has a ring of truth, but why us?' Bonnie asked.

'Every one of us who has been brought here has a particular skill set,' Thom answered. 'Me, I'm a seaman. Before, I was an international ocean racer—sail and power. I've sailed every ocean, sea, and most of the lakes in the world so I know navigation. Not the electronic version, but the old-fashioned by-hand methods.' He paused, taking a long draw from his coffee cup. 'Candy was a computer programmer and systems analyst, one of the best.'

Reg interjected. 'She's the one who gave us access to all the satellites floating overhead. She also decrypted the control and weapon systems on all the ships we have. Her loss was monumental.' Reg's tone showed Clyde he had genuine remorse for what happened.

'And me, what skills do I bring?' asked Bonnie.

'You, my dear, are a trauma specialist... or were,' answered Reg 'You worked in one of the busiest hospitals in Melbourne during the start of the terrorist attacks. Plus, you were a reservist. That's where you got your weapons training.'

Clyde sat quietly, trying to be invisible. 'I'm almost afraid to ask about me.'

Thom replied. 'You are an enigma; Special Forces, trained in all the nasty arts needed for the job, and qualified to fly every plane we have here. You also hold a Master's Certificate in international navigation, are an expert in hand-to-hand combat, and know almost any weapon ever used, guns, knives ... hell, you were even an Olympic archer in your youth.'

Reg leaned forward. 'From what we have been able to find on your history, you even staged out of this facility for a number of operations. As for your competence, I'll tell you a story.

'When Australia's civil war was raging, Victoria suffered badly. It had always been a very left wing socialist state and with the massive influx of refugees, had descended into a total fear zone, with terrorist killings and bombings happening on most days. The government tried desperately to hide the problem, but it's awfully hard when one of the major cities in a country is constantly burning. The story goes that it was all planned by one man. No one ever saw him; no one really knew who he was.

'You, my friend, managed to infiltrate his base and get yourself captured. Your adversary saw your capture as a fantastic chance to gloat, to use your execution as propaganda. He wanted to show the infidels just how weak they were. He set up a broadcast and you were brought in, bound, and blindfolded. They sat you in a chair and started their usual religious diatribe. When he finished, the leader brought you a piece of paper and a pencil—he had a confession you were to sign—but with your restraints, you couldn't comply. Your right hand was freed and the pencil handed to you.'

Thom chimed in. 'Cool as a cucumber, you took the pencil, rammed it into his left eye, drove it fully into his brain, spun him around, and grabbed his AK. You then killed the other five in the room before, and I'll never forget this—best bit of TV I'd seen for years—you dragged the terrorist leader to the camera, ripped off his face covering, and spoke. I even remember the words.

*'Think on this, arseholes! I've just killed this scumbag, in his base, in a room filled with armed terrorists. Now, listen up. If I can do this, how safe are the rest of you? Time to decide – either you all leave my country or I'll come for you and I'll kill every last one of you and your extended families.'*

'Fucking awesome; but there was an outcry, the usual cry of "victim"; you were charged and cashiered, but strangely enough, twenty-four other terrorist leaders and extreme clerics met similar fates in the two months after you were cashiered. Not long after, the attacks stopped and there was a mass migration out of Australia.'

'Okay, so I've been a badass. Why bring me here? Sounds like I'm dangerous,' Clyde asked.

Reg placed his empty coffee mug on the table and smiled. 'We need you to retrieve something for us. Something that potentially could, and I emphasize *potentially could,* save the human race.'

'Right... and here I was, thinking that I was some sort of stud in a breeding program?' Clyde replied.

Reg hesitated, carefully considering his answer. 'Well, the breeding thing was a total failure, but you had skills we needed, and still do. As for the job, it is possibly dangerous, but definitely difficult. Before we go any further, I think we should talk to the Garibaldis. They're the ones who need to convince you.'

Bonnie stopped the conversation. 'Reg, this is all well and good, but let me recap. Somehow you went back in time, kidnapped us, deleted our memories, and brought us here. What I don't understand is why we still have some of our skills – and what about the incongruity of young bodies and old heads?'

Reg considered his response for a few moments. 'As I said before, we have a huge amount of very advanced technology, most not of Earth. One unit is a very advanced bed; I suppose you would call them. They allow us to treat many things without resorting to invasive options. These we found could help rejuvenate bodies, so we used them as part of your treatment, hence your physical changes. As for your faces, we decided to leave them, to give you some reference for any memories that may return, and as for the memory thing, that was a side effect of the time travel, or so the experts tell me.'

Thom went on to confirm Reg's explanation as well as reiterating his and Candice's memory issue when they were brought forward.

'Hang on,' Clyde said, 'these beds… I remember some vague reference to 'Med Beds' from before; why couldn't you use them to reverse the fertility problem?'

Reg shook his head. 'Probably best if I let the Garibaldis explain the detail, but the issue is in DNA. The virus has modified our DNA so much that it is now impossible to reverse it, at least without fully understanding the technology.'

# FOURTEEN

Zena Garibaldi stepped away from the computer screen.

Her eyes were tired, dry, and itchy; she'd been either studying images on the screen or through a microscope for hours. She knew what she was doing was hopeless; they just didn't have the correct base to start from. But she was determined to keep trying, however hopeless it might seem.

As soon as she and Anton had arrived, they had left the others and had been brought to the research centre. What they discovered proved that Reg hadn't been joking or embellishing when he first discussed them leaving their home and coming to the islands. They had marvelled at the vast array of equipment available and all were in pristine condition. Reg had explained that the facility had been left on automatic operation, meaning the power source was kept on and the normal filtering and air purification was running. Even though the site had been uninhabited for a few years prior to Reg and his crew arriving, it was still in what Reg called, 'self-care and maintenance' mode.

The first day, they spent cataloguing what was at their command then, while Anton began to design the research methodology they would need, Zena had started to see what they had to work with.

'It's hopeless... it's just not here!' she screamed to no one in particular. She hadn't slept since arriving and she knew she desperately needed to sleep. She saved her work, shut the system down and left the room, heading for their apartment and bed.

Anton met her in the corridor, the bags under his eyes telling a similar story. 'Time to rest,' he said his voice croaking with exhaustion.

Hand in hand, they trudged back to the elevator. The door opened onto the main foyer of the accommodation area. Heads down with exhaustion Zena didn't see the group of people on the opposite side. Her only goal was to reach their apartment and sleep for several hours.

*** 

Reg stopped. 'I think we should let them rest. I don't think either of them could put two words together coherently at the moment. Thom, maybe this would be a good time to show more of what we have? I've got some other matters to attend to now.'

Thom agreed and led the way to one set of elevators. 'Okay, training and evaluation; who's up for it?' Thom asked.

The elevator dropped fast and when it stopped, the door opened and they exited into a large concrete area. It was open and looked like a parade ground, but would prove to be much more.

'First,' Thom said, 'wardrobe; you all need kitting out.' He turned and strode towards the far wall, through a door, and into a smaller change room.

'Right,' Thom grunted as he opened a large cupboard to his right. 'Ladies here you'll find a stock of women's fatigues; select what you need and then change. There are lockers you can use to leave your clothes.'

'Why do we need this crap?' Allison asked.

'Because you're not going on my range dressed like that. I'd hate to see that cute arse of yours scraped over that nasty concrete out there. Now get dressed!' Thom retorted.

'Bossy bastard,' Allison huffed under her breath.

'Clyde, there will be some fatigues for you over here. Thom indicated the row of lockers for Clyde. Quickly Clyde chose his own gear and dressed before re-joining the group.

The training was carried in a classroom and on the wall were many weapons. Thom selected each one and then gave detailed instructions on stripping, cleaning, and assembling it. He also gave an evaluation of their use and effectiveness, including any of the idiosyncratic problems that almost all weapons have. Clyde, as expected, instinctively knew each weapon. Bonnie was almost as good and, with both having had military service in their past, this was no surprise.

Allison, on the other hand, had none of the almost instinctive knowledge the other two had, but she was a fast study and within an hour, was almost as good as them. He noticed her penchant for the small, but deadly, Mini Uzi and her disdain for the larger M4, but it was her ability with the Fostech that surprised Thom. It seemed she had already chosen her kit.

Something in the back of Thom's mind caused the hairs on the back of his neck to rise—these three appeared to be a tight, complementary unit already.

'Good! It seems that you all know how to strip these things, but let's see if you can shoot them,' Thom teased as he led them out the door and down another corridor. The range they entered was for static firing. Each shooter had an enclosed range with a movable target, making it possible to test accuracy at various ranges up to two hundred meters.

As the three began firing, Allison continued to impress; her ability and accuracy were uncanny.

After two hours, Thom called a halt. 'Clear and lock your weapons and stand back from the range.' When the three were standing two paces from the range, Thom stepped forward and checked each weapon. Satisfied all was correct, he addressed them. 'Good, very good,' he looked directly at Allison. 'You're a surprise. You're almost as good as these two and believe me; they have both had a lot of training, even if they can't recall it. Now, as it's nearly two. I think a little lunch is in order. Follow me.'

While they had been testing the various weapons, Thom had called for some lunch to be delivered. It was a simple affair of sandwiches and a fruit platter, but it was gratefully received by the hungry crew. Coffee followed and Thom began to discuss the next phase. 'Next is some fun, with a serious side. You will be put into a simulated combat scenario. You will have ten seconds to evaluate and select the weapon or weapons you wish to use. You will then proceed onto the range. The object is to make it to the other end but on the way, you will encounter a number of obstacles and challenges.'

His smile turned to a leer as he spoke. 'There will be some bad guys. You need to take them out – and some good guys – please don't kill them. Time is also important as there is something that must be retrieved in the time allotted. Miss the time and you fail. Kill the wrong person and you fail. Now a word of advice: nobody, and I mean nobody, has completed this course the first time, and some of the people here have had military service. The standard is around five attempts. So, remember you need to make it through and kill all the bad guys. Ready?'

Allison was the first on her feet. Bonnie and Clyde finished their coffee and fell into line behind her. They entered a small control room. Windows covered the wall opposite the door, but only blackness was visible through them.

Thom went to a console, activated it, and entered a series of commands. A large screen on the wall to their right burst into life. 'This is your mission briefing, so pay attention. The building here,' Thom tapped the console and a building illuminated, 'is your target. You must reach it and you have ten minutes to do so. Between you,' again he tapped the keyboard and another building illuminated, this time at the opposite end of a narrow street from the first building, 'are ten bad guys. Now, we know some of them are holding hostages; they are all well-armed and have orders to stop anyone from getting to the target. Remember, you will have ten minutes to achieve your objective, concentrate on the console, examine the scenario, and make your plan.' Your time starts now!

Clyde was ready three minutes later; Bonnie took seven, while Allison needed every second; at exactly ten minutes the screens shut down.

'Please follow me.' Thom led them out of the control room and down a flight of stairs. They each stood in front of a bank of doors. 'Behind that door you are facing is your range. When it opens, move forward to the yellow line. When I signal, the weapons safe will open and you have twenty seconds to select the weapons and ammunition you want. After twenty seconds the safe will close. There is no second dip. Are you ready?'

Allison's throat was dry, but she managed to croak ready. Bonnie and Clyde responded the same way. Thom left and they stood silently facing the door. Each door swung open and the three moved to their respective yellow lines. As the door closed behind, the gun safe opened and they all made their selection quickly.

Clyde took his favoured M4, a Desert Eagle; two spare mags for the M4, and four for the Eagle. He only had time to grab two grenades, but he was satisfied he had enough for the task at hand.

Bonnie opted for an MP9, four spare mags, and a Glock G45 with four magazines.

Allison chose her beloved Mini Uzis, clipping them quickly to her harness. She grabbed six magazines which gave her 360 rounds of ammunition. She donned her glasses and stood on the ready line, nervously looking to either side, knowing this would be the last time she would see either Bonnie or Clyde until each had completed the course.

The door opened to each range and the lights began to glow. Thom's voice boomed from hidden speakers. 'It's early evening and the light is bad – time to play.' His voice had a cruel edge to it as he activated the scene.

Instinctively, Allison ducked to her left and sprinted to an abandoned car. She took a few seconds to allow her eyes to acclimatize and scanned the area. She saw a movement to her right behind a broken window—her first encounter. She ran, crouched, and sprinted to the side of the building. Looking to her left, she saw a figure pointing a rifle her way. She hit the target with a short burst from her left-hand weapon. Simultaneously, she moved under the window sill to the other side of the building and sent a short burst inside. Lady Luck was with her—she managed to score a kill shot and no collateral damage.

She continued down the street, using debris and destroyed cars as cover. Three buildings along, her instincts told her to duck. She did and rolled to the curb just in time to see a figure in the window. But she didn't fire; something told her not to, and she was right. The figure was a child, so she kept moving. Three more times she fired, each time hitting her target. She stopped, taking cover behind another wrecked vehicle, changed magazines in each gun, and surveyed her surroundings before continuing.

So far, she had accounted for eight of the bad guys. There were only two left and there were still three minutes on the clock. The steps leading up to the target were close, with only one building on either side still to clear. She knew that crossfire was inevitable. Carefully, Allison checked the building to her left. A shadow behind a window told her there was a target there, but friend or foe, she didn't know.

The building on her side of the street was her main problem. She was too close to see anything or anyone inside. Time was marching forward—only two and a half minutes to go—she had to make a choice and act.

Then she remembered some of the computer games she had played at uni and this scenario seemed very familiar. She scanned the building ahead, noting a dark doorway just past the last window. Adrenalin again coursed through her body and she was ready for action. A thin smile crossed her lips.

Allison steadied her breathing and focused on her next move. She broke from her cover, emptying the left-hand Uzi into the window to her left. She ducked down and rolled under the window to her right, sliding into the doorway. She stood and ducked into the building.

A door was to her left. She raised the Uzi, kicked the door with all her strength, and leaped through. There was a bad guy in front of her holding a woman and hiding behind her.

Allison fired instinctively, just as she had done in the computer game years previously. She fired three shots in rapid succession. The first hit the hostage's arm but penetrated through and into the bad guy. The other two had a similar trajectory but as the target dummies were programmed to react as would be expected, the bad guy lost his grip and the victim dummy slipped to the floor just as two rounds hit the target in the head.

Instantly, the room was bathed in a red light, signalling a failure. Allison swore. 'Fuck off. I cleared the bad guys and I still have sixty seconds to get to the target.'

Thom's voice echoed through the room. 'Yeah, but you shot a hostage – automatic fail.'

Allison wasn't about to let it slide. 'Maybe if you check the dummy, you'll see it's just a flesh wound in the arm. She'd survive in the real world. The test was to not kill a hostage, just bad guys. Check your data. You'll see I've done that.' Allison spun on her heels and sprinted out of the building and up the stairs to the target. She made it with seconds to spare.

***

Bonnie made similar progress to Allison and also got caught at the final building. Being on the opposite side of the street, she fired two rounds at the hostage situation first but caught the hostage in the leg. The dummy's reaction was as designed and her second shot took the bad guy between the eyes. Another fail and another argument for the de-brief session.

***

Clyde made it through without shooting any hostages. His sixth sense had warned him that one of the two final buildings would be the usual no-win scenario, so he got creative. He entered the second-last building to his left and made his way to the second floor. From there, he had a better view of the hostage situation and made good use of the accuracy of the M4.

One shot and the bad guy dummy's head exploded. Following that shot, he raced down the stairs, kicked the interconnecting door to the next building down, and dispatched the single bad guy in there. He made the target with a full minute to spare.

***

Thom called time and instructed the participants to follow the illuminated path to the de-briefing room. He knew he was in for a discussion or more probably an argument. When they were disarmed and sitting, he began, 'Well, one pass and two fail!'

He was immediately cut off by Allison. 'Utter bullshit. My hostage would have a superficial wound to her upper arm. The bad guy was dead so, according to your parameters, I passed. I didn't kill any hostage!' she fired at Thom before he could speak again.

'And mine has a minor wound to her left leg,' said Bonnie. 'The bad guy is dead and, from a medical perspective, the hostage would survive without any permanent damage.'

Both women glared at him.

Clyde added to the conversation. 'I'm afraid they're right, Thom. That part of the test is supposed to be a no-win scenario, but we have just shown that none of us will accept that, so I reckon they should pass.'

'Thom, do you know where that scenario came from?' Allison asked.

'No, it's part of the training system left by previous owners,' he answered cautiously.

Allison smiled. 'Well, I do. During my time at university, I played a game called *Insurgent*. Actually, I was the campus champ for those three years. That scenario is part of the game, the exact same situation, and that's one of the acceptable solutions, so we win.'

Thom knew they were right. His own words in the initial briefing had been the key—*no hostage is to be killed*. Also, he was aware of the solution. It was in the instructor's notes, but this was the first time anyone had got it in their first attempt. Some of his better students had failed a number of times before deciding that wounding the hostage was acceptable.

'Okay, I accept that, and you're right, Allison, but nobody has ever got it this fast. but now you've done the individual thing, let's see how you work as a team. Bonnie, you're team leader for the first exercise. It will be different, so keep your wits about you and follow the leader.'

Thom went back to the console, brought up the scenario, and started the briefing. This time they would be in a large building, trying to rescue a hostage, with twenty bad guys to contend with. For this exercise, they were given comm units. Each kept the weapons they had chosen but were allowed to collect more ammunition.

When they were equipped, they stood on the ready line. This exercise was far more taxing—the building was multi-story and had seen much damage; with a time limit of twenty minutes they had to hustle.

Halfway in, Thom called a halt and told Allison to take the lead. This was unexpected, but the team obeyed, more bad guys showed up and progress stalled. Time raced by, but they were now on the top floor, the only place left for the hostage to be found.

Clyde retrieved a small telescopic mirror from his vest, extended it, and slowly scanned the area before them. They had taken refuge near an old elevator shaft; the car had long ago fallen to the ground. 'Bingo,' he hissed, 'found our hostage.' He kept scanning, trying to locate the six bad guys he knew were still unaccounted for.

Finally, he retracted the mirror and put it into his vest again. 'Here's the situation.' He began drawing in the dust. 'The hostage and three guards are here.' He placed the letter 'H' for the hostage and 'G' for the guards. 'There are two more in the rafters equipped with rifles so I think they're snipers. That leaves one I can't find.' He turned to Allison—she was the leader and this was her decision.

Allison looked at the rough map Clyde had drawn and then looked up to the top of the elevator shaft. The ceiling material was gone from the building but there was an access walkway running around the shaft, just below the roofline. She stuck her head through the open elevator door and quickly saw what she needed.

'Clyde, can you climb up the service ladder to that landing?' she asked.

Clyde quickly looked inside and nodded. 'About three minutes,' he replied to the question she hadn't asked.

'Good. Bonnie, you skirt back around the stairwell and come at the hostage and guards from there. I'll break cover and try to take the snipers out and draw their fire. Clyde, you find that last bastard and finish him – all clear?' Both Bonnie and Clyde nodded and started to move away.

Allison took her position, reloaded both Uzis, and waited.

'*Clyde in position,*' Clyde's voice rang in her ears. Bonnie replied in the same way. Allison waited; hers was the hardest part—break cover, try and kill the snipers, and not get killed herself.

She took a deep breath and raced forward toward some debris she had selected as next cover. The staccato bark from her Uzis breaking the silence, she hit one of the snipers immediately, but she missed the second. A suppressed pop from Clyde's M4 finished that one as well. Bonnie broke her cover and dropped two of the three guards, exposing the sixth man in the process.

Clyde dropped the last guard, but the sixth bad guy was in a good position to kill Bonnie, but Allison wasn't having any of that. She leaped from behind her cover and propelled herself headlong at the bad guy, slamming into the dummy with a sickening thud. The dummy fell forward and she fired a short burst into it for good measure. Bonnie and Allison moved to release the hostage—mission complete.

'Well done, and time to spare.' Thom's voice echoed from the hidden speakers. 'That's all for today. Head back to the briefing room.'

This de-brief was quick; all three were exhilarated by their success.

'Enough of the self-congratulations; hit the showers and change. Get some rest because tomorrow is a quantum leap in difficulty and the bad guys can shoot back.' Thom called the session to an end and the three left for the showers.

Allison was sore; the dummy had been more solid than she thought.

'I think I'll defer to a spa if that's OK?' she suggested. Both Bonnie and Clyde had similar ideas. They had a quick shower, just to wash off the dirt and sweat, changed, and followed Thom back to the accommodation block.

# FIFTEEN

Bonnie started the spa, selecting a temperature to soothe sore muscles. She added a couple of essential oils that were also supposed to help and removed her clothes.

The door opened and Allison walked in, naked. 'Clyde's being a prude; he says we can have this to ourselves.' She pouted as she spoke, her disappointment obvious.

'Not bloody likely,' Bonnie said as she left the room. She found him sitting in the lounge area and quickly convinced him that returning to the spa with her was his only choice.

They entered the spa and all lay back, letting the turbulent water sooth their aches away. They had been in the spa for ten minutes when Bonnie noticed the huge purple bruise forming on Allison's right shoulder. She slipped across to the young woman and inspected the damage, gently touching the area.

The response from Allison was immediate. She let out a groan of pain and moved away. Bonnie reached for the spa control, turned it off, and called to Clyde.

'Wake up, Allison's hurt.'

Clyde responded and soon saw why Bonnie was concerned. 'Shit, Ali. You must be in agony. I think we need to get that x-rayed.'

'What? I was just getting up the courage to jump you. Not fair.' She protested weakly, the pain etched on her face. Quickly, they dried her as gently as possible, dressed, and called for a med team. The x-ray showed a fracture in her collarbone and extensive bruising to the shoulder area.

'That dummy was tougher than I thought,' Allison said as her father entered the room.

His concern seemed genuine as he spoke to his daughter. 'What happened?'

'Training accident; Allison crash-tackled one of the dummies – turns out, they're tougher than she expected. I'll say one thing for your daughter, she's got balls. I'd hate to get on the wrong side of her.'

Bonnie returned as they were talking. She'd been with the trauma team discussing Allison's treatment. 'She'll be fine; it's not that bad a break, but she'll be out of action for six weeks or more.' Bonnie smiled as she moved to Allison's side. 'You just rest and get better. Tomorrow, they'll start some treatment that may speed up things, but you'll be laid up for a few weeks.'

Allison smiled weakly, the drugs taking their toll as she slowly began to drift off to sleep.

Clyde explained what had happened. 'I've never seen instincts like hers. She summed the situation up and acted. Usually, that takes years of training, but Ali did it instinctively.' Clyde chuckled. 'She just didn't realize the dummy was a machine and a very solid one. She dropped it, no hesitation! In real life, she would have saved us.'

They talked for a few minutes more before deciding to call it a night. It was just after ten and another long day was planned for tomorrow. Reg told them he had arranged an early meeting with the Garibaldis, and left Bonnie and Clyde to return to their apartment.

✳✳✳

Bonnie walked into the main living area just after 07:00 the next morning as Clyde slid a perfect ham and cheese omelette out of the pan onto her plate.

'Morning, sleepyhead; breakfast is ready.' Clyde took the plates to the table and returned for the coffee pot.

Bonnie began eating, savouring every morsel. The combination of two cheeses, deeply smoked ham and the herby chives was just what her taste buds needed. 'You know Ali was going to jump your bones last night.'

'And you're okay with that?' Clyde asked.

'Well yes, and after this delicious breakfast, no – I mean, you're free to screw whoever you want, so am I, but I really, really love your cooking, so I might just have to convince you that I'm the better proposition,' Bonnie replied.

'But what about I have both? That'd work,' Clyde suggested almost salaciously.

'If you think you're man enough – have a go, stud,' Bonnie challenged, but the conversation didn't get any further, the door buzzed and Reg entered. It was time to meet with Anton and Zena.

✳✳✳

Gaining access to the lab wasn't easy. First, they had to strip and shower with a foul-smelling soap, next they stood in a cylindrical enclosure while they were bathed in various coloured lights. The glasses they had to wear were the tell-tale—this was an ultraviolet decontamination unit. Finally, they entered a dressing room, where Reg handed each of them a bundle—clothing, footwear, and a small package.

'Sorry, but we must use these.' He held up a tampon. 'I'm afraid we need to seal every part of the body.' He motioned for them to go behind a couple of screens for a little privacy.

Shortly after, Clyde emerged dressed in the one-piece coverall that he had been given. The coverall did exactly that—from head to toe, they were covered, a thin gossamer veil covering their faces. Reg went to a cupboard and handed them what looked like a space suit and helmet, complete with attachments for a breathing tube.

'These two connections,' Reg pointed to an air fitting on the helmet and another on the rear of each suit, 'will supply purified air for breathing, and to inflate the suit; we must be at a positive pressure so we can guarantee that nothing can enter. And this part is critical — you must be extremely careful, a cut to this suit could be fatal. There are some very nasty things in here; if you snag on anything, get back to this airlock immediately, understand?' His voice was firm, conveying the seriousness of the situation. Both nodded their agreement.

'Now, the process – we enter the first section of the airlock and will be decontaminated again. I suggest you hold your breath; the decontaminant is foul. Next, we pass through to the second chamber, where the suits will be dried and checked. Finally, we enter the last chamber, connect our air supply, and in we go.'

'Great, now you've scared the shit out of us, what's in there?' Clyde asked.

Reg shook his head. 'Sorry, my bad; this is a level-five containment lab – nothing gets in unless we want it to and, more importantly, nothing gets out. We have a number of nasty biological and viral agents we're working on. In truth, any one of them would wipe this facility out in a matter of hours.'

'Then why couldn't we just meet in an office? Do we really need to be here?' Bonnie's voice had an edge of fear to it.

'The Garibaldis are in there, and you need to understand what they're trying to do and what they want you to do. Ready?' Reg donned his helmet and then helped Bonnie and Clyde with theirs, then he opened the first airlock door and they stepped through.

Clyde found walking in the inflated suits rather comical — it felt as if their bodies and limbs were much larger than before — but his mind kept reminding him of the reason for the suits, keeping him focused on avoiding sharp objects.

Reg led the way past rows of gleaming equipment, none of which he recognized.

Bonnie noticed that the technicians were less inflated than they were. 'Reg, how come we're so pumped up we can hardly waddle and the techs aren't?'

'Easy—you're at a higher pressure as a safety precaution. They've all been inoculated against everything that's in here. You haven't, as yet.' Reg's answer was casual and to the point. 'The higher pressure should give you a safety margin to get back to the airlock if you pierce the suit.'

Bonnie accepted his answer but the 'as yet' comment kept repeating in her head.

They followed Reg until they caught up to Anton and Zena, both concentrating on a screen. The image on it looked something like the result of a heavy night followed by a bad kebab. The vomitus image kept swirling, making Bonnie a little queasy.

Anton pushed back from the console. 'Another failure!' he mumbled, and then spoke into a comm unit. 'Destroy all samples in batches Zulu one five and Bravo three four.' He pushed back, turned, and saw Reg. He reached for Zena's shoulder, 'Zena, our guests are here.' As Zena turned, Anton offered his hand to Clyde and shook enthusiastically. Zena repeated the greeting; her voice sounding a little disconnected through the suits.

'Well,' she said to Bonnie, 'what do you think of our facility?'

'To be honest, I have no idea what most of this does, but it is impressive,' Bonnie answered.

Zena laughed. 'Then we'll just have to bring you up to speed.' She led the way and gave a running commentary on what each piece of equipment was for. Bonnie noticed that triple redundancy was behind the design of the lab. Zena also ran them through a sample of what they were trying to achieve. First she took one of the virus samples they had, all locked away in a sealed chamber; then worked the remote arms to carry out her tasks. Clyde thought it looked easy, but soon discovered the skill to handle things properly eluded him; thankfully Zena made sure he only handled empty vials. The tour lasted over an hour, but finally they were back at the airlock.

'So am I right? You have three of everything?' Bonnie asked.

Zena answered. 'Yes, triple redundancy. Only a few agencies could ever afford that. Anyway, let's get out of these suits. We can discuss things much easier out of here.'

The five entered the first chamber and quickly cycled through to end up back in the changing area. Reg and Anton helped Bonnie and Clyde in removing their helmets and placing them in special containers. Next, the suits were removed and similarly disposed of. All five were standing naked, Clyde showing his awkwardness.

'Sorry for the lack of privacy, but it is essential that we check each other for any signs of infection or irritation,' Zena explained as she quickly examined both Bonnie and Clyde, giving them the all-clear.

'Now, unfortunately, you have to go through the decontamination process again.'

Fifteen minutes later they all met again, this time clothed and a little more relaxed. They climbed up two flights of stairs and entered an observation room, where coffee and refreshments were already laid out for them. They sat in silence, sipping the coffee, and watched the action below.

Bonnie was the first to speak. 'I know my memory isn't complete but I'm sure I've only ever heard of level four containment; you said this was level five?'

Reg answered. 'Yes, this was a military or quasi-military research lab. They were working on bioweapons, hence the added layer of containment. And before you ask, this was not the site that bastardized the Garibaldi virus, or so we believe—we're still to find that one.'

'But wouldn't the thieves need a similar site to produce enough virus stock to infect the entire bloody world?' Clyde asked.

Anton stood and moved to the window as if to watch his team at work. 'Not really,' he said. 'Even a level four could, in theory, weaponize the virus, but once it had been weaponized, it could have been grown in any one of over a hundred facilities around the globe;

probably in more than one. Once weaponized, the risk was minimal until it was released.

'There were labs in rogue states, commercial labs that had a habit of fudging documentation if the price was right. Worst of all, some governments would have assisted due to political or ideological beliefs. No, Clyde, once it had been weaponized, it was easy to grow but, how to distribute it... that was the real kicker.'

Anton lowered his head, as if ashamed of what he was about to say. 'In the end, we did the job for them. The same system that delivered the binary virus was used to spread the killer. From what we have uncovered, there was someone very high up who allowed the weaponized virus to replace the benign one. Who, we'll never know, but it doesn't matter—they're probably dead anyhow. Greed, arrogance, or just stupidity would have been the driver, but the end result is the almost hopeless mess we have now.'

Bonnie shook her head. 'You said they used the same delivery method as you did for the first part of the treatment. I'm almost afraid to ask what that was.'

Anton and Reg shared an almost embarrassed glance before Reg answered. 'After the virus and vaccine debacle of 2019 to 2022, there was a huge reluctance by all people to trust government-sponsored vaccines. You probably don't remember, but in Australia, the problems with that particular Vaccine caused massive political upheaval. Politicians and bureaucrats were eventually arrested and tried for treason and crimes against humanity, and Australia wasn't the only country. The vaccine proved to be worse, long-term, than the virus it was supposed to defeat.

But I digress; these actions and consequences meant that a covert delivery system was needed so we turned to one that had been used for... other purposes.'

Reg stopped as Clyde held up his hand. 'Aerial dispersal... chemtrails; you arrogant bloody fools... you had the primary virus designed as an aerosol, then used planes to spread it over the whole planet, didn't you? I remember something about this being one of the huge conspiracy theories from back then.' Faint memories were beginning to resurface as this conversation progressed.

Clyde's was angry, and he showed it; he couldn't believe how stupid this entire situation was. 'And because of your blind faith, one could actually call it arrogant stupidity, you did it anyway,' Clyde turned away; his anger beginning to take over, when he calmed down he made the connections. 'And in the end the terrorists used the same system. I'm right, aren't I? Maybe the world is better off as it is. At least humans can't fuck it up anymore.'

Clyde really didn't want to ask the next question, but he knew he had to. 'So just exactly what are you doing down there?'

Zena drew herself to her full height, held her head high, and answered. 'Trying to fix the mess; there's nothing we can do about the secondary virus; it's already done the damage and has died out. But the binary virus, if we can reverse that, the human race has a chance.'

'But you've hit a snag, right?' Bonnie asked

'Right; we just don't have any of the original base viral stock. Without that, we're just playing with the toys. Don't get me wrong, what we are doing down there is good. We're isolating a number of very nasty bioweapons and destroying them. We're also isolating some of the nastier disease and virus stock so we should be able to make vaccines quickly if needed. But it's all academic if we can't reverse the binary virus.'

Clyde moved to Anton's side. Down below were twenty techs working at various stations. 'All this gear and it could be for nothing.'

Anton nodded. 'Unfortunately, yes. That suit you wore, we have several hundred. Each one of them cost over one hundred and fifty thousand dollars. The window in front of you is very special—it has five layers. Each is filled with an inert gas and connected to the decontamination system. It's also bulletproof; anything short of an RPG will just bounce off. See that piece of equipment just to your right?' Anton pointed. 'That's a relatively cheap unit, cost just over two hundred thou, and we have three.

'The way the lab is set out, in three rows so everything is triplicated, each row would have cost over one hundred million. The lab itself, with its level five rating, would have cost over a billion, and in the end, it may be totally worthless. How's that for irony?'

Bonnie had been watching the faces of Zena, Reg, and Anton during the conversation. The furtive glance she saw caused her hackles to rise. She looked at Clyde, the concern etched on her face.

She put her cup down and moved to his side. 'This has been interesting. It's truly amazing that you have all this equipment here, but what does it have to do with us?'

Almost as one, Reg, Zena, and Anton found something on the floor to fix their gaze on. It seemed there was something they needed to address but were afraid to.

'Look, just tell us. What has all this got to do with us?' Clyde repeated Bonnie's question.

Reg was the first to look up. Hesitantly, he started to speak. 'Everything... but first we need to discuss something.' He looked at Anton and Zena. Both had an almost panicked look on their faces. 'You've been led to believe that returning to your own time is not possible.'

'Reg, stop – no more!' Zena burst out.

'No, Zena. They need to know the truth.' Reg sat and beckoned the others to do the same.

When all had taken a seat, he continued. 'The initial plan was to bring people here that had skills we needed, nobody was brought just to be a breeder; we don't have that luxury. Everyone we recruited had to have two uses: the ability to breed and a skill set we required. Sadly, Candice's death proved how wrong and misguided we were. As you have both guessed, you have military training and in your case, Bonnie medical training as well.'

'Clyde, when I found you, you were a mercenary, but research showed you were Special Forces. I found out later the merc role was an undercover operation. You were part of a black ops group, sometimes based here, but mainly out of Darwin. Bonnie, you were a talented reservist, trained in weapons and unarmed combat, but your normal job was as a trauma surgeon based in Melbourne.'

'We decided we needed both of you and proceeded accordingly. By this time, we knew that gentle recruitment took too long and we were running out of time.'

The look on his face showed he was reliving something painful. 'So we just snatched you, suppressed your memory, and began the rejuvenation process. We did this because the skills you had were important, but the council had ruled that no-one could be brought here if they couldn't procreate, hence the rejuvenation process. While this was going on, we did our research. For example, we found out that one of your best mates, Clyde, had a boat like yours. You spent a fair bit of time on it, so we went back again and commissioned one to our specs and brought it here. The rest you know.

'But we need you much more than you need us. We need your skills, but we will not force you. We **can** take you back to your time, if that's what you really want and you can live the rest of your lives there.' He looked over to the Garibaldis. 'No more lies, no more deception. If they want to leave, they can. But if they choose to stay, it must be their decision.'

Clyde smiled. 'Now what that Malabo woman said makes sense. She was going to try and force us to do what you want. Fuck, I should have shot her when I had the chance.' He looked hard at Reg. 'Eventually, someone will have to.'

He studied the faces of the others; fear, hope, and embarrassment all evident. Then he looked at Bonnie. 'Bonnie?'

Bonnie thought for a moment. 'You want us to retrieve something, something essential.' She gazed at each face in turn. 'You want us to retrieve some viable base binary virus, don't you? That's the only thing you need.'

Clyde smiled; they had come to the same conclusion.

Anton spoke softly. 'Yes, we believe some has survived, but we have already tried to retrieve it. No one came back. We sent a team of technicians to find it. None returned and we don't know what happened.'

Clyde stood and started to pace around the room. 'And you're sure you can reverse the damage if we get the virus?'

Zena held her hand up to silence Anton. 'No, we're not. But without it, there's absolutely no hope. With it, we have a fighting chance.'

She chose her words well, intimating that the decision Bonnie and Clyde had to make was one between certain extinction and possible continued existence. Clyde recognized the tactic, impressed with Zena's attempt. 'So we have to decide. If we do this, you can still send us back if we want?'

Reg answered. 'Yes, but we can't reverse the rejuvenation process. You'll be as you are—old heads on young bodies.'

'Sounds like a dream come true.' Clyde chuckled.

'Hang on a minute,' Bonnie said. 'All this time travel crap. As I understood it, that was impossible. As far as I knew, nobody had even got close to or invested in the research. Hell, even with all the money spent on space travel we were still using geriatric technology, chemical rockets, and shit like that. To travel through time would mean that there was some incredible technological advance made in a very short time. Sorry, but I don't buy it.'

Reg stood and went to her side. 'I never said humans had made any breakthroughs. There's still a lot you need to know before you decide. Come with me.'

Both Anton and Zena began to protest, but he brushed them aside. 'Full disclosure and the truth, nothing less,' he countered forcefully.

Bonnie changed the subject. 'Well, continuing on that theme, what about these magic medical beds you have?'

Anton answered. 'We are really not the best to show you. I'll call down to the hospital and clear you through security. We only have two of these units fully operational. There are another four that we are working on, but at this stage, they can only monitor patients.'

He left the group and made the call, returning a few minutes later. 'Doctor Matthews will see you now. Please understand that these units are still under investigation and we can't use them for everything, Allison's injury being a good example. So head down to the hospital reception and learn what you can.'

* * *

Doctor Matthews was a great source of information. He showed the beds and started his diatribe on their capabilities. The two that were more functional had the capability of being able to monitor the physical condition of a patient and carry out very intricate surgery.

'We had one patient who had a bullet lodged in his spine, very close to the cord,' the Doctor began. 'No one here had the skill to operate and we were faced with him being incapacitated totally for the rest of his life. Then one of the techs who were working on the unit suggested using the capabilities of the bed. As you can imagine, there were some heated discussions. If we failed, he would be paralysed, or worse.'

'In the end, it was left to the patient and his family. They opted to try and the result was an outstanding success. The operation was completely automatic even so; we had a full surgical team on standby just in case.' Matthews was obviously proud of this achievement.

'These look familiar,' Clyde said. He walked around the unit. It was shaped like a normal bed but with a half-circular cover. This cover had a number of strange instruments and screens. 'I've got it!' he said. '*Star Trek*, they had things like this in their sick bays.'

Bonnie had a similar revelation, but Doctor Matthews looked blank.

'It was a sci-fi series that ran for many years on TV. I loved it and I remember these from that show. So, is this alien or Earth technology? Also, I seem to remember there was a story—perhaps another conspiracy theory—that some medical equipment companies were working on this technology.'

Matthews shook his head. 'We really don't know. It could be either, but the main thing is it works.'

The discussion followed this theme for a while until Reg called a halt.

* * *

Allison was frustrated and bored. She'd been in the med centre too long.

She climbed out of bed and began to dress, her injury making it slow and painful. She had just finished with her clothes and was trying to tie her shoes when a nurse came in. She brushed Allison's hands aside and completed tying the laces. 'You really are a piece of work. You'll be bloody sorry if you damage your collarbone again. Now, come with me.'

She led Allison to the nurses' station and gave her a form to sign and some meds for the pain. 'You're free to go, just be careful. You still have a few weeks of healing to get through. The doctors want you back here in a week. Sooner if anything happens.'

Allison smiled. 'Okay, next week or sooner if it gets too bad.' She smiled as she hurried away.

Her first instinct was to call Bonnie but instead found herself activating her father's number.

'Denham here,' Reg answered.

'It's me, Dad. They released me. Are Bonnie and Clyde there?' she asked.

'That's great. Now take it easy, you don't want to do any more damage. Bonnie and Clyde are with me. Tell you what; meet us at the train stop, near the Med Centre on level six, sector eight. There's something I'm going to show them, maybe you should see it too.'

Allison ended the call, found the map app on her phone and followed the directions it gave her. It was a short walk to the correct sector and she reached the stop just as the others arrived.

Allison rushed to greet them, Bonnie gently hugging her. After both she and Clyde had welcomed her, she turned to her father. He cautiously embraced his daughter and they held each other for ages, neither wanting to break apart. It was as if the broken bone was a catalyst for a thaw in their relationship. When they finally separated, Reg leant forward and gently kissed his daughter on the forehead, adding to the impression of reconciliation.

The train arrived and they boarded. Six stops later, they left it and walked toward a nondescript office block. The block was empty except for three guards, which seemed out of place given the empty building they were in.

Reg approached the guards and spoke quietly. He then beckoned the others and they took one of the elevators. He pressed a button on the control panel and it slid aside. He entered a code and looked into an iris scanner that opened in front of him.

The elevator began to fall fast. Reg smiled. 'I take it you are familiar with the rumours about a place called Area 51?' He didn't wait for an answer. 'Well, here is the truth.'

The elevator stopped and the doors opened. 'Area 51 was only one of a number of sites around the world where evidence of alien visitation was held, but the main ones were in Russia, America and Australia.' He turned to Clyde. 'But you never heard about that one did you? Seems the Aussies were much better at keeping secrets than the others. To cut a long and involved story short, most of the alien technology ended up here, and now it's ours.

'Most of what we have here is a mystery; we have no idea what things do or how they work, but we are always researching. The unit that allows us to travel in time is just up here.'

He led the way forward to a door that looked like it could withstand a nuclear blast. Once again, Reg activated the security system and the door opened, lights came on and they entered.

Inside, the room looked like any messy electronic nerd's party room. Computers, cables, monitors, and other bits of hardware were everywhere, but in the centre was a table with a dull grey box on it.

'We had no idea what this ugly box was, but one of our computer geeks figured out how to interface with it; then everything changed. We believe that this unit folds space and time, allowing us to move back and forth. We can't go forward—that is further forward than our inception point—but we can travel back down our timeline to the past.

Reg activated one of the computers as he spoke. The system came alive and the grey box started to hum. Beside it, the air seemed to glow and shimmer.

'When the system is set, an event horizon forms, just like a vertical mirror; you simply step in there and emerge where you have selected. Coming back is via this little gadget our techs have come up with.' Reg held up a small device that looked like a garage door remote. 'You can attach this to a key ring and nobody is the wiser. It's coded to the DNA of the user; only one who has gone through can return.'

'Are you serious?' Clyde asked.

'Well, you're here, aren't you?' Reg's logic was sound, he deactivated the system. 'We don't believe this was designed for time travel, but we think it's part of some sort of intergalactic drive, something that might generate a wormhole. One day we hope to figure it out. The problem is that while it seems to be working, we can't form an event horizon. But, our techs are confident this will be sorted very soon, and when it is, we can send you back.

'Now you see how we brought you here. If you want to know more, the actual physics will have to wait — it's way beyond me. We do have a few physicists who believe they're close to full understanding, so you can talk to them if you like. But for now, you need to take some time and think about what we have suggested. In the end, it's your decision.'

Reg held the door open for them to leave. They walked back to the train stop in silence, each caught up in their own thoughts. The train arrived, reversed, and headed back to the main compound.

Reg took Clyde aside. 'Genesis is fuelled and back at the dock if you want to take her out.'

Clyde thanked him and left with Bonnie for their apartment. Allison went with her father, giving Bonnie and Clyde space to think.

They arrived at their apartment and Clyde poured two large glasses of scotch. He and Bonnie took the drink out onto the balcony. The sun was setting and the sky was a constantly changing palette of predominantly pinks and purples, morphing and transforming into different shades. The beauty of what they saw added to the weight of their decision.

# Sixteen

Reg entered the detention block, his heart heavy.

The guard opened the door to the interview room and ushered him in. She was waiting, defiant and arrogant. Zuri Malabo glared at him as he entered. 'Come to gloat, have you?' she hissed.

'No, Zuri, just to talk. Tomorrow, you'll be formally charged. The legal team is still working on the charges, but they'll be multiple. I just want to know what you thought you would achieve,' Reg asked.

'What you'll fail to do—force him to get what we want. I did it for the good of everyone,' she replied defiantly.

'Bullshit! You did it just to grandstand and because of you, he may refuse to help.'

'My way was better; he'd have no choice but to comply.' Her voice was hard and emotionless.

Reg shook his head. 'Your problem is you don't know who Clyde is, what he is capable of. All your way, as you say, would have achieved is the destruction of the virus and possibly this sanctuary. He would never capitulate to threats. All his life he has fought against exactly what you planned.'

'But he doesn't remember all that. He's like putty. I could mould him into what I wanted, but now you've stuffed that up. You and that murderer of a daughter you have.' Malabo's rage came to the fore as she spat the words at Reg.

'You actually believe that, don't you?' Reg shook his head in disbelief. 'And you're wrong. Clyde's actions are almost instinctive; years of training and operations have forged him into who he is. We may have suppressed his memory, but we can't change what he is. If you had tried to secure Bonnie, he would have killed each of you, and don't carry on about your guys being armed. They're just thugs, not a trained killer like he is. If I was a betting man, I'd have put money on Clyde and ordered an extra coffin for you.'

Reg stood and went to the door. 'It's sad; you could have contributed so much, now... well, I think the outcome will be very different.' He left Malabo sitting alone in the room.

*＊*

Bonnie woke slowly and lay listening to the regular breathing beside her. She thought back to the previous evening; she had sat on the balcony with Clyde, watching the sunset.

The scene had been amazing. As darkness slowly defeated the light of day, the sky transformed into an amazing colour show; she and Clyde sat, spellbound, absorbing the scene. Neither had spoken, both electing to keep their own counsel. Then, as the final battle for the sky eventually dissipated, he reached out, taken her hand, and led her to the bedroom.

What happened next could in no way be termed making love. Their passion was primordial, almost violent, as if they were trying to fuck away the situation and the decision they must make.

Bonnie remembered orgasming three times, with Clyde showing amazing stamina and control to get her there. Then his needs took control – Clyde's climax was noisy and brutal; she slid her hands down her hips. *Yeah, that'll leave a bruise.* Bonnie smiled to herself.

She looked across at the now waking form. As he rolled over, his chest bore testament to her own actions.

'Morring stud,' she teased.

'Morring,' Clyde smiled in return.

Bonnie gave him a wicked, challenging smile. 'Now, lover, after last night, are you still interested in that threesome we discussed?'

Clyde feigned indecision before answering. 'I think I'll reserve my decision on the grounds that right now, I'm in no fit state of mind to decide.'

His answer earned him a gentle punch and a command. 'Okay, smart arse, get up and make breakfast.' Bonnie used her feet to push him out of bed before grabbing the sheet and covering herself in a display of mock modesty.

Clyde obeyed and went to the bathroom returning a little while later freshly showered and dressed in shorts and tee shirt. As he passed the bed he called. 'Come on, get up. If you're late, your breakfast will go in the bin.'

Twenty minutes later Bonnie entered the dining area, just as Clyde was serving one of his special breakfasts onto her plate. This one he called his Man Fest—steak, smoky bacon, two hash browns and scrambled eggs all surrounding a pile of baked beans. He stopped for a second. 'Ever wonder just where all this food comes from? Thom told me they had things called stasis lockers, something like fridges but different, but it seems to be a never ending supply.'

'Yes, I have been thinking similar things; maybe we should have that discussion later?' Bonnie sat and looked at the meal before her. 'Do you want me to get fat?'

Clyde kissed the top of her head and gently slid his hands over her shoulders, moving slowly towards her breasts. Bonnie's response was immediate. 'It's a foolish man who tries to grab a lady's tits when she's holding a knife.' As Clyde removed his hands, Bonnie continued. 'Besides, the way they feel, I'm sure you gave them a workout last night.' Her smile was cheeky and challenging.

'Speaking of last night, it seems I had an encounter with some native beast; I've been scratched all over. I think I need to go to the med centre maybe for a shot or something.'

Bonnie's put her knife and fork down. 'No, but I think we should both stop avoiding the elephant in the room.'

Clyde sat ignoring his meal. Bonnie was right—they hadn't said a word last night, just watched the sunset, had a couple of Scotches, and gone to bed.

He pushed his chair back and swung on the back legs. 'All right, let's talk. What's your take?'

She stared at him before speaking. 'In reality, we have no decision. It's a rock and a hard place situation. If we refuse, we condemn these people to a slow death. If we accept, we could be killed, fail and condemn these people to a slow death. Either way, we're screwed.

'But if we accept, there's no guarantee the Garibaldis can reverse-engineer their virus, so it could all be a waste of bloody time,' Bonnie replied.

'Agreed, but can we live with ourselves if we refuse to try, and there's a possibility that Anton and Zena can succeed? Plus, we can go back at any time if we choose.'

The last words stunned Bonnie. She turned, tears in her eyes. 'Is that what you want? To go back?' she asked, her voice quivering with emotion.

'I don't know. This is a great place, we could have a good life here, but what if we have people back then? Maybe you were married, had kids. Wouldn't you want to get back to them?' Clyde asked.

'There's no one, for me at least, but you, do you remember someone?'

Clyde stood and moved to her side. 'No, I think there may have been someone at some time, but not anymore. I know that.' He reached out and drew Bonnie into his arms. 'Now there's just you and me.'

They clung to each other, the decision made silently between them.

Clyde gently pulled away. 'Do you think you could look at these wounds? The animal that attacked me was vicious.'

Bonnie gave him a gentle punch to the ribs. 'Fuckin pussy!'

'That's what caused this attack,' Clyde added with a devilish smile.

Any further banter was cut short by the buzzing from the door. Clyde answered it and let Allison and Reg enter. Allison rushed to Bonnie and hugged her as best she could with her injury. 'Have you made a decision? I hope you're staying.'

'Leave them alone Allison. They'll make their decision in good time.' Reg turned to Clyde and handed him a thin folder. 'This is our constitution and laws. In light of recent events, I thought you should understand what we're trying to do and how we see the future.'

Clyde opened the folder as Bonnie returned to his side. Inside were four sheets of A4 paper, printed on both sides. Clyde handed it to Bonnie. 'You read first. I'll make coffee, then we can talk.'

Clyde returned to the kitchen while Bonnie led the others to the balcony. When he returned with the largest coffee pot, filled with a steaming brew, Bonnie had finished reading and handed the folder to him to read.

The document was simple and written in plain language that even the dumbest person could understand. It was based around individual liberty and individual rights and responsibilities, unlike the old western world where everyone demanded rights, but no one wanted the attendant responsibilities. One clause was clearly taken from the old USA constitution, giving all citizens the right to bear arms and to protect themselves and their property.

The laws were similarly simple—you can do this, you can't do that—and there was zero leeway in interpretation and punishment. If a crime was proven, then the punishment was set out clearly; no discretion as to the punishment imposed. This was complemented by the fact that there were no lawyers or judges. A person accused of a crime had the right to a defense but only by themselves; no other representation was needed, as the laws, rules, and regulations were simple and clearly defined.

'We also have eliminated any judicial corruption or jury rigging. The investigation panel and jury are different, but each is made up of nine randomly selected people. We settled on an odd number to eliminate a hung jury. A simple majority is sufficient to convict or exonerate,' Reg said.

Clyde sat back. 'That's great I seem to remember one of the worst things we had back in the day was the legal system. It was overtly corrupt and essentially useless. Judges were given too much leeway and that caused loads of problems. They used political correctness to justify protecting entire communities of criminals, and worse.

'I like this. It would have solved a heap of problems if we'd had it back then.' He glanced across at Allison, expectation and fear etched in her features, then down at Bonnie, who nodded almost imperceptibly. 'We really didn't have a decision to make. Of course we'll help you, but as for staying, we still have some things to work out.'

'Then I'll tell Thom,' Reg said.

'Hang on, what about me? I need the training more than they do,' Allison said.

Bonnie had a solution. 'The Garibaldis said they needed at least a couple of weeks to inoculate us and train us in the correct protocols for the lab. If Ali is to come with us, she needs that as much as we do. The lab training shouldn't cause any problems with her healing, plus, if the speed with which she recovered after being shot and nearly bleeding out is any indication, three or four weeks may be all she needs.'

'And she still has one hand. She can still exercise and train with her left hand. Could be good for her,' said Clyde.

Reg said nothing; he was not about to put any strain on his renewed relationship with Allison, knowing full well he had no say in the matter anyway.

✳✳✳

The lab training was mainly in a meeting room initially. It consisted of lectures, visual training, and tests. According to the Garibaldis, the base virus they sought was the most innocent and least dangerous substance they were going to encounter. All the discussion did was raise doubts about, not only the possibility of success but also about the wisdom of trying.

'To counter possible infections, you will all need to be wearing a portable, self-contained biohazard suit,' said Zena. 'But even that may not be enough. So tomorrow, we will be starting a series of inoculations to give you an added layer of protection. Unfortunately, we can't vaccinate you for every possible disease you will almost certainly encounter, but we will give you the best we can.'

The session concluded at 14:30 and Thom pulled Clyde aside. 'Time for another reef run – meet me at the dock at four.' He turned and left before Clyde could respond.

*Four? That's a bit late*, Clyde thought as he watched Thom walk away. He did some mental calculations and realized the return run would be in the dark.

He accessed one of the consoles in the room and checked the tide charts. His fears were confirmed; they would be returning during the worst tidal change. 'This should be fun,' Clyde said out loud.

'What should be fun?' Bonnie asked.

'Nothing, just another reef run session,' he replied, keeping his thoughts to himself.

They returned to the apartment and Clyde began working on the reef run, checking the tides and looking for what he could expect.

Finally, he managed to superimpose the various bits of information onto one screen.

What he saw was challenging, even downright dangerous. The design of the reef, which he now knew wasn't all natural, made for some very turbulent water in the channels. And there would be no moon to guide him, just knowledge and instruments.

At exactly 16:00, Clyde entered his code and scanned his iris. The door to the RIB dock opened and he walked through. Thom was waiting in the boat. They greeted each other and quickly had the boat in the water.

They were making their way through the restricted zone when Clyde broached the subject at hand. 'Coming back in is gonna be interesting.'

Thom smiled. 'Done your homework I see.' His face changed and he was suddenly all business. 'I'll level with you. Of all the boatmen I've trained, you've got it quicker than the rest. Tonight's exercise usually doesn't come for weeks, but you've got here in three sessions. Pass tonight and I'll certify you; fail and it's back to school for you.' Thom's smile seemed cruel and sardonic in the late afternoon sunlight.

Clyde smiled and pushed the throttles to their stops. 'Then you'd better hang on.' The RIB was the larger unit they had and it responded to the urge from the twin three-hundred horsepower water jets in the stern. It literally leaped out of the water, but settled quickly onto the plane and was flying across the smooth water at a little over fifty knots.

They arrived at the entrance to the reef channel. Clyde throttled back and dropped the buckets into the reverse position. The RIB stopped almost instantly and when all motion had ceased, he checked his instruments, trying to gauge the speed of the water starting to flow out to sea through the channel.

'When you're ready,' Thom said, stopwatch in hand.

Clyde nodded, lifted the buckets, and turned toward the channel entrance. 'Ready.' He opened the throttles until he reached the speed he had worked out earlier. The boat responded beautifully, with only a slight change of attitude required to counter the outgoing tide.

At the recommended speed, it would take just over an hour to navigate the reef. Clyde considered running it faster but knew it would achieve nothing. Thom had planned the run and failing light was one of his test parameters. No matter what he did, he would be doing the return run directly into a setting sun and a full outrushing tide.

One hour and twelve minutes later, they reached the open sea. Clyde kept the boat running for a few minutes more before stopping. He had a good view, probably his last, of the spectacle that was the tidal change.

He remembered something from his past, something from Western Australia. Mental images of reefs emerging from the sea, huge tidal shifts, and massive disturbances. He couldn't retrieve more, but at least he had a distant familiarity with what he now faced.

'Just hang around here for ten minutes,' Thom instructed, 'then we'll have some fun.' He checked their safety gear. The suits they wore were made of a Kevlar-based fibre, highly resistant to cuts, tears, and abrasion. They also incorporated a full buoyancy system. If they were thrown from the boat, it automatically inflated, keeping the wearer afloat. Their helmets were designed to take heavy impacts as well as house secure comm gear.

But the best survival tool was the boat. It was completely self-righting and very tough; one reason why they'd both donned the harness the seats were equipped with.

Time passed and Thom finally spoke. 'When you're ready!'

Watching the developments in the channel facing them was cause for alarm, and this was the easy bit. The worst part was halfway through and looking at the mess of angry water in their path, it would be terrifying.

Clyde swallowed hard, gripped the throttles and called, 'Ready.' He pushed the throttles forward and lifted the buckets into the forward position. The boat surged forward. Clyde adjusted the trim, lifting the bow slightly just as they hit the first tidal surge.

They climbed over it, almost as if it wasn't there, and with his confidence returning, Clyde opened the throttles. A little more power was one thing, but momentum was what he needed to counter the force of nature he was battling. Even with six hundred horsepower, the three-ton boat was nothing compared to the energy the sea could release.

The first waypoint came up. Clyde turned the boat easily without losing any forward momentum but was forced sideways by the force of water cascading off the exposed reef to port. The boat slid violently towards the still submerged reef to starboard. Clyde slammed the throttles to the stops, and the jets behind him gulped water and spat out huge volumes, correcting their drift, with only meters to spare.

Back on course, he approached the next and probably most difficult section.

Reefs to both sides cascaded millions of litres of water into the channel every minute as the tide changed. The channel reminded him of the memory from his past and his confidence evaporated.

This channel was a series of quick 'S' turns, four in total. The only safe passage was in the centre, but that was a maelstrom of violent rushing water. In the navigation channel, the water reared up, forming insane, rushing white peaks. But he had no option; it was either win through, 'Or kiss my arse goodbye,' Clyde said out loud.

He only had a couple of seconds to decide, and then he saw a possibility. *Brains or balls*, he thought as he pushed the throttles forward, hard.

*Balls it is.* His decision made, he threw the boat into a violent left turn, and settled it back onto the new course, all the while keeping one eye on the instruments in front of him. They were his guide, but his gut was making the decisions, and he instinctively knew never to second-guess his gut.

Playing the throttles and bucket controls like a master conductor in front of an orchestra, Clyde guided the boat through the first turn, aligned it for the second, and drove forward. He won through and repeated this at the third direction change.

Now the fourth and final leg of the turns loomed. The water ahead was impossible. It boiled and washed in every direction at the same time and Clyde couldn't see a way through. To make it even more challenging, he had to make his final turn only meters past the mess in front of him. If he was too slow, the maelstrom would slam the boat into the rocks. Too fast, and he'd overshoot and suffer the same result. But there was no alternative. He couldn't stay there and he couldn't retreat.

'Fuck it!' Clyde shouted as he pushed the throttles to the stops again. The RIB powered forward, the bow slamming into the first wave front. It leaped skyward, the jets useless without water to feed them. They slammed back into the water, but even then, it took a couple of seconds for the twin turbines in each drive unit to develop enough thrust to push them forward; a couple of seconds that proved critical.

The force of the water pushed them back toward the wave front they'd just conquered, the jets only defeating the force of the tide at the last second. Clyde steered the boat toward the final test, the water again standing much higher than the boat. This time he changed the angle of attack, taking the wave front slightly off the starboard bow.

They hit the wave at full throttle, the boat again flying off the top of the crest. This time it landed quickly, but the tidal flow pushed it towards a jagged rock outcrop to port. The jets started to grip again, but it was not enough. As the power began to flow through the drive, Clyde dropped the port bucket into the reverse position, causing the bow to turn suddenly in that direction.

Instantly, he lifted the bucket back to full forward and dropped the starboard bucket, causing the boat to jump in the opposite direction. It worked—the rock outcrop passed behind them without incident. Later, when they watched the feed from a drone that had been tracking them, it looked like the RIB had danced its way past the danger.

The water was calmer now, still running fast, but with much less violence. Clyde throttled back and negotiated the final sections in an almost casual fashion.

As they entered the main lagoon, Thom unbuckled himself and went back to Clyde. 'I'd say that was a pass. Now you know why we don't run the reef on tide changes.' He chuckled. 'Let's go home. I think a drink is in order.'

## SEVENTEEN

Bonnie heaved again.

Nothing came from it; she had nothing left to throw up. Slowly, she removed her head from the toilet bowl, flushed, and sat back against the wall. Gradually, she dragged herself to the vanity, pulled herself up to her feet, and looked into the mirror; the face reflected wasn't someone she recognised. The eyes were red and sunken, the nose seemed larger and very red and the face had a deathly grey pallor. She rinsed her mouth and washed her face. 'Fuck, I hate you, Zena Garibaldi,' Bonnie grumbled, just as she heard Clyde retching into a bucket in the bedroom.

'Fucking bastards,' she heard Clyde moan as she left the bathroom. As she entered, he rose from the bed, took his bucket, and swapped rooms. Bonnie collapsed onto the bed, sweat pouring from her body.

Clyde returned, cleaned up but still clutching his bucket. 'I'm gonna fucking kill those bloody Garibaldis, I swear.'

Yesterday, they had started on their inoculations with a warning that they might experience some nausea; there was no mention of spending the entire night throwing up violently.

'Shut the fuck up and let me die in peace,' Bonnie moaned.

A painful cry from Allison's room took them both by surprise. Gingerly, Bonnie climbed out of bed and trudged out of the room.

She found Allison huddled on her bathroom floor, clutching her shoulder, her sling nowhere in sight. The look of pain on Ali's face told Bonnie all she needed. She retrieved the sling from the bedroom and reattached it to her patient. Disorientated, it seemed Allison had slipped and fallen; she had landed on her good side so any possible damage to her healing collarbone would be minimal, but she would need constant assistance until this nausea diminished.

Bonnie helped Allison up. Together, they went back to the main bedroom. Allison couldn't stay in hers—she'd made such a mess. Bonnie took her into the bathroom and cleaned her up; her clothes were stained so they had to be removed.

After a quick shower, Allison looked and smelled much better.

'Right, young lady, into bed,' Bonnie ordered. Allison obeyed and lay beside Clyde, Bonnie close behind her.

They slept for hours and when they finally woke, long shadows were creeping across the room.

Allison turned to her side. Clyde wasn't there. Then she heard the shower.

A wicked grin crossed her lips. She started to move to the side of the bed when a warning from Bonnie stopped her.

'Don't even think about it!'

She turned to see Bonnie watching her through half-closed eyes.

'Just my luck – I finally find myself in bed with both of you and we're too sick to have any fun.' She pouted.

'Don't worry, that can wait. It's your shoulder I'm worried about. How do you feel by the way?' Bonnie asked.

'Except for the shoulder, I'm fine,' Allison surprised herself with her answer. 'I guess that injection isn't going to kill us after all.'

Bonnie dragged herself out of bed and stood in front of Allison. 'No, it just feels like that would have been the easier option. Now let me have a look at that shoulder.'

Clyde returned from the bathroom, selected some clothes and began to dress, totally ignoring the two naked women in his bedroom. Normally he would have reacted, or made some ribald comment, but he didn't feel strong enough for either. 'I'm definitely killing those Garibaldis,' he mumbled to himself.

'Clyde, there's a mess in Ali's room. Can you clean it up?' Bonnie asked as he left the bedroom.

She wasn't kidding. Allison hadn't managed to get to the bathroom and the sheets were evidence of that. He quickly gathered them up and went to the laundry area, placed the sheets into the tub, and filled it with water. While he was waiting for the mess to soak off he returned to Allison's room with some cleaning gear and started to clean the bathroom floor.

Thankfully, the mattress had been spared any staining, so the clean-up was easy. When he'd finished, he returned to the laundry, rinsed the sheets and protector off, and placed them in the washer. With that sorted, he went to the kitchen. Coffee was all he could think of, but the thought made his stomach rumble, so he opted to make a large pot of peppermint tea instead.

He checked the clock—17:30— they'd been there for twenty-four hours.

Bonnie came out of the bedroom, Allison following slowly behind; her movements seemed strained. Even though she couldn't be feeling any better than he did, Allison didn't waste the chance to tease. She gave Clyde a suggestive smile and turned to give him a better view. Clyde shook his head and went back to his tea.

Ten minutes later, they both joined him and gratefully accepted the tea.

'I'm going to take Ali to the med centre and have her x-rayed, just to be sure.' Bonnie was back in charge. 'You need to call Zena, let her know we're OK.'

'More likely I should just shoot her,' Clyde grumbled.

'Oh, come on, I bet you've had worse hangovers... big baby,' Bonnie chided as she kissed his forehead. 'Now be a good boy and call her while we're gone.'

The two women finished their tea and left. Clyde sighed and made the call.

✳ ✳ ✳

The next three weeks were hectic. There was training every day consisting of lectures, lab work, and hazmat retrieval, plus one inoculation each week. These had much less effect—mild nausea, headaches, and some muscle and joint discomfort—but they passed quickly.

When Clyde broached the subject with Anton, his reply caused the hackles on Clyde's neck to rise.

'My dear Clyde,' Anton said, 'you're going into a military facility, so we need to give you military-grade immunity.' Anton refused to be drawn further, simply stating that things would become clear later. His dismissive attitude only deepened Clyde's concerns.

On Thursday evening, Bonnie and Allison returned from the med centre with good news. Allison was healing faster than any thought possible and she no longer needed the sling or cuff. The other positive aspect was the advice that she needed to start exercising her arm. Swimming was suggested and they decided that they would do this every afternoon, starting that day.

Both were talking and laughing happily when Bonnie opened the door to the apartment; their mood was suddenly sliced away by what they saw. Out on the balcony were Thom, Reg, and Clyde, and the conversation was anything but cordial.

'I'm sick of the bullshit.' Clyde's voice was angry and loud. 'Either you tell us everything now or you can fucking well send us back – your call Reg!'

The interesting part of the scene was Thom, who was standing shoulder to shoulder with Clyde. 'That goes for me too. It's time to level with us.'

Thom's words seemed to hit Reg like a hammer blow. He slumped back into his chair as the two women walked through the door.

'Clyde, what's going on?' Bonnie asked.

'Reg is about to explain what is going on... the truth this time,' Clyde replied, his voice cold and hard.

When Allison and Bonnie were settled, Reg started. 'We're not trying to deceive you in any way, but you are correct in some of your concerns. The simple fact is we know **what** we need you to retrieve; we just don't know exactly **where** it is.'

'What?' Thom exclaimed. 'We're training our arses off, being stuck like pincushions with who knows what shit and you don't know where we need to go?'

Reg slumped into one of the chairs. 'Thom, please just listen; when the Garibaldis sold their research to the Australian government, it was taken to a special military facility, and that's where we have our dilemma.' He looked at Clyde hoping some memories were starting to surface. 'I think you have some idea of what I mean, Clyde?'

'I remember something about joint venture bioweapons research, nothing specific though,' Clyde answered.

'Yes, US and Australian agencies joined forces to try and counter a growing threat by various dissident and terrorist groups using biological weapons. The problem we face is that there are three possible locations, each with its specific challenges and dangers. That's why you've been given three different inoculations.

'Each site had a different brief and therefore, different hazards.' He turned to Thom. 'That's why the sub went back. They're checking on one of the possible sites. Hopefully, we'll know more when they return. All I ask is please trust me. I'm not trying to con you, but I didn't see the value in discussing this until we had more information.' Reg finished and sat back.

Thom broke the silence. 'This training schedule, let's talk about that. First you asked me to do it, to find out just what skills they could remember; then today you gave me three sets of possible scenarios to work towards. What it told me was there would almost certainly be some sort of urban action.' He held up the schedule.

'But there's also some aquatic training and high temp, dry land work. Care to explain?'

Reg sighed. 'This is what I was trying to avoid, but here are the facts, as far as I know. One possible site is a couple of hundred kilometres south of Darwin, another is in an underground facility in Tasmania only accessible underwater. The third, and most probable, is located in the city of Newcastle; exactly where we don't know, but it's the one I'd put money on.'

'Why?' Clyde asked, his memory slowly recalling the city.

'Simple. It had three things going for it. First, it was the home of Edmund Clements; we think he weaponized the virus. Second, the university had both the technology and necessary staff and finally, it was defended—an army base just up the road and an air force fighter base just out of town.

'Other reasons are that the Northern Territory facility is far too remote, making transport an issue, and the other site had been compromised by Green activists, at one stage. No, I'd bet my balls on Newcastle; nobody knew it existed.'

Clyde thought for a few minutes, trying to recall any detail that might help, but those memories were still blocked. 'All right, let's assume it's Newcastle. What can we expect in resistance?'

Reg looked at Thom. 'Your turn – I gave you all the details I have; you tell them what we know.'

Thom shook his head. 'No, I think we should cover this tomorrow.' He turned to Clyde. 'We have some plans of the town and some of the facilities but I need them to show what we know.'

'So Newcastle is the only location you have plans for?' Clyde asked.

Thom nodded.

'Then I think that settles it – Newcastle is the target.' Clyde said. 'Tomorrow we go through this. I want everything you have, and I mean everything; no more bits left out, agreed?'

Reg agreed and left them.

Clyde turned to Thom. 'I take it you already have an equipment list?'

Thom's smile showed genuine excitement. 'Yeah, and I reckon you'll love going through the stores.'

With the meeting over, they decided to have dinner at one of the bars in the common area. The sun was setting, the sky bearing witness to the day's demise, delivering a magnificent colour show.

Clyde stood gazing at the sky show, lost in thought as he felt a hand slide into his.

'Penny for them?' Bonnie asked.

'Nothing, really,' he answered. 'Just seems a shame. If we fail, there'll be no people left to see sights like this.'

'Well, that settles it. We can't fail,' Bonnie announced with conviction. 'Come on, I'm starving.'

* * *

Thom's presentation was very detailed. He had plans for each facility, layouts of labs, and even security specifications. There was only one thing missing—the location of possible entrances. The University of Newcastle (UON) site had been set up as a training and research facility and was partially incorporated into the University Science Faculty, but the real biotech part had been kept secret.

There was the same problem with the second site. In 2020, the expansion of the John Hunter Hospital (JHH) had commenced and this was where Thom believed the real bioweapons facility had been built. There plans showed extensive subterranean work, listed as mine subsidence rectification. As the site and indeed much of the old city had been extensively mined, this made sense. But again, there was no indication of any entrance, or even of any underground facilities.

'As you see,' Thom said, 'the plans show some detail of what look like rooms, or could be labs, but the actual detail is very poor; plus, there is no indication of any entrances. The subsidence rectification story looks firm.' He sat, clearly frustrated with the situation.

'But,' Reg said, 'we hope our latest foray will deliver some good news.'

'What foray?' Allison asked.

'We have one sub active and it has been down there for the last six months, gathering intelligence. It's due back here this week and they believe they've found the information we need, but we still have to wait for them to return.'

'But what about resistance – any idea of what we'll face?' Clyde asked.

Reg looked at Thom before answering. 'Truly, we don't have much. We believe the local population is a few thousand, all armed and prepared to defend what little they have. We have taken some losses just looking around so it's fair to say that the best plan is to avoid the locals. But they're not the real problem. We don't believe that Clements would release the virus without having some personal protection, an antidote, or something else.' He turned to Thom. 'Put up the revised plans please.'

Thom obeyed and the screen changed. Now it showed the JHH site, but it was different— much larger. Reg continued. 'This is what we believe is one possibility. Clements had a secure bunker built close to the facility, a bunker capable of holding up to one thousand. I know Edmund, and he would never release the virus without a plan to survive and he knows that you need numbers, facilities, and supplies. Believe me; he would have set all that up before he released the virus to his brother-in-law.'

'What do you mean – brother-in-law?' Bonnie asked.

Reg stopped and sat down. 'Edmund Clements's wife was Lilah Mustafa; sister to Ahmed Mustafa, the nut job who we believe was the ultimate terrorist who released the virus. The rumour was that Ahmed kidnapped Lilah and her two children to force Clements to do his dirty work, and is seems it worked.'

'He threatened his own sister and her children?'

'Bonnie, he's a total sociopath. He claimed to be everything and everyone, from the leader of the Muslim world, an ancient Hebrew general, through to the reincarnation of the angel Gabriel. He didn't care, as long as it suited and advanced his plans. Thankfully, we believe he was one of the first to die in the plague,' Reg explained.

'I wouldn't bet on that,' Clyde replied as he studied the bunker plan. 'My gut tells me that there is someone calling the shots, and this Clements isn't that person. He slapped the desk and smiled. 'Look here.' He pointed to one end of the bunker plan and then the other. 'These are access tunnels and they lead off in two directions.'

He brought up one of the original area maps that Thom had used; then he superimposed the bunker plan and matched scales.

'Clever bastard; I'll bet he's built this in an old mine. I believe this is a totally separate facility and that it's connected to both other sites. We're not looking at just one facility. He used both.'

The mood changed; now they had compounded the problem. If Clyde's theory was correct, they had to find both facilities and it was entirely possible that they were still in use. And with a possible thousand defenders to contend with, things just got a little harder.

'Anyhow, it's only a theory. Maybe we'll know more when the sub returns.' Clyde mused. 'Thom, let's have a look at the equipment you think we need.'

The meeting broke up and Thom led them to the armoury. 'I thought we should start here.' He smiled as he operated the security system. It only allowed one person in at a time. Each had to be scanned—iris, biometric, and palm print, coupled with their codes.

Once inside, Thom quickly began his tour. 'Most of the weapons here are from Evans Engineering; they supplied the Australian military from 2024 on. Seems someone finally realized that the military needed a reliable source of supply and buying everything overseas was just a recipe for disaster.'

Well that decision was overdue,' Hurray! Clyde exclaimed. 'The morons that infested politics in my day thought they should stop all manufacturing in the country and outsourced as much of our manufacturing as they could; bloody traitors.'

'Well, it finally bit them in the arse. When the threat of attack became a reality, the army panicked. They had just three days' ammunition stockpiled, and fuel was even worse. Evans jumped into the fray, began making ammunition, and solved that issue. The fuel problem took a bit longer and needed a referendum, but finally new processing plants were built, old ones were re-activated and Australia became self-sufficient once again.

Bonnie interjected. 'I seem to remember that we were dumping fuel powered vehicles and going solely to electric?'

Thom smiled. 'Yeah, well, that sort of vanished when they couldn't be charged. One of the insurgent's first targets was electrical infrastructure, wind farms, solar farms; even poles and wires. It was a total surprise just how little had to be destroyed before the grid totally fell over.'

'While all this was taking place, Evans kept pushing forward. He began designing new weapons, making them far superior to what the military was using. Thom paused as he picked up a pistol, 'This was one of the first ones —the Evans side arm.' He handed the pistol to Clyde and then gave one to Bonnie and Allison. 'Get the feel of it.'

'It's big but feels light,' Allison observed.

'Give the girl a prize. You're right. It's lighter than any other weapon like it; manufactured from a combination of light, extremely durable matrix of metal and composite materials; even now we don't know the formula. The man was a genius.' Thom picked up a selection of magazines and ammunition. 'Mags from ten to sixty rounds, single shot, semi-auto or full auto, this thing does it all. Don't worry; we'll have time to play later.'

He led them to the next aisle where there were assault weapons in locked cabinets. Thom opened the first one and handed each a rifle. 'The Evans assault rifle, in ten millimetre – it has a higher rate of fire than your old M4; it's lighter and more durable than even the old workhorse, the AK. This weapon made Evans the major supplier to the military forces.' Thom waited while his charges had a quick familiarization with the weapon.

'Two mags, thirty and sixty rounds semi-auto or full auto at a flick of the switch, and the ejection system, safety, and fire selector make it ambidextrous. This version has the enhanced sighting system. You can use this baby at any time: night, day, in smoke or fog. Shit, I've even fired it underwater.'

'Sounds like true love.' Clyde chuckled.

Thom reached into a separate cupboard. 'This is my personal weapon, complete with forty mill grenade launcher.'

Clyde smiled. 'Now you're talking. I'll take one.'

'You might want to wait until you see the next one.' He led them further down the aisle, unlocked another storage cupboard, and brought out his final unit. 'The Evans SSMG or Squad Support Machine Gun; it's chambered in twelve mil by seventy-five. It packs a huge punch, believe me. Here, feel it.'

Clyde took the gun, surprised at the lack of weight for a weapon of this size. 'Same construction I take it?'

'Same secret formula, yes,' Thom replied.

Clyde handed the gun to Bonnie.

'Hell, even I could use this, it's so damn light,' she said as she handed it to Allison, who responded with similar comments.

'Okay, now let's head to the range and give them a run-through.' Thom didn't have to wait for an answer; everyone was eager to try the new toys.

The armoury had its own five-lane firing range that could be set anywhere from five to two hundred meters. They entered the range officer's office and Thom entered an ammunition request into the console on the range commander's desk.

'The ammo will be delivered here, and I'll hand it out.' Packages slid gently into a receiving basket. He took them out and handed magazines for the pistols to each person. They each had two fifteen-round mags and one sixty.

'Okay, load these and we'll see what you think of the pistol.' Thom watched as they filled the magazines, satisfied with the ability of each. While the weapon was large, it didn't feel cumbersome. The look on Ali's face told Thom her much-loved Uzis may actually have some competition.

They took their positions and Thom sent targets to the five-meter mark.

'Okay, the bad guy there is your target. A double tap centre of mass please,' he ordered as he checked their readiness.

'All ready, here we go.' Thom had control of the target. At the moment, sideways to the firing line, all the shooter could see was the thin target backing plate. With a tap of a switch, each target snapped to full frontal.

Six shots reverberated through the room, and the targets swung back to their neutral position. He retrieved them and tallied the score; they had done well, considering this was their first time using the weapon.

The process was repeated out to fifty meters, and each time the results were impressive.

'Now, you each have one sixty-round mag. Please load the weapon and make it safe.' They all complied while Thom set up the final exercise. 'This time, we'll start at twenty-five meters and the target will run toward you. Your job is to stop the target and survive. Imagine he has a weapon and is firing at you. Ready?'

The targets snapped and began to move at a running pace. Bonnie and Clyde opened up; Allison waited a couple of seconds then fired. The results were interesting. By waiting, she inflicted the most damage, concentrating her fire in the centre of mass in short bursts. All thirty of her bullets hit their target, a huge hole where the heart should be.

The trials continued with the other weapons, and each time Thom was impressed. 'Good shooting, but we still have a couple of secrets with these weapons.' He typed another ammo order into the computer and packages started to arrive. 'As I said, Evans was a successful engineering company and they started this venture as an ammunition manufacturer, something they took great pride in.' He opened the three packages.

'I'm using the pistol for this. The results will be similar with the bigger units. This is a true anti-personnel bullet.' He handed each person one of the rounds.

'Looks like a standard RIP unit,' Clyde observed.

'Good, you're right, except these will do more damage than the others you've seen, same with these penetrators.' Thom held up another round. This one looked like a drill bit. 'The secret of both is the material and attention to detail. But this one is the daddy.' Again, he handed out bullets to each. These looked like a penetrator except they had a different, dull grey nose.

'Are these explosive?' Clyde asked.

'Well-sighted; each one contains a small charge of a binary explosive. The design allows them to penetrate bulletproof glass, some armour plating, and even Kevlar armour. The explosive is in two parts. They mix only when the round hits the target. It takes less than a millisecond for the reaction to take place; then they explode.

If it's still in the armour plating or Kevlar, the explosive finishes the job. If it's through the protection, well, I don't want to be in the same room with it. Follow me.'

Thom led them to another room.

'We don't fire those in the range for obvious reasons. In here, we have the facilities to demonstrate them.' He took a pistol, loaded one round, and went to the glass panel in front of them. Lights came on behind the panel and they saw a second room. In the centre was a dummy wearing a standard combat vest. Thom placed the pistol onto a cradle, opened a firing port in front of it, took aim, and fired.

The dummy exploded, bits of it flying around the room. Not only did the bullet tear through the body armour, it decimated the entire dummy body. The room now resembled something out of a horror film; there were only a few identifiable body parts to be seen.

'Fuck me,' Clyde whispered.

'It will most definitely do that.' Thom chuckled. 'Now for the interesting bit – the military tested but rejected this bullet, citing some international convention bullshit. But the guys who resided here took a different approach. They obtained every round that Evans could make for each of the weapons. In total, we have over a million rounds for each gun and, more importantly, the tools and equipment to make more, including the only known copy of the explosive formula. We may be facing huge odds in Newcastle, but I think this will level the playing field.'

# EIGHTEEN

Clyde clawed his way through the dark fog of a deep slumber.

The incessant buzzing in his head was calling him. The door; someone was at the door. It was 04:30; the red numerals glared in his face as he checked the time.

A groggy voice beside him spoke. 'Who's here at this time?' Bonnie was also being disturbed.

Clyde rose and stumbled to the front door, checking the monitor. 'Thom, what the fuck?' Clyde grumbled as he operated the lock.

'Sorry, thought you'd like to see this. The sub's returning. She'll be coming through the reef very soon so you better get dressed,' Thom announced excitedly.

Clyde just stood still, not completely comprehending why the sub returning should interrupt his sleep. Then his memory clicked into gear. Thom had told him that he needed to see the sub's entry and Clyde had agreed.

'Right, give me a sec to get dressed.'

He went back to the bedroom, selected some clothes, and dressed as quickly as he could. He was about to leave when the sleep-slurred voice again came from Bonnie.

'What's up? Why are you dressed?'

Clyde chuckled; sometimes Bonnie took ages to regain cognitive functions when she woke. 'I'm just going with Thom to watch the sub come through the reef. Go back to sleep.' Bonnie didn't need any encouragement—she rolled to her left side and instantly dropped back into a deep sleep.

Thirty minutes later, Thom and Clyde were sitting in a RIB in the middle of the seaward lagoon.

'Well, if you wanted to take me for a moonlight boat ride, you've succeeded. What are we doing here?' Clyde asked.

'Remember I told you that the reef is only part natural,' Thom explained, 'and that most of it was built by the previous operators.'

Clyde nodded slowly as he recalled the conversation.

'Well, now you're going to see part of that man-made bit in action.' Thom pointed to a dull blue-white light just off their starboard quarter. 'Watch that spot. Things will get interesting in about five minutes.'

Clyde kept watching the light, using his peripheral vision to keep it locked. Then something seemed to change. 'Either my eyes are playing tricks or that light is moving.'

'Your eyes are okay – this is what I wanted you to see. This part of the reef is artificial; we move it aside to allow larger vessels in. There's a fifty-meter-deep channel down there, enough for us to bring in all the big ships we have. And to answer the question now in your head... no, the carrier couldn't make it in here; too bloody wide, but we're working toward a solution.'

Thom handed Clyde the binoculars; something was breaking the surface out to sea. The sub was surfacing and heading for the channel. The whole process took twelve minutes: three to open the channel, six for the sub to enter and transit, and another three to close the gap.

'Impressive,' Clyde commented. 'You'd never know what just happened – so what now?'

Thom checked the time. The first rays of light had begun splitting the dark sky; once again the cycle of day and night was starting. 'It's after six-thirty. You could go home, get a few minutes more sleep or we could follow the sub and see if they have any data for us.'

Clyde smiled, he indicated that he wasn't interested in sleep and they set off, trailing in the wake of the sub. They kept a good distance between the two vessels and Clyde took the opportunity to give the sub a once-over through the glasses.

*'Thomas, is that you in the rowboat?'* the heavily accented voice of Ivan Milosevic, the sub commander broke the silence.

Thom picked up the mike and responded. 'Yes Ivan, it's me. How was the trip?'

*'Sad, my friend; we didn't bring all back alive so now we have some difficult time before us.'* The voice coming from the radio was heavy with grief. *'Give me some time. I will call you later.'*

Thom brought the RIB to a halt. 'Deaths – they were on a recon mission; there was no need for contact.' His voice reflected the shock he was feeling. He turned the RIB and they headed back out of the tunnel, both men silent.

The rest of that day was sombre. The news that six had lost their lives in what should have been a simple recon exercise hit like a hammer blow.

Around 16:00, Thom arrived at the apartment. 'Reg wants to see us.' His voice was quiet and out of character.

'Everything all right?' Bonnie asked.

'Not really, I had some good friends in that operation – two didn't make it,' Thom replied, his voice filled with sadness. He waited at the door as the others grabbed their gear and followed him.

Reg was waiting in one of the meeting rooms; several others who Bonnie and Clyde hadn't met were with him.

'Bonnie, Clyde,' Reg greeted them. 'I wish we had better news. Please let me introduce some people: Captain Milosevic, the sub commander, Professor Andreyev, our leading physicist, and Julie Barnes, the leader of the recon team.' Reg stood aside as greetings were made, but there was no small talk; the mood was far too serious.

Reg indicated for all to sit. 'Julie, run us through the operation.'

Julie began. It had started like so many other similar operations. The sub had dropped them off and then slid away to hide in the depths – it had been scheduled to return three days later.

The op had started well—they'd made good time and were in position in the bush behind the old hospital the next afternoon. There they waited for darkness before venturing further. They had entered via a maintenance workshop at the rear of the main building, split up into three groups of four, and begun their sweep. Two hours later, they had found nothing except indications that people still used the building from time to time.

Next, they had turned their attention to the research wing, the newest extension to the rear of the main structure.

'This is where the whole thing fell apart,' Barnes said. 'We missed the security system and we must have triggered some type of alarm.

Within minutes of entering the facility, we knew we were on the right track. It was orderly, clean, and showed signs of constant use.

'Then the defenders sprung their trap, must have been thirty of them, all well-armed and trained. They pinned us down in a corridor, with a well-planned crossfire ambush. Bullets were everywhere but we couldn't get an accurate bead to return their fire; someone had really planned this ambush bloody well. That's where Harris and Stevens bought it. We managed to find some cover and returned fire; that seemed to disperse them. We grabbed a couple of trolleys, loaded the two dead on them, and started for the exit. Our second fuck up; they were waiting. We were trapped. They held the high ground and had the only way out in a pincer grip.' She took a deep breath before continuing.

'That's when Sarah Roberts came up with the solution. She loaded her forty mil launcher and sent four grenades back into the complex. That dropped the roof in the corridor, removing the threat from the rear, but we were caught in the open; Sarah took three rounds for her effort. Then everyone loaded their grenade launchers and let loose. We had a good idea of where the enemy was, so we simply demolished any spot we thought they were hiding in. Bloody effective; their return fire became sporadic and ineffective.

'I took this opportunity to send two guys off to find transport. There was no way we were leaving our dead and we couldn't carry them all the way back. Anyway, they returned with one of those huge American utes. We loaded the dead and wounded into it and took off. We managed to break through the cordon and headed out to the main road; here we found another obstacle.

'The roads are a mess. No maintenance has them busted up all over. Plus, there are vehicles everywhere. People must have died in their thousands trying to drive somewhere, anywhere. But, our friends have cleared a path through the worst of it, so we took it and not a moment too soon. We heard the sound of a chopper starting and believe me that spurred us on.

'We had just made it to the end of Croudace Road when a sniper hit Hopkins; bloody good shot considering we were driving like lunatics. Anyway, we had to follow the path they had cleared and that gave the chopper the advantage. To cut a long story short, the pilot wasn't very good and he hesitated. We let him have a full mag from the SSMG and that was the end of the pursuit.

'We made it back to the rendezvous, hunkered down, and waited for the sub to return and here we are.'

Reg stood and started to pace. 'And the entrance to the hospital?'

'No way in there unless our friends clear it,' she answered. 'Sorry about that.'

Thom spoke next. 'Doesn't matter; somewhere between the university at Shortland and the hospital, there is a larger habitat development. From this report, it seems there are still quite a few of them so we need to either avoid them—which will be difficult—or we take them out. Simply finding another entrance will do nothing except get us killed.' He looked at Clyde, who seemed to be miles away. 'You got something on your mind Clyde?'

'This is how I see it,' Clyde replied. 'You want us to go to Australia, find an entrance to a fortified habitat, breach it and deal with God only knows how many hostiles. Then retrieve something, but you don't know exactly where it is; bring it back and then maybe the

Garibaldis can figure out a reverse-engineered virus. How's that so far?' He waited until Reg nodded in agreement.

Clyde continued. 'We're going about this the wrong way. We have a time machine, or so you say. Why not simply send some of us back to before all this started? We neutralize the threat and destroy any evidence of the research.'

Rudy Andreyev answered in a dismissive tone. 'It simply won't work.'

'And why bloody not?' Clyde asked indignantly. In his mind it was simple: go back, destroy the research, maybe even kill the Garibaldis —if required—and save the world.

'A thing called the time paradox, that's why,' Andreyev answered. His attitude showed that he had little time for silly ideas, and this was one of the silliest.

'Come on, the least you can do is explain why!' Clyde demanded.

Andreyev stood and moved to a large whiteboard. 'It's complicated and involves a lot of theory and not much fact.' He began drawing while he spoke. He drew a straight line from one side of the board to the other. Then he drew one that started halfway and diverged at a forty-five-degree angle.

'Okay, time paradox for dummies. The straight line represents the time flow we were in when all this shit started,' he made a point two-thirds the way across the line, to the right. 'And this is where we are now. You have been brought here and now want to head back and fix the problem. Well, you can't.' He held his hand up to stop the question he knew would be coming. 'Please, allow me to finish.

'Let's say we do as you ask Clyde. We send back a team to fix the problem.' He moved his pointer to the intersection of the straight and angled line. 'Here you go back and fix the problem; but that will also change history completely.' He moved his pen down the angled line. 'This will be the new reality your actions will create but, and this is the paradox, the timeline that sent you back to do the deed will not exist, ergo, we will not be here to send you back. One possible reaction may be you simply cease to exist. Who knows? This is all theory. The only fact I know is that changing the past, in any form, will be disastrous.'

'And what we have now isn't a disaster?' Clyde asked.

Andreyev shook his head sadly. 'Yes, it is a disaster, but it's one we need to fix here and now. We simply can't go back and change any event. To do so would see this timeline,' he erased the horizontal line, their current timeline, 'simply cease to exist from this point.' Again he moved his pen back to the point where they wanted to be sent back to. 'The angled line would be the new timeline.' He waited for some comment, anything that might show understanding, but the faces before him showed very little.

'Now this is where arguments start. One view is that the new timeline will become the new reality and history will progress—without the virus in this case. The other view is that because of the paradox, you can never complete the mission, because as soon as you do, that version of reality will vanish, which means we were never here to send you back. Now, I don't think anyone here is qualified to argue this, and believe me; it can really fuck with your head. So please listen to what I say. That option can never work.'

'Hang on; if we go back and fix the problem, you're saying that it will be as if we never went back?' Clyde asked.

'Exactly – the problem with the past is that it is the foundation for the present and therefore, the future. Change the past, even by the minutest bit, and you dramatically alter the future – so I'm sorry, you just can't go back and stop the development of the virus.'

'But what if we took the Garibaldis back and let them sabotage their research?'

'Then you're changing the past and thereby changing the timeline. This reality would still cease to exist. You can't change the past. That's all there is to it.' Andreyev made it clear that he considered the matter closed.

'But, if what you're saying is true, didn't bringing us here, from the past, change things? What I mean is isn't there something that we might have done that now affects today?' Bonnie asked.

Andreyev smiled. 'Bingo, and that's why people go crazy trying to figure out this bloody time paradox thing. I'm just glad the damn machine is now off line, as I have told Reg a number of times, we don't understand it enough.'

'Alright, enough of this time travel crap; we're back to plan A. We find the base virus and hope the Garibaldis can fix the problem in this timeline,' Thom added.

Clyde glared at Andreyev. 'So Professor, I take it that there is also zero possibility of us ever getting back home?'

Andreyev gave Clyde an appreciative look. 'Astute, very astute; I've been trying to tell Reg that for ages. If we send you back, it must be accurate to the nanosecond, or better. And considering where we grabbed you from, I don't think you'd want to go back in any case.'

Reg stood, calling for the meeting to end. He thanked them for their attendance, advising that the funerals for the dead would be held in the morning. The meeting broke up, each person going their own way.

***

Bonnie woke slowly, as she usually did. She reached out, lazily searching for Clyde, but his side of the bed was empty.

She sat up. No sounds came from the bathroom or the lounge area. She left the bed, threw on a robe and went to the door, listening for any sounds from Allison's room. The thought of Clyde and Allison together both excited her and caused a sharp pang of apprehension. These feelings were foreign to her, or so she thought. As she quietly crept down the lounge room to see if she could get a better take on what might be going on, she felt the excitement start to manifest itself between her legs.

Bonnie stopped. All she heard was gently rhythmic breathing. Confused, she turned to go back to their room and then she saw Clyde, standing on the balcony, staring out into the dawn light. She went through the large doors and onto the balcony before he was aware of her presence. Gently she slid her hands up his strong back until they reached his hair. She playfully ruffled it between he fingers. 'Deep thoughts – care to share?'

Clyde turned. 'Take a look at this.' He gestured toward the ocean. 'It's beautiful. I mean, I've probably seen many sunrises as good as this, but I've never taken the time to **really** look at them.' He stopped as Bonnie moved to his side and slid her arms around him.

'I know; I feel the same. Things I used to take for granted I now pause to appreciate. This place has changed me.'

Bonnie's response caught Clyde off-guard. 'Really?'

'Yes, really; now I take time... just like you do. But that's not what's bothering you, is it?' Bonnie pulled away. Her body language told him she wouldn't take any bullshit.

'No, this time paradox stuff that Andreyev spoke about – I've heard it somewhere before; I don't know where, but I know I have. It makes sense—we can never return to our old lives. This is now our reality and it has been since we arrived. All Reg's crap about sending us back was just smoke and mirrors,' Clyde said angrily.

'I don't think so. I think he genuinely believes that they do have the ability to return us. But Andreyev said that it's all theoretical because so far nobody has proved any of it,' Bonnie returned. 'But what does any of this have to do with us? If we're here then that's it. Or did you have something else in mind?'

Clyde turned back to the sea. The sun was about half risen and looked like a huge fireball climbing out of the ocean. A brilliant yellow/orange path seemed to lead to their island, and the sound of birds greeting the new day echoed over the complex.

'We could take the boat and just leave. Maybe find an island of our own and live our lives there. We seem to be compatible. In any case, the sex is great and we get along. We don't owe these people anything. They owe us!' He turned back to the sea.

Bonnie watched him, standing as if about to step off onto that orange path between them and the sun. For a moment, she felt he could be right, but only for a moment. 'Clyde, I understand how you feel, but the simple fact is we do need them. We need to be part of a community to survive. Hell, you're the one who convinced me of that, so what's really up?'

Clyde stood still, staring out to sea, seemingly ignoring Bonnie's words. She moved forward and placed her hand on his left shoulder. Clyde took her hand and moved her to his side. 'So far, they have lost over a dozen people in this quest. Now we're supposed to succeed where they've failed? Why? Are we that much better than them or are we just expendable?'

'Do you trust Thom?' Bonnie asked quietly.

'Yes, he's one of us—a captive.'

'Is he? I think you'll find that he's as committed to the mission as Reg or the Garibaldis are. I think you'll find that he's now an integral part of this operation just as we can be, if we want. As Reg said, the decision is ours, but in the end, I think you're right, we really have no option. I don't think either of us could live knowing we had condemned everyone here to extinction.

'And before you say anything, yes, I know it may be a fruitless gesture. Anton and Zena may not be able to reverse the binary virus, but at least we will have given it the best chance of success.' Her voice was calm and soothing as she reached up and kissed him. 'And yes, I feel the same way about us.'

Their lips joined again, with more passion this time. Clyde pulled away and looked into her eyes. 'Then don't come on the mission. Stay here; give me something to come back to.'

Bonnie chuckled. 'And leave you and Miss Horny Knickers together in close quarters for the duration of the trip? Not bloody likely. If anything happens, it's the three of us or nothing.' She gave him a wicked grin and dropped her robe. 'Right now though, judging by your growing interest, I think you might want something?'

Bonnie parted her legs, inviting him in. Clyde leaned in closer, nibbling her neck. She rubbed back and forth on his hardening member, teasing and lubricating at the same time. Their hands roamed all over each other until finally Clyde cupped her buttocks and lifted her. Bonnie wrapped her legs around him, opening herself to his raging passion. He began entering her, an inch at a time, teasing, and then began lifting her slowly up and down before finally dragging her down on his full erection.

Bonnie groaned. 'Harder, yes! Come on, ram that thing in.'

Clyde obeyed and moved to the glass wall separating them from the apartment. With better support he began obeying her demands, slamming harder into her. Her breathing became shallower; her fingers tore at his back, and gripped Clyde with her legs, helping his thrusts, increasing their ferocity.

'Yes, oh God, yes!' Bonnie cried as her orgasm slammed through her body. Her legs tightened around him, keeping him locked deep inside her. The rhythmic contractions of her orgasm driving Clyde to the brink himself – he tried to withdraw, but Bonnie's legs gripped tighter.

'No, I want you inside me!' she gasped breathlessly and pulled his hips closer, locking him where she wanted him. Moments later, she got what she'd demanded as Clyde climaxed.

They stayed locked in the position for what seemed like ages before Bonnie gently nipped Clyde's earlobe. 'I love you Clyde.'

With these simple words, Bonnie released her hold and slipped to the floor, turned, and started into the apartment. Clyde grabbed her arm, pulled her to him and kissed her, before standing back and mumbling.

Bonnie smiled and placed her left hand over his mouth. 'No need to reciprocate. I think I might have just shocked myself as well!'

# Nineteen

They entered the lecture room of Thom's training facility; a strange-looking suit was hanging beside the lectern that he was leaning against.

'Good morning. I hope you all rested well?' Thom's tone was slightly sarcastic. Clyde was about to make a comment but a quick punch to the ribs from Bonnie stopped him.

'Well, I know I did,' Allison replied.

'Good, then this morning will be a breeze. I know you're all looking at the garment beside me; we'll get to that later. Right now I have thirty volunteers who want to come on this mission. Today we've got to select the ones we want; your thoughts, Clyde?' Thom moved away from the dais and joined the others.

Clyde pulled four chairs into a semicircle and they all sat as he began with his thoughts on the requirements. 'I was thinking of four teams of five, with a fifth in reserve for backup. Each team should have one medical person and one Squad Support Machine Gun (SSMG).'

'Why only five in each team?' asked Allison. 'Surely it's better to have more. Why not two teams of ten? After all, we only seem to have two possible entry points.'

Clyde considered her option before replying. 'The main reason is stealth. A smaller number will be harder for any adversary to detect. Also, it will make our job of covering multiple entry points much easier. Remember, we don't actually know where the entry points are, but we hope that the plans and maps that the sub brought back will give us a clue.'

With that issue decided, they started on the requirements of each person coming with them. Thom had a dossier on each candidate so they studied and discussed each person's strengths and weaknesses.

Two hours later, they had sorted the pool into five groups and selected a team leader and medico. The rest were there in order of perceived attributes.

'Before we make any final decisions, I want to see them in action.' Clyde turned to Thom. 'First on the range, next on the combat course - let's get them in here and talk to them.'

Thom agreed and sent for the thirty candidates. When they assembled, he explained the situation, emphasizing that not being selected wasn't any reflection on their ability. They only had twenty-one spots and thirty candidates. Someone had to miss out.

Thom addressed the assembled group. 'The first thing is on the firing range. Each of you will be checked against each weapon we'll be using on the mission. Tomorrow we'll be on the combat course. There will be three scenarios that you will need to complete, first individually, and then, the next day, as a team. Four of you are certified med techs.' He read the names. 'This gives you an advantage, but you still have to complete the selection process. Fail and you don't go, medical certification or not.'

The four med techs nodded their understanding as Clyde took the stage. 'From now on, this will be a military operation. Each team will have the same structure: a team leader, a second in command, and so on. The teams will be identified as: Alpha; Bravo; Charlie; Delta and Echo teams. The leader of Echo team will be Echo One; the second will be Echo Two, and so on. Each team will have one SSMG and that will be Echo Five, for Echo team. Once the teams have been selected, there will be no names used, and that includes here on the base.

'Thom will become Bravo One, and that is how we all will refer to him. Never under any circumstance use anyone's name. This is critical for security. Does everyone understand?'

Clyde waited while they agreed. 'Once we have set the teams up, we will all move into a new training site for final preparation. There will be no communication with the rest of the base so I suggest that if you have family or other attachments, make the next few nights count.' He let them have a few moments for the message to register, then spoke again. 'Okay, now let's see if any of you can shoot.'

The rest of the day went quickly. Each candidate was taken through various weapons and their proficiency noted. It was Allison who noticed a glaring problem. One of the med techs was a terrible shot, but his medical skill and qualifications made him almost an essential inclusion, and Bonnie agreed.

'All you've concentrated on is the Evans gear,' Allison said. 'What about the Fostech? I really think we should have at least one of them in each team. To be honest, from what I've seen, it'd be of more value than the SSMG.'

'Why? The SSMG can put down a fantastic field of fire,' Thom asked.

'Yes, on open ground or even in an urban setting, but we're going underground, into a tunnel and maybe even a cave system. Don't you think that the SSMG may be limited in that scenario? I'd prefer to take one instead of the assault rifle. I'll still have the pistols, and yes I want two, so the Fossy will be my choice.' Allison stood, firmly challenging Thom.

Clyde intervened. 'She's right. We've been concentrating on getting to the facility and that may be the easiest part of the job.' Deep down, Clyde knew what Allison's suggestion meant. 'We'll need to add a member to each team. Let's break out some Fostechs and see what happens.'

Clyde and Thom had designed the teams around a specific fighting style and adding another member was going to confuse things, but they couldn't just substitute one of the assault rifles with a shotgun without compromising the team's firepower. Now they needed six per team.

As the day wound down, Thom called the candidates together and asked if any had ever used a shotgun. Six answered in the affirmative. He then gave each a Fostech and directed them to the range. Three would shoot at a time. Clyde didn't like even numbers in a team, so he elected to include an extra person on each.

The teams had gone from five to seven but even Clyde had to admit, it was for the better. The firepower was now greatly enhanced and would consist of one SSMG, one Fostech, five assault rifles, and seven pistols. Ammunition was another concern. As they had no idea what opposition they would face, each team needed to carry enough to meet whatever they encountered, but that came with a weight penalty.

Allison was a good example as they tried to work out what she needed to carry for survival, as well as the munitions she wanted to take. The whole idea of this mission is to get in, grab the loot and get out without any problems, Allison's initial ammo load suggested she was preparing for an extended battle situation and the weight penalty she would incur would see her exhausted very quickly.

The discussion continued for another hour until everyone was satisfied with the load each team member would be required to carry. In the end, assault rifles would have one, one-hundred-round double drum magazine fitted and one spare; each pistol would have one fifteen-round mag fitted and six spares. Allison was the only exception—she wouldn't budge from her choice to carry an extra six; sixty round mags for the pistols, her rationale was she had reduced her Fostech load considerably so there would not be a weight penalty.

In addition, each member would carry four fragmentation grenades, three smoke canisters, and three flash-bangs. When the SSMG came up, the decision was to add another double mag and drop the grenade load down to two fragmentation units.

'Finally, that's settled.' Clyde breathed a sigh of relief. 'Now, Thom, what's this suit you've got?'

Thom stood and walked back to the black garment hanging on the dais. He took it down and brought it to the group. 'It's called a battle suit. I told you this place had many functions; one was to look through all the wacky ideas that came from fiction and movies, specifically science fiction.

'Back in this place's heyday, they had almost as many people reading futuristic books as anything else. This suit came from a combination of writers' ideas. It's made of a special Kevlar-type material so it's effectively bulletproof. It has a personal function, as it has to be matched to the wearer's DNA and body structure. It then monitors the condition of the wearer and can administer certain drugs—for example painkillers —if needed. It also can process urine and sweat into drinkable water. Unfortunately, we haven't been able to replicate the fictional ability to process shit; that still needs to be done the old way.

'One thing we have to do is remove all body hair. The inner garment must be in total contact with the wearer's skin for it to work.'

'That won't worry me,' Allison piped up. 'I don't have any anyhow, but you and Clyde do. So, in the interest of your survival, I'm willing to shave you both.' Her broad grin left no doubt about what she was suggesting.

Thom answered her challenge disappointingly. 'Sorry to rain on your parade, but shaving just won't do. We have a process that we will all have to go through to make sure everything works.'

* * *

The next day saw each person run through three scenarios on the combat course. Clyde was quietly impressed with the result, but when they started into the team operations, things went awry.

Every person in the facility had to qualify on these courses individually, but when placed into operating as a team, egos and personalities were causing problems. No team survived even the first scenario.

Thom and Clyde were livid and it showed. Everyone had gathered in the briefing room when Thom let fly. 'Just what the fuck was that shambles out there? Every person in this room is fucking dead. He glared at each person in turn, heads suddenly finding something to study on the floor as he looked at them. 'This isn't a pissing competition and I don't care what plumbing you've got. A team is only as good as the weakest link and from what I see, you're all bloody weak links.'

Clyde moved to his side and Thom sat down. 'Thom's right. Not even we survived.' He pointed to the four red blobs on his fatigues. 'And how did I get these? My team broke and everyone went their own way. Now, go home and reflect on what a fucking pack of pussies you were today and report back here at zero six hundred tomorrow and we'll do it all again. But dwell on two things: One; fail tomorrow and the mission is scrubbed, and you know the consequences of that; Two, I want each of you to write the word "team" and show me where the letter "I" is! – Dismissed!' Clyde watched as the group of very dejected people left, waiting until they were gone before leaving the dais.

Thom approached him. 'Clyde, I'm sorry. I thought we had the right group.'

Clyde smiled. 'We do, they just don't feel it yet. At the moment each of them is trying to impress, trying to stand out; it's normal. A good team comes with time for each member to be ready to place their life in the hands of every other team member. To be fair, they didn't do as badly as I expected. You wait; tomorrow will be much better, but now it's time for a drink and sleep.'

Clyde was right. The next day three teams made it through the scenario and achieved their goal, one with zero casualties. The other two still had a few egos to deal with. Thom took them as de and didn't mince words. Then they tried again; this time they made it.

The scenario was simple, designed to show why teamwork was important. All the planning was done and each player's actions pre-determined. The debriefing proved interesting, giving Thom and Clyde a deeper insight into their teams.

'Congratulations, today was better, but tomorrow it gets harder,' Thom announced as the debriefing was winding down. 'Tomorrow, we simulate live fire. The suits you wear will give you a close representation of injuries on the battlefield. If you are hit, believe me, you'll feel it. Now, before you leave, we need to sort out the body hair issue. From now on battle suits will be your fashion of choice. So head down to the showers and we'll meet you there.'

Ten minutes later, Clyde and Thom walked in, Allison and Bonnie close behind. Bonnie took charge.

'Now listen up. Some of what happens now will be difficult for you but believe me when I say it is necessary. You'll be fighting with the operative next to you, behind you, or in front of you. Their gender is unimportant. What is important is that each of you will have every other life in your hands. You must totally believe, I repeat—*totally believe*—that they'll have your back.' Bonnie stopped and gazed around the assembled group.

'Now, across that hall is where we need to go, so strip off and assemble back here in five minutes.'

'What, you want us all to assemble here, naked?' a voice whined.

'Who said that?' Bonnie called back.

'I did. Michelle... I mean Echo Six,' she corrected herself quickly.

'Understand this, all of you! You will not be working with a man or woman beside you; they will be another operative. Imagine this: In the heat of battle, you get injured, your team needs to inspect the wound and they cut off your suit, blood spurts everywhere; an indication of an arterial wound.

'For a split second, the male beside you hesitates; he's just seen your tits. His basic instincts kick in and he hesitates for the slightest moment and he misses the piece of shrapnel in your neck, slightly hidden by the battle suit. With his interest on another part of your anatomy, he cuts the suit away and drags it off your torso. He has just dragged the piece of metal out of its hiding place that was covering and sealing, the slit in your carotid artery, blood spurts everywhere and you die in those precious seconds. But let me not be sexist. He might be injured and you cut his suit off to reveal his rather large penis. For the briefest moment you hesitate; you've just discovered the operative beside you could really tickle your tonsils, if given the chance, in your distracted state you see the large piece of shrapnel sticking out of his groin and, without another thought you remove it. Instantly you're covered by blood spurt from his Femoral artery, the shrapnel had nicked it but, while it was still embedded it had sealed the wound. Now you're both dead.' Bonnie stopped to let this sink in.

'You must all get used to each other; so much so that you stop seeing different plumbing, different genders. All you will see is an operative who has your life in their hands. Now, Echo Six, do you understand?'

'Yes Ma'am, I do!' she replied.

'Good. Now, get going, you're wasting valuable time,' Bonnie ordered.

Exactly five minutes later, a naked Bonnie strode purposefully back to the group; Allison, Clyde, and Thom were three strides behind her. Bonnie smiled inwardly; it was exactly as she'd pictured it. Everyone was standing slouched, using hands and arms to hide behind.

'Aten-hut!' Thom called and slowly the assembled group came to attention, their arms finally locked by their sides. 'There, that's not so bad, is it?'

Thom, Clyde, and Allison left the room and opened the door across the hall. Lights came on and they disappeared inside.

'Right... now I want you to form a line, five paces apart, and start walking over to that room,' Bonnie commanded.

They obeyed and the process started. Allison was waiting inside the door and asked that they remove any body jewellery. Only two had an issue, one of the men had a number of rings through the head of his penis and nipples, and another woman had her nipples, navel, clitoris, and labia pierced. It all had to come out as the suit couldn't work with the metal in their skin. Their option was simple—keep the jewellery or be part of the mission. Both chose the latter.

Next, Thom fitted each with a helmet. Facial and head hair was allowed but it needed to be protected from the process. Then Clyde guided the first operative through the first tank. There were three tanks. Each one had stairs down into it and a variable-height walkway on the bottom. This allowed for people of differing heights to be processed.

Each tank was five paces long and at the end was a shower. They walked through one tank and had the residue washed off; then repeated. The final process was timed for exactly one minute from exiting the tank; enough time to walk to the final deluge. There, the water came in a huge rush, washing away the last vestiges of their body hair.

Bonnie was there to carry out a final inspection. Only one needed to repeat the process. Delta Two was the hairiest man Bonnie had ever seen but the second pass cleared him.

As each person passed her, Bonnie told them to head for the normal shower but not to dress. The next phase was to fit them for their battle suits.

The fitting process was fairly simple. Each person stood inside a clear circular enclosure, feet placed on marked spots and arms stretched above their heads. A laser beam washed over each body and fed the information to a computer. This, in turn, designed the suit for a perfect fit.

Clyde led the procession. 'Alpha One,' he said as he entered. Three minutes later, he was told to exit. His suit had been designed and the next station was for head gear. This was more complex as four cerebral interfaces needed to be fitted.

Again, the process was expedited by automation. The position of the interfaces was deduced by the computer and the four almost microscopic implants were placed under the skin in exactly the right place. Next, the computer ran a number of tests and simulations to calibrate the implants and acclimatize Clyde to having a connection to external sensors.

He left the booth after twenty-three minutes. Thom was waiting. 'This is the choke point. Your installation was quick; the average is thirty-five minutes, so we're looking at over twenty hours.'

'Then we better stagger it; work in shifts so we get it done by this time tomorrow. By the way, what's the time?' Clyde asked.

'Around seventeen hundred I think.'

'Okay, work through the teams alphabetically. That way we can keep working on the fitting. Once everyone is fitted, we'll have a break for a day and then get back into training.'

Clyde and Thom were walking as they talked and arrived back at the locker room, where they got a pleasant surprise. Everyone was still naked, but the awkwardness and embarrassment had dissipated. Now the teams stood or sat talking among themselves with no recognition of their state of dress.

'Can I have your attention, please?' Clyde asked. 'This whole process will take longer than we'd anticipated, so we'll be working on it through the night. We should finish by late tomorrow afternoon. Bravo One,' Clyde indicated Thom to the group, 'will work out the schedule. Once this is done, I suggest you get something to eat and then some rest. The bunk room at the end of this hall is fully equipped and I'll arrange for the mess to be staffed and opened; any questions?' Clyde waited, but none came. 'Excellent. We all have things to do so I suggest we get at it.'

By 20:00, everything was working normally. Thom spoke to Reg and arranged for another implant system to be activated; speeding up the process and reducing wasted time. Clyde had a little more difficulty in getting the mess sorted, but finally got through to Reg again and things started to move. Soon staff arrived and the kitchen began to hum. This would be everyone's home for the foreseeable future so he wanted things to go smoothly.

Once measured and fitted with their implants, the crews donned fatigues and began filing into the mess. When Clyde entered, he saw Alpha and Bravo teams sitting at separate tables. He smiled, filled his plate at the buffet and joined them.

# TWENTY

Clyde woke suddenly, the incessant chiming from his communicator dragging him back to consciousness.

He checked the time, 05:45. 'This better be fucking urgent,' he grumbled as he climbed out of bed. Bonnie didn't stir; she was exhausted, having only come to bed a couple of hours ago. He quietly went to the next room and answered the call.

'*Clyde, it's Reg. There's something you need to see.*' Reg's voice sprang out of the speaker.

'Do you have any idea of the time? Shit, we only got to bed a few hours ago!' Clyde complained.

'*Sorry, but I think you'll want to see this, believe me.*' Reg sounded excited, like a small child opening presents. '*I've sent a driver to collect you, should be there any time.*'

'Okay, give me twenty minutes. I need coffee and a shower,' Clyde replied.

'*You've got about ten.*' Reg cut the call.

Clyde dispensed with a shower. Instead, he stuck his head under the cold tap. It worked and he started to come alive. He dressed quickly in training fatigues; the coffee was percolating, filling the rooms with that unmistakable aroma, waking Bonnie in the process.

'Coffee, just what I need,' she commented as she stumbled to the kitchenette. 'So why are you up this early and who called?'

'Reg says he has something I need to see now.' Clyde was interrupted by a knock at the door. He turned to Bonnie. 'That'll be my driver. You'd better go back to bed. I don't think you want to greet guests dressed like that.'

'Good point. I'll see you later.' She blew him a kiss as she shuffled back into the bedroom.

Clyde opened the door and, coffee in hand, followed the driver to the waiting car.

It took a full twenty minutes to reach their destination. Clyde didn't recognize anything. 'Where are we? I don't think I've been here before.'

The driver didn't answer. He stopped the vehicle, got out and held the door for Clyde to do the same.

He'd no sooner left the vehicle when Reg came rushing through the door in front of him. 'Come on Clyde. You've got to see this!' Reg urged Clyde towards the doors.

'Reg, slow down; where are we?'

Reg stopped and answered. 'This is an old NSA control hub, one of a number they had around the world. They used them to control many things—drone aircraft, drone vessels—but what we're excited about is that this facility is one of only two that controlled God's Eye.'

Clyde stopped in his tracks. 'What did you call it?'

'God's Eye, why? Do you remember something?'

'Nothing specific; just a familiarity with the name that's all,' Clyde responded cautiously.

'Let me fill you in. The NSA had many spy systems in the air, on land and sea. But their crowning glory was what you're about to see.' He entered a code into a pad on the wall. A small ocular reader popped out of a concealed alcove and Reg looked directly into it. A thin blue beam scanned his right eye and a door began to slide open.

'There's only a few — outside the operational staff — who have access. You'll see why very soon.'

Reg led the way down a long downward sloping corridor. At the end, there was another security scan and another door opened, this time into a room full of consoles and operators. Reg led Clyde to an observation room high at the rear of the room. Once inside, he pressed a button on the console and spoke. 'Where are we up to people?'

A voice sprang from concealed speakers in response. '*Just over Sydney now... we should have a good scan of the CBD in a few minutes.*'

'Just what is God's Eye, Reg?' Clyde wanted answers.

'God's Eye was a joint venture between Australian security services and the US NSA. It's a combination of sophisticated satellites and various drones, as well as manned systems. By combining these they could find, identify and eliminate enemy forces up to two hundred meters below ground. You'll see what it can do in a couple of minutes.' Reg replied.

'*Satellite coming online now,*' the voice from the speakers announced. Reg stood and beckoned Clyde to come closer to the glass screen. The main viewer flickered and settled. It showed a skeletal vision of buildings down through car parks and deeper, into the very bowels of the city.

Reg spoke excitedly. 'There... those small red dots... they're people deep into the underground system, and a lot of them.'

The image changed as the satellite sped overhead. It seemed that thousands of people were in the old transport tunnels, with large concentrations at the old stations. But above, there were more, hanging in space, inside the skeletons of the buildings.

'Now you see what God's Eye does. This is where the system changes. If those were targets, the coordinates would be set into the drone's mission package and any site selected would be obliterated. Effective and economical, no losses on our side,' Reg said. 'Now we move it to Newcastle and start to investigate. How's you group coming on?'

Clyde gave an honest update and Reg appeared pleased with the progress. They agreed to meet again in five days to gauge the group's progress and study whatever the satellite had discovered.

'I agree that the system gives us an advantage,' Clyde remarked. What I don't understand is how you've managed to gain control.'

Reg nodded as he guided Clyde out of the control room. 'Simple. When it hit the fan, one of the last things all agencies did was to put their assets into a sort of holding pattern. This facility is one of only two in the world that has the capability to activate and control these assets. The other had to be neutralized first and that was completed during the last escapade to Australia. Now we are the only control hub still active – gives a shitload of capability.'

Clyde quietly absorbed what Reg had said. If he was telling the truth, then the only real power left might be this small group and this was one scenario he was uncomfortable with.

* * *

The next two days were slow and revolved around fitting the battle and training suits and downtime. On the third day the group gathered in the locker room at 05:00, where they donned their practice suits and headed back into the briefing room.

At 06:30 everyone was seated. Thom took control of the briefing.

'Listen up! Today is about battle readiness. The suits you are now wearing have the ability to simulate injury; get shot and you will know it. The pain level will be similar to an actual wound, as will any delay. For example, there are recorded instances where soldiers have been badly wounded but because of the adrenalin and other hormone levels, they didn't realise it until later. Some didn't ever realise it—they just died, eventually.

'What these suits will do is induce pain and other responses according to many years of research. If you are wounded, the real test is how you and your team react to it. Any questions, you'd better ask now.'

There were a few nervous comments but no serious questions so Thom handed the floor to Bonnie. She stood to the lectern and studied the faces before her. 'Most of you probably think I'm coming along as Alpha Two, right?'

There was a general affirmative response.

'Well, you're wrong. One of the benefits of the suits is the ability for remote tracking and monitoring. I'll be with a special team of medical operators monitoring each of you. We will be able to see if you are in trouble and respond accordingly. Anything from adjusting your adrenalin and hormone levels to administering pain meds to pulling you out of the op, that's our call. Today is also the first run through for my team— Zulu —and we will all be evaluated too. '

Bonnie's team of medics entered. She introduced them, with her being Zulu One to the last member, Zulu Nine.

'Now, before there's any comment, we have two extra members purely so we can make sure you are all being backed the best way we can. We'll begin in ten minutes so take the next five to get acquainted.'

Ten minutes passed and Bonnie called her team together. They followed her to a different room where monitors for each team had been set up.

The mission scenario was simple—all teams were to approach a target from different directions. Resistance was programmed to be heavy, so stealth and cunning would be just as important as combat skills. Assembly points and basic strategy had been worked out. Clyde—Alpha One—was overall commander with Thom—Bravo One—as second in command. The teams quickly moved to their assembly points and, on Bonnie's command, the simulation began.

Each team had to make their way through the undergrowth, approach the target—in this case a small cave system that was part of the training facility—and successfully infiltrate that system. In theory, it was simple enough, but there were many traps along the way, traps that in the real world would kill. In the real mission, one team would be held in reserve in case things went bad. But today, each team needed to feel the heat, feel the pain, so there were five tracks being used to approach the village.

Each team had their own strategy, including the line-up for the trek. Clyde set his up with Alpha Seven on point followed by Four, One, Three, Two (the medic), Six (Fostech) and last, Five and the SSMG. His instructions were clear: keep eyes peeled and be aware of everything around you. He had finished his team briefing by telling them an old motto he'd heard somewhere—*make haste slowly*.

There was a little over a kilometre to traverse to make the target. Clyde's team was only two hundred meters in when a loud bang sounded and then screams of pain to their left filled the air. As one, they all dropped to the ground, assuming the cover fire positions they had drilled in. Clyde called his team to sound off, and was relieved when they all reported; from where the sounds came it was Delta who had been hit. Now was the time when the team's potential would be tested. They had a mission, one of their teams had suffered, but Alpha was intact. Clyde gave the order to move out, and was relieved when each member stood and assumed their correct position, their dedication to their mission overcoming the urge to help their friends. As they moved forward the screams died down.

***

The mission scenario was played, with bravo team reaching the objective first. Delta wasn't the only one to be hit. Charlie team also incurred casualties, but they elected to continue. In all, there were five deaths and seven serious injuries.

With everyone now back in the room, Clyde began his debrief. 'Delta One, what happened in your team?'

Delta One replied, giving all a good description of the events. Delta team had run tripped a nasty booby trap. The point man had triggered it, but it was designed to wait, let at least one more past, before detonating. Point and second took most of the blast, with Delta One also copping some minor damage.

Delta tried to silence his point man, Delta Four, by placing a hand over his mouth and telling him to shut up, knowing that in a real battle scenario, the screams would be a beacon to any opponents. He noted that Four's suit was covered in small red dots—paint indicators to show where he'd theoretically been hit. His wounds were multiple and looked very serious, but gradually he began to relax as the suit simulated administering pain relief.

Delta One then discussed the options with the team medic before calling Zulu team and making the decision that Delta team was out of the mission. He then rearranged his team placement for maximum cover before calling Alpha to announce his team's exit from the mission.

'We were in too much of a hurry; we rushed and missed the booby trap – seems we were trying to prove ourselves.' Delta one finished his report.

'I hope we all learned from this debacle today; too much speed and a team desperate to shine, wasn't observant enough. The same can be said for some of the other teams, Alpha included.' Clyde had experienced some resistance in slowing the pace and it was only after Charlie team had been hit that his crew had started to think and slow down.

'Seems that we've all learned some lessons today; go and clean up, have some chow and be back here by fifteen hundred to plan tomorrow's operation.' Clyde dismissed the teams.

The next day was a repeat, but this time, all teams came through without injury. The following days saw more complex and dangerous scenarios, with the final day set as the make or break. This time, not only did they have to make their way to the cave system, each team had to navigate a village that was filled with resistance; both booby traps and simulated defenders.

Clyde called the four team leaders together. 'Here's how I see it. We have to enter the cave system and locate the target, grab it and get out.

'Alpha and Bravo teams will lead. Charlie will follow and take up a hold point here.' Clyde took the map Thom handed him and indicated the spot where the hold point should be. 'Delta will set up at the cave mouth as a defensive measure. Allison's observation that SSMGs could be more of a problem in the caves may be correct, so Alpha and Bravo Five will stay with Delta. Okay, everybody is to check their ammo load and be ready in three minutes.'

Each leader went back to their team and the ammo check was completed. Echo One set up a defensive ring to cover any approach to the cave mouth while the other teams gathered at the entrance.

'Once we go, move any wounded inside, that way they can still give support without compromising the team's effectiveness.' Clyde issued the instruction and led the way into the cave.

Once they'd moved a few meters inside, the light disappeared. As one, each team member activated the low light system in their helmet. Five minutes later, they reached Charlie's hold point and that team dispersed to give cover to Alpha and Bravo.

Bravo took the lead, with Alpha team covering their rear. *'One hundred and fifty meters, then turn right.'* Clyde's voice sounded in Thom's ear. Bravo reached the intersection and Bravo Three moved forward, rewarded with a burst of machine gun fire from the tunnel. She ducked back, no wounds evident.

The scenario played out with more tests and traps, but both Alpha and Bravo teams showed they were up to the task. Alpha was surprised when machine gun fire came from their rear. Alpha Four was hit in the leg and Three took a simulated round in the arm, but the return fire from the team removed the threat. Bravo continued to the target, retrieved the flag that signified it, and returned. They encountered some resistance but the cover from Alpha made the return relatively easy.

An hour later, all teams had returned, the dead and wounded brought out of the course with them.

Bonnie greeted the teams. 'Looks like a success and the casualty rate is good. Well done, all of you. I think it may be time for a celebration. Hit the showers and report to the briefing room.'

The teams walked past her, heads held high. Finally, each person realised that they were a part of something bigger than themselves.

Clyde and Thom were beside her. 'Well done, both of you. It's quite amazing looking at the difference today. You've turned a group of individuals into a team.' She planted a kiss on each of the men's cheeks. 'Yes sir, I'm proud of you, but you both need a shower, so get moving.'

# TWENTY ONE

The celebration for completing the training was well received.

At Clyde's suggestion, a fire pit had been dug and half a steer was roasting over it. A couple of kegs and a few cases of wine were set up on the beach a few meters from the fire. Chairs, tables or rugs were spaced round and everyone grabbed a place as they returned from the debriefing.

Clyde stood as the last person joined them. 'This is the last official thing I'll be doing tonight. I hope each of you is proud of what we've achieved. I know I am. In just two short weeks we've gone from a group of individuals to a fairly well-oiled team.

'Now the training is largely over, our next scenario will be for real, so enjoy tonight and rest well – I have a feeling we'll be leaving soon for the real thing.' Clyde resumed his seat as one of the mess staff brought the first tray of meat to the long table.

The feast was in full swing when Reg arrived, Julie Barnes at his side. Clyde stood and invited them to join the celebration, spare chairs were brought and they both sat.

'We have some good intel about your targets. How's your training schedule?' Reg asked.

'To be honest, we're as ready as we'll ever be. The next few days will be lighter and mainly weapons based. Why?' Clyde replied.

'I'd like you and your team leaders to view what we have ASAP. Tomorrow would be good.'

Reg's answer left Clyde with a feeling that something was still to come. 'And that's not all, is it?'

'No, but we'll discuss it tomorrow.' Reg wasn't giving anything away.

Clyde looked at Reg and then Julie. 'You want to come, don't you?'

Julie smiled, her eyes sparkling. 'Yes.'

'That might be a problem. We've worked hard to get the teams set. Adding another member isn't something I really want to do so you'd better have a damn good reason.' Clyde's mind was racing. Julie had just returned from a disaster, that was the only way he could describe her mission, and now she wanted to join his group? The only reason he could fathom was revenge, and that would only lead to more trouble.

'Can you, Thom and I discuss this somewhere more private??' Julie asked.

In the end, Bonnie joined the group and they moved slightly away from the gathering. 'Right, we're out of earshot, what gives?' Clyde asked, his voice reflecting his disapproval already.

Julie's face was a mask of concern. 'There's no way to say this easily. My team was set up. They knew we were coming. There's a bloody leak here somewhere!'

'Have you spoken to Reg about this?' Thom asked.

Julie fidgeted, and then gave Thom a hard look. 'No, and I'm not going to.' She reached into her trouser pocket and brought out a small mesh container. Inside was a tiny electronic device. 'A tracker; we found one on every member of the team. The only place they could have been put on us is here.' She passed the small device around.

The temperature suddenly seemed to drop.

'And you suspect Reg?' Clyde asked.

'I don't fucking know. To do this would require a lot of access, and as far as I know, there aren't too many people with that sort of clout. Reg is one.' Julie left the comment hanging, like a rotten fish.

'How many of these?' Thom asked.

'There was one on every member of the team, but that's only part of the story. We all have these when we go on a mission. Our security installs them and we are all monitored. These were additional.'

'Bullshit. Weren't you scanned as you left the sub?' Clyde said.

'Yes, and all passed. These must have been activated after we left.'

'And the skipper of the sub reported your departure; standard procedure. Someone here must have activated them.' Clyde turned to Thom. 'Can we get access to the security logs? I want to know who was where on that night.'

Julie answered. 'I can get access.'

'Then why are you only bringing this to us now?' Clyde asked. 'You could have done this a few days ago.'

'I didn't know if I could trust any of you, but with your teams so close, I had to take the risk.'

Clyde nodded his acceptance and held his hand out for the bug. 'Give it to me.'

Julie handed the case to him.

'Bonnie... you, Thom and Julie head back inside and get some weapons. It's time for answers.'

He turned and walked back to the gathering; spirits were high and he hated the fact that he must now pour water on the evening.

He approached Reg. 'Is there a problem, Clyde?' Reg asked.

'You fucking know there is.' Clyde handed Reg the mesh case. 'Explain this and then give me a good reason why I shouldn't kill you.' Out of the corner of his eye he saw Thom and Julie take out the two escorts Reg had brought with him. 'Don't worry about the muscle, they've been dealt with.'

Reg looked at the case in his hands. 'We use these to track our people in the field, same as you used to do.' Reg looked genuinely confused.

'Then explain how Julie's team was compromised.'

'You think these caused the problem?' Reg laughed. 'Not possible; these use a randomized frequency. The only way to track them is by a special algorithm. Without that, these are just a pretty button.'

'Well, Julie's convinced that they were tracked. Every one of her team had two of these on their gear—one for your security to monitor and the other?' Clyde spoke through clenched teeth.

Reg shook his head. 'Not possible. All our teams' gear is monitored. We would have noticed something like this.'

'Well, it appears you didn't. Now, who has access to the program?' Clyde asked.

'Only the operators; and they're all vetted!' The colour started to drain from his face. 'And the programmers, they also have access.' Reg stopped in his tracks. 'Oh shit, Malabo. One of her sons used to be a programmer. He was caught trying to hack the security system and was removed from the team.'

'But could he still have accessed the trackers?'

Reg lowered his head shamefully. 'Yes.' The word was almost whispered.

'I fucking told you we should have shot the bitch when we had the chance.' Clyde turned on his heels and started for the entrance to the complex. They reached the two security escorts, both unconscious.

'Was that really necessary?' Reg asked.

Clyde marched determinedly through the entrance. 'They're still fucking breathing aren't they?' They located the others, now clad in battle suits. 'Thom, Bonnie, get the teams geared up. Locate all of Malabo's family and as many of her supporters as you can and bring them to the holding cells. It's time to finish this!' Clyde removed his clothes and began suiting up.

By the time he was dressed, the teams were already starting to change. Echo one called. 'What about the two security types?'

'Just tie them up. We'll be back for them later,' Thom replied.

'Clyde, what are you intending to do?' Reg asked.

'Finish this, once and for all. Alpha team, on me – the rest of you, Bravo Two is in command. Zulu One, is your team ready?'

'We'll have all of you on monitor before you arrive; comms are now live, check.' Bonnie ordered. As each team member sounded off in turn, Zulu confirmed the comm system. 'All in the green, we're good to go.'

Thankfully, Thom had thought to call for transport. They left the compound and Alpha team took one of the assault vehicles from the garage, Bravo commandeered the second. Charlie, Delta, and Echo boarded the POD and left the training facility.

***

Alpha's vehicle stopped outside the security compound; Reg and Clyde exited and walked to the guard room. A short conversation ensued and the gates opened and the truck headed for the decline – the destination was deep below this surface level.

'Alpha team, listen up. We have no idea what resistance, if any, we will meet so here are the rules of engagement. Give any hostile five seconds to disarm. If they don't comply, take them out. Understood?' Clyde waited as the team chorused the answer. 'It's underground so I don't want too much noise. Fix suppressors.' He reached for his weapon, took the suppressor and quickly locked it into position.' He turned to Julie. 'Stay on me, Barnes.'

The truck wound its way down the decline until the road flattened and the roof began to rise; now they were in the central security operation hub. They came to a standstill outside the main entrance; two guards outside and another four just inside. Reg approached them and he was instantly recognized and they admitted him. Clyde listened to his conversations. He'd secretly placed a tiny bug on Reg as they'd left the training facility. So far, he was following the instructions Clyde had given him.

The conversation was short and Reg turned to beckon Clyde inside. The rear hatch on the vehicle opened and the team exited, heading for the main door. Clyde and Julie made it inside before the two behind the desk saw the team. They paused for a second too long. The next thing they saw was Julie's shotgun – the sight of the weapon stopped any warning they may have been thinking about sending.

Alpha team secured the building in minutes, while Reg, Julie, and Clyde took the elevator down to the main operations room. The scene from above repeated and they were given access, the weapons clearly unsettling everyone. Clyde signalled Julie to tone the threat down and both put their weapons in a carry position. Now it was Julie's turn; she sat at one of the consoles and began her sweep of the security logs.

'*Alpha One from Bravo One, we have the targets and are moving to the lockup.*' Thom's voice was scratchy; the depth of the security compound was causing problems.

'Bravo One, Alpha One, signal is weak, but I got the message. Proceed with next phase.'

'*Copy.*'

Now it was all up to Julie. Ninety minutes later, she stood from the console, a look of triumph on her face. Clyde went to her side.

'I got it,' she announced. 'But I think you already had an inkling of what I was going to find.' She called the operation chief to her side, explained what she had done, and asked him to confirm. Sixty minutes to isolate the traitor and ten for the chief to confirm. He looked very small as he admitted to Reg what he now saw, and it had happened on his watch. Clearly, he thought his life would be over.

Reg simply replied. 'Welcome to the club. They fooled us all.' He turned to Clyde. 'Well, here's your evidence. What now?'

'Julie, bring it with you,' Clyde ordered and turned to Reg. 'You don't have to come; we can handle it from here.' He was trying to give Reg an out, but to his credit, Reg declined, saying that the problem was one of his making and he needed to be in when it was fixed.

The operation chief spoke quietly to Reg, then to the others. 'We have isolated the location of their system. I apologize. We should have detected it much earlier.'

Clyde shook his head. All this hindsight was a good teacher, but it wasn't going to solve anything. 'Look, the past is just that—over and done with. Learn from it and don't let it happen again.'

'Echo One from Alpha One, do you read me?' Clyde called.

*'Alpha One, signal is weak but readable.'*

'Echo One, the following coordinates are for a high-value target. Apprehend all operatives and neutralize the site. Confirm?' He then repeated the coordinates.

Echo One repeated the coordinates and confirmed their mission. The target was as good as out of commission.

Clyde turned back to the chief. 'I suggest you do a full sweep of the entire complex, just in case there is a backup.'

'And make it part of your regular scans,' Reg added. 'Now let's talk with Malabo.'

By the time Alpha team reached the detention block, Charlie and Delta teams had rounded up most of Malabo's supporters and were holding them all in three cells. The conditions were cramped, to say the least, with standing room only, but they were contained.

Clyde walked briskly up to Delta One and had a brief conversation.

'Sampson Malabo,' Delta One called.

A tall, heavily built black man stood and approached the bars. 'Who wants to know?' He scowled in response.

'I do,' Clyde replied and then to Delta One. 'Get him out here.'

'I'm comfortable in here, so fuck you!' Malabo replied and extended the middle finger of his right hand.

Clyde smiled and glared back. 'It wasn't an invitation.' The team brought their weapons to bear on Clyde's signal. 'Now, tough guy, either you come out or we take you all down. Either way, I don't care; you're a traitor so ending you would save a lot of trouble.'

Malabo looked around the cell. The faces that stared back were confused, some even angry. 'All right, I'll come out.' He pushed his way to the door. It opened and two of Delta's team grabbed him, cuffed him, and led him away.

Meanwhile, Reg had gone to see Zuri Malabo. Her cell was much more comfortable, but it was still a cell. He had her moved to one of the less intimidating meeting rooms and sat down to explain what they knew. That's where Clyde found them as they pushed Sampson through the door.

As the door closed, Echo One called Clyde and told him they had found the transmitter. 'But skipper, it was sending a location signal. Someone's coming, that's certain!' Echo One's voice was agitated as she spoke. Clyde gave the order to disable the transmitter, but not to destroy it. Somewhere in the back of his mind, the germ of an idea was forming.

Zuri looked up at her son. 'Sammy, what have you done?'

'What you didn't have the guts to do. This asshole,' he nodded at Reg, 'has kept us down long enough. Clements promised a better deal, so when he arrives, we'll get what we want, what you've wanted all along.' He turned and smiled smugly at Reg. 'Your days are over. Clements and his force will be here very soon and there's nothing you can do. While you've been stuffing around trying to find his base, he's been building up his forces. And now they know where this place is, you're finished.'

Zuri stood and walked to her son, looked him fiercely in the eyes, and slapped him hard. 'You moron – you've done a deal with the one person who makes the devil look benevolent. How could you be so stupid?'

Sampson looked bewildered. 'But it's what you wanted... to end Reg's reign. This way we'll be able to run the place. Clements has agreed.'

'How could I have raised a son so stupid? Edmund Clements is the most duplicitous, lying asshole I've ever met. Hell, I'd rather a hundred Reg Denhams to one Clements, and you're wrong. All I want is more representation on the council and a stronger hand on the wheel. I didn't want what you've done!' She turned to Reg. 'I need to talk to my people. We're all in deep shit now and we're in it together.'

Reg nodded and escorted her back to the cells.

Clyde watched as Thom was busy on his communicator. When he'd finished, he beckoned Clyde over.

'What do you want to do with him?' Thom gestured toward Sampson.

'Shove him in solitary. No visitors unless we approve. That goes for his mother too,' Clyde replied. 'What was the call about?'

Thom smiled. 'Let's get him sorted and then I'll show you.' He issued instructions to his team regarding Sampson. Clyde dispersed the other teams to perform roving patrols of the most sensitive areas of the complex.

Thom turned. 'Walk this way.'

'If I walked like that, I'd be arrested.' Clyde laughed and fell into step beside his friend.

# TWENTY TWO

Fifteen minutes later, Clyde and Thom arrived at the main operations centre.

They were greeted by the operation chief, Madeline O'Mara. 'We've just launched the cloud and we're sending a few drones out in the meantime,' she announced. 'It'll take the cloud nearly three hours to get on station.'

'Don't worry, I know about clouds,' Clyde replied. He sensed O'Mara didn't believe him and began to explain. 'A cloud is a lighter-than-air ship; basically, a hi-tech blimp. Used primarily as a sensor platform. Has a crew of twenty, working in equal shifts, and can stay in position for weeks at a time. They also were used as refuelling stations. I didn't know you had one.'

'Actually, we have four,' O'Mara added 'three remotes and this manned version. One is currently down for repairs and the other two remotes are deployed, so we launched our only manned unit. The drones will cover much of the area until it reaches its operating location and we have every sonar and hydrophone station online. If anything moves out there, we'll know it.' O'Mara was obviously proud of the units under her command.

'Thanks, Madeline. We'll be in tactical if anyone asks.' Thom guided Clyde through two sets of security doors and into a large, almost empty room. The floor was four meters below them as they entered the room. Darkness was quickly thwarted as the lights came on. The room was twenty meters square and a series of gantries crossed it. The walls below and above were covered with computer hardware and a number of very large screens.

'I'm familiar with this room,' Clyde said softly. 'Don't know how, but I recognise it.' He moved to one of the consoles, entered a code, activating the viewing system. The floor seemed to glow and the lights dimmed. Moments later, the floor looked like an ocean. Clyde entered more into the terminal and a grid pattern covered the ocean.

Clyde activated the intercom. 'Ops!'

'O'Mara here.'

'Madeline, can you feed your data into the tactical system?' Clyde asked.

'I can, but we can't get that system working.' Her voice sounded wary.

'Well, Clyde got it working, so send the data and get in here,' Thom responded, sounding like an excited schoolboy.

Seconds later, the scene changed. The feed was now coming directly from the three drones speeding toward their patrol zone. Any sounds from the sonar/hydrophone network were digitized and displayed as varying-coloured dots. Black was for very large biologicals, such as whales; blue for smaller fish species, and red for mechanical signals. So far only black and blue were visible.

On the wall opposite was a large screen; Clyde activated it and brought up the map. Australia was in the far-left corner and their island network showed as being approximately six thousand kilometres to the northeast. Onto this, he superimposed the flight path of the drones, the image just changing as O'Mara entered.

'How...?'

'I could tell you, but I'd have to shoot you,' Clyde joked. 'I somehow knew the code.'

'How could you? We've been trying for years, and we failed all the time.' O'Mara stood, hands on hips, her demeanour demanding an answer.

'That's obvious,' Thom replied. 'He's been here before.' He looked at Clyde; an explanation was needed. 'Clyde used to be SAS and after that a special group that was sometimes based here, that's all we know but Reg might know more.'

O'Mara nodded slowly. 'But to remember the code, to even have the code, says you were very senior. And you don't remember more?'

Clyde shook his head. 'No, not really; I get flashes sometimes, like when I remembered the code, but that's all. That part of my life is still locked away. One day maybe I'll remember.'

They went back to studying the data coming through, but Clyde had a feeling they were missing something. 'Do we have any more drones?'

'Yes, quite a lot, but we don't have the crews to man them constantly,' O'Mara answered.

'If I remember correctly, they have a swarm feature—they can operate independently, correct?' O'Mara nodded and Clyde continued. 'From what Sampson said, and the fact that he has been sending the location signal for quite some time, I don't think this is where they'll come from. It's too obvious.'

Clyde scoured the map, and then he put a new course into it, from Sydney, passing to the east of New Zealand, then to the island. 'No, this is the course I'd take. Look closely. The listening system is weakest here and we assumed they would take the quickest route, but I'll bet they are on this course, and fairly close by now.' He turned to O'Mara. 'How quickly can you get those drones in the air?'

'Ten minutes.'

'Good, then get cracking. I have a bad feeling we've been blindsided. I'll send you the course I think they should take at maximum spacing to cover the most area.'

Clyde began to enter the course data as the door opened and Reg stepped inside. 'O'Mara, move the cloud as well. Make sure it covers the area I've just sent you,' Clyde called.

She hesitated, looking at Reg for an answer.

'You heard him. Do what he said,' Reg replied to her unspoken question. He let O'Mara pass and closed the door after her. 'Well Clyde, you seem to have started something. I'd like to hear what.'

'I know we are wrong looking out there.' Clyde pointed to the original search area. 'It's just too obvious and we now know they've had weeks to get into position.' He brought up another image. This time the island complex was shown on the floor, with twenty kilometres of ocean around it.

'Here is where we have been thinking the attack will come from, but...' he enhanced the western side of the island, 'here is where I'd try and infiltrate. What assets do you have there?'

Reg didn't answer; it was Thom who had the information. 'Not much. Because of the terrain we never gave it much thought. I think the previous occupants had more, but we've never had the time or the people to find out.'

Clyde looked like he was about to burst. Something was bothering him, something deep in his psyche. He knew much more, but those memories were blocked and it was very confusing. Sometimes he would remember the strangest things, like the code, then other things that he wanted to remember, still eluded him. 'Look, I know I've been here. I know that I even ran ops from here, but for the fucking life of me any real memories are gone and I need them now!' He glared at Reg. 'What happened to my memory? What in the name of God did you do to me?'

'Steady on,' Thom said. 'Remember, any of us who were brought forward have differing degrees of memory loss – me included.'

'Bullshit. You've got most of yours back,' Clyde spat back.

'Yeah, and I've been here a bloody lot longer than you. It came back gradually,' Thom said.

'Stop it, both of you. The last thing we need is you two falling out. Thom's right—his memory came back in stages but there may be a way to get yours back quicker, although you need to consider this. The process could send you mad, totally psychotic. It's happened before and we ended up having to euthanize that person, so you better be sure it's what you want.' Reg's stern tone caused Clyde to stand back.

Clyde spoke softly. 'Reg, if there are things that I know but can't remember, things that may help win this coming battle, then I think the risks are worth it.'

'Maybe you need to discuss this with Bonnie first?' Reg suggested

'Discuss what with Bonnie?' No one had been watching the door as Bonnie entered. 'Just what are you three planning?'

Clyde stood, no words coming to him. Reg inclined his head toward the door; Thom took his cue and followed.

'Well, that's telling, those two leaving. Just what is going on Clyde?' She watched the door close behind the other two.

Clyde cleared his throat. 'I'm going to have Reg restore my memory,' he stated quietly.

'Oh, are you?' Bonnie stood defiantly. 'And when did we make this decision?'

Clyde started to move toward her, but her raised right hand stopped him in his tracks. 'It's the only solution,' he said. 'I know I've been here before. I know I have much more information hidden deep down, information that may just be the key to beating Clements. I have to do it!'

Clyde finished believing his logic was sound, but Bonnie wasn't interested in his logic. 'You really thought this through.' She held her hand up again, stopping Clyde's interjection dead. 'We are stuck here, you know that. There's no way we can ever return and we agreed that we'd start a new life here together. The first chance you get you want to bring back the past; revert to whoever you think you may have been. Well, what about us? Where do we fit in with your new assumption? You don't bloody well know, do you?

'We know the process is dangerous. In fact, it has never been done successfully. Did Reg tell you that?' Clyde looked away. 'Look at me, you big fool!' she commanded. 'Let's look at the most likely scenario. You have the procedure, go insane and have to be shot. Where does that leave us? Where does it leave me? Bloody hell Clyde, I thought we had started something!' Her eyes were now full of tears.

'I have to do it,' he blurted out. 'It may be the only way to save the island.'

'Bullshit,' Bonnie shot back. 'You're starting to believe all the bullshit about yourself. You think that nobody but the great Clyde can save the day! You arrogant arsehole! How about thinking of me for a moment? We made a pact and now you just want to throw it away, just so you can play Dudley fucking Do-right. Sorry, but you'll be playing it alone.'

Bonnie turned and walked to the door, but stopped when an alarm started to chime. The insistent sound brought both of them back to reality. Clyde went to the main console. 'It's too late anyway... they're almost here.'

The door opened and Thom and Reg entered, looking at the group of red dots showing on the floor display.

'Looks like our visitors are getting close,' Thom said as he worked a console, changing the display to now include distance measurement.

'That makes your idea a bit redundant, Clyde,' Reg said quietly. 'They're too close to risk the process.'

Clyde didn't answer. He stood still, like a lump of rock. His breathing had slowed and his eyes were fixed on some point a thousand meters away. Bonnie moved to his side, took his hand, and whispered to him. His eyes slowly regained focus and his breathing increased. Finally, he moved, taking Bonnie's hand and drawing her to him. No words were spoken; they just stood clinging to each other like their lives depended on the contact.

Bonnie slowly eased away from Clyde, looking directly into his eyes. 'You remember something?'

Clyde nodded, the memories starting to come back faster now. 'Yes, I know how to beat them – how long, Thom?'

'They should be in range early tomorrow morning, why?' Thom replied.

Clyde grinned. 'Time for us to go shark hunting,' he moved to the large wall map of the island. 'Reg, have you explored this part of the complex?'

Reg shook his head. 'Not really. We know it's there, but we just don't have the people to do everything. There is a rail line that goes there and I believe a road tunnel, but I don't know much more.'

'Well, you're about to find out a hell of a lot more. Have the ops group man this room. Alpha, Bravo, and Echo teams come with us, the others stay here and remain on watch,' Clyde said as he turned to Bonnie. 'You were right. Sorry, I sometimes get delusions of grandeur.' His words were rewarded with a gentle punch to the ribs.

'Come on, let's get moving. Let's see what else you have remembered.' Bonnie led the way out of the room.

***

Three personnel carriers left the ops centre at speed, Clyde driving the lead truck. They drove towards the west, taking roadways and tunnels that were rarely used, until they reached a blockage.

Clyde pulled the heavy vehicle to a standstill, left the driver's seat, and opened the side door. He walked from the vehicle to inspect what was hindering their progress; Thom and Reg were close behind.

'Well, that's it. This must be as far as the road was built,' Reg said, his voice filled with disappointment.

'You reckon?' Clyde threw in.

Reg's initial assessment seemed correct. The road stopped at the solid rock wall, evidence of tunnelling staring them in the face.

Clyde pushed past the others and approached the rock wall to his left. He started to move slowly along it, looking for something. A few minutes later he stopped, placed his hand on a smooth, rounded rock protruding from the wall, and pushed it. It moved, retracting into the wall and another section slid down to reveal a security access point.

Clyde placed his hand on the scanner and waited. A small ocular reader opened and he placed his left eye on the scanner.

'*Welcome, Colonel Pearson,*' a computerized voice said. At the same time, an electric motor started to hum and the rock wall blocking their path slid slowly to the left, revealing a complete tunnel.

Clyde felt a hand on his shoulder. 'Well, Colonel Pearson, shall we continue?' Bonnie's voice had a slightly sarcastic edge to it, but her smile told him a different story. 'Now we know your last name, the rest should be easy.'

They resumed their journey. Clyde knew which branch to take when there was a choice. Finally, he stopped the vehicle outside another set of doors, repeated the ID process, and access to the section was granted. This time progress was slower, the sounds coming from beyond the door indicating some sort of air transfer.

'All these sections would have been set to auto maintenance and care when they were closed down', Clyde explained. 'All the air would be removed and replaced with inert gas, no corrosion and no degradation of the systems, and the power system is fully autonomous once shut down is initiated.'

As they entered the building, lights came on illuminating their path, revealing another tunnel; this time only large enough for a small ground transport or pedestrians. Clyde turned left or right whenever an intersection was found and everyone followed.

It took about fifteen minutes to reach his destination. He stopped outside a set of familiar-looking doors, except the inscription was different. UUV CONTROL was emblazoned on the doors.

'This is what we need,' Clyde said as he accessed the door control. Once again, they were delayed as the air inside was changed. The lights came on as they entered, revealing the control room. 'Right, Reg, can you access the comm system and get O'Mara on the line? Echo One, I want a full sweep of this place ASAP.'

He pulled up a schematic on a console. 'Use this to plan your op. Bravo One, below us there is what looks like a hangar. I need to know what assets we have in there. Now, before anything happens, you all need some security clearance, so just give me a few minutes.'

Clyde moved away to another console and began entering commands. Soon he had what he wanted and called Thom, Bonnie, and Allison to him. 'This is where we may have an issue. Down here, I'm the only one who has total clearance. Don't ask why, we don't have time. So I'm setting you three up with the next level of access. The others will have the access they need, but no more.'

He was interrupted by O'Mara's voice over the comm. 'Reg, what's going on? We've just lost control of everything including God's Eye.'

'Now it hits the fan,' Clyde whispered, and then took the comm. 'Madeline, the system now recognizes me as the senior military commander on the base. All control functions for all military and covert systems come through me. Don't worry; I'll reinstate control in a couple of minutes.' He looked across at Reg; he was trying to access the terminal. 'Won't work Reg, you don't have the clearance, yet. Just give me a few minutes and it'll be fixed. Please send me the list of people and their function to this terminal.'

Clyde watched as names and functions began streaming over his terminal. As quickly as possible, he sorted people into groups, allocated relevant clearance, and activated their profiles. O'Mara, he gave Green Two clearance to, the same as Bonnie and Allison. Thom got Green One clearance, just one step below Clyde, but Reg was the sticking point. Clyde still had trust issues, —even though Reg had showed he could be an asset— so he decided to limit any and all of the academic and political group to Blue Two level.

'There, Madeline. Everyone is back online.'

'With one exception – it appears you, and you alone, have total control. Why?' O'Mara asked.

'For the moment, that's the way it needs to be.' Clyde refused to enter a discussion.

Reg's support was a surprise. 'Madeline, it's for the best. Believe me, I know why this is happening and I agree totally with Clyde's actions; just follow his orders!'

'Okay, everyone knows their function. Let's get moving; we don't have much time.' These words from Clyde saw everyone resume their jobs. 'Madeline, I'd like you here. Can you prepare a team to join you and another to run ops there?'

'Affirmative, give me half an hour.'

'No rush, we'll be there to escort you in about an hour,' Clyde responded. He turned to Bonnie. She was working on the console and, as he moved to her side, the huge view screen covering the wall in front of the banks of workstations came to life. It didn't show much, but at least she'd got it working.

'Bonnie, can you and Allison return and pick up O'Mara and her team?'

'No problem... when?' Bonnie asked.

'I gave her an hour to get prepped.'

Reg was now behind Clyde. 'I'll go with them. You're going to need supplies and mess staff and I can still organize that.' He held up his hand to silence Clyde's comment. 'I know why you did what you did. I'd have done exactly the same thing, so let me help where I can.'

Clyde nodded and thanked Reg as Bonnie led the others out the doors.

# TWENTY THREE

Like the Island community, Edmund Clements lacked people.

There were many old Australian naval vessels he could use, but the lack of people and skills made it difficult. His rag-tag fleet was now approaching the island chain; another twelve hours would see them arrive.

Edmund watched as another RIB deposited the last of his commanders on the deck. *Show time*, he thought as he turned for the bridge door. While his fleet was made up of commercial vessels or pleasure boats, it still looked impressive. Twelve ships, all converted to a more sinister purpose, bristling with machine guns, and a few rocket launchers on the larger trawlers, made for serious firepower.

Three of the large trawlers had been stripped of all their fishing apparatus and converted to carry a number of RIBs and personnel to fill them – his assault force. In all, he could land one hundred and fifty people at one time using the twenty RIBs from what he called his assault ships. His one regret was not being able to use the ships the old navy had left tied up when the world fell apart.

Edmund shook off the feeling and started down the passageway toward his meeting room. Moving quickly in the narrow passageways was not possible. Sometimes, Edmund regretted not spending more time exercising, but at sixty eight, he believed that a little extra bulk came with the territory. Regardless, he still made good time, arriving just as the last group commander entered the room. There was no leaping to attention. No one moved, just as Edmund wanted it.

He greeted the room. 'Good afternoon,' a chorus of replies followed.

'Now for the good news – we're very close to our objective!' He pointed to the rough model on the table. Instead of taking a seat, he preferred to move around the room as he talked, believing it gave him a better insight into his people. 'Our agents on the island were able to provide enough information for us to build this model. As you can see, there are no active defences, and if there were, they have the same issue as we do—not enough people to man them. So what does this mean to us?'

He paused to allow anyone to answer. One took the bait, a young man whose eagerness to impress his commander showing in his demeanour and enthusiasm. 'We'll have an easy ingress, no resistance.'

Clements smiled. 'A wonderful thought but don't get complacent. Remember our objective. We must take this facility. They have the equipment we need if we are to solve the problems facing us. So listen up—the equipment is of paramount importance, and second to this, the Garibaldis. Save them if we can. Everyone else is expendable. But the equipment must not be damaged. Is that clear?'

A chorus of agreement ranged around the table.

'Good, now we will be in position to launch the RIBs by three tomorrow morning. Make sure your teams get a good night's sleep, it might be their last for a few days.' Clements retrieved a tray holding glasses and a large decanter. He poured everyone a good measure of the amber fluid and raised his glass.

'To success and our new world order – remember, we are the future of the human race so we **must** succeed!' Clements said reverently.

'To success and our new world order!' The mantra was echoed by all as they drained their glasses. The meeting continued with logistic reports and a final run of their attack scenario.

The target side of the island, while seemingly undefended, still caused problems. Steep sheer cliff faces, dangerous reefs, and rock outcrops left only one area that could be used. A small, crescent-shaped beach was the only possible place the force could land.

The downside was the possibility of defense. Even a small squad could hold the beach against a superior force, such was the topography. The success of the mission now rested on the accuracy of their Intel.

The meeting broke up with each commander returning to their troops and Clements heading for his stateroom, the plan for the next day playing continuously in his head.

***

In the makeshift operations centre, a sonar operator thought he picked up something.  He interrogated the system and started to track the object, breathing a sigh of relief as he cancelled the tracing.

'Do we have a problem, Sailor?' The watch commander asked.

'No Sir, just another glitch. Thought I had a contact; turned out to be a biological, probably a shark.'

'Well, at least you caught it and identified it. Well done.'

* * *

Thom shook his head in disbelief. 'You just sent that Drone Shark directly under them and they didn't see it; bloody amazing' He had been watching the data transmission from the UUV that had just passed under the attacking fleet. When the data indicated that the unit had been detected, he thought the whole shark thing was over. But he was amazed when it passed behind the felt and looked to Clyde for the answer.

'UUVs mimic a shark in almost every way. Their outer she l is similar to shark skin and the way they move, everything says shark... that's just what we want them to see,' Clyde answered with pride.

Any further discussion was interrupted as O'Mara and her team arrived. 'We're here, but I really don't know where *here* is.'

'This part of the installation is purely military. More of my memory is returning and this is what came back this time. The computer knows me as Colonel Pearson and I have full access, but I still don't know how or why,' Clyde replied. 'I do know that I need you and your team manning things so I can run the battle.'

'You're sure there'll be a battle?' O'Mara asked, her voice betraying her concern.

Clyde nodded and beckoned her to follow him. They moved into a separate, small room where Thom activated a hologram of the island.

'We're certain they'll attack here, probably early tomorrow morning. It looks like an easy target, but in reality, it's the only place they can land. We have a squad down there now, digging in. Believe me, tomorrow, Clements is getting a big surprise!'

'I'll get the team set up. O'Mara replied. 'We'll have this place humming in no time.' She smiled as she left and Clyde noticed she had a different stance, one of more confidence. He was grateful for that; it meant that any further explanation wasn't needed.

Clyde turned back to Thom and the hologram. 'Okay Thom, what've we got?'

'Heaps and heaps but given the timeframe, I think the sharks are the best option. They're easy to pilot, they can run autonomously if we need them to, and they pack a punch. Some of the other stuff... it'd take too long to work them out.'

He changed the display to show what he had in mind. Clyde watched the scenario run, appreciation for the ability of his deputy growing each second. 'This is what I'd do...run a dozen of them autonomously, with another six under human control, mainly as backup. If we get them into position early enough, Clements will pass right over them without realizing what's below him, as we've just demonstrated. Even with larger numbers, it'll just look like a pack of sharks.' Thom chuckled.

'It's your baby, you run it!' Clyde was about to continue when he saw Alpha Two striding toward the room.

'We're dug in, we took Bravo's SSMG, but we're terribly short on ammo.' The haste with everything the day before had caused issues with supply. 'We all thought we were just policing, so we only took a couple of mags each.'

'Do you know what you need?' Clyde asked.

'Yes Sir, I have a full requisition in my head.'

'Right, go see Echo One. She has the run of the place. She'll escort you to the armoury. Take whatever you need. Do you have enough guns?'

'Yes Sir, the way we've set things up any more would see us crossing fields of fire too much. It'd be counterproductive.'

The confidence in the man's voice told Clyde things were running as he wanted. 'Good... but remember, Echo team is available if you need them; and you have a new call sign. You're now Alpha One.'

'Thanks, Clyde. You won't regret this,' he said and left.

Thom clapped Clyde on the back. 'A few weeks ago, these guys were a rabble. Just look at them now.'

'Yeah, but it's about to get real. That's when we'll separate the chaff from the hay.' Clyde's voice carried concern. Somewhere in the depths of his mind he had doubts, believing he had seen situations like this before. But the die was now cast and they were all committed.

* * *

Bonnie and Allison returned from their second trip to the main complex in separate vehicles. Allison drove a personnel carrier filled with support staff, cooks, cleaners, maintenance personnel;

the backbone of any operation. If the troops weren't fed or looked after, then the whole operation would fall over.  She also had three medical people who would assist Bonnie if needed.

Bonnie drove a large transport loaded with food and everything needed to keep the place running. She reversed the truck into a loading dock and leaped out of the cab. She ran to the dock and straight to the nearest restroom. Allison saw this and decided to follow her, entering the bathroom to the sound of Bonnie retching into a toilet bowl.

'Bonnie, are you OK?' Allison called, only to be rewarded with more heaving from the cubicle.

'I'll be out in a minute,' Bonnie replied weakly. Shortly after, the sound of the toilet flushing announced Bonnie was returning. She went to the basin and washed her face, rinsing her mouth at the same time.

Allison moved to her side and held her palm on Bonnie's forehead. 'Are you OK? Maybe you picked up some bug. Maybe it's something from the inoculations...' Her voice trailed off and her face changed, as realisation dawned on her. 'Bullshit. You're pregnant, aren't you?'

Bonnie turned to look at her. Allison spoke enthusiastically. 'You are, aren't you?'

'I'm not sure. I'm two weeks late, but it could be a false alarm. Please don't say anything, Allison, promise me you won't say anything.'

'So you haven't told Clyde yet?'

'No, not until I'm sure. Now promise me you won't say a word!' Bonnie demanded.

'All right, I promise, but under protest.' Allison smiled as she spoke. 'Damn, I suppose that puts an end to our threesome.'

'Hey, I might be having a baby, I'm not becoming a nun,' Bonnie said as they both burst into laughter.

When the laughter had subsided, Allison looked at Bonnie. 'Now I know why you got so pissed when Clyde wanted to go through the reversal procedure. Maybe you should tell him before he has another delusion of grandeur and offers to sacrifice himself again.

'No, not until after this thing is over. If I tell him now, he'd just ship me back to the complex. I think I'd be better here watching him, just in case,' Bonnie answered.

'Come on then, let's get back.' Allison replied and they left for the control room.

* * *

At 02:00, Clements rose from his bed. He quickly dressed and headed for the ops room. It still held a slight odour of freshly caught fish, reminding him of its hard-working history.

He checked with the sonar and radar operators—all clear. Next, he consulted the hydrophones operator, but with the ship still at full speed, his equipment was almost useless.

'It seems we are still on track and undetected. Thank you all. I'll be on the bridge if you need me.' He turned and left. Next call was to the galley, where he ordered a snack of ham and cheese melt and coffee for himself and also a plate of mixed toasted sandwiches for both the ops crew and the bridge.

He opened the door and stepped onto the bridge. 'Morning all, I trust everything's okay?'

'Morning, Mister Clements,' the captain, Phillip Davis, responded. 'All seems quiet and we're on schedule. It seems you made the right decision.'

Clements knew he was referring to the longer voyage. 'Hopefully, we'll see the benefit of the extra few days. By the way, I ordered a plate of toasted sandwiches for the bridge, should be here soon.' Clements smiled; satisfied that everything was progressing as it should.

***

Clyde stood at the rear of the ops control room, watching the game play out.

'The cloud is now on station. Recalling the drones for refuelling,' one of the operators called.

O'Mara approached Clyde. 'We have six wasps armed and ready. They can be on target in twenty minutes.'

'Excellent Madeline, keep them on standby. We may need them a little later.'

Clyde reviewed everything. So far, they were fully prepared. He couldn't think of anything else he needed to do. 'Right everyone, now we wait. I know this is the worst time but don't let your imagination get the better of you. We just need to do our jobs.'

But his thoughts were anything but confident. Something was nagging at the back of his mind.

# TWENTY FOUR

E dmund Clements felt a swell of pride as he watched the RIBs launch.

Almost as one unit, their engines started and they peeled away from their respective mother ships and formed up into a staggered five-by-four pattern. Soon all he could see were the remnants of the boats' wakes.

He checked his watch—03:15. Another twenty minutes and his first wave would be ashore. The RIBs would then return and be loaded with the necessary stores and support personnel; they should leave the flotilla just before five. Everything was running on time. Clements grinned and walked back to the bridge.

A fresh pot of coffee had just arrived from the galley. Clements took a mug and filled it with the steaming brew; he turned to the captain. 'Captain Davis, in twenty minutes; reduce speed to slow. Please inform the other ships.' He moved to the port side of the bridge and sat on the lounge. The well-worn seat, a remnant of the ship's fishing past, had served as the captain's ready room when the fish were on.

Davis approached. 'Edmund, are things going as you planned?'

'My dear captain, at this stage, I would say an emphatic yes but, as with any military incursion, it remains fluid. Our main advantage is our intelligence. Our friend on the island has given us a great chance of success. So, to answer your question directly, yes, things are going as planned.' Clements studied the bridge crew for a few moments, noting a slight change in their stance and smiled. As he hoped, his confidence had infected them all.

***

Clyde was pacing; something he'd started doing as more responsibility was passed to him. He felt something touch his arm.

Bonnie was beside him, her left hand resting on his right forearm. 'What's wrong? You're like a caged lion.'

Clyde stopped and stared at the screen. 'Look at this madness. The world is decimated, billions dead and here we are starting another fucking war, and for what – a possible solution – something that in the fullness of time **might** offer a glimmer of hope? And how many will we kill to achieve it? Since we arrived, we've done our fair share of killing. How many were on that freighter?'

He was starting to sermonize, but Bonnie stopped him. 'All right, what do you intend to do about it? Just stand here and deliver a sermon? Or did you have something real in mind?' Her hands were firmly on her hips, her lips slightly pursed, telling Clyde that he'd better have a solution, not just a whinge. When she had this look, Clyde knew he better deliver.

He started to calm down, his mind ticking over silently. 'I've got a solution; get Reg on the blower!' He moved to the comm unit. 'Echo One from ops... come in.'

Echo One responded to his hail.

'Echo One, hostiles are inbound, twenty mikes out. We need to modify our strategy. Come back to ops double time!' Clyde left no opening for a refusal as he cut the link.

'I have Reg,' Bonnie chimed in, unsure what was happening.

Clyde reached for the unit and thanked her. 'Reg, this is Clyde. We're changing our strategy, here's what I want you to do.' He moved away from Bonnie and continued in hushed tones.

Allison entered as Bonnie sagged into a chair. 'Bonnie, are you all right?'

'Just a little dizzy; I'll be fine in a moment,' Bonnie assured her.

Echo One entered and waited in the doorway. Bonnie beckoned her over and called to Clyde. He turned and finished his conversation. 'I don't give a rat's arse – do as I ask or suffer. Remember, I have control now. Echo One, show me your disposition.'

Echo One moved to the console and brought up the beach, superimposed the layout of her men and equipment, and stood back.

'Five rows of mines... and they're remote?' Clyde asked.

'Yes, standard anti-personnel units.'

'Good, here's our new strategy; I don't want to kill anyone unless there's no other alternative.' Clyde's words brought a look of relief to the team leader. 'First, we've got to stop any retreat,' he turned to Allison. 'Ali, race down to the armoury and bring back two Fostech mags and one hundred round mags loaded with explosive rounds.'

Allison nodded and ran for the door.

Clyde turned back to the screen. 'Here's what I believe they'll do.' Clyde spelled out his plan; Echo One appeared to get his strategy.

Allison arrived back as they finished and handed the two drum magazines to Clyde. He handed the mags to Echo One. 'Good luck!' She smiled, thanked Clyde, and left.

Bonnie looked at Clyde. 'Okay, what now?'

'Now we're in the hands of one Reg Denham. It's all down to him now.'

***

Reg Denham sat at the comm console in the central operations room, debating with himself. Clyde had just ordered him to do something he thought was stupid and a waste of time, but how could he refuse? Since he had activated the military section, Clyde had been in command and no one could override his commands.

As he battled his thoughts, Reg set the frequency on the comm system. As much as he disliked this idea, he had no option. He pressed the transmit button and started the call.

***

The insurgent force approached the beach; twenty RIBs took up their positions with four boats depositing their men at a time. The beach was narrow, making it impossible to all land at the same time; the others held back, behind the small breakers that signalled the fast shoaling of the beach bottom. Each RIB carried ten fighters and they quickly leapt from their boat and assumed covering positions while the boats changed their positions. More insurgents arrived and the first wave stayed in position while the new arrivals sprinted and took positions a few metres ahead of them. Their operation was smooth and efficient and it only took ten minutes for all two hundred to be deposited on the beach. The RIBs then moved to the southern end of the beach, while the insurgents ranged across the beach in a haphazard skirmish line.

The first indication of any action was the dual report of two Fostech shotguns. Two RIBs exploded. One had its bow torn open; the other took a direct hit on the stern. Both started to fill with water instantly. More reports were heard and three more RIBs were side-lined. Then there was silence as the gunners moved slightly, not a second too soon, as the twelve-millimetre machine guns from the remaining RIBs opened up.

Once again, the two Fostechs fired, and another three boats holed. One veered off course, its driver hit by shrapnel, slamming into another boat to its left, both exploding as one of the Fostech rounds hit a fuel tank. The area was now covered with a growing field of burning diesel fuel. Boat crews desperately tried to escape, but with the sea surrounding them now an inferno, none could and their screams were heard by all on the beach. The remaining boats tried to escape, but the wall of flames and the two Fostechs claimed all of them.

While all this was happening, the insurgents on the beach lost their purpose, the horror of what was happening on the water seemed to diminish their resolve. They began milling around unsure of what action to take.

Echo One watched, the horror of the scene not lost on her, or the team, but it was time for them to enter the fray. 'Now,' she called and her 2IC flicked the detonator to fire and hit the detonate button. A line of mines, just behind the insurgents exploded, spewing sand high into the air. The central SSMG opened up and sent a long burst across the front of the group, stitching a line of sand geysers across the whole beach. The insurgents turned back to the beach, trying to find where the attack was coming from. Their ranks broke; total confusion now reigned as they concentrated their positions trying to get closer to another human being, for some sort of psychological support.

Echo One picked up the microphone and switched it on. 'Attention, insurgent force, this is Eden Island Security!' She'd thought up the name on the spot, believing it sounded official. 'You have illegally invaded our territory. You will disarm yourselves or be destroyed. First, remove the magazines from your weapons and clear the breach. Next, throw all weapons and magazines back into the water...' She never finished her speech.

'Fuck off, bitch!' The words flew from one of the insurgents as he fired toward where the voice seemed to be coming from. All he did was blow foliage off a couple of trees and condemn his compatriots to death. As one of the three SSMGs began firing, the squad's 2IC activated and detonated the second row of mines, directly under the main body of the attackers.

Arms, legs, and other body parts flew in all directions, the mines doing their job with cold efficiency. The three SSMGs cut a swathe through the masses, inflicting horrendous damage as they fanned the area.

***

Clyde was watching from his command centre. 'CEASE FIRE!' he screamed into the comm system. But he quickly realised that this was a useless gesture. The noise of the battle, coupled with the huge adrenalin rush meant that no-one in Echo actually heard his command. Clyde had another memory flash; he'd seen scenarios like this before and he knew there was nothing he could do to stop it. He watched in impotent awe as the whole force was decimated in seconds.

***

Finally, Echo One managed to regain control and called a halt. The silence on the beach could almost be felt, only broken by the crackle of burning RIBs. She led her squad out from their cover and slowly walked through the carnage, checking for any life, but there was none. The ambush had been hideously successful—a full forty-five seconds of insanity—with the result now before them. Two survivors from the boats were swimming toward the beach. There was nowhere else to go; the water seaward was still burning. Two of the squad raced to help them out of the water, quickly restraining them.

Echo One was numb; strangely she felt nothing, no revulsion, no horror; just total numbness. The scene was surreal. The sand was mostly red and brown, with dead and destroyed bodies everywhere, some intact, others totally unrecognizable as a human being.

She looked to her left. Two of the toughest men in her command were vomiting. Still, she felt nothing. She regained some composure and called for a sound-off. All members were alive and none were wounded. Only a couple of the invaders had actually opened fire; the others had died before firing a shot. Further investigation showed that most still had their weapons switched to safe.

'*What a stupid fucking waste!*' she screamed as she turned to reorganize the squad.

***

Clements sat on his seat at the port side of the bridge. He understood his limitations and operating a boat was one of those, so he made sure to keep out of the way.

He checked his watch. The first boats should be about to land. He smiled; soon he would have control of the most powerful operation still in existence. His smile broadened into a huge grin. He knew he could soon be the most powerful man in the world. He would be free to mould society, or what was left of it, into his own vision.

His musings were interrupted by a call from the captain. 'Mister Clements, it seems you are being hailed on an amateur frequency.' The captain indicated for Clements to take the handset.

'Really? Put it on speaker,' Clements replied, intrigued by who could be calling.

'*Edmund Clements, this is Reg Denham on Eden Island. Please respond.*' The voice echoed around the bridge.

Clements chuckled. 'Seems our adversary wants to talk,' he couldn't hide the excitement this contact brought to him. 'Who knows – he may want to surrender.' He heard a murmur of approval from the bridge crew.

Clements stood and took the mic. 'Reginald Denham, this is Edmund Clements, it's been a long time since I heard your voice. How may I help you?' Clements couldn't hide the pompous arrogance in his voice.

'*Edmund, stop being a dick; call off your attack, you can't win!*'

'My dear Reg, I have no idea what you mean. What attack?'

'*The one you have committed twenty RIBs to, trying to land on Half Moon Beach on the western side of the island. The first boats have landed. Either you stop it and withdraw or we'll be forced to destroy them.*'

Clements got the sense that he had his opponents on the back foot. 'My dear Reginald, if we are indeed doing as you say, my suggestion would be for you and all your followers to surrender. I have superior forces, what can you possibly do to concern me?'

'*For one, we can destroy your small force, and then the fishing fleet you are following with.*'

Reg's words caused Clements to take a step back. How could they know about the make-up of his fleet? 'This is your last chance, Reginald. Surrender, or face the wrath of my forces.'

'*You were always an arrogant bloody fool, Clements. All your posturing will do is guarantee the deaths of everyone with you... is that what you want?*'

Clements thought he heard a hint of desperation in the voice on the radio and responded. 'This conversation is over. I'll see you very soon, and then we can discuss your surrender in person, Clements out.' He cut the comm and looked to Davis. 'Let them stew on that for a while.'

Clyde was listening to the conversation. '*Clements, this is Colonel Pearson, commander of the military installation you have foolishly tried to attack. Your landing force has been destroyed. Check and you will see burning RIBs and dead bodies. I give you thirty seconds to surrender or I will take out your entire flotilla.*'

The new voice caused Clements to stop. The person, whoever he was, was impersonating someone who Clements believed had died decades before. 'Do you want me to believe you are Colonel Benjamin Pearson? Sorry, whoever you are… he's dead,' Clements replied.

'*Twenty seconds.*'

'You have nothing. This is just a bluff. I'll deal with you later.' Clements' voice faltered slightly, his air of confidence was greatly diminished. If this was who the voice said it was, then there could be some problems.

'*Ten seconds; any last words, Clements?*' Clyde's voice was cold and devoid of any emotion.

'Yes, fuck you, whoever you are!' Clements shouted. He was angry at this development and also at himself for believing, even for a second, that the voice had anything behind it. Pearson was dead, he knew that for certain. He turned to the captain. 'Bring all ships to full speed – time to take the fight to them.'

His words were drowned out by a huge explosion to port. The pressure wave from it slammed into the large trawler, forcing it sideways and heeling it over to starboard.

'What the…' Clements cried.

'That was our main fuel ship. She's gone,' the captain replied. The flotilla had two trawlers converted to carry fuel, two others as munitions carriers. One of their fuel supply ships was a huge fireball.

Seconds later, there was another explosion, followed by thousands of smaller reports. 'They got one of the ammo carriers.'

*'Edmund Clements, will you surrender now?'* Clyde's voice cut through the cacophony on the bridge.

**'NEVER!'** Clements screamed.

Suddenly, three UAVs appeared and started a strafing run over the flotilla.

The three planes dove toward the ocean, their robot eyes coldly watching the targets, and transmitting the images back to the island. They opened fire, one drone for each line of vessels. The twin twenty millimetre multi-barrel guns mounted under their wings spat flame and armour piercing rounds toward the fast-approaching ships.

On board the lead vessel, Clements watched the first signs of the attack, having difficulty believing his eyes. Several small waterspouts erupted as the first rounds hit the water, then the drones found their target. Clements had set his flotilla in three lines, each vessel separated from the next by one hundred meters; an ideal setup for this attack.

'Where in the name of hell did these come from? Where's our radar? We should have had some warning!' Clements screamed; desperation now etched in his voice.

Each drone flew as slowly as it could to maximize its time on target. Even doing this, the run only took a few seconds and six more vessels were left burning. As the drones passed over the last ship, they broke to port and accelerated away, just as three more started their run from the rear.

This attack was even more frightening as all the defensive weapons had been turned forward; no-one expected a rear attack. The drones followed the first attack, in reverse order. Slowing as much as they could, their cannons cut a huge swathe down the length of the remaining vessels. The effectiveness of the attack was frightening—now only Clements' ship and one other were still under power. The others were in varying degrees of destruction. Fires raged on most and even Clements' was filled with holes and starting to take on water.

Clyde's voice again broke through all other sounds. *'Now will you surrender?'*

'Never! We will fight until our last breaths, our...' Clements' voice was cut off, replaced by a new one.

'Colonel, this is Captain Davis, commander of the lead vessel. We surrender, please call off the attack!' Clements stood, firmly held by two burly sailors, screaming and swearing at the captain.

Davis turned back to Clements. 'It's over Edmund; one more strafing run from those planes and we're all dead.' Clements stared belligerently at Davis, but the reality of what had happened in just a few minutes was all around them—burning ships, men frantically taking to life rafts, destruction everywhere.

Clements seemed to fold back into himself as the realization of his failure hit home. He tried to speak, but no words came.

One of the sailors produced a pair of large zip ties, fashioned them into rudimentary hand cuffs and restrained him. This final humiliation was drowned out by the sound of large rotors beating the sky. Three large twin rotor helicopters had arrived to assist with the rescue; Eden had more but not the crews to fly them. They hovered over the madness engulfing the sea below and winched survivors to safety.

Of Clements' twenty ships, 'Sea Otter' and 'Mermaid', were the only ones still under power. They were instructed to head for the island, under the watchful eye of the drones. Clyde sat watching the screen in front of him, showing the feed from six UUVs, the ones that had fired the first volley in the engagement. He could see them now lurking deep behind the two ships limping toward land. The first of the choppers passed overhead, returning to the island with survivors. It was to be the first of many trips that morning.

*** 

Captain Davis was directed towards what he thought was a rock outcrop, but as he got closer, he saw it was a concrete and rock pier. 'Clever, very clever,' he mumbled as they approached. To his left he saw the remnants of the RIBs, some still smouldering; and on the beach, lines of full body bags. A huge sadness seemed to crush the breath out of him. He averted his eyes and concentrated on bringing his crippled ship to the dock.

With both vessels now tied up, he saw a squad of military types approaching. Davis led Clements out of the wheelhouse and they climbed the few steps to the dock. The squad broke formation and took up positions along the dock, giving them a good field of fire over both ships. As this happened, two UUVs surfaced as a show of force. They were sinister as they rode low in the water, their forward torpedo tubes menacingly visible just below the surface. To add to the ceremony, both flights of drones passed low overhead; another show of power.

'I take the point,' Davis said as Clyde approached.

Clyde smiled. 'Captain Davis? And this must be Clements.'

'Correct, but I must ask... what is to be the fate of the crews?' Davis asked.

'First, we'll get them what medical treatment they need, then clothes and food. I'd like you and Clements to come with me. We need to work out a lasting solution to this dilemma.'

Clements turned to Clyde, with a look of total defeat and confusion. 'Colonel, how is it you're here? I remember reading about your death years ago.'

'Didn't anyone ever tell you not to believe everything you read? Now, please follow these two.' He ushered them behind Echo Three and Four, Bravo Three and Five bringing up the rear.

Clyde turned as Thom double timed up the dock. 'It appears that our ambush was bloody effective.'

Clyde shook his head. 'Maybe too effective; take over here. It's time to settle this mess once and for all.'

Thom nodded as Clyde fell in behind the squad marching toward the complex entrance.

# Twenty Five

Reg entered the conference room attached to the main security section. His surprise was evident when he saw who else was present.

'What's she doing here?' he asked Delta One indignantly.

'Clyde's orders; she's to be part of this,' Delta One replied.

Reg moved to the opposite side of the table and glared at the person opposite. Zuri Malabo simply smiled and shook her head.

It was three hours since Clyde had arranged this meeting and he was still absent. Reg was beginning to worry but the door opened and in walked Clyde. Behind him, escorted by four guards, was Edmund Clements.

'Reg, Zuri, I believe you both know Edmund?' Clyde announced as he took his seat. Edmund was directed to the seat at Reg's side. Clyde sat beside Zuri. 'I think we can dispense with the restraints. After all, the only ones with guns are you guys.' The escort agreed and removed both sets of restraints. Clements had just been freed when the Garibaldis entered the room and took seats at the table.

'Now, let's get started. Edmund and I have had a good long talk and there are a few interesting developments you both need to know.' Clyde turned to his prisoner. 'Edmund, the floor is yours.'

Clements cleared his throat and took a swig from the glass of water in front of him before starting. 'First, I'm not going to apologize for anything I've done. There's too much history for that. I know you want to obtain a sample of the base virus to try and reverse the sterility problem we have. You have the equipment but no virus. I have the virus and no equipment. Believe it or not, it was all destroyed when the shit hit the fan.' The animosity in the room was palpable, but he still continued.

'One thing you don't know is that Mustafa survived. He came to Australia, located me and we started the dance all over again. He secured my wife and daughter. She's fourteen now, and said that if I didn't take this installation, he'd give my daughter to his men as a sex toy.'

'Bullshit. You're so fucking full of it, Edmund. Always have been,' Reg yelled. 'And let's face it… who cares if this is true? Look at what you've done to the world. Sorry, but this tearjerker of a story means absolutely jack.'

Clyde stood and called for calm. 'Reg, I know how you feel, but hear him out.'

'What the hell do you know? You didn't live through what he did.' Reg glared at Clyde. 'And in any case, just who in the hell do you think you are, telling me what to do?'

Clyde spoke quietly but firmly. 'I'm the guy who just saved your arse and I'm also the guy who has total control of this installation. In other words, Reg, for the moment, I'm the damn boss, so shut up, sit down and listen. When you've heard everything, then we'll decide what to do, okay?'

Begrudgingly, Reg sat and remained quiet.

Clyde turned to Clements. 'Please continue.'

Clements started and took the next hour to describe what had transpired and what was supposed to happen now.

At the end Reg spoke. 'So you're supposed to call Mustafa when you secure the complex, then he'll bring the live virus here so you can start work?'

'That's correct.'

'And how is he getting here?' Zuri asked.

'We have a large seaplane. He was to use that to bring the virus and twenty more men, more as his body guard than to secure the compound. Then another flotilla is to bring the rest of his people and this base would be his.' Edmund said.

'And what happens to our people?' Reg demanded.

Clements didn't answer.

Clyde entered the fray. 'That's not important now. Here's how I think we should proceed. We clean up the mess from the battle, have Edmund call Mustafa and delay him for a couple of days; we can't risk any longer. While this is going on, Edmund will keep up a steady report schedule and then declares he has the island. And don't worry; he'll be using a script we'll write, so we'll be in full control of the dialogue. Any attempt to warn Mustafa, Edmund dies.' He turned to Clements. 'What was your original timetable?'

'Forty-eight hours max. After that, Mustafa will launch his own attack.'

'Okay, let's say we use an extra thirty-six as our base. Reg. get crews organized to speed up the clean-up; nothing perfect—it must look like a battle ground. We lure Mustafa here, take the virus and his people, free your family and send a patrol to intercept his flotilla. Sounds too easy, I know,' Clyde admitted, 'but I don't have any other ideas.'

Clements looked at the others. 'Reg, Anton, Zena... once we were friends, colleagues. We even worked on projects together. We can do that again. Together, I believe we can sort the mess out, or at least we can give it a good try. Look, I realise you have problems with trusting me, but you all know my family, know that I'd do anything for them, and I know you would do the same if you were in my situation.'

'But to weaponise our work – it was supposed to protect us all, not kill us!' Zena said, emotion welling in her voice. 'And yes, I know Lilah and Salma and I sympathize, but look at how many have died. You knew just how violent and insane Ahmed was. You must have known how much damage your mutation would cause, and still you obeyed. Forgive me if I seem less than enthusiastic at your proposition.' she stopped, as if considering something. 'Edmund, do you know exactly where the virus is?'

'Yes, where it has always been—in the bunker under the old John Hunter Hospital. Your last infiltration was so close they could have almost touched it,' Clements replied.

Zena looked back at Reg and the others and her eyes filled with tears. Her voice was heavy as she spoke. 'Then we have the only true solution—the Wrath of God.'

Reg looked as if he had been physically hit. 'We can't.'

'But we must. For the sake of everyone, we must!' Zena cried passionately.

'No, you misunderstand,' Reg replied. 'We simply can't access the system. It's locked and we don't have the code.'

Silence fell on the room as all eyes turned to Clyde. 'But he does,' Reg announced. 'Do you remember anything about it?

Clyde responded. 'Not much, just words, things like it's a partner to God's eye and the sword, another part of the weapon system. How did you even know it existed?'

'We managed to unlock some files about the system; nothing specific. All it told us was that there was a massively efficient weapon system attached to the eye,' Reg answered.

'But you don't know what the weapon is?' Clyde asked.

'No, we assumed it was some sort of nuclear device.'

Clyde sat back; his eyes seemed to be focussing on a distant object. The fact was his memories were surfacing much quicker now, and not always in the most convenient situations. After several minutes, he started to re-focus on the room and those in it.

'Now I remember. Wrath is a whole lot more than a nuke; in fact, it makes nukes look like Stone Age weapons. If we use it, it'll vaporize everything in the area to a depth of at least one hundred meters; no sound, no radiation, just total destruction. We could use it against the lab but, if my memory is right, not only will it destroy everything deep down, it will have a destruction radius of up to twenty kliks.' Clyde spoke with authority.

'How do you know all this?' Clements asked.

'I was in charge of this project before...' he stumbled; something from his past was still blocked. 'Anyway, I'm probably the only person alive who can operate it, and I'll tell you this ...I don't want to. I'd rather try the other way.' In the end it would be up to the council to decide, not him, and he was thankful for that.

Reg stood and faced the others. 'I'll call a meeting of the council this afternoon. Clyde, how soon can the weapon be ready?'

Clements cried. 'My family, you'll be killing them. Please, no!'

'And how many of us were you prepared to kill?' Reg hissed through clenched teeth. 'You were willing to kill us all. Remember the billions you have already killed or relegated to a slow and lingeringly hopeless death? You did that and justified all those deaths by conning yourself into thinking you were doing it to save your family, but how many families had to die for that, how many mothers had to watch their children die horrendously, and you want us to feel some sort of compassion for you? Given your actions, that's a big ask.' He looked at Clyde. 'Now, are you going to work with the council or try and institute a military dictatorship?'

Clyde returned Reg's stare. 'I never wanted this, but you forced it on me. I have done what you required; I have routed the attack and brought Clements before you to tell his side of the story. In essence, I'm just the muscle, but you are the elected leader of the council, and whatever the council decides, I'll abide by. If we're to have any future, military control isn't going to be part of it.'

Reg held his hand out. 'Thank you.' Clyde shook it.

Clyde called to the guards. 'Return Edmund to the brig. He sees and speaks to no one, got it?'

One of the guards replaced the restraints before taking Clements into formation. Two guards led, followed by Clements, with two guards at the rear.

Clyde checked the time, 15:30. He had missed lunch and so had his prisoner. He called to the guards and ordered them to make sure their charge was fed; then headed back to his op centre.

***

*Thirteen; what a bloody rotten number*, Reg thought as he watched the other twelve members of the council take their seats; even Malabo was present. There was no part of the constitution that they could use to preclude her as she was a formal member of the council. This was something Reg made a mental note to look into.

The council room was finely furnished with mahogany and teak woodwork and joinery, leather seats and chairs. The massive oak table that graced the centre of the room gave the impression of importance. The full-width window filled the room with light and gave a panoramic view of the bay and reef; a beautiful sight in anyone's mind. But right now, all this beauty and opulence held no value; the decision the council must make would shape their lives forever.

Peter Knowles opened the meeting. 'So the options are: we allow this Mustafa to come here with armed troops, subdue him and take the virus. Then the Garibaldis attempt to reverse engineer the damn thing and maybe, I emphasize that word, *maybe*, give some the chance of having children,' Knowles was an expat Brit and a bit of a stuffed shirt, but had a keen intellect and wasn't given to emotional decisions. 'Does anyone have an idea of what the chance of success is?' He turned to Zena and Anton who, although not members of the council, were considered expert witnesses.

Zena stood. 'Mister Knowles, to be totally honest, no we don't. We have been trying since we got here with samples from our inhabitants, with no luck.'

'And this base virus will increase your chances by how much?' Knowles asked.

The question was loaded, but she had to be honest. 'I have no idea... it's only a theory. If we have un-mutated virus and we can compare it with our present samples, there is a chance we will find an answer.'

'How much of a chance?' he asked.

Anton replied to this. 'Peter, we have no idea. The whole thing may be a waste of time. It may be impossible to alter anything, but we do know that continuing as we are will generate nothing; we have proved that. Our only hope—and I will be brutally honest, it's just a hope—is that the base virus will allow much more scope for research.'

The meeting kept going, swinging back and forth with argument and counter argument, until Reg called a halt to the discussion; it was going nowhere. 'We've been here for hours and still we have nothing. I'm sorry, but we must make a decision. Time is a major factor now.' He checked his watch. 'We only have thirty hours left. I move for a vote.'

There was a knock at the door. Reg opened it to see Clyde, resplendent in his full-dress colonel uniform. 'Reg, I apologize for the intrusion, but I have some information and an alternative. I'd like to address the council.'

He turned back to the room, still blocking Clyde's access. 'Councillors, Colonel Pearson wants to address us before we decide. How say you?' Almost as one they agreed and Reg stood aside and introduced Clyde.

Clyde stood and addressed them in a military fashion. 'I have remembered quite a lot more about the weapon and this course of action. The facts are that it will destroy everything in a twenty kilometres of the target site, down to a depth of at least one hundred metres. Now, to some this might not seem much, but if you look at the old maps we have of the site, you will think again. It is my view, and that is supported by some of your own people, using this weapon against Mustafa's site will destroy what is left of Newcastle. Remember, the city has been heavily undermined in the past and the energy of this weapon will, in the opinion of your own scientists, permanently destabilise the entire area. Everything will die, and the geological structure will be permanently changed. How, we don't know and without a detailed analysis of the area, we never will. This is one of the reasons it has never been fired – but I may have an alternative.'

Clyde proposed a possible way to secure the virus, rescue the Clements women and neutralize Mustafa as well. 'This plan  isn't foolproof; it doesn't guarantee success and it still doesn't improve the odds of Zena and Anton being successful. But it does give us the possibility of having a go at solving the problem. I will await your decision.'

Clyde stood and prepared to leave.

'No wait, Colonel,' Knowles said. 'I for one would prefer you to stay and watch the vote. I move we adopt the Colonel's plan. Will someone second?'

The room was quiet, then a female voice. 'I'll second.'

Reg spoke next. 'We have a motion that we adopt the plan of action from Colonel Pearson. We also have a second. I call for all members to cast their vote.'

The councillors reached for the paper and pens before them, recorded their vote and placed the piece of paper into the bowl. As chairman, Reg's vote was withheld—his was always the casting vote in the event of a tie. He passed the bowl to Clyde. 'It's your plan, Colonel. Maybe you should count the votes.'

Clyde started to check each paper, putting the ayes to his right, nays to the left. In the end, there were even piles; six each. He turned to Reg. 'Looks like you have to break the deadlock Chairman.'

This would be the hardest decision Reg had ever made. He looked at Clyde, then the Garibaldis, then at each of the councillors in turn. He took the paper, looked at it as though it was going to bite him, before taking the pen and casting his vote. He folded the paper and handed it to Clyde.

Clyde looked at it and handed it to Knowles. 'Mister Knowles, please read the chairman's vote.'

Knowles smiled. 'It reads aye.'

Reg nodded. 'That makes it seven to six in favour of the motion. I declare it carried. Thank you all.'

***

Ahmed Mustafa lay naked on the bed. He was a tall man, well built and he had never had a problem attracting female companions. He had a commanding presence, something that had ensured his rise to power. This presence was only equalled by his arrogance; he was, after all, the chosen one of God, at least in his own mind.

He rolled over. Two young, naked female forms were beside him, snuggled together as if to lock out the world. He remembered the pleasure these two had given him last night. Laying there with the early morning light gently caressing their bodies, he felt a surge of passion begin to flow through his body. He slapped the one closest to him on her shapely backside. 'Wake up, whore. I am in need of servicing.'

The one he'd slapped moaned and rolled toward him. Mustafa grabbed her by the hair and forced her head to his groin. She was barely awake, but she complied. To refuse would mean a whipping, or worse.

Mustafa's pleasure was interrupted by a knock at his door. A scared voice emanated from the other side. 'Master, there is a communication from Clements.'

Mustafa groaned and looked at the girl. 'You seem to have been relieved of your task, but I'll see that your talents are not unused.' He leered at them as he climbed out of the bed. 'I'll be there in five minutes. Find a dozen men. There are a couple of infidel whores here who need educating.'

'Yes, Master,' the voice replied as Mustafa walked into the bathroom. He took his time to prepare and dress. He was always conscious of his appearance but to others it was extreme vanity. His beard was perfectly trimmed and combed; his hair always tied up under his keffiyeh.

Finally, he was ready, his five minutes turning into half an hour. He left through the bedroom, the two girls still waiting on the bed. He didn't even look at them. Their duty to him was done. They were now the property of the dozen men he had asked for.

His military boots shone as he marched down the corridor. His uniform was perfectly pressed and showed him as holding the rank of general; five stars in a circle on his epaulettes. His chest bore many medals. Mustafa had a penchant for giving himself a medal whenever he believed he deserved one, and he believed that quite often.

He strode into the communications room, everyone leaping to attention as he took his seat. 'Now, what does Mister Clements have to say?'

Clements' voice boomed from the speakers. '*Ahmed, resistance is heavier than we anticipated. Our advance team has secured the beach and the entrance to the complex. We are proceeding to disembark our main force, but this will take longer than planned. We'll need at least another seventy-two hours.*'

Mustafa didn't flinch. 'You have thirty-six, that is all; Mustafa out!' He signalled for the comm to be cut and turned to his second in command. 'Abdul, are we ready?'

Abdul Nazari had been Mustafa's right hand since they'd first formed the Ummah Liberation Army, the army that was supposed to bring about the formation of a worldwide caliphate. He was Mustafa's only true friend and believed totally in what they were fighting for. He was a zealot and true believer.

'Master, our main force is awaiting orders. They have boarded the ships and are ready,' he replied.

'Excellent, my friend; give the order and send them now. And the plane... is it prepared?' Mustafa enquired.

'Prepared and ready for whenever you need it – shall I prepare the hostages?' Nazari asked.

'No, they're not going anywhere. If Clements thinks he has won their freedom, he's very mistaken.' Mustafa looked at his friend. 'I promised the girl to you and you shall have her... after we have flushed all the infidel vermin off the island.

'Abdul, we have almost succeeded. Allah saved me for a reason. Very soon we will be the only power in the world. Everyone will either convert or die. We will win. Allahu Akbar.'

On cue, everyone in the room shouted their praise. Mustafa smiled. His dream was almost a reality. Soon the whole world, or what was left of it, would be his followers. He knew he had been saved so he could unite the world—even the infidel plague hadn't killed him. He knew Allah had great things planned for Ahmed Mustafa.

# TWENTY SIX

Clyde stepped back. 'Thank you, Edmund.'

'But what about Reg and his council?' Clements asked.

'Need to know. At this stage everyone, you included, knows just what they need to.' Clyde replied.

'Now, the guards will take you back to your accommodation.' Clyde opened the door and two guards escorted Clements back to a secure room down the hall.

Clyde left the building and took one of the ground vehicles. He needed to hurry; time was a real issue. He drove like a man possessed, exceeding every speed restriction until he reached his destination—another massive underground facility. This one was different; still solely under his command, but it housed various aircraft, and a lot of them. He stopped the vehicle outside a large hangar area. Even underground, some of these areas had doors to conceal what was inside.

Thom was waiting outside as Clyde's car stopped. 'Morning boss,' he cheerily greeted his friend.

'Morning, Thom. Clements did it! You've got thirty-six hours. Can you do it?' Clyde asked.

'There's no can, we **have** to!'

Thom led the way into the building. Before them were three strange-looking aircraft. The wings were short and thick and at the end of each was a large nacelle; in this was a huge Rolls Royce jet engine. The exhaust nozzle of each was moveable, giving the plane VSTOL capabilities. 'Just like the old Osprey, except better; carry more, fly further and faster. Have a look... she's loaded and ready to go.'

Clyde walked up the rear loading ramp. Inside was Bravo team, two APCs and all the equipment they would require.

'Great, isn't she? Charlie and Echo teams have the other two. The tankers have already left, as well as that insane mother ship 'Eight Hawks'. I still can't believe eight of those drones can be operated from that plane.' Thom slowly shook his head. 'And all this was locked up in your memory. Unbelievable.'

'Yeah... and I wish it still was; it'd mean that we had a simpler life,' Clyde responded.

'I hear you.'

'It's time, I'd better let you get moving. Remember, Wrath will be on target in twenty-nine hours, after that you better be a long way from that site.' Clyde's voice was firm, commanding as he spoke. 'The council has decided; they don't want Mustafa's forces to have any hole to hide in. We'll take him out here. You make sure you get the hostages and get the hell out of there, got it?'

'Roger that; there's no way I want to be around when you fire that thing!' The sound of the jet engines starting emphasized the timing.

Clyde clapped Thom on the back. 'Go kick arse, mate, and kick hard!' He turned and sprinted down the ramp, just as the loadmaster started to close it. He stood back as the planes started to taxi out of the hangar, watching as they rose gracefully into the air and exited through the cave mouth. Moments after the last plane had left, the runway extension retracted and the door closed; from outside, he knew it again looked like one solid mountain of rock.

He'd left Alpha and Delta teams planning the final stage of the operation—the welcome for Mustafa and thought it time to check their progress. He walked into the meeting to find everyone almost relaxed, most with a coffee or tea in hand.

'I take it you have a plan?' Clyde asked, his tone conveying his fear that they had not achieved what he wanted.

'We have,' Alpha One replied as he switched the lights to dim and activated a holographic display in the centre of the room. 'Here it is.'

Clyde examined the plan and, try as he might, he couldn't find a major flaw or defect. He suggested a couple of minor improvements but, overall, it was sound. 'Well done. I suppose you had better get things set.' He was impressed, and it must have showed. The whole group seemed to stand a little taller.

Clyde watched as they all filed out, took one more look at the hologram and then switched it off. He slowly left and closed the door. Walking down the corridor, aromas from the mess reminded him that he hadn't eaten since lunch yesterday, so he took a detour.

The mess was empty when he entered. Being just after 11:00, breakfast was finished and lunch was about to start. He went to the counter and waited until one of the staff noticed him. He quickly ordered a steak and moved to a table.

Clyde sat alone and reflected on what had brought them to this point and what was about to begin. He felt very alone, everything was his responsibility. If he was wrong – Clyde shook his head to clear it. He couldn't afford any second guessing.

'Fuck it, we're all in now!' he said aloud just as one of the kitchen staff brought his meal.

'Play Poker, do you Sir?'

'Badly my friend, unfortunately,' Clyde chuckled as he started on his meal.

*** 

Three thousand kilometres south of the complex, the cloud dawdled along at twenty thousand meters, its vast array of detection systems constantly scanning both the skies and the ocean.

'Contact,' one of the operators reported. 'Surface contact, five vessels bearing to port – range one hundred klicks.'

'Log it, and send coordinates to control,' the OOD replied. Lieutenant Rickard Mossman, a tall swarthy man surveyed his team with pride. Although it was sometimes hard to discern, he was immensely proud of them, but he rode them hard — constantly training — but always with a word of praise or encouragement when needed. Now all the training and effort was being rewarded.

'Contact,' a female voice to his right called. 'Single aircraft heading for the complex, speed three-twenty knots; course, three one five magnetic.'

'Relay the data to control. Great job, team! We found the bastards, exactly where the Colonel predicted. First round will be on me when this is over; now you know why we train so hard.' Mossman smiled.

* * *

Ahmed Mustafa sat comfortably in the leather seat in his aircraft. Behind him in the cargo section was the virus, still frozen in its cryogenic capsule; with the island now under Clements' control, his mission to save humanity could begin. He smiled, his immortality was now certain, but just in case, he had with him twenty-five of his most trusted men, each armed and ready to respond to any threat.

Mustafa felt safe and confident. The fool Clements had done as he promised—he had delivered the means for Mustafa to save the world and, in his mind, any man who could save the world from a slow and pointless end, would be hailed as a new prophet.

He initially had a tiny fear that Clements would fail, but now his faith had been justified. Once he was in full command of the complex, the work could begin. One piece of information Clements had accidentally given was that the Garibaldis were there, hastening his own death. With the two who had invented the binary virus now his captives, Clements's usefulness became far less. After all, any man who would betray his people and faith for a woman was not a man.

He turned and surveyed his men—hard, tough and loyal. Each was prepared to die for their leader. *Just as it should be,* Mustafa thought.

'Master,' Nazari's voice interrupted Mustafa's thoughts. 'What is your plan for when we land?' Nazari was a practical man, always planning for variable scenarios and today was no different.

'Simple,' Mustafa replied, his smile conveying confidence to those around him. 'We land and taxi towards the dock; five divers slip out the rear of the plane and head for the shore. We have some difficulty in docking to allow them time to reach land; then we tie the plane up and exit. The twenty will form an honour guard for me; a bit of ceremony will work wonders on these fools. I alight and our five commandos infiltrate the complex and remove any resistance. I don't expect there to be any though because Clements is too afraid for his family to risk angering me. No, my friend, this will go smoothly.'

'And what happens when Clements realizes his family isn't here?'

Mustafa laughed. 'He never will. You will have killed him before he learns anything.' His laughter echoed round the plane, infecting the others; all except Nazari who gave a discreet chuckle. Deep inside, he was concerned that the plan was too arrogant, too reliant on Clements' devotion to his wife and child.

*No, Nazari thought, I must keep an open mind. I must be alert for any dangers.* His thoughts trailed off as the mood in the plane began to infect him.

* * *

Thom's plane was last to land. It came in low and fast, just as the others had, transferred to vertical operation and dropped onto the ground. The rear door opened and the two vehicles it housed roared out. The landing zone was an old private aerodrome just north of the old city of Maitland, now nothing more than rubble.

Beside the three teams, each plane carried fifteen well-armed security personnel. Their job was to secure the landing field and planes and keep them safe. They filed out and began setting up their perimeter and launching small surveillance drones. These would be monitored from the planes and could extend the normal detection range many kilometres in all directions. As soon as the engines had stopped, the crews began to cover the planes with camo nets.

Thom called Charlie and Echo One to him. 'You know your objectives. Now, let's set the timing. We have seventeen hours until Clyde obliterates the target. It'll take two to transit, another two to return. That leaves us thirteen on site. I don't want to be there a second longer than we need, so saddle up and let's get this show on the road.'

It should have been easier, but the old bridge over the Hunter River was gone so a longer route had to be taken. The three vehicles closed their doors and headed off, the extra transit time a major concern.

'Sir, the drones are on target. Data feed is coming through now,' Bravo Three announced as she fed the data into the vehicle's computer.

'Thanks, Three. Keep monitoring,' Thom replied.

The APC looked more like a snow cat than an ATV. Each was driven over ground by four triangular track systems, powered by a nine-hundred-horsepower diesel engine. As they set off, the vehicles accelerated to seventy kilometres per hour, well below their max of one hundred, but enough to get them to the target in plenty of time. Thom had selected the landing area with time and distance in mind. The range of the APC — at their present speed — was four hundred kilometres over open ground. Normally the trip would have been easy, and done a little slower, but with the bridge issue, their planned distance of sixty kilometres had blown out. Now both time and duration could be an issue.

Adding to Thom's worries was the problem of river crossings The APC was amphibious and could run at ten knots in water, but all this came at a cost—fuel consumption. Running over bad terrain, avoiding ruined roads and having to traverse rivers all took fuel, and lots of it. Thom's calculations gave them less than ten percent margin, not nearly enough. To alleviate the situation, he had one of the drones check on an alternative extraction point—the old Rutherford airfield. He hoped it wasn't necessary to use it as it was close to what was left of Maitland and he knew people were still living there; people who he had no knowledge of. For all Thom knew, they all might be converts to Mustafa's cause. But it did give them an alternative.

He decided to ignore the issue. They were committed to the mission and the rest would fall as it did. He couldn't alter that now.

## TWENTY SEVEN

T hom's plan was simple.

He believed they would encounter fewer people by using backroads through old farming areas. He reasoned fewer people would mean fewer blockages and less possible hostile encounters.

But he was beginning to see flaws in the reasoning. He had drones programmed to follow the route and warn them of any obstructions or other possible deterrents. The feed coming from one of the drones made his heart sink. He checked the others, quickly realizing that it wouldn't be long until their covert operation was discovered.

'Charlie One,' Thom hailed the second team, 'are you seeing the drone feed?'

*'Yeah, looks like we'll be discovered if we follow our original plan.'*

Thom agreed; the original plan was sound on paper, but on the ground there appeared to be many small bunker-like constructions, all close to roads they had planned to use. He called for the formation to slow down. Thom needed time to think.

*'Bravo one from Delta three; I may have a solution. We could use the Paterson River; it has some possible civilian problems, but a hell of a lot less than our present course.'*

The road ahead was clear for the next twenty kilometres, but then it converged on the old residential area of Bolwarra and Largs and they needed to go through these areas to get to the river.

Thom took Delta three's suggestion seriously and studied the map. Scrolling through screen after screen, he eventually found a possibility. He called for two drones to be re-directed. He had a hunch and ten minutes later, he had his answer.

The APCs started again, this time on a new route. They ran cross country until they reached their destination—the small farming village of Woodville. There they switched to silent run mode and took the trucks into the Paterson River. This would take an hour longer, but they should be able to avoid any entanglements.

Now he had to call the island and tell Clyde the bad news.

Clyde listened to Thom's report.

*'Sorry, boss, we have no other alternative.'*

'Don't worry, it couldn't be avoided. Our intel was too thin. I have a couple of ideas re an alternative exfil point. You get to the objective and secure the target. I'll work on your escape from here, Pearson out.' Clyde cut the transmission and looked at his timetable. It wasn't good. Mustafa would be arriving in a little over two hours and now they had to stall until Thom could complete his mission. Clyde let his thoughts wander down an all-too-familiar path. He stood and called Alpha and Echo leaders. 'Change of plan. Meet me in ops.'

* * *

Mustafa craned his neck, trying to take in everything he saw below. The plane banked steeply as it circled the lagoon.

'A beautiful sight, is it not Nazari?' Mustafa called to his 2IC.

Abdul Nazari nodded. 'It is a most agreeable sight. We should be happy here.'

Mustafa smiled. All the doubts his friend had previously had seemed to be gone, now they were so close to their victory. Behind them, the twenty-five armed men were making final preparations.

The plane straightened and flew back out to sea, descending as it did. The pilot kept his heading until he turned and lined the plane up with the widest section of the lagoon for its final approach.

***

On the dock, the welcoming committee watched as the huge, ancient plane gently kissed the surface of the lagoon and sped past them, the un-muffled roar of the four huge radial engines, assaulting their ears. As the plane's speed washed off, it passed the dock, slowly settling and allowing the hull to float, the four propellers still providing the diving force.

'Where did they find that museum piece? It must be a century old,' Reg commented.

'There's always someone who restores old things,' Clyde replied. 'I think I know this old girl.'

They all watched as the huge plane slowly turned and started to taxi back to the dock.

*'Five divers in the water – tracking them.'* The voice of Echo Four came from Clyde's earpiece. As the plane turned and retraced its

path, five of Mustafa's men had dropped out of the rear access door. Clyde said nothing.

*'They're all heading towards shore. Looks like they are trying to surprise you from the rear,'* the voice advised. Still Clyde didn't respond.

The plane finally made it to the dock. Three men accepted the tethers thrown from the plane and quickly secured it. The main door opened and ten heavily armed men disembarked. They formed a cordon down each side of the dock as another ten men, similarly armed, formed an honour guard from the main door.

Mustafa waited just inside the plane to give his five insurgents time to get into position. At length, he stepped out of the door, resplendent in his brilliant white robes. He stood, taking in the sight. 'My dear Clements, well done... and Colonel Pearson, I've wanted to meet you for a long time. Your face looks the same, but you carry yourself like a much younger man. What miracles have these evil men worked on you?' He waved his hand. 'No need to answer. We'll have many hours to discuss that, along with other matters.

*'All five insurgents down – repeat, all insurgents down,'* the voice was music to Clyde's ears.

'My family, where are they?' Clements called.

'Do not worry; they are safe, for the moment. Once you complete your work, they'll be brought here,' Mustafa replied.

He started to walk toward the group; Clyde needed to delay him.

'Not so fast,' interrupted Clyde. 'You agreed to bring the base virus with you. Did you at least speak truthfully about that?' Clyde's words were an insult; he was basically calling Mustafa a liar.

'Yes, I did, but what is it to you? Only Clements or the Garibaldis know what to do with it and now I own them!' Mustafa spat back.

Clyde smiled as he quietly said three words. 'Execute, execute, execute.'

Four automatic weapons opened up from below the dock. The twenty guards spun and danced as their bodies were riddled with twelve-millimetre explosive rounds. Before the honour guard could respond, each of them was dead, the massive damage from the ordinance Clyde had chosen riddling their bodies.

'Clements, you fool! You have just killed your wife and daughter,' Mustafa screamed. His words were cut by the report from Clyde's pistol. Mustafa slowly dropped to his knees. Blood started to dribble down his forehead, a look of surprise on his face.

As if in slow motion, he dropped face down on the dock just as two men clad in wetsuits and carrying pistols entered the plane. Two shots echoed from inside the plane and one of the men returned, carrying a small portable Cryo-pod.

'Is this what the fuss is about?' he asked as he placed it on the ground.

Clements turned to Clyde. 'You fucking fool. You've just killed my family!' He launched himself at Clyde, only to be unceremoniously knocked to the ground. Reg and Anton quickly restrained him.

* * *

As soon as Clyde had given the *execute* order, things happened in other places. South of the islands, six heavily armed drones— in a staggered formation from six different directions— began their pre-programmed attack on Mustafa's rag tag fleet. His fleet consisted of twenty converted vessels — mostly large trawlers —

but their sensor systems, radar included, were compromised by the jamming from the drone's mothership which was orbiting above.

The first wave saw six vessels either on fire or blown apart. There was no defensive fire; the attack was too swift. The second wave was almost as successful; as the drones began to attack, heavy machine guns opened up from all the boats. Men screamed as they were engulfed in flames, but they kept firing until the end. Five more boats were disabled but the defensive fire started to have the desired effect. The fire from the boats concentrated as command was re-established; now the planes had to negotiate a withering barrage. Two drones were hit, one exploded in mid-air. The other damaged unit dropped to sea level; the gunners changed their target to the next two drones approaching.

The damage to the drone now just above the waves was too great for it to survive and the AI made the decision to use it as a weapon. A few of the gunners saw what was happening and turned their fire back to this unit. It tried to avoid the barrage from the remaining boats and with it now close to the water, only a few of the guns could depress low enough to target it. The drone accelerated and turned, slamming into closet boat at over six hundred knots.

The vessel it hit was the largest in the fleet and had been converted to a troop carrier. Two hundred of Mustafa's fighters lined the decks as the drone impacted, detonating all its remaining weapons as it did. The resulting explosion was horrific: flames, debris and bodies flew in all directions. Drums of fuel and cases of ammunition exploded spectacularly, sending fireballs and sheets of flame in every direction.

One vessel was too close and was engulfed in the conflagration, as the remaining drones pressed their advantage and attacked the last four ships. Each was turned into a raging inferno. Men leapt into the sea and desperately tried to swim away, but the sea was awash with burning fuel and oil. Survival in this environment was impossible.

Now back in the command centre, Clyde watched the feed from a surveillance drone over the sea battle

'Clyde!' Bonnie's voice slammed into his ears. 'They're just men. Mustafa's dead, his plot is finished. Do something for them!'

Clyde turned and what Bonnie saw frightened her. 'There's nothing I can do. We don't have any assets close to them.' His words sounded empathic, but his face... Bonnie knew she'd never forget that look.

She turned and ran from the room.

***

Thom cursed his luck. Running silent slowed them down. Over water, the extra muffling dropped the engine efficiency hugely and their speed was halved.

He consulted his calculations again. 'Fuck it!' he yelled to no one in particular.

He pressed the transmit button on his comm unit. 'All APCs secure from silent, accelerate to full speed. We're out of time.'

The order was instantly obeyed and the three boats leapt forward, their speed racing up toward their maximum of fifteen knots. The downside was the noise. With the silent muffling removed the full report of the huge v10 diesels powering each APC reverberated across the water and into the small fishing community that was Old Hexham.

Thom didn't care; they had less than two hours to complete their mission.

The river ran parallel with and very close to the old highway. Thom could see the remains of cars strewn along it, but he knew he had to exit the water very soon if he was to make it to his destination.

He saw a clear patch of road. 'Driver, up there... get out of this damn water.' The driver obeyed, turning the craft towards the bank and initiating the track drives. This was when the APC was most vulnerable; the transition from water to ground craft took time.

'Charlie and Echo teams, form up for land transition,' Thom called into the comm system. Both APCs complied; their speed dropped, and their weapons turret was activated. Now their job was to cover Bravo team as it transitioned and exited the water. In total, it only took five minutes for each to transition and exit water ops, but it was five minutes of vulnerability.

'Okay, we all have our ingress points. Let's get moving.'

The three vehicles accelerated down the eerily empty highway. They turned off at the university exit and Thom was surprised to see that this was also clear. Minutes later, Charlie team peeled off and began to race through an old golf course toward its ingress point below what used to be the science department.

Echo left next, heading toward the old engineering faculty buildings; from information they had from both Clements and previous incursions, this was known as one of Mustafa's strong holds. Thom and Bravo team kept racing for the main entrance. He checked his watch. Time was too tight, but they had no other option.

Thom saw a possible shortcut and called to the driver who slammed the big vehicle into a hard left turn, raced up the embankment and over the rise. He backed off as they reached the top of the embankment and started down the other side.

As they reached the roadway below, the unmistakable sounds of small arms munitions hitting the armour of the machine assailed Thom's ears. Immediately, the twenty-millimetre cannon in the turret opened up, its eight barrels sending explosive rounds towards their attackers. The short burst from it almost demolished the building that had been the source of the attack. Once again, the only sounds were the engine and the howl of the tracks on old pavement.

The driver slewed the APC into a right turn and raced down another road. A few hundred meters later, he did the same, this time to the left, and moments later, their objective was in sight. The old Chancellery Building and, according to Clements' information, Mustafa's headquarters, was now to their right. The turret rotated to cover the building as Thom and the team leapt out the rear of the APC. There was no need for stealth; anyone who wasn't aware of the attack was probably dead anyhow, plus the sound of another twenty-millimetre firing elsewhere should convince people to stay away.

Thom reached the main door; it was locked. He attached a breaching charge and retreated. The door exploded inwards as he tapped the detonator. Two by two, the team entered the foyer. It was a shambles; the shock wave from the breaching charge had slammed into the old foyer and debris was strewn all over the place.

Thom looked at the floor plan they had previously uncovered during one of their recon missions. He led the team down a corridor and directly in front of them was a blockage. They crashed into two doors on opposite sides of the corridor just as automatic weapons opened up from the pile of tables and junk sealing the corridor.

Instead of returning fire, Thom and half the team opened an adjoining room and raced to the end of it. There they placed more breaching charges on the wall facing the corridor and retreated to the first room.

The sound of weapons firing told Thom that his team was following the plan. He tapped the detonator button and the wall of the next room and the corridor exploded, the force of the blast knocking the defenders down.

Thom led his group through the hole in the wall, quickly dispatching the two defenders left alive. He heard a door slam to his right, spinning to see where it came from. He saw another defender running toward an office at the end of the corridor. Thom raised his weapon, taking aim as he did, and squeezed off one round. It hit the fleeing man in the back and he was catapulted forward, the force of the twelve-millimetre projectile and his own momentum slamming him into the door.

The door shattered under the impact to reveal their targets. Both were tied to chairs and there was another defender standing beside them, not where Thom and the team were expecting them to be.

'LEAVE! LEAVE NOW OR I KILL THEM!' he screamed as he raised his rifle and turned towards the two women. Thom fired three shots toward the captor. The unmistakable sound of the AK74 the captor carried hit Thom's ears like a hammer blow. Had he been wrong? Had his action caused them to fail their mission?

These thoughts assailed his brain as he ran toward the open office. It seemed like forever before he burst through the doorway.

The scene was surreal. The captor was dead, his blood splattered over the rear wall of the room. Thom turned toward the two chairs, where the women were tied.

'Fuck!' he cried and then into his comm unit. 'We need a medic here now!' Both women were covered in blood—, old and dried, with fresh blood running down the older woman's right arm.

The team medic raced into the room and started to examine the two captives.

'They're okay, Bravo One. Both women are okay!' The medic's voice sounded a thousand miles away; Thom tried desperately to understand what the words meant.

'Boss, they're both *okay*,' the medic shouted. 'Mrs. Clements has a couple of cuts from the glass in the door. That's all.' She turned away and continued treating her charges as Thom's mind came back to reality.

An explosion brought home their real situation. Delta team had executed their diversion, now it was time to leave.

'Can they move?' Thom asked.

'You better believe we can,' Lilah Clements replied. 'I've had enough of being locked in here.' But when she stood, her legs gave way; the medic grabbed her and supported her as they began to walk forward. Two more of the team rushed in and assisted both of the women.

The medic led them back through the rubble. Thom brought up the rear, checking that his team had completed their tasks. They all piled back into the APC just as a large four-by-four vehicle came screaming round the bend behind them. It sported a fifty-calibre machinegun mounted in its tub and began firing. The sound of heavy calibre bullets slamming into the APC was deafening.

The twenty-millimetre in the turret of the APC returned fire, six hundred twenty-millimetre explosive rounds versus unarmoured SUV; the battle was over in moments.

'*Bravo One from command, please respond,*' Clyde's voice echoed.

'Bravo One here. Package secured, exit now.'

'*Bravo One... coordinates for new extraction point coming now. Time is critical, you have twenty minutes. Please acknowledge.*'

Thorn acknowledged the transmission and fed the new data into his data pad. He looked closely at it, the driver doing the same.

'Shit boss, that's in the old wetlands. It's been a wet few months and it'll all be marsh now. We'll never get there in time.'

Thorn studied the area. The driver was right. With all the rain that had fallen, even the APCs would find it difficult crossing the ground.

Then it struck him. 'The railway, we could run on that. It's above any flooding and it's still solid. The extraction point is the old service yards; tons of room for the planes to land and us to board.' He reached for the comm unit and called the other two APCs and gave them new orders.

# TWENTY EIGHT

Thom tightened his seat harness as the driver slid the APC off the road and down the embankment towards the rail corridor.

*Now for the fun stuff,* he thought as the vehicle bounced up onto the rail line. While it wasn't designed to run on rails, the width between the drive tracks of the APC meant it could comfortably straddle the rails. Thom watched as the other two APCs formed up behind his unit. Delta team was rear guard and the turret on the top of that vehicle turned back to cover their escape.

'*Heads up!*' Clyde's voice broke through the ambient sounds of the vehicle. '*We have three drones covering you, but our friends are in pursuit. Six vehicles are coming down the track behind you and three more are in front.*'

'Roger that,' Thom answered as he adjusted the optics on the front cameras. 'Echo One, six bogies will be coming up behind you very soon. Take them out. Charlie One, assist with the rear action.'

The screen in front of Thom showed three large SUVs parked across the tracks, rear facing his advance. On the back of each was a fifty-calibre machine gun and while these were nothing to be concerned about, the four men kneeling on the ground, each with a shoulder-launched anti-tank weapon could be a real problem.

They were still three kilometres away from the blockade, too far for the twenty-millimetre cannon to be really effective. It would come into range at about the same time as the rocket launchers. The first to fire might just win. This was going to be tight.

At two klicks, the unmistakable roar of the twenty-mill cannon echoed through the vehicle. The ground just ahead of the blockade erupted as the bullets exploded on the ground. As the dust and smoke cleared, Thom saw the four men with the launchers get back into position and take aim. If they fired at this range, a hit was assured—the APCs had nowhere to go.

Explosions and flames leaped from the ground around the blockade. Three of the enemy rocket men simply disappeared. The fourth was knocked off his feet but regained his weapon as the Hawk drone flashed overhead.

'Gunner, take him out!' Thom shouted. He was rewarded with another long burst from the eight barrels above him. The result was devastating; the body was torn apart as the three hundred explosive rounds hit it and the ground around it. But the weapon had still been fired, the smoke trail from the rocket confirming it.

'**Incoming!**' Thom shouted.

About a hundred meters ahead, the rocket hit the ground, the explosion rocking the APC. A twenty-meter section of rail was blown apart. Now the APC was racing toward a jumbled mess of twisted steel. A huge hole had been opened in the corridor. The driver began an emergency stop, calling to the following vehicles as he did. Thom saw an opportunity. They had been running on the old coal corridor and to their right across a small divide; was the old passenger and general freight line.

'To the right, the old passenger line!' Thom called.

When the APC had slowed enough, the driver threw it to the right, mounted the cable box dividing the two corridors, and resumed traveling in the other lanes.

Thom smiled. This is what they had trained for—working as a team and being able to take the initiative when needed. The other two APCs followed.

'Echo One, do you have any mines on board?' Thom got an affirmative answer and ordered them to seed the track. Just before their pursuers reached the mines, one fired another rocket. This time it was more effective. Just as the SUVs set off the mines, the rocket slammed into the rails just ahead of Echo team. It tore the rails up and blew another hole in the ground, too close for any evasive action.

Echo team's APC slammed into the crater and twisted rails at speed. It stopped instantly.

Thom called for his driver to stop and reverse. Both remaining APCs did the same, Charlie team crossing the rail line again to cover the others. There was nothing to cover from at this stage; the minefield had done its job. Four of the pursuers had been destroyed or disabled and the wreckage, coupled with the damage caused by the rocket attack, had the other two blocked.

Thom raced back to the damaged APC. Both front tracks were badly damaged and it appeared that one of the twisted rails had penetrated the bottom of the body. This unit was going nowhere. The two medics from his and Charlie team wrenched the rear door open as the rest of their teams formed a protective cordon around the vehicles. Thom was first to enter.

Inside the APC was chaos. Two members had been slammed into bulkheads as the vehicle stopped from seventy KPH in an instant. The others were all strapped in but were still injured.

*'Thom, what are you doing? Time's running out.'* Clyde's voice broke through Thom's earpiece.

'Saving survivors... what the fuck does it look like?' Thom replied venomously.

*'Well hurry the fuck up! Wrath is closing.'*

'Then delay the bloody thing. We're not leaving people,' Thom yelled back.

*** 

Back on the island, Clyde fumed. 'Fucking useless; they'll all be killed!'

Bonnie's quiet voice asked, 'Why?'

Clyde turned and confronted her. 'Because they all knew the risk and now Thom is hell bent on saving them and time is almost up. I can't delay Wrath - either I fire it when it's on target or I lose the window.'

'Well the answer is simple — lose the damn window!' Bonnie screamed.

'We've got the chance to wipe out every one of Mustafa's followers, to finish this bloody crap once and for all. Besides, this is what the council ordered, it's their decision not mine!' Clyde fired back.

'Bullshit! You're the one with his finger on the trigger, not the fucking council. Those people are our friends, and you're prepared to murder them; and then hide behind the council?' Clyde didn't answer and she continued. 'I've been looking into Colonel Ben Pearson. You were quite a bastard. Last commander of this facility until something went wrong and it was closed down. What happened Clyde? What did you do?'

Clyde didn't respond. He just glared at her.

'I'll tell you. You sent a team to one of Mustafa's strongholds. The mission was to take him out. But it went haywire, didn't it? The team was captured and used as propaganda. They were tortured and butchered, all on national TV. I even remember the horror and the outrage; you and your group let it happen; you did nothing. All this capability and a few rag-tag terrorists in some desert shithole made you look stupid.'

Clyde turned. 'Yes, you're right. I let it happen. We were ready to launch a counter-strike when the politicians caved. They gave in to the PC bullshit of the day and shut us down. *They* killed all those soldiers, not me. And now I have the chance to level the score, and you think I should stop? You're just like them...' The look in Bonnie's eyes stabbed at his conscience.

She placed her hand on his right arm. 'No, Clyde I'm not. And neither are you. You set off that damn weapon; you'll kill every living thing in a twenty-klick radius. Not just Mustafa's people, but everyone else. You'll be worse than him and you'll be alone. I won't live with a homicidal maniac.' She looked deep into his eyes. 'Ben Pearson is dead. He died years ago, and you are not him, so don't try and resurrect him. Just be my Clyde – do the right thing.'

Clyde stood perfectly still; then his hands started to shake. Bonnie saw the signs and grabbed him, held him tight, blocking everyone else's view. Clyde finally broke away and went to the Wrath control.

Everything from his past screamed for him to fire the bloody thing, but Bonnie and the possibilities for the future demanded something different. He held his hand over the control panel; the fire and safe buttons side by side mimicking his dilemma. He closed his eyes and pressed.

WRATH IN SAFE MODE

The message flashed on the main screen and a collective sigh of relief sounded through the room.

'Release the eye's drones; send them to assist Thom, but keep recording everything the eye sees ... we may need it later.' Clyde sank into his chair and called Thom. 'Bravo One, Wrath has been disabled. Three more drones are on their way, but you still need to secure the landing zone.'

***

Thom stood and looked down the rail line as his comm unit received the call.

'Roger that. We have recovered all the injured and are proceeding to exfil. Bravo One out.' He turned and entered his APC. They started down the final couple of klicks to the landing zone. He had set the self-destruct in the damaged APC and just as they entered the old rail repair yard, it detonated. Nothing was going to use that rail corridor again for many years.

There was very little resistance—about twenty opponents, and they were only lightly armed. The firefight was short and one-sided, with the defenders giving up very quickly. Thom called the planes and almost instantly he was rewarded with the sound of the huge Rolls Royce engines transitioning the planes to vertical landing. Loading was done quickly and with great efficiency, once they were all safely inside the planes left and were soon climbing out of harm's way. Now they could finally sleep; it was a long flight home.

***

Clyde waited just inside the cave entrance, scanning the sky with a pair of field glasses. It was fourteen hours since they had left the old rail complex and they should be landing any minute, but still, the sky was empty.

He felt something touch his hand, Bonnie was at his side.

She looked into his eyes. 'Thank you.'

Clyde feigned ignorance. 'What for?'

Bonnie replied. 'Thank you for realizing who you really are. I thought I had lost Clyde, and I really didn't like Colonel Pearson.'

Clyde nodded his head resignedly. 'Neither did I. In fact, it was the reason all this was closed down.' He checked the sky again; still empty. 'We have time, so I'll explain. It's all come back to me. I remember who I was and what I did, and I don't like it. Mustafa brought it all home.

'He was very young, only about fifteen, I think, when he leaped to fame. He did things—killed indiscriminately, raped, pillaged—everything a warlord does, and all in the name of his prophet. But we always knew he had his own agenda; even then he was really ambitious. He attacked one of our embassies. My team was charged with rectifying the situation. I won't go into detail, but that was when I went rogue.'

Clyde gathered his thoughts. 'I took a small group into the lion's den and wiped out over one hundred of his closest followers. But I missed him and he retaliated. I saw his anger. The things he did infuriated me, just as he wanted. I hit back—and almost got him—but we did get another fifty of his followers. Mustafa was always too slippery. We never got close enough.

'Then the politicians got involved. They wanted to solve the situation with diplomacy so, as politicians do, they caved in, gave ground and Mustafa won. That's when I closed this operation. Yes... I closed it down. I set all the codes so I was the only person who could ever activate it again.

'Now, am I proud of what I did? No, but it was essential at the time. Am I glad I shot the arsehole? Definitely, and I'm just as glad you stopped me from pressing the wrong button! You were right; if I'd gone ahead, I'd have been no better than him, so thank you for making me see who I really am. Ben Pearson is now gone. I never want him back. I like being Clyde.'

He stopped and reached for Bonnie. She melted into his arms. 'I like you being Clyde, too.' Then she crushed her lips to his just as the PA system announced the planes were returning.

***

The weeks went by very quickly. A second foray to Newcastle was activated; this time Mustafa's group was located and offered the chance to surrender. They refused and a surgical drone strike was called in. Both the hospital and university sites were taken out and any survivors sealed underground. Three additional entrances were found and similarly demolished.

With the end of Mustafa's reign, locals started to emerge with horrific stories of what life had been like in the old city. Under Mustafa's reign fear and hopelessness were their constant companions. At any time day or night, his troops would raid, take anything they wanted especially young women, and they were almost never seen again. Food was in constant short supply and any that did find its way to the people was always a target for Mustafa and his goons. Water was another problem, all fresh drinking water was controlled and rationed sparingly, except to Mustafa's followers, tales of people not having any drinking water for days, while being forced to watch his troops cavort in large pools had forced a number of rebellions, always with the same result, anyone who rebelled suffered horrendous torture before being killed.

Clyde and Reg met with local leaders and a dialogue was started, the locals were wary, at first, but as discussions moved forward they saw that life would only get better. A small enclave was established so that progress with rehabilitation and rebuilding could begin, the eventual goal was to return to Australia, but that was many years away.

Clements and his family were reunited and work on reversing the effects of the virus began. Again, time was going to be an enemy; every year that it took guaranteed fewer people could breed. But at least there was hope.

* * *

Clyde and Bonnie walked slowly along the beach, the sunrise throwing up its amazing colour show. They were clad in swimming costumes.

Bonnie began to laugh.

'What's so funny?' Clyde asked.

Bonnie ran her hand down her belly, caressing the small but unmistakable baby bump. 'I'll soon look like a hippo!' She laughed again.

'Well, if it's going to be that bad, maybe I should get Allison to move back in.' His attempt at humour earned him a solid punch.

'Yeah, I'm sure Thom would agree to that.' Bonnie giggled at Clyde's surprise at her suggestion. 'What, you didn't know? Maybe you guys should actually talk more. Besides, this is all your handiwork, so you're stuck with us,' Bonnie retaliated.

'I could think of worse fates.' Clyde pulled her close and they watched as a pod of dolphins frolicked in the surf.

End.

through several dimensions, a definitive plan is needed. Petra makes a discovery and must risk all to warn the 12th Realm, if she fails it will be her lover who kills her.

**Chronicle of the 12th Realm Book 3: Hunt for Balerophon**
Has the human race won the battle for freedom and survival? Does the enemy have anything in reserve? Aaron and Petra discover the Sedition's final solution, one that if implemented will change everything. Once again they are forced into action, but is it all too late? Their initial raid on the enemy facility has deadly consequences; consequences that force Petra embrace her Vargan heritage and race to confront the ultimate evil that has been haunting humanity.

**Freebooter Foundation:**
Murphy's Law, ever heard of it? The crew of the trade ship Drake discovers just what it can do, in a perfect storm of impossible events. A tiny meteorite, an improbable double power failure causes Drake to be stranded in a sector of space humans avoid. Freebooter is an adventure of survival, both physical and political as a coup is enacted on earth, a coup that would mean the end of freedom; but a new and unlikely ally may be the key to victory.

**Prequel to Chronicle of the 12th Realm: Incident at Zyralin 4**
A simple training mission to to the remote planet as a qualifying trial for Allan Dean's promotion to Captain 4th Grade, goes terribly wrong. His small task force is almost destroyed, only one ship survives, and questions must be answered. What happened to the science station on the planet? Why were Coalition ships attacked

in their own territory, and by who? Against a backdrop of political intrigue and treason as court of inquiry must find the answers.